All That I Want

A Queensbay Small Town Romance - Book 6

Drea Stein

GirlMougl Media

Contents

Chapter 1

C olleen McShane pulled the tap and let the Guinness pour slowly into the glass, watching as the dark liquid crept to the top. Not too fast, not too slow, but just right, and she smiled in satisfaction as just the thinnest layer of foam settled at the top. She maneuvered the glass underneath the tap, and her smile grew even wider. She'd managed to draw the shamrock symbol in the layer of foam and, as she set the glass down in front of her customer, she was rewarded with a cheery "thanks" and the push of a bill across the polished expanse of the bar.

She moved gracefully down the length of the high counter, checking on her patrons, noticing when one needed another round and when others wanted to be left alone. Wednesday night at Quent's Pub, one of Queensbay's two drinking establishments, was in full swing, and for a small town in New England before the start of the tourist season, things were hopping.

She didn't usually work Wednesday nights, but Quentin Tate, the owner, had called Colleen and begged a favor from her, mentioning something about a family emergency, which was odd because as far as she knew, Quent didn't seem to have a family. He was an enigma, who, according to local gossip, had turned up in Queensbay a few years ago, started working the bar at the Ship's Inn, and when Sully, the owner of the Ship's Inn, had wanted to retire, had bought him out with a suitcase full of cash.

Quent had surprised everyone and completed a renovation that had transformed the former dive bar into an upscale sports pub, complete with big screen TVs, a decent bar food menu, and a décor that was homage to all things English, the island from where Quent claimed to hail.

Colleen, having spent a decent amount of time there, was pretty sure that Quent's accent was London by way of Brooklyn. But she enjoyed his cheery "luvs" and colorful slang as much as the next person and the patrons ate it up. In keeping with the British theme, Wednesday night was New Wave night, and the classics were playing: U2, The Cure, Oasis, and Coldplay. Colleen was in charge of the playlist, and she was getting all of her favorites in.

She surveyed the landscape, wiped an imaginary water spot off the bar, and smiled. She had called in her own favor from Mrs. Halifax to watch Adele, since her mom was working the night shift at the hospital, but the tips were definitely worth it. Colleen poured the remains of a drink down the drain and set the empty glass into the sink. She needed to get a whole stack of glasses loaded into the dishwasher, but the tap on the keg of light beer was starting to act up. Nothing she couldn't handle, but without backup, she didn't want to be fiddling around with things while customers went thirsty.

"Are you new here?" asked a woman. Her tone was curious, friendly. She'd been watching Colleen for a while, with a cool, appraising stare, but this was the first question she had asked. Her accent was from well south of the Mason–Dixon Line, a slow, syrupy drawl unlike the cool, clipped tones of New England.

"Sort of," Colleen said. "I used to work at the Osprey Arms but heard there was an opening here. Another?" The story rolled off her tongue easily enough; though it stretched the truth, it would do for now.

The woman nodded, and Colleen pulled out the bottle of nice French white that the woman had asked for specifically. Quent had told her it was only for special customers.

"Quent around?" the woman asked, casually enough, but Colleen detected a tone of interest in her voice. The woman had glossy dark hair that hung in waves below her shoulders and wore a dress that Colleen envied, which would have been more at home at an elegant restaurant than a townie bar in Queensbay.

"Family emergency. Least that's what he told me."

"Really?" the woman said, one dark eyebrow curling up in surprise.

Colleen knew the other woman was thinking the same thing she had. Quent didn't seem like he had any family who would have called him to an emergency. Colleen threw her a smile in sisterly agreement as she wrestled with the finicky tap. It took a while, but she finally got a decent beer poured and sent it down to the middle-aged man at the other end of the bar. He was not so discretely eyeing the woman chatting with Colleen. Colleen wiped her hands and looked a little more closely. Beautiful, yes, she thought of her conversation partner, but maybe not as young as Colleen had first thought. Not that she was judging; hell, she'd be pleased as punch to look that good at any age.

"By the way, I'm Eleanor DeWitt, but my friends call me Ellie," she said. "As you can tell, I'm not exactly from around here. After my husband died, I came to Queensbay to be closer to my son. He runs a car dealership in town."

Ellie held out a beautifully manicured hand, and Colleen took it, shaking it lightly.

"Nice to meet you, Ellie, I'm Colleen McShane. Born and bred in Queensbay."

"You don't look it," Ellie said, "and sugar, I mean that as compliment. You're not quite as preppy as the rest of the locals, with their Vera Bradley and L.L. Bean, if you know what I mean. I'm pretty sure the top you're wearing wasn't bought within five hundred miles of here."

Colleen laughed at the assessment. "I just moved back from Paris. I came back to spend more time with my mother." Another half-truth, but Ellie was having none of it.

"Well, if that isn't a way to say that there was a man involved, then I don't know what is."

Colleen shrugged and said, "I didn't think it was that obvious."

"Oh, darling, there's always a man, in my experience."

Colleen fell silent. She'd never meant to have her life defined by a man. After her father had walked out, she'd vowed never to rearrange her life for any man. But, looking back now, that was exactly what she'd done. No more, however. She had moved back home to start over. It wasn't the first time she'd reinvented herself, but this time she was taking her time with it.

"Don't worry. I can see you don't want to talk about it," Ellie said, with a wave of her hand. "Well, no worries, you can tell Ellie when you're ready. Anyway, here's to starting over."

Ellie raised her glass and Colleen lifted the cup of club soda she kept handy behind the bar, and they toasted. Colleen smiled, feeling the tension she'd been carrying around ease just a bit. The trouble with coming back home was that it felt like all eyes were on her, to see if she was just like she had been before she had left. Ellie, new to town, wouldn't remember the old Colleen, which felt like a good thing.

Colleen worked while she chatted with Ellie. Colleen had a feeling that Ellie was keeping an eye out for Quent, but she was friendly enough and nicer to talk to than the guy at the end of the bar, who had parked himself there just as happy hour had begun and hadn't moved since. She called him Chino Charlie, since she was fond of alliteration. He had told her to call him Charlie when he sat down and plunked a hundred-dollar bill on the bar, as if that would buy him her full attention.

She had studied him, sizing him up. He wore a pair of tailored chinos, expensive loafers without socks, and an aggressively blue and white striped dress shirt, wide open at the neck with diamond-studded cufflinks at the wrists and an obscenely expensive watch. He was just past middle age and had been getting friendlier as his alcohol intake began to affect him. First it had been a bourbon on the rocks, and then he had switched to beer, but it was obvious he was feeling a little loose. Usually when Quent was working, he would handle guys like that. He ran a tight ship, and customers weren't supposed to be ogling the servers. At least that was what he'd told her.

She had snorted at that and responded that she'd been tending bar since she was eighteen and knew a thing or two about handling a drunk. Still, she usually had backup, but tonight, until Quent got in, it was only a skeleton crew in the kitchen, none of whom looked tough enough to throw this guy out. Still, she had a few tricks up her sleeve, and she was prepared to use them.

"You're not the usual bartender, are you?" Chino Charlie asked, trying to be friendly. She'd already heard about his car, and his boat, mostly because he'd kept dropping hints about the size of its cabin. She knew that he had a house on the water in the next town over, an apartment in the city, and a share in a private jet. She didn't believe half of it but nodded and tried to be polite but distant. There were a set of keys in front of him, and Colleen was already planning on the best way to cut him off, swipe his keys, and find him a cab ride home.

Quent had warned her not to try that trick on her own. That, he had told her, required sturdy backup of the male kind. Colleen sighed. She was quite capable of taking care of herself, and Chino Charlie, with his spare tire and flushed face, didn't seem like he'd be too hard to handle. The music switched over to the B-52s' "Rock Lobster." Technically, they weren't British at all, but she had a soft spot for them and their upbeat, happy style. She loved how the mood of the bar shifted, right along to the music.

One of a group of women down at the end of the bar waved her down, enthusiasm radiating from her as she sang along to the lyrics. Colleen judged it was girls' night, or book club night or, maybe it was just "it's Wednesday night and the week was half over" night. The group was drinking Cosmopolitans, more than was probably good for them. The one who had been corralled into being the designated driver dutifully sipped a sparkling water as the level of giggling rose up around her. Colleen was sure that most of them would regret the Cosmos tomorrow morning, but they were appreciating the fun they were having tonight.

They ordered another round, and as Colleen broke the shaker in half and poured two perfect drinks into the wide-lipped martini glasses, she told the water sipper, "Next time you come in, and you're not the driver, first drink is on the house."

"Thanks," the woman said and gave Colleen a smile, slightly less morose at the thought of her good deed paying off.

Colleen twirled away, feeling good about the energy. She hadn't had a drink herself tonight, but she loved the festive atmosphere. It was like planning and throwing a really great party, except here she was getting paid. She moved along with the beat of the music, glad she had on her favorite jeans, the pair she had painstakingly tracked down in a beloved Parisian boutique, as well as a shimmery sleeveless top she had picked up at Wal-Mart. Ellie had been only half right as to the origin of her clothes. But no one needed to know, and Colleen loved the mix of the high and low.

Chino Charlie was getting to the bottom of his beer and doing his best to catch her eye, but she danced away and pretended to be busy checking the level of alcohol in some of the bottles. The door opened, and

Colleen's whole body registered that someone new had entered the pub. An instant later, she knew who it was: Jake Owen.

Their eyes met across the long expanse of the room. Just then the audio slipped, and Bono's haunting, sexy voice seemed to linger in the air, catching them in a web of old history, broken trust, and too much attraction. Then, just as suddenly, everything righted itself and the music went on, and the babble of the customers filled the air as if no one else had noticed what had just happened. And Colleen supposed they hadn't.

I should do the same thing, she thought, as she turned her back to him, telling herself that it was no big deal that Jake Owen had walked into her bar. She used the mirror behind the bar to her advantage and watched Jake as he squared his shoulders and started to wade his way through the crowd toward her.

He walked easily enough, his confidence evident as he traversed the length of the room. People called out his name, slapped him on the back, and shook his hand. He was the big man around town and had been since he'd been the star of the high school football team, so good some had thought he'd make it to the NFL. That hadn't happened, of course, those kinds of things almost never did, but he still took the recognition as his due, moving through the crowd, slowly, deliberately, giving everyone a little bit of time.

In one part of her mind, the one that was a healthy, red-blooded, living breathing woman, with a pulse and eyes in her head, she registered his broad shoulders and the way his body tapered to his trim waist and then to his long legs. She admired the way that the sleeves of his shirt stretched tightly over his

8

muscled arms. His hair was short, shorter than the last time she had seen him. He must have gotten a haircut. She liked it longer, she decided, even as his dark blue eyes, under the strong slash of brows, caught hers in the mirror.

She looked away first, focusing on a getting a martini ready and finding what she needed to whip up another batch of Cosmos. Chino Charlie was done with his drink and signaling to her for another, but she continued to ignore him and everyone else until Jake was finally at the bar and standing in front of her. Looking up, Colleen carefully added three olives to the martini that Alfie, one of her favorite customers, liked dirty.

Jake stood, fingering the collar of his dark blue polo shirt, which was embroidered with the name of his construction company.

"How are you?" he asked.

She said nothing as she put the drink on a napkin and placed it in front of Alfie.

"Working," she replied. "Are you drinking or standing?"

A slow, half-smile crept over his face, and he said, "I think I'll stay and have a drink." He took her up on her challenge and planted himself right at the bar.

She scowled. She had meant to frighten him off, by being curt with him, knowing it was better for them both. She'd been doing that for the past few months she'd been in town, doing everything she could to let Jake Owen know to stay away. She'd even taken to crossing the street when she saw him, so they wouldn't have to talk and, on those rare occasions when they did cross paths, she'd been downright rude. He should know without a question that she was trying to avoid him.

But here he was, like he'd known just where to track her down.

"Small town, only a couple places to drink," he said. "Guess you're stuck seeing me around, right, Colleen?" he said with a smile that was aimed only at her.

And it was the smile that let her know. Or rather the way the smile made her feel. She was in trouble.

"Oh, sugar, you're always around," Ellie chimed in with a laugh.

"You two know each other?" Colleen looked between them, trying to not to let her thoughts show. She knew that Jake couldn't have stayed alone all of these years, but Ellie was too old for Jake - wasn't she?

"We're neighbors, in the apartments in the Annex over at that Marina," Ellie said, her tone mild, as if she had guessed what Colleen was thinking.

Colleen nodded. Okay, that explained it. *No need to get worried.* Not that she was, in any case. She was going to make sure that there was nothing between Jake Owen and her, no matter how many times he kept showing up in front of her.

"Is this a better gig than the Osprey Arms?" Jake asked casually, mentioning the other place she'd worked until recently.

"Sure. Better tips, boss is nicer," she said and flicked a towel over another invisible spot. She'd switched jobs for a couple of reasons, none of them having to do with the size of the tips. Mostly it was because Jake was too frequent a customer at the Osprey Arms.

"Going to take up space or order something?" she said, turning her back on him.

"A beer," he said, putting a fifty-dollar bill on the

table.

"Queensbay IPA?"

"You remember?"

"It's my job," Colleen said as she poured the amber liquid into an icy glass. She didn't want him to think that it was anything special. She remembered people more by what they drank than by their names, another bartending trick. Have a customer's drink ready as they walked in, and they tipped well. Simple math, good business.

She set it in front of him and leaned on the counter, watching as he took his first sip.

"Did you come here to find me or avoid me?" she asked before she could stop herself.

He smiled at her, and her stomach did a little flip.

"Let's just say I knew exactly where you'd be."

She pulled back slowly, but he kept looking at her, his eyes level with hers, and she felt a slow flush creep up her skin. It was a compliment, sly and sweet, and it had her completely undone.

She had always thought of Jake Owen as the boy next door, the hometown boy that made good. He'd never really left Queensbay but hadn't let that slow him down. He owned his own construction business. Word was that he was invested in more than one commercial property around town, and he drove a shiny new truck. Colleen knew he had a sweet little fishing boat parked down at the marina. Fortune had smiled on him, and, goddammit, people liked him for, well, being himself with them. People liked Jake Owen because he was a good guy, which meant that he was so not her type.

So she pulled back, gave him the briefest of

smiles, and told herself to stop flirting with him because he was safe. It wasn't nice to let him think there could be something between them. Chino Charlie was calling to her, his finger swirling around his empty glass. She swung a towel over her shoulder and decided that it was time to deal with him. Out of the corner of her eye, she saw Jake shoot Charlie an angry look, but he said nothing.

"How about a cup of coffee?" she offered, using the towel to hold her hands steady.

"I don't want coffee. How about you pour me another beer, honey?" Chino Charlie said, his words slightly slurred; his eyes were unfocused, and his face flushed. She thought he would have been handsome, except for the extra weight he carried around his face, which was beginning to shape into jowls, probably from too many nights like these.

"Sorry, I think you've had enough." She kept her voice cheerful as if she had just agreed to pour him another.

"I'll tell you when I've had enough," he said and slammed his hands flat on the bar top. The sound was loud and sudden, and Colleen winced despite wanting to appear tough. He was loud enough that the other patrons noticed, and the bar quieted just a fraction, so the upbeat tune from The Police suddenly became very clear. She noticed that Jake had tensed, leaning in toward them. She didn't need a white knight to get involved with this. Her job, her mess to clean up.

So she held firm. If it got ugly, she'd have to call for backup, but in the meantime she wanted to try and avoid a scene. A scene was bad for business.

"Sorry, sir, I think the Guinness tap might be out.

If you can wait a moment while they change it out, I'll get you a water."

"I'll have a shot of bourbon," he said, his voice low and menacing.

She nodded as if considering it, meanwhile thinking that he wasn't going to back down and gracefully accept a cup of coffee.

So it was time to play tough. She was aware that Jake was off his bar seat and moving in. She didn't need his chivalry. She'd been taking care of herself for a long time, and she wasn't about to stop now.

She leaned over the bar, looked Chino Charlie straight in the eye and said, "Last thing you need is more bourbon."

"If you won't serve me, I'm sure I can find someone else in this town who will," he said and made as if to pick up his keys.

Colleen was faster and managed to swipe them just out of his reach. She jumped back in success and to make sure there was a decent distance between her and him. His face darkened and she took a deep breath, ready to weather the storm.

"Give them back," he yelled.

"No way."

He leaned in and planted both hands on the bar, getting right in her face. She swallowed and held her ground. Now she was rethinking her decision about not calling for backup. Even the skinny dishwasher would be something.

"Do you know who I am? I'll get you fired if you don't give me those keys. Give them to me now."

They were at a stalemate, but Colleen was ready, had a plan worked out, and was ready to implement it.

"Hey mister, I think the lady here told you to back off." Jake Owen's voice was calm but loud enough to be heard above the beat of the music.

She blew out her breath, not sure with whom she was more annoyed: Jake and his assumption that she needed help or Chino Charlie and his belligerent attitude.

"I don't need your help," she hissed at Jake and shot him a look for good measure, one that had withered many a man who had stood in her way, but he held his ground, his eyes focused on the drunk Chino Charlie who was standing, albeit with a bit of sway, as if the floor itself was moving.

She turned her attention back to Chino Charlie and smiled. It was the smile that Olivier had told her had won his heart. It was the smile she thought she would always wear, a lifetime ago, back in France, when the days had been sunny, and her life had seemed dreamy. It stopped the drunk, and he looked at her, desperately trying to focus on her. She was pretty sure he was seeing doubles of her.

"Look, sailor," she said, her voice pitched low. He grunted, pleased.

She leaned in. "You don't want to go out there now. It's dark, and I hear there's a storm heading in."

"My boat's berthed at the marina. I just have to get there. Maybe you can help me find my way?" he said. Colleen kept smiling. She wasn't going to walk him to the marina and she wasn't going to give him his keys.

"How about this. I'll call a cab and the front desk at the hotel at the marina. You go back to your boat, get a good night's sleep, and I'll make sure breakfast is on the house tomorrow. Chef there makes a great Eggs

Benedict. You can pick up the paper and your keys then. What do you say?"

The man straightened up and seemed to realize that he was being offered a lifeline. Colleen was aware that most of the bar was watching this little scene, including Jake, who looked like he wanted to hit someone. Chino Charlie sensed that public opinion was not on his side. Or maybe it was the sheer bulk of Jake standing near him that had him rethinking his attitude. At last, he smiled, as gamely as he could, and asked, "Are you going to be serving me the coffee?"

"Guess you'll just have to stick around and see." She added a wink for good measure, and the jerk took it as a sign of goodwill and nodded.

The tension eased out of the room; already, Colleen could feel the vibe picking up, as the rest of the patrons turned their attention back to themselves and their own good time. She kept the smile up, but clenched her hands together so that no one could see them shaking.

She called back to the kitchen, got one of the dish washers, whose cousin drove a cab, to call it in and had him walk the guy out into the fresh air and the bench conveniently located just outside for such situations. Drama handled, Colleen was about to go back to work when she felt his stare on her. Jake was looking at her hands, a slow deliberate look, then he met her eyes. She unclenched her hands and placed them on the bar, willing them to be steady. The confrontation had left her a little shaken, the surge of adrenaline coursing through her, wearing itself out. Jake stood there, his own arms crossed over his chest, his eyes dark with suppressed emotion.

"What?" she demanded.

"Nothing," he said, the word conveying that it was anything but.

"Fine," she said with a shrug. "Are you going to keep drinking, or just stand there and take up a paying customer's spot?"

Colleen turned away and sighed as she pulled down the tap, letting the beer run down the side of the cold glass, annoyed at how the situation had gotten out of hand. She'd misjudged how belligerent Chino Charlie would get. Still, she had taken care of the situation, and she hadn't needed any help, not really. She watched Jake. He had taken a seat at the bar, near Ellie. He was slowly sipping his beer, watching her, his jaw tight with tension.

He looked angry. At her. She didn't know why. She hadn't done anything. If anything, she should be angry with him for butting into the situation.

"Taste better than warm beer from the can?" she asked and was rewarded with a smile and laugh. She meant it as a jab, but he returned it with a flash of humor.

"One of the pleasures of being a grown man. I can now drink beer in a glass. In public."

She nodded and started to slip away, suddenly needing to be away from the intense way he looked at her. Like he cared about her.

"You okay?" he asked, his voice low, laced with concern. It confirmed her worst suspicions.

"Why?" she said sharply, as she stopped.

"The guy was getting in your face, and he didn't seem like a nice guy."

"Happens," she said. "It's part of the job. I was

16

going to offer him a cab home, make him come back for the keys in the morning no matter what. I was handling it."

"So you didn't need any help?"

"Didn't need any help," she confirmed as she wiped down the bar between them.

"Had it under control?"

"Totally under control."

Jake shook his head and kept looking at her, making her think that he was seeing too much of her.

"Collen McShane, you always did have to be the smartest one in the room," he finally said.

It was her turn to snort with laughter, the tension partially broken.

"It was high school in this hick town. The standards weren't that high," she said.

"And here we are, both back in the same hick town."

"Guess that means I'm still the smartest one in the room."

"And, I guess that just makes me the dumb quarterback looking for a good time."

"Am I going to have to kick you out, too?" she said and meant it as a joke.

He had said his line with practiced good humor, and she had no doubt that if she told Jake Owen to bug off, really bug off, he would. But just for a moment she was enjoying it, the little flash of flirting, even if she knew it could go nowhere. He smiled at her and, for just a moment, she felt her heart skip a beat before it settled down with a flutter. *Traitorous hormones*, she thought. Jake Owen was too damn easy on the eyes, always had been, even if he wasn't her type. Nope, she liked her guys more refined, less muscly, less like the buff, tanned, former quarterback sitting here in front of her. Of course she did, she told herself.

"Not tonight," he said.

She didn't have to say anything more because someone called for her, and she was back in the moment, working, doing what she did best.

Chapter 2

He watched her the rest of the night, knowing she knew that he was watching her. Earlier, he'd been evasive in his answer to her. He had come to Quent's because he knew she would be working there. He'd heard from his bookkeeper, who'd heard it from the sous chef at the Osprey Arms that Colleen had been asked to leave her employ there because the owner's wife wasn't all that fond of her.

Since Jake felt partially responsible for that particular situation, he'd swung by Quent's Pub and found that Quent could use a little help behind the bar. A tip to his bookkeeper, who had tipped off the sous chef, who had tipped off the owner, Sean, and Colleen had found herself smoothly out of one job and into the next. So yeah, he had come in here to check on her and see how she was doing. Word on the village streets was that she was a hit, wresting away control of the playlist from Quent and bringing a much-needed bit of feminine softness to Quent's old-school but gruff style of hospitality.

He'd deny any part in it, of course, but he couldn't say he minded watching her tend the bar. She was elusive to track down, but whenever they were together, tensions ran high, usually in a simmering, slightly sexy kind of way. At least they did for him. For her part, she seemed content to ignore him, and it was driving him crazy.

Seeing her in Quent's, in her quicksilver top, with her smile and her whirlwind command of the place had been like a jolt to his system. Sure, he'd seen her around town, but she usually crossed the street when she saw him coming, and she'd always been more clothed. She favored dresses that were flowing rather than clinging and coats and rubber boots or ballet flats, scarves, and sunglasses. Very Parisian, Jake imagined, thinking that he could sketch a picture of her sitting at café table in front of the Eiffel Tour and title it "Parisian at Rest."

So it was a surprise, a nice one, to really see her, to see her wearing jeans that hugged her curves and a shirt that showed off her toned arms, a deep V of creamy flesh around her neck, and hair that flowed over her shoulders in a tumble of golden brown waves. And her smile. He hadn't seen that in a long time. Of course, it wasn't directed at him. At everyone but him and, by the size of the tips he saw left on the bar, Colleen McShane was working her magic. He settled into a spot where he could keep an eye on her, while talking to some guys he knew about baseball, fishing, and the usual. He listened mostly, so that he could focus on her.

He would look up, every once in a while, pulled out of a heated discussion about local politics or the game or plain old gossip and look at her. And half the time he was surprised to find that she was looking right back at him. Not staring at him, and certainly not so much that she didn't move with the grace of a conductor behind the bar, filling drinks, cleaning old ones, making guys laugh and getting women to spill their guts to her. But nope, they were now, unofficially, he thought, keeping an eye on each other.

Jake watched closely, looking for anyone else in the mood to hassle her, but unfortunately no further need for him to get between Colleen and some other guy with too much to drink occurred. He stayed the rest of the night, until last call when she made it clear he needed to get out. He wanted to offer to help, but she didn't need it. She was orderly, easy, and confident, but there was no mistaking she was tired all the same. He saw her shoulders sag when she thought no one was looking. She arched her back and dug a fist into the small of it, as if it hurt.

Not for the first time in the last few months, he wondered just what Colleen McShane was doing back in Queensbay, lifting trays of glasses and pouring drinks. Last he had heard, she was living in Paris, working as an interior decorator, shacked up with a count or duke or whatever they had over there. Whispers had abounded of a flat on the Left Bank and a chateau in Provence. Queensbay, as charming as it was, was a far cry from that kind of life. Paris was the type of place she had always wanted to be, something she had confessed a long time ago to him in one of their brief moments together. And he had never doubted she would get what she wanted.

But now she was here, slinging drinks and doing her best not to notice him noticing her. His attention made her mad, he could tell. Was she mad because she hated his guts that much, or was she mad because she didn't hate him enough? He would just have to find out because he couldn't stop thinking about her.

Now, after last call, he was waiting outside on the small bench. The village was quiet, mostly dark, though the marina lights still shone bright, lighting up the sky near the harbor with a softly glowing aura. They wouldn't dim until later, but the whole village had a sleepy, settled air. He took a deep breath, clearing out the smell of the bar with the tang of sea air, seaweed, and salt. It was a bracing, distinctive scent, and you either loved it or hated it. He loved it.

"Need a ride home?" he asked when she finally stepped out, a jacket covering her bare arms. Good thing, as the air was chilly. Clouds piled in, scudding across the half moon. Rain by morning, he expected, which was good, as he was told the flowers needed it.

"I can walk," she said, a stubborn tilt to her chin.

"It's a bit of a hike," he said, knowing she was living at her old place, halfway up the hill toward the back of town, the side without the water view, the side that gentrification hadn't quite hit.

"I'm used to it."

She said it like that was the end of it. The drunk was safely tucked into his boat at the marina. Jake had made sure of that with a few quick texts to the harbormaster, but still, he had no intention of letting her walk home alone. She started off, and there was nothing to do but follow her.

"I don't think so," she said, stopping and turning around suddenly enough so that he found the palm of her hand on his chest. She snatched it back as if she hadn't meant to do that. She didn't have a ring on, he had never seen one, and that gave him hope. Maybe the count could be counted out of the picture.

"You shouldn't be walking alone," he said as

22

reasonably as he could.

"It's Queensbay," she said, as if that should have explained everything, and normally it would, but not tonight.

He shook his head. "You saw what happened in there. I'm not letting you walk home when there's a creep like that around."

"That one is passed out on his boat and is going to wake up tomorrow with a headache and bad case of embarrassment."

He shook his head again and said, "You don't know that he's the only one."

"You are not walking me home," she said and turned. Her stride was quick but he caught up.

"Seriously, I'll call the police," she warned.

"Officer Sisson's a friend of mine. I am sure he will agree that having someone walk you home is the safest thing."

"You're not walking me home," she repeated, picking up her speed.

She stopped after a few paces and turned half way, looking at him.

"What are you doing?"

"Not walking you home," he answered and also stopped, so that a gap remained between them. He could play this game too.

"You're following me?"

"Yup. Not walking you home. Can't stop me from following you to make sure you get home safely."

"Who's the creep now?"

"You don't have anything to worry about with me. I'm not a creep."

She looked at him, as if deciding something, then

shook her head. "Just until my street, then you can go."

He pretended to think about it for a moment, before agreeing.

He kept his pace just off hers, deliberately hanging back just a little. He decided that this was a little game and he was starting to enjoy it. Sure, he had chased a few women in his time, but this was different. Colleen seemed perfectly comfortable ignoring him, as if she weren't aware of him at all. Time to remind her that he wasn't going anywhere. Just when he had made the decision to stop mooning over her and start pursuing her, he couldn't say. Sometime between getting her a new job and seeing her at it. Colleen McShane was not an easy woman to forget, and Jake thought that this was his chance to see if he wasn't ready to get over her.

"Lovely night back here. How is it up there?" he called to her. The clouds were coming in faster and he wondered if the rain would come sooner than he'd thought.

"Shhh, you'll wake the whole town," she said, without even looking over her shoulder.

He looked around. No one would ever accuse Queensbay of being the kind of place that never slept. They were almost past the part of town that had most of the shops, and they were all closed and dark. In half a block, they would be in a residential area, the streets of houses gradually rising up the bluffs. Along the hills that hugged the harbor was the section of town known as The Heights. Solid, large Victorians and Craftsman houses sat, interspersed with some more modern homes, all covered with windows to take advantage of the water views.

Colleen's house was in a different section, the

one that was straight behind the commercial strip, a cluster of smaller homes, from genuine saltboxes and Colonials to more recently built Cape Cods, all on postage-stamp-size lots. In this part of town, a person had better like their neighbors. The boom in fortunes that had hit the rest of Queensbay had passed this part of town over. The old iron and gas street lamps that were a distinctive feature of the commercial section of the village, gave way to more utilitarian fiberglass and fluorescent lights that pooled in dingy yellow circles, illuminating the tired-looking cars lining the streets.

"We're the only ones up," he pointed out.

"These people have to get up early. You know, the bus drivers, the construction workers, the fishermen, the worker bees."

He caught up to her, until he was just behind her.

She turned. Her blue eyes were dark, searching. Once, a long time ago, she had been a bright, sun-drenched blonde, but her hair had darkened to a richer brunette. There was no smile on her face.

"This is my street. You don't have to come any farther."

He nodded. He knew that her house was about halfway down the block, a late Queen Anne Victoria, on the small side, but with some nice detailing. He also knew that it needed a paint job, or at least it had the last time he had driven past. He tended to notice these things, and the details stuck with him. In fact, he knew that the house next to hers had gotten a new roof last year, and that the one three doors down needed one.

"I don't mind going farther," he told her.

"I can still call the police and tell them you followed me home."

He shrugged and held up his hands. "Fine, have it your way."

Her eyes narrowed, and her lips twitched as if she wanted to say something. Instead, she shook her head gently, her expression growing almost sad. He wanted to ask her what was wrong, but she just turned, hiking her bag higher on one shoulder and took off down the street. It wasn't quite a run, but it was quick enough that she was to her house and up the steps before he could say anything more. He stood there, for a moment, in the light spilling out from the street lamp. Somewhere, down the road, a dog barked, and the wind rustled through the trees. He felt the rain drop, just as he heard the first splat of water, big fat drops, against the pavement. He cursed, wishing he had brought a jacket or maybe an umbrella, then turned and walked quickly back toward town and his apartment.

Chapter 3

Jake moved through the throng of bodies gyrating to the thump of the music. Whoever controlled the playlist had decided to channel a club-like vibe, and the music had no words but a beat that made it easy to dance to. Red plastic cups were held high, definitely not filled with soda, their red-colored contents jostling and spilling over as the guys and girls jumped up and down in a drunken approximation of dancing. No one cared. It was prom night, and everyone was in a party mood.

The night was warm and close, a haze of humidity settling down over the scene. The only thing heavier was the fog of hormones, all too palpable. He surveyed the scene, feeling both detached and superior. Been here, done that, even it had just been a year ago. Wait until these kids got to a big time frat party. He took a sip from his own Solo cup. Some sort of punch, fruity with a definite bite of alcohol. He should know, since it had been his job to bring the liquor. He was pretty sure that was reason number two Darby Reese had asked him to go with her. Reason number one was that he was Big Reg-approved. Reg was Darby's father, and he wasn't going to let just anyone take his precious daughter to the prom.

Prom night: full of anticipation, fear, and excitement. These kids didn't know what life had in store for them. How good high school had been. But he did, now that he was a freshman at UConn, soon to be a sophomore, and *he felt lordly with the wisdom a year of college had given him. High school had been simple. Easy. College was harder. Playing football was harder, school was harder, everything was more complicated, more pressure. The question of what he was going to do with his life seemed to lie heavy on him. Taking Darby to prom had seemed like a nice way to forget about all that.*

Of course Big Reg, Darby's dad, had made the rules clear. He would be allowed to take Darby to the prom, and he would be allowed to escort her to the after party, and he would be allowed to bring her home by her curfew. But, in between he was to make sure that no one, and that included him, touched Darby.

Big Reg, who had hands that could have doubled as meat hooks, had poured him an ice tea and made him a hamburger, on the house, since the whole conversation had taken place at the Reese family deli. Funny, the burger, which was one of Jake's favorites, had tasted like sawdust in his mouth after Reg's lecture on respect and description of what he, Big Reg, would do to anyone who touched his precious Darby. Not that Jake liked Darby that way. They'd grown up together; their fathers were the best of friends. She was like a little sister to him, an attractive, smart little sister who had looked pretty damn good in her dress, but still, a little sister.

So now he was here playing bodyguard to a girl who had no intention of keeping her promise to her daddy to behave. The seniors of Queensbay High had taken over a no tell motel, its only distinction being that it was close to the water. It had a crappy pool, skanky rooms, and beach access to the placid waters of Long Island Sound. But, no one cared. The music was turned way up, prom dresses and rented tuxes had been shed for shorts and skimpy t-shirts and people were promising to be best friends forever and to never lose touch and remembering all the good times they had.

Jake kept pushing through the crowd. He had lost sight of Darby and that was not good. She had tried to kiss him, a real kiss, and he had been tempted to kiss her back, but the thought of Big Reg had effectively stifled all desire. Besides, to him, she was just Darby, so he had pushed her away, and she had shot him a challenging look that only meant he was going to have trouble tonight and disappeared into the crowd.

He had meant to follow, but then thought it would be a good idea to give her some space, so he had gotten a drink, then run into a few guys he knew and had spent a while answering questions about what it was like to play college ball. He realized that Darby had been gone a while, and when he started to ask where, someone had said that they had seen her go off with Aaron Miller, and that was not a good thing. Aaron Miller was a tennis player and one smooth bastard. Darby had seemed intent on having something happen with someone tonight, and Aaron Miller was probably not as afraid of Big Reg as he should be. Jake didn't like to think what would happen to him if he failed to keep Darby out of trouble.

He moved more quickly, giving nods to people who seemed to know him. He stumbled out toward the end of the row of rooms, to where a tall tree speared up toward the sky. Grass and sand mixed together, and he thought he saw her sitting there, head down on a bench, silhouetted in silver in the dim light of the moon. Goddammit, it looked like she was crying. He wondered what Aaron had done to her. Whatever it was, Jake would make sure he paid. He stepped out onto the sandy path, his feet sinking into the sand and *muffling his footsteps. It was quiet here, the music and the sound of drunk and happy kids muted to background noise.*

She looked up. It wasn't Darby. He should have known. She was too blonde, the hair turning to silver in the moonlight. Colleen McShane. Jake swallowed. She wore cut-off jean shorts and a tight little tank top that exposed just a bit of her belly, which was flat, tan, and just a little too enticing. They had been in an art class together, and once she had said that he was a good artist. Then he had watched her in the school play and in a practice debate that the whole school had been forced to sit through. Something about her caught his eye, and he had made a few attempts to talk to her. He had even asked her out on a date, but she had coolly ignored him.

"Sorry, I didn't mean to interrupt," he said, which came out as a stammer, and he swallowed. There was no need to be nervous, he told himself. He wasn't some high school kid. He was a college man. But there was something almost like scorn in her eyes as she answered.

"You're not."

Once again he had the sense that Colleen McShane could care less whether he was there or not, lived or died. He simply didn't register for her. Still, he couldn't help but notice that her eyes were blue, a dark, deep blue, hard to see in the dim, washed light, but now he was certain that they were glittering, as if filled with tears. Colleen McShane had earned a reputation as an ice queen. She was a cheerleader, a great student, and hot. Yet she said no to all dates and appeared aloof as if she were better than the rest of them. It had only made her more desirable.

He wanted to turn away. He needed to find Darby. If Darby found out he was talking to Colleen he would be in for it. They were considered frenemies, who couldn't decide if they liked or hated each other. The latest disaster had something to do about the vote for class president, if he recalled correctly. But Colleen looked like someone had just run over her dog. He couldn't bring himself to abandon her.

"Are you okay?" he asked, and he should have turned away then, should have run far away, but he was curious. On a night when every one of her classmates was celebrating, what could be so bad that it would leave her here instead, alone, at the edge of the crowd? If she said she was fine, he would leave and continue on with his mission of rescuing Darby from the clutches of Aaron Miller. Do the job he was supposed to do.

"Want to take a road trip to Vegas, pull my deadbeat dad out of the Elvis chapel, and tell him to come to graduation?"

Her voice was flippant but she turned away immediately, as if embarrassed by what she had said.

He couldn't leave now, as much as he might want to. There was something about the look in her eyes, the way her lower lip trembled, the way a twinkle of light caught at the necklace that hung down, dipping below her tank top, right there to the swell of her breasts. He swallowed. He should not have looked there. He carefully brought his eyes up to her face.

A road trip with Colleen McShane had some definite possibilities.

He went and sat down next to her.

"Think we could make it back by Monday?" he asked. "Don't you guys have a week of school left? Finals?" He could play this game too.

"What do you care about finals, Jake?" she said and raised her chin just a little. She was prettier than he remembered, not that he had been thinking about her much. Okay,

31

so maybe he had made a sketch or two of her in his notebook, but he hadn't gotten the nose right. He'd drawn it too straight and in real life, it curled up, slightly pert, and it gave her face much more animation.

She had said his name as if she knew him. Sure he had been the quarterback of the football team, but he was used to such disregard from her that he couldn't help the flicker of excitement sparked by her recognition of him. She had said his name, and now she was looking at him, her blue eyes level and clear, as if she were waiting.

She smelled good, sweet, like lemon and flowers, and her hair was soft. He reached out and touched it. He didn't mean to. It just happened, and she didn't hit him or tell him to go take a hike.

In a moment he was kissing her, and she was kissing him back. He grew bolder, and touched her and again, when she didn't resist, his let his hands roam over her, feeling her warmth. She was curves and strength, smooth skinned and beautiful, and he wanted her. She seemed, unbelievably, to want him. Somehow, and even in this dream, especially in the dream he could never quite figure out how it happened, how within minutes they seemed to find themselves in a room together, laughing, touching, kissing, all the while him trying his best to keep his cool.

He was a college man and this was supposed to happen to him all the time, though it had never quite happened like this, this smoothly, this perfectly with a girl who took his breath away. He ignored the misgivings that pricked at him, that this was too easy, that this wasn't supposed to happen this way because she was laughing as clothes came off, and he was laughing with her and that everything about it was perfect.

Until the moment when the door was flung open, a

bright hard light came on, and the covers were thrown off and a frighteningly calm Darby Reese said, "You have got to be kidding me."

It was then that Jake always woke up. Well, not always. Once, the dream had kept going, and he and Colleen McShane had had their moment together. But this morning, in the bright cool light that came in through the bare window, the dream ended as it normally did, leaving him both aroused and disappointed. He lay there, as the dawn slowly gave way to the morning, light pouring into his windows. He had come home last night, soaking wet from the unexpected rain shower and hadn't been able to fall asleep, tossing and turning and thinking of Colleen until finally he had started to dream of her.

This wasn't the first time he had dreamed of her. All that summer he'd been tormented by thoughts of her. Over time, when he had realized that she wasn't coming back, the dreams had faded. The memories, too, became muted. Then a few months ago she had quietly slipped back into town, and now he dreamed of her all of the time. Now he went out of his way to find her and be near her. Half the time she ignored him; the other half he fancied that he sensed a weakening of resolve. He never saw her with anyone else, a point in his favor. She seemed unreasonably opposed to him and just him. But last night had marked a thawing in their relationship. She had actually laughed at something he'd said.

This slimmest of openings was something, and he would take it. He needed to get up soon and go to a job site that he knew was behind, and he was supposed to deliver a bid on a new commercial building. One of his crew had just had a baby, and he was sure that he was supposed to do something nice about that. Yet all he could think about was Colleen McShane, and the way the streetlight had made the back of her shimmery shirt glimmer as she had all but run away from him.

Rolling over, he punched the pillow as if that would give vent to some of his frustration. He knew exactly why he couldn't stop thinking of Colleen McShane. She was the one that had gotten away, the one he couldn't stop wondering "what if" about. And now she was here again, right in front of him, and he couldn't get her out of his head.

Chapter 4

The morning came all too soon was Colleen's first thought as the sun hit her face, and she was pulled toward consciousness. She'd been right in the middle of a dream, a very realistic, detailed dream that involved her and Jake Owen getting to know each other very intimately. The room was too hot, the one window that was propped open not providing enough of a cross breeze to combat the stuffiness. Or maybe she was just hot and bothered. Her breathing was fast, and her whole body tingled. The dream had been complete with activities in which she hadn't engaged in a very long time. Not that she needed to, she told herself. There were plenty of other things to think about besides sex. She groaned, reminded herself to buy a fan, and gingerly opened one eye, and was met with a solemn pair of dark blue eyes and a tiny forehead wrinkled with concern.

"Bunny is sick." Adele's voice was a whisper as if merely raising it would cause Bunny to feel even more ill.

Colleen smiled and managed a surreptitious look at the clock. Six o'clock a.m. was early for someone who worked at a bar, but not for a five year old. It had been almost one o'clock before she had gotten home, just ahead of the rain and almost another hour before she could settle down and sleep.

All of it was his fault. Jake's offer to walk her home had kept him on her mind more than she should have allowed it to. Her only consolation was that he had probably gotten wet walking back. There'd been no sign he was prepared with an umbrella or a jacket. *Served him right*, she thought as she brought her attention back to the matter at hand. Bunny's glassy brown eyes stared back at her while Adele's blue ones were round and worried. Colleen reached out her hand and touched Bunny's plush head.

"He feels fine to me, hon," she said, though in truth, Bunny, the stuffed dog, felt a little sticky. Probably from the toast Adele liked to have each morning. White toast with strawberry jam. Two pieces. Lightly toasted. Only about one and half ever eaten. The other half Bunny was supposed to eat but somehow never did.

Colleen sat up. The secret to surviving late nights and early mornings was regular Pilates and plenty of water the night before. She didn't believe in sampling the wares while she was working, so at least she was only tired, not hungover. Tiredness could be cured by a strong cup of coffee. And sleep. Someday she would sleep again, on a regular schedule.

"I think he needs to go see the doctor. You know, the special doctor, the whatchamacallit, the wet," Adele said.

It took a moment for Colleen to process what her daughter had said. "The wet? Oh you mean the vet. It's short for veterinarian. The kind of doctor who takes care of animals," Colleen said, but didn't bother to mention that the vet was only for real animals. Adele was four going on forty, and Colleen treasured the moments when she still sounded like a little girl.

Adele's forehead pinched together in concentration, then she nodded in comprehension as she processed the new word. Her daughter knew both French and English, but since they had moved back to Queensbay, Colleen had used English more and more with her daughter. Still, some words, like "veterinarian," were tricky. She knew that focusing on English wasn't very sophisticated, but she didn't care. A new town meant a new language. Adele could learn French again if she wanted.

"So Bunny should go see the vet," Adele said, enunciating the word clearly and emphatically.

Colleen pushed herself up. There was no going back to sleep, at least not until later tonight. She was off from the pub tonight, thank goodness, which meant that she could, if she wanted, go to bed when Adele did.

She held out her arms, and Adele crawled into them. Colleen hugged her little girl and felt the warm sun on their faces. Adele curled into her, a warm, cuddly ball of love. This, she thought, this was why she had done what she did, why she was doing what she was doing now. These sweet, unsullied, uninterrupted moments with her daughter as just the two of them made a life for themselves, without waiting for anyone else.

"The vet is only for real animals. I think we can take care of Bunny just fine by ourselves."

Adele squirmed around, and Colleen leaned down and touched her nose against her daughter's, slightly snubbed, freckled one. Adele smelled like strawberry jam.

"Did you already have breakfast?"

Adele nodded. "Grammy made it. Now she's gone to bed."

Colleen's mother often worked the night shift as a nurse in the hospital and was a natural night owl, and even when she wasn't at work, still kept to a graveyard shift schedule, rattling around the house, drinking herbal tea and watching cop shows on TV, then sleeping during the first part of the day.

"Bunny is real," Adele insisted, not to be deterred. Colleen admired her daughter's determination, while she hugged her closer and thought for a moment about how best to answer.

"He's real to you and to me, of course, but I don't think he would be real to the vet," she said. "I am sure if we give Bunny lots of hugs and kisses, he'll be just fine."

"If we had a real dog we could bring him to the vet."

So this was where Adele's thoughts were heading, Colleen realized. Adele had wanted a dog for a long time, stopping ones on the street to give hugs and pet them. Olivier had said something about getting a dog once, something Adele had not forgotten. To her, he was just an uncle, a friend of her mother's, but sometimes Colleen wondered if Adele knew the truth. Colleen sighed. The last thing they needed in their life was a dog. Adele had been through so many disappointments that this was one promise Colleen intended to keep, but not today.

"And I told you, someday, not too far from now, we can get a dog."

Adele gave her a look that was both imploring

and reproachful. The real question, and Adele knew it, was when. Colleen sighed. How did she tell a five year old that she couldn't put a date on getting her crap together, that these things, even though Colleen had a plan, took time? More time than seemed reasonable to a little girl; that much was obvious. It would all work out in the end. Colleen would make sure of it. All that crap about the journey being the most important part was just that, crap. Right now, she would have been happy to snap her fingers and get to the destination.

"Soon, honey, soon," was all she could answer, and for the moment Adele seemed assured by it, or maybe it was Colleen's rhythmic stroking of her hair that reassured her. She asked no more questions, just burrowed more closely into Colleen.

Colleen let the moment linger, loving the warmth of her daughter sinking into her, ignoring the cracked plaster in the corner of the small room that had been her childhood bedroom, ignoring the fact that it hadn't changed in years, ignoring the fact that it needed new paint and that the window pane had a hairline fracture in it, shutting everything out but the small, warm little body that was curled up against her.

Soon, a small voice told her. Soon things would get better, more stable. She had a plan, a big one, but she was convinced that it could work. She would make a life here. Adele would grow up in a small town, safe, loved, and stable. She would be able to give Adele everything she'd never had. Their life before, in Paris, would fade, even as Olivier and the pain of his not being around would fade. She couldn't afford and had no time for pity, and she couldn't let Adele see her as anything less than strong and assured that the future was going to be better. Colleen wanted to pretend, to imagine for herself what their life would look like, and because she wanted to force herself to keep a promise, she asked, "What would you name this dog of yours?"

Chapter 5

"What are you up to?" her mother asked when she wandered into the kitchen, a bathrobe tucked tight around her, her eyes red rimmed, and her hair messy from her mid-morning nap. The tone in her voice reminded Colleen of her teenage years.

Colleen shut down the cover of her laptop out of habit. She'd been looking at paint colors, trying to decide between cloud white, snow white, and something called vanilla bean. Vanilla bean was slightly creamy, slightly warmer, and she was pretty sure that would be her choice. Of course what she had really been doing was trying not to think about Jake Owen. Either way, she was antsy and distracted.

"Just some email," Colleen said.

Her mother shot her a look as she made a beeline for the coffee machine. "What are you really doing?" Her mother's voice was gravelly, a holdover from the years she had smoked. She had quit, along with the drinking, quite a while back, but Maura McShane had a roughhewn edge that clean living wouldn't ever quite undo. Her mother poured a cup of lukewarm coffee, took a sip black, and frowned in disgust.

"I'll make you a new pot," Colleen offered and pushed up to get started. She didn't want to discuss her plans with her mother.

Her mother waved her away. "Not if it means you're going to grind the beans, then get out that fancy schmancy pot of yours. I'll just stick it in the microwave."

It was Colleen's turn to make a face. Her mother was talking about the French press and coffee grinder she had brought with her from Paris. Every morning Maura watched Colleen make a pot of freshly brewed coffee with barely disguised irritation. It was all too fussy for her.

"Nothing wrong with coffee from a machine," her mother answered.

"But the way I make it is so much better," Colleen protested.

"To you, maybe," her mother said, putting the coffee in the microwave.

"I hardly think I'm the only one."

"Nope, I'm sure you're not."

Maura jabbed the panel on the microwave, which was old like everything else in the house and on its last legs. She had to apply an inappropriate amount of force to the start button before anything resembling reheating would begin.

"So," her mom said and looked around while the microwave gave off a hum as loud as a jet engine behind her, "were you running another one of your cost models? Working on a blog post?"

"What?" Colleen couldn't keep the surprise out of her voice.

"Paint's cheap enough, I suppose," Maura grunted

and turned as the microwave beeped, surveying the rest of the kitchen.

"And, I suppose we can—what do you call it—repurpose the cabinets. I don't have any money for anything new."

"Sure. We can repurpose the cabinets," Colleen agreed, surprised that her mother knew the meaning of the word.

"Maybe," her mother said, taking another sip of her coffee and rolling it around in her mouth before she swallowed it, "we can get a tax break."

"What do you mean?"

"Can't we write off the supplies if you put it on your blog? It's your business, right?"

"What?" Colleen asked; the conversation was obviously moving too fast, and she reached for the coffee. She definitely needed some more caffeine.

"You know," Maura said, "your blog and that book. I thought it was all part of your career back in Paris, part of running that shop there. Isn't the bartending supposed to be a temporary gig? The hours suck, but I suppose the tips are good. I heard Joan at the Garden Cottage is looking for some part-time help. Maybe you should walk on over and give her your resume." Her mother paused, then said, "I also sent for some catalogs from the community college. They have a good nursing program. I should know. The hours suck at first, but they get better. And benefits," she said and shrugged. "Pretty sure Quent doesn't give you those. Of course, if you just sold the building, then I don't think you'd have to worry about any of it."

Colleen sighed. They'd been over most of this before. Her mother was just trying to help, she knew, and she didn't want Colleen to take on any more risk than she had to. Her mother had been dropping hints about nursing school or network administrator courses since she moved back to Queensbay. Her mother had her best interests at heart, but Colleen had a plan that went in an entirely different direction. And her mother thought she was crazy.

It was a big step forward, something she had dreamed of doing, but now she had finally been forced into the reality of it. Maura wasn't a fan of taking risks, sticking her neck out. She would probably quote the statistics that four out of five businesses failed within five years. Colleen didn't need any more self-doubt. She had plenty of that to spread around.

"Some," Colleen admitted. The blog had started out in college as a way to document her hobby of taking second hand furniture and refinishing it. Before she'd known, though, it had grown from a hobby into a business selling furniture and taking on design clients. Finally she'd garnered a big enough fan base that a publisher had offered her a chance to write a book, a nice, glossy hardcover book. She'd poured her blood, sweat, and tears into the book. It was good, but it hadn't quite made her into a household name. Still, it was a start, a foundation, and Colleen was determined to build on it.

"Well then, there you go," her mother said. "See if you can expense the paint, and then we can go shopping." Her mother laughed, and a spark of humor danced in her eyes. Colleen knew her mother was trying to distract her, figuring if they started on a project like the kitchen, then maybe Colleen wouldn't go forward with what she had in mind.

Colleen had to give her credit. Caffeine worked

just as expected on her mother, turning her into something resembling a pleasant human being. To her credit, Maura knew this and did her best to stay away from the public until she'd had at least two cups.

"I didn't know you knew so much about the business of blogs."

"Or that you had one?" Maura said pointedly, eyebrows raised and looking at Colleen steadily. "Don't you think I've been paying attention all these years?"

Colleen shrugged, not knowing what to say. The messy, complicated truth was that she had hoped her mother was paying attention but also had wanted to be as far away from her mother and all Maura McShane represented as possible.

"I read your blog. How else would I find out how to make lavender lemonade?"

Colleen narrowed her eyes. "You never made lemonade unless it came out of a plastic barrel."

Her mother snorted and said, "True. I still like looking at the pictures."

Colleen frowned. "I think that's the only thing people like to do."

"You always have quite a few comments and lots of likes on social media," Maura said, and Colleen knew that her mother meant these things encouragingly. "Apparently that's how you know you're an influencer, right? And you're a good writer, too."

"I didn't know you read the book."

"What kind of mother do you think I am?" Maura asked in a voice laced with testiness.

"I mean of course you did," Colleen backpedaled hastily.

"I did get it from the library."

There was a silence while Maura looked out serenely over the rim of her coffee cup. Then she laughed. "I'm just kidding, you know. I bought a copy and one for the library too."

It was Colleen's turn to laugh. "Well, I guess that accounts for fifty percent of my sales." She had gotten the book deal after her blog had been successful. She had worked for months on the book, assembling her best recipes, tips, and photographs for living a *La Belle Vie*, A Good Life, the French way. Olivier had been proud enough of her, insisting on displaying the book in the store, where it helped to promote the design side of his business, not her own.

"Just remember, I was here, right where I've been all these years," Maura said as she drained her cup. "I never wanted anything but the best for you, all mothers do. At least all the decent ones do. I know that maybe you didn't think I did right by you, but I did my best. The best I could at the time." Her mother smiled softly.

Colleen nodded. Her mother had done her best, but Colleen hadn't thought it was good enough. Now as a mother herself, she could recognize that her mother had done more than she credited to her. There had been a roof over her head, food on the table, and if the lemonade had come from a plastic barrel with nary a hint of lavender in it, then so be it. So what if her mother hadn't asked if she was doing extra credit or taken her on college tours or hired an advisor on how to fill out financial aid requests? Colleen had learned to figure all of that on her own.

Her mother had done what she could to the best of her abilities and had said nothing when Colleen had asked to come home, except to say, "It's your house too, Grandma left it to the both of us."

And so now Colleen took a deep breath, and said, with wisdom from life experience and now being a mother herself. "I know you did, Mom."

"Now you do."

"Yes, now I do," Colleen said and held her mother's gaze, and Maura nodded. Colleen couldn't quite help but notice the slight glittering in her mother's eye as she gave a snort and tightened the belt of her robe.

"No, you don't, not really. Not even close, but you will someday, now that you're a mother. Of course, Adele will probably have to break your heart by going to live in Timbuktu or something like that before you'll learn, but that's the way it is."

"You have to get knocked down before you can get back up again," Colleen said. It had been one of her mother's sayings, long ago, when life seemed to be knocking them about every damn day.

"Something like that. I never could tell you anything. Always wanted to find out for yourself, certain you could do it on your own."

"And look where I am now."

"There are worse places. You have a roof over your head, you have got a sound mind and able body. You're not afraid of hard work, I'll give you that. And, you've got Adele, who's the sweetest thing ever."

"Must come from a different side of the family," Colleen said and smiled.

"Oh that's for sure," Maura agreed, then her voice softened, and she said, "It's just a rough patch, Colleen, just make sure you don't let it get you down. You won't, because you're stronger than I ever was. Always knew it, even when it broke my heart to know it. Just be careful. Don't try to run before you're ready to walk."

"Thanks, Mama," Colleen said, and she knew that her mother was really thinking of her. Her mother would think she was just being realistic, by telling her not to dream.

"Well, enough of that," her mother said briskly as she pulled herself up from her chair. "See if you can do something about the linoleum floor while you're at it."

"What's my budget?"

"A night's worth of tips. See, that would be a good blog challenge, kitchen redo on bar tab budget."

Colleen laughed as her mother left the room.

"I'm serious, you know," Maura called from the other room. "Bet it would be way more popular than lavender lemonade."

Colleen let her laughter die and looked around the room. The house was from Queensbay's Victorian era. It had been in her mother's family forever, built by one of her ancestors who'd been a carpenter in the shipyards. The workmanship showed, even though everything was tired and a little rundown. Nothing a few simple repairs and paint couldn't fix. *Maybe, just maybe, her mother was onto something,* Colleen thought as she pulled her computer toward her.

Chapter 6

"Y"ou are about to experience some up-heaval."

Jake almost did a one-hundred-and-eighty-degree turn when he saw what was going on in the break room, but he reacted too late. Madame Robireux, Queensbay's only psychic, had already seen him. "And you, Mr. Jake, you must come in, come in. I am reading tea leaves. I will read yours." Her voice was heavy with an accent of some indeterminate Eastern European nation.

Madame, as she insisted on being called, looked the part of the psychic. She channeled her supposed Gypsy origins into a modern-day interpretation that ran to long flowing skirts, peasant-necked blouses, and a scarf wrapped in her wild, brown-gray curls. She was draped in beaded necklaces. Jake was pretty sure she had rings on her fingers and toes.

"No thanks, Madame, I just need a cup of coffee," he said and tried to bypass her, but she reached out and practically dragged him into the plastic chair across from her at the small round table. When he and his partner had redone the building that housed their construction business, they hadn't the heart to kick out

Madame, who had occupied a small space on the third story.

His nerves jangled as he looked into her dark, kohl-rimmed eyes. Hell, they'd been too chicken to ask her to move, not wanting to court bad luck or an ancient Gypsy curse. So they had done what seemed like a nice thing at the time and offered her a long lease and a new paint job. She had expressed her appreciation by using their break room for free cups of coffee and impromptu tea leaf-reading sessions. He looked around for rescue but Tory Somers, who worked in the building, just shook her head and smothered a smile.

"Traitor," he mouthed to her, over Madame's bent head.

Madame took his palm in her strong grip and began to closely scrutinize it. Unsettled but curious, he waited as Madame ran her fingers over the lines in his palm, all the while making strange cooing and clucking noises.

"See this here?" she said, pointing to a line that ran downward.

"What is it?"

"Your love line."

He could see that Tory was rolling her eyes behind Madame's back. Tory did not believe in reading tea leaves or waiting for destiny to happen.

"What's wrong with it?" he asked.

"Yours is squiggly."

"What does that mean?"

"It means you're looking for love in all the wrong places. Love isn't found in bars."

"I don't find love in bars," he said.

Tory's eye rolling turned to a laugh that she

covered up with a cough.

"Or hotel rooms," Madame added with a disapproving shake of her head.

Jake pushed back: "I don't go to hotel rooms."

"Not since you finally moved out on your own," Tory pointed out.

She had lived next door to him until she moved into a beach cottage with her fiancé, Colby. Now Ellie, Colby's mom, lived in Tory's old apartment, right next to him, just another of those small town connections.

"You," Madame said, one slightly crooked finger waving sternly at him, "need to grow up. Or you'll never find true love."

"Who says there is anything like true love?" Jake asked, but Madame gasped.

"For you there could be, but you squander it chasing after anyone that makes eyes on you."

"I do not," he said and managed to snatch his hand back, fighting the desire to wipe it down on the side of his leg. Squiggly love line indeed. He'd only been chasing around after others because the one he really cared about had moved an ocean away.

"Don't you?" Tory said, with a toss of her head as she looked him.

"It's not like you were ever interested in me," he said. He'd made a half-hearted attempt to see if there might have been something with Tory, but thankfully they had both realized that it wasn't right.

She shook her head sadly and said, "Serena, Gwen, Amy . . . I could name a few more, and that's just in the last while."

"That's enough," he said, his voice rising. He did not want to talk about the list, especially about Amy.

Madame was ready to go, but not before she sent a warning look in his direction and gave him one last prediction: "You treat love too lightly, and it will kick you in the face." Her accent faltered only slightly, betraying her New England roots. With a tinkle of jewelry and a swirl of incense, she left the break room.

Tory gave him a one-shoulder shrug and headed back toward her office.

Jake got up, pouring the coffee down the drain. He wasn't thirsty anymore.

He didn't treat love lightly. He had never told any woman on that list that he was in love with her, especially Amy. In fact, he'd been quite clear on that point. It wasn't his fault that maybe one or two of them had thought that they could change him. *Why*, he wondered. He hadn't wanted to change any of them. He had liked everything about them for what it was and as long as it lasted. He liked women, but no one ever quite measured up to Colleen McShane. He rinsed out his mug. That was the problem. She had stomped on his heart, and like a little puppy dog, he was ready to come back to her, if she'd take him. And last night she'd been... nice. And now his hopes were riding high. Just maybe they were at a turning point.

He put the mug in the rack to dry. She was a bartender. Of course she was nice to everyone. Except for that creep Charlie last night. Charlie was lucky Jake hadn't decided to punch him for talking to Colleen the way he had. He felt a sudden, hot intense flash of anger. He needed to settle down. Colleen hadn't wanted him to interfere, but he had felt compelled to. He would have done it for anyone, of course, because that's what a nice guy does, but he knew that he wouldn't have cared about the outcome as much. Nope, he had it bad for Colleen McShane and had for over a decade. With Colleen back in town, his longing for her, his desire to be with her had only gotten more intense.

He flexed his palm open and looked at the squiggly lines. They meant nothing to him and he didn't believe in Madame Robireux's predictions at all. Like Tory, he was pretty certain that luck didn't have much to do with destiny, and success was more about hard work, persistence, and dedication to goals. Colleen McShane was definitely one of Jake's goals. She just didn't know it yet.

Of course, he thought with a half-smile, she didn't really know Jake Owen 2.0, the grown-up, mature Jake. Not the horny teenage football player who had nothing more pressing than thinking about where he was going to take a girl on Saturday night. Hard work, persistence, and attention to detail were all things he was good at. Those were traits that had made him a good football player; now those traits made him a good businessman and an excellent builder. He just needed to turn his attention fully in her direction, give it the full court press, the old college try with the home court advantage. He walked out of the break room, whistling, his head filled with a litany of positive sport analogies that made him smile. He was about to make a play for Colleen McShane.

Chapter 7

After her surprising conversation with her mother, Colleen had walked her daughter to Happy Face Pre-School, where Adele spent a few hours a day playing, learning, and making friends. It was a nice, normal, perfectly small town thing to do and though Colleen missed Adele even for the few short hours, her daughter was always happy.

Now that she had a few hours to herself, she planned on making the most of it as she walked through Queensbay. Last night's rain was merely a memory, but it had left the village looking freshly scrubbed and sparkly clean. The morning air was still cool, but a promise of warmth to come hung in the air, and a wonderful spring breeze rolled in off of the harbor. A few fat, puffy clouds dotted the blue sky, but the sun shined with gentle warmth.

She stopped for a moment along the boardwalk and soaked it all in. The harbor was spread out in front of her, so that she could see the long, encircling arms of hills and land that hugged the water, along with the hulk of the Queensbay Showhouse, and beyond that, Middle Island with its distinctive stubby lighthouse. Farther out, across the Sound, so far away it was but a low line of gray, was the low-slung coast of Long Island. It was the kind of day meant to be immortalized on a postcard, and she savored it.

Despite having grown up in Queensbay, she hadn't spent much time on the water. Her family, she laughed at the thought of calling it that, had never owned a boat. Sure, she had used a friend's canoe once or twice or been out on some other friend's boat, but during high school she had been so focused on leaving that she hadn't had much time for friends or parties. Homework had been the priority because good grades were a way out, the basic tool of building her escape plan. Colleen had been a cheerleader, more because that was what the cool girls did than because she liked it as a sport. Debate club had been something she had done because it had felt good to argue. She joined drama club because although her singing voice was decent, not spectacular, she had loved being an actress. She felt as if she was acting most of the time anyway, playing a part. She liked imagining herself as someone different. She could fake accents, copy mannerisms, always had been believable in whatever role she was playing.

She turned onto High Street, taking in the buildings lining both sides of the street. She loved this section of the village, with the beautiful, well-kept houses, small trim Colonials painted creamy white or buttery yellow, with their tall black shutters. Then there were the later Federal and Greek Revival styles, almost always in austere white, columns strictly at attention. After those, came the Victorians, simple to grand, their bright colors popping. Finally a few Craftsman styles filled in the gaps, solid and boxy with aggressive porches, perfect for catching the shade.

And the gardens. Gardening was a bloodsport in Queensbay. They abounded and it seemed like everyone had a green thumb. For now, the early spring bloomers like the dogwood and cherry trees were starting to bud out, and she was eager to watch the procession of color as the seasons progressed.

Later in the summer, the sunny side of the streets would be ablaze in lavender and rosemary, coneflower, and foxglove. Riots of color would poke out from white picket fences or more ornate iron ones. Overflowing pots were hung from porches and giant classical urns filled with flowers flanked walkways and brightly painted doors.

The tourists would be in town by then, walking in and out of the shops including *La Belle Vie*, her store, and that was the secret she was keeping from just about everyone. Her own shop, something she had wanted and dreamed about for years, but had never been certain she'd take the leap to do it.

She knew just how she would stock it. A mix of inventory, from antiques to newer furniture she would restore herself, to housewares, linen, jewelry, and even some clothing. Her idea was to embody the idea she had created with her blog. A little bit of the French philosophy on living a good life on any budget, right here in Queensbay. And of course, she could ship anywhere in the world. She might be based in a small town, but there was no reason she couldn't go global. And she'd take on clients, those who wanted to hire her to decorate their homes and their offices.

Nothing like that existed in Queensbay yet. And as she stopped in front of the ramshackle front of Phil's Queensbay Treasure Emporium, she realized that she was a long way from her dream of *La Belle Vie*.

It was still hard to believe that Phil's Queensbay Treasure Emporium, long a mainstay of town, was hers. Somewhere along the line, Colleen had become an heiress and that was a thought that made her want to laugh out loud. She had worked for Phil Sattler in his dusty Treasure Emporium back in high school. He'd been old even then, but kind, and once he realized that her interest in antiques and furniture was genuine, he became her mentor and taught Colleen about buying low and selling high.

She in turn had been fairly decent with computers, and once she'd set him up with a website and an online auction account, there had been no stopping him. Phil's Treasure Emporium had shipped all over the world, or at least throughout the continental United States. There was no telling what people would buy off the Internet, he always said and Phil had taken full advantage of that fact, happy to turn one man's junk into another man's treasure.

She had stayed in touch with Phil over the years, answering his technical and not-so-technical questions via email. He came to Paris and visited her and they had gone on a wine-fueled treasure hunt through the famous flea markets of the city. He had followed her blog and ordered ten autographed copies of her book. He sent little presents to Adele and antique postcards from Queensbay's past that he turned into humorous missives when he decorated them with slightly off-color comments. He'd been like a grandfather to her, and she had thought they were close. Apparently they had not been close enough for him to tell Colleen about the cancer. It had taken him quickly, so quickly.

The only thing more shocking was to discover that he had left her everything. She knew that he had no relatives, was the last of the Sattlers. His estate had proved to be surprisingly robust. It included the building, which he owned outright, several bank and investment accounts, his inventory and online auction account, which she had diligently kept up while trying to decide what to do. A five-star rating was nothing to sneer at, and she knew Phil, wherever he was, would be happy to know that his "treasures" were still finding their way into the hands of people who appreciated them.

At first, she had been enticed by the suggestion that she sell the building and liquidate the accounts. The lawyer who handled the estate said that there was a lot of interest in a commercial building in the heart of the village. He promised a quick deal, money in the bank. It had been especially tempting as things with Olivier dissolved. But Colleen had sat down, opened up a spreadsheet on her computer, and done some computer-aided math. Along with her own savings and what Phil had left her, she could open her own store. A place of her own where she could sell the furniture she restored, and things she loved to discover and tell the world about, all the things she had highlighted and talked about on her blog.

It had long been a dream of hers to do it, and Olivier had made vague promises to help her with it, but she had soon realized that those promises were empty ones. If she wanted to do it, it was up to her and her alone. And suddenly, with that random twist of fate, she'd inherited a commercial property in the small but vibrant tourist town.

Of course the reality of dealing with the remains of the Treasure Emporium and a rundown building had proved somewhat overwhelming. She was focusing on the inside, but she now looked at the outside of the building critically. Someday it would be nice to have the building restored; for now, just a good coat of paint on the front would do. She had taken the shutters down and they were in the workroom in the basement of the shop, leaning against the wall in various stages of undress, as she thought of the stripping and sanding she was doing.

She looked to her left. Only three doors down, the neat and trim façade of the Golden Pear Café beckoned her. She could almost smell the aroma of the dark, rich coffee wafting down the street. It reminded her of the Paris cafes where she had loved to sit and watch people when she had first moved to the city. She'd heard that Darby's *pain au chocolat* was fantastic as well. She thought longingly of being able to breeze in and order, without things being awkward. After all, ten years had passed since Darby had flung open that motel door, and she and Jake hadn't even been a thing. So it should have all have been okay.

She'd thought when Darby's husband, Sean, had hired her at his restaurant, The Osprey Arms, that bygones were bygones. Then Darby had dropped by and seen her there. The fight between Sean and Darby had been muted, quick, and fierce. After it was over, Sean had looked like he was truly in the doghouse, but he hadn't said a word to her.

The last thing she wanted to do was to cause trouble with anyone's marriage, though from what she'd heard, they were sickeningly in love and had one adorable baby to prove it. Still, she was not that kind of woman, so she took pity on Sean and quit before he had to figure out a way to fire her nicely.

As she was walking out, head held high, Oswald, the sous chef, had told her Quentin Tate was looking for some help at his sports bar. She stopped by Quent's that same day, and before she knew it, she as pulling in a few shifts. Of course, she didn't have to work, not with her savings and what Phil had left her, but she'd made a vow not to rely on a man, any man, even if he was dead and had left her all his money. So she worked for the principle of it, figuring that the bar patrons might very well become her customers, and serving drinks was one way to reestablish herself in the community before she risked it all and opened a business.

She had not seen Darby since that day at the restaurant. Colleen knew that part of moving back here meant atoning for her past behavior. She'd been a classic mean girl in high school, so ready to get the heck out of this town, she hadn't cared whose toes she stepped on.

It was that Colleen McShane who had thought nothing of giving in to her desires and making out with someone else's prom date because she had lost the election for class president to Darby. In high school, Darby had everything Colleen didn't: a loving, over-protective father; a sweet, PTA-bake-sale-baking mom; a happy home life. Colleen couldn't let her win. But that was the old Colleen. Back then she'd believed life was a zero-sum game. That to get what she wanted, someone else had to lose. Being buffeted around by life had taught Colleen that sometimes she would win and sometimes she would lose. Life, and happiness, were a marathon, not a sprint. And she had come to realize that the life she thought she wanted had turned out to be all wrong.

When she'd decided to come back to Queensbay, she knew she'd have to make amends, prove she wasn't the same person she'd been. It was obvious to start with Darby, but she hadn't had the courage. Yet. Colleen squared her shoulders. This was her town, just as much as it was Darby's. They'd both grown up here, both gone to school here, and now they were both business owners. It was part of Colleen's job description to get along with the other shopkeepers in town. Retail business owners found strength in numbers. Besides, *La Belle Vie* was going to be the type of place people sought out, a special, one-of-a-kind magical shop that catered to people with money to burn. They would be very happy, Colleen told herself as she forced her steps toward the plate glass windows of the café, to shop and then go get lunch and coffee at the café just a few doors down.

The coffee she'd already had was making her stomach churn. Tea, maybe something herbal would be better for her, she thought and a croissant to put her in the Gallic mood as she worked on her designs for the store. She could take pictures of the croissant for the blog post. Maybe get some business for Darby. She'd be bound to appreciate that.

She pushed open the door and a bell, strong, certain, announced her presence. There was no going back now. A few people sat, scattered at the round tables, reading the paper, checking their phones, and sipping coffee, enjoying a peaceful interlude. Colleen could appreciate the sense of style in the place, beachy and cozy, with good hardwood floors and white wainscoting that climbed halfway up the light gray walls, a simple, effective backdrop for the large black and white framed photographs. The photos featured local scenes, sailboats, the lighthouse, and the cottages out on the point, maritime without being kitschy. Music played, contemporary coffee house rock, neither too loud nor too low.

Not quite a Parisian café, which tended to have an excess of subway tile, dark wood, and the smell of very strong coffee, but this suited Queensbay. People here didn't seem to mind a little sand between their toes. The fragrant smell of buttery baked goods mixed in with the scent of what Colleen was sure was going to be the soup of the day, a lobster bisque. That might be a lunch worth coming back for, but first she needed to get through coffee.

A blonde was working behind the counter, and Colleen breathed a sigh of relief. Darby was a redhead, and this girl was not. Still, she silently berated herself for her cowardice. She was a grown woman. The past was the past. She was about to go up and place her order when the swinging doors to the kitchen opened, and Darby appeared, dressed in pink rubber clogs, checked pants, and a white chef's top coat, her name stitched across it. Her red hair was pulled back away from her face and there was a spray of freckles across her nose. Darby was talking over her shoulder to someone in the back, shouting something about fresh mushrooms over the sound of running water.

She held a tray full of cookies and turned to speak to the girl manning the counter: "Melissa, make sure you get the brownies cut from the pan and put out in the case."

Darby whirled around, balancing the tray as she dodged the swinging door and the scurrying of Melissa to get to work. Colleen tried to hide the smile. Darby had always been a bundle of energy, able to do a million things at once. It used to be organizing school dances and agitating for better cafeteria food. Now it was cooking and running a café.

But Darby froze when she saw Colleen. It was only an instant, but she saw the recognition and annoyance flash across Darby's face before she set the tray down and began filling the case. The silence stretched out between the two of them. Colleen wanted to break it, but she thought that maybe Darby should, maybe with a simple, "What are you having?"

And, then Colleen would say, "A coffee please. And one of those *pain au chocolats* I keep hearing about."

And then Darby would say, "Ah yes, thank you. I took a pastry class in Paris."

To which Colleen would answer, "I used to live there, you know . . ."

And then they would talk about how wonderful Paris was, and Colleen would invite her to *La Belle Vie*'s grand opening and ask her to make some appetizers.

But the question never came. Colleen waited, the silence stretching between them, until she was sure that everyone must have noticed. Darby finished placing her croissants on the rack in the case and then, without a word, disappeared back into the kitchen.

Colleen blinked. Nothing. Not a word.

Melissa, the blonde girl, was looking at the swinging of the kitchen door with a slight frown of confusion, as if she wasn't sure what had just happened. But once her boss was gone, her training took over, and she snapped to attention: "May I help you?"

Colleen just shook her head, felt the shaking start, and turned heel and ran out into the fresh air. The sun was higher now, the air warmer. It promised to be a splendid day, and a whole future awaited her. She had thought that it would be easy, but she was wrong. It wasn't going to be easy. But there was no place else to go. She couldn't go back to Paris. She'd thought she could come home again.

She squared her shoulders and faced the shutterless façade of the Treasure Emporium. This town was hers just as much as Darby Reese's. And eventually, Darby would come around. They had been friends once. You didn't just give up that much history over something that had happened long ago.

Chapter 8

The light poured through a tall, high window, turning the faded red velvet curtains into something resembling gleaming swirls of drapery, revealing a hint of former glory. If Jake closed his eyes and concentrated, really concentrated, he could almost imagine what it had been like in here, in the building's heyday.

Dressed up in their finest clothes, white tie and tails for the men, gorgeous gowns and tiaras for the women, couples mingling before the show began, making small talk, sipping champagne, listening to snatches of music playing from the orchestra as it warmed up, overlaid with the sound of laughter, of stories being told, stock tips exchanged, the news of the day hemmed and hawed over. His eyes flew open as a shadow crossed them. He caught a glimpse of fluttering wings, heard the shuffling sound of pigeons high above him. The mood broke, and he wondered what the hell he had been thinking. This place was nothing but a dump and needed lots of work, more than he'd ever undertaken.

His idea was crazy as hell, and he was starting to feel like he was just as crazy. Of course, it didn't help that he'd been thinking about Colleen again, all evening, all night. He just couldn't get her out of his head. He flipped open his notebook, looked at the page where he'd drawn a few sketches. A newel post that he wanted his carpenter to recreate for a house he was fixing up in the Heights. Then there was a doodle of a roof line for a more modern house he was restoring in the woods, and then came the sketch featuring Colleen.

He hadn't realized as he was doing it that he'd been drawing a memory of that night, after the prom when he'd found her, alone, vulnerable and upset. She had said something about her father not making it back in time for graduation and she had started to cry, hadn't she? Or had they started to kiss? Either way, it had landed them in a tangle of limbs and lips and clothes that needed to come off. And then . . . it had been interrupted. They had met up again and for a few brief weeks they had shared everything about themselves, except for being with each other. They had decided to take that part slow, but the connection between them had been intense. And then she had disappeared. Literally, there one day, gone the next, off early to college and some job. And she had never once come back. Until now.

He was about to rip out the page and crumple it up, as if that might make him forget, but he heard the creak of the door. Quickly he closed his notebook and looked up. Jackson Sanders, his business partner, stepped into the gloom of the Queensbay Showhouse carefully, as if afraid of getting his fancy shoes dirty. Jake had sensibly dressed in work clothes and boots and didn't care that they were probably already covered in pigeon crap.

"Are we supposed to be here?" Jackson asked, as his eyes scanned the space.

"I used a key," Jake answered. Jake could tell when Jackson's stare landed on a couple of the pigeons on one of the tall clerestory like windows. A frown crossed Jackson's face, and Jake fought back laughter. Jackson didn't like pigeons, never had, and after a particular incident in third grade had never quite forgiven the breed. Manfully, he squared his shoulders underneath his tailored jacket and stepped further into the shadowy gloom.

"You mean the key that didn't work?"

"How do you know that?" Jake said, but guilt tugged at him. It had been a long time since he'd done any breaking and entering.

Jackson gave a short bark of laughter. "Even I can tell when wood's been broken. What did you do, jimmy the wooden bar off the door?"

"Details," Jake muttered. He had thought that the key would work, and he'd be sure to nail the board back on before he left. Jackson said nothing, just arched an eyebrow and took a slow, deliberate circuit of the main floor of what had once been the Queensbay Showhouse. Built in the 1870s by a Gilded Age robber baron with a "summer estate" along the shores of the harbor, he had wanted to bring the show to him, rather than have to travel to New York City for opera, musicals, and other entertainment.

The theater had been a jewel set among the hills of the harbor, an ornate, square building with so much fancy work that it resembled a wedding cake. The good times had ended sooner rather than later, when the robber baron had gone bankrupt. Ill-fated revivals of the place had occurred over the decades, like summer stock theater and then when that failed, a townie movie theater that had survived until the multiplexes up on the highway had moved into town.

Since then the building had been empty, dormant. Now it stood in ghostly disrepair, owned by the town's historical society. They had tried to raise enough money to restore it, maybe turn it into a museum, but Queensbay already had one museum, and the building needed a lot of work. For as long as Jake could remember, the Showhouse had sat vacant, on its own little high spit of land, slowly tipping closer and closer to the water, dangling precipitously over the edge, like an actual wedding cake that had been kept out too long in the heat of a crowded ballroom. Still, it had always fascinated him, and he had always wanted to get inside, to see what treasures the building held. Now that he was in here, his mind was racing. The smell of old wood and possibilities was exciting to him.

"Look at this place. The workmanship, the detail," Jake said to Jax and swept his arm around, trying to take it all in. Ornate carved moldings, the curving staircase to the second floor. And that was just the lobby. The actual auditorium had frescoes on the ceiling and some of the biggest chandeliers he had ever seen. Of course the power didn't work anymore, and he'd heard more than his fair share of scuttling feet that surely indicated a rodent problem, but there were ways to fix all of that.

Jackson grunted, and Jake tried not to laugh. His best friend was a tried and true modern type of fellow. Jax preferred clean lines over ornate details, straight edges over curves. Even his house, which had once been a boxy, mid-century ranch, had been completely redone into a sleek glass, concrete, and dark wood bachelor pad. Now that Jax shared it with his wife, Lynn, a few feminine touches had been added, but the two of them were well matched when it came to keeping things clean and simple.

"Doesn't the history of the place get you excited?"

Jackson shook his head, and Jake could see from Jackson's expression that the cost calculations were starting to race through his mind.

"Do you know what it's going to cost to fix this place up?"

"Not exactly," Jake said. He had an idea, but he knew that Jackson wouldn't like the answer.

"More than it's worth," Jackson answered, unnecessarily.

"But look at that," Jake said and strode to the side of the theater, the one that faced the water. Curtains, tattered, faded, probably once velvet, most definitely moth bitten and mouse gnawed, practically fell apart in his hands as he yanked them open.

"All right," Jax agreed. "It's a good view."

"A good view?" Jake sputtered. "It's an amazing, awesome, awe-inspiring view."

"It's a little cloudy out there. Hard to see anything," Jax said and stood with his arms crossed.

Jake looked at him. True, clouds were starting to roll in, but the air was still perfectly clear. The surface of the harbor was a flat, stone-like gray. Sunny, no, but it was still majestic.

"People will pay a fortune for this view," Jake answered, and he knew they would. The old real estate cliché about location, location, location was true for a reason. Waterfront property sells.

"What, are they going to look at the view while they watch some third-rate off-Broadway show?"

"Huh?" Jake pushed back his cap and scratched his head.

"You know, some second-rate revival of *Cats* or *Phantom of the Opera*. Or maybe you plan on renting it out to the Queensbay players? Or maybe you want to let the high school use it for the annual production of *Our Town*?" Jax was gesturing now, really getting into it. "I can't quite imagine Mrs. Sampson, singing, trying to hit the high notes, can you?"

Jake couldn't help laughing as an image came into his mind with sudden clarity.

"What's so funny?" Jax asked, stopping. He noticed he was standing on a stain of something indeterminate and moved a little to the side.

Jake took a deep breath and said, "You think I want to turn this back into a theater?"

"Yeah," Jax said slowly. "You did play the part of the Prince in *The Little Mermaid* in eighth grade."

"I just did that to impress Amy Waters."

"Still, it was quite a performance, even if you were trying to impress her. Who are you trying to impress this time? Is it the waitress at the bar up on the highway, the one who's just doing it until her modeling career takes off? You know, I am pretty sure there are easier ways to get in her pants."

"I don't want to get in her pants."

Jax raised an eyebrow, his expression disbelieving.

"Well, I don't, honest," Jake said and meant it. He

70

couldn't even remember that girl's name; she was of no interest to him. Her pants were not on his mind at all; instead, he had to push a sudden of image of Colleen and her form-fitting jeans aside. He was talking business now and needed to stay focused. "That's not what I want to do with this place."

"I don't think trying to turn this back into a movie theater is a sound business plan either. You know they have the multiplex up on the highway with the big seats and the waiter service. I don't think an art house theater is going to survive that kind of competition."

"Do you think I'm crazy? I know none of that stuff will fly. I love culture as much as the next guy," he said and waited while Jax stifled a laugh. "I'm not a complete moron."

"Never said you were," Jackson said, but his voice held a ribbing tone as if he still thought Jake was crazy.

"So I like movies better than the opera. Sue me."

"I'm with you there, brother. Seriously, man, what do you want to do with this place?"

Jake waited a beat before he delivered his announcement. "Apartments. Actually high end, retirement community apartments. For empty nesters."

Jackson was silent a moment, and then he slowly turned, looking around, and Jake could see that he was considering the place in a new light. Another pigeon winged its way over their heads, flitting from one sunny window perch to another.

"Apartments," Jackson said, an interested grin on his face. He clapped Jake on the back. "Now you're thinking."

Jake waited.

"You know it would be a big job."

"Huge," Jake agreed.

"We'd need an architect."

"Absolutely."

Jax rubbed his jaw. "Are you sure we could even sell them for what they're worth?"

"Absolutely, especially with the views and the amenities we're going to add. And, I'm pretty sure that dock is fixable."

"You mean sell them with boat slips?"

"Yup, and I was thinking that there might be space to add a small restaurant too. Waterside dining open to the public, with space for boats to pull up."

"Very, very interesting," Jackson said, then added, "It's a gut job."

"Totally."

"Who owns it?"

"Historical society."

Jax nodded. "Tricky group of people to deal with. Mrs. Sampson's the president."

"She loves me," Jake said, knowing that Mrs. Sampson was seventy if she was a day.

"I don't think your usual strategy of loving and leaving them is going to work on her."

Mrs. Sampson had been married to Mr. Sampson for fifty years. Jake knew because he'd built a dance floor for their backyard anniversary party.

"I guess I'll just have to rely on my charm," Jake said.

"Do you want me to handle it?" Jax asked.

It was Jake's turn to smile. Jax was talented at many things, but people skills weren't his area of expertise.

"Thanks. I'll handle the public relations aspect of it. Maybe you can start talking to an architect, figure out some cost models, and research similar projects."

Jax nodded, and Jake was pleased to see that the wheels of Jax's methodical brain were already hard at work. Jake turned around, looking at the shadows and feeling that spark of excitement that always preceded a challenge. This, his idea, could really happen.

Chapter 9

After leaving the Golden Pear Café empty-handed, Colleen had settled for a cup of strong tea made from the ancient plug-in kettle in the back of the shop. It looked just as junky as everything else in the store, but the water was reliably hot. As the morning wore on, she grew hungrier and thought longingly of the lobster bisque she'd scented, but decided to settle for the granola bar she'd stuffed in her purse. There was plenty to do in the store, mountains of it, and she didn't need to waste her precious time or money on eating at restaurants. Not when she had a budget figured out to the last penny.

She lifted the lid of the dark wood-and-glass display case and spritzed the cleaning solution over the inside of the glass, wiping away a thin layer of grime. The display case was solid and handsome; it just needed some elbow grease to bring it back to life. When she had first opened the door to the shop, she had inventoried everything, and this had contained World War II medals, pillbox hats, and ladies' gloves.

"Why the heck did you put World War II medals and hats together?" she said to herself, though she was really invoking Phil. He had always seemed to know where to find any piece of his inventory, no matter how small or obscure, but she had been lost when she took over.

After many long hours of sorting things out, Colleen realized that there was a method to Phil's madness. Chronological organization, of course. As she cleaned the case, she almost laughed as the answer came to her. "Because World War II was the last time anyone had worn hats."

The medals and the hats had gone downstairs, gotten inventoried, and been stacked in boxes on the shelves. She had found that there was a lively online auction market for them, and she had slowly been selling things off, pleasantly surprised at the trickle of money pouring into the bank account and the excited emails of the buyers.

Working for Phil in high school had been her first exposure to old things, well-worn and well-loved antiques. Before that she had been surrounded with old, but it had just been, well, old. His passion for treasures had transferred to her, though she'd taken a different approach. She'd gotten into college in Manhattan, excited by the thought of leaving the small town behind. She needed money to pay for it, so Phil had set her up with a job at an antiques store in New York City. Still, she'd barely been able to afford rent, so she'd gotten a second gig bartending. Both the antiques store and bar had been strictly second tier. The great thing about the city was that everyone, even the A-listers, had a favorite dive bar.

The one she worked at happened to be a favorite after work hang out of a restauranteur who owned one of the hottest night clubs downtown. Soon, Colleen had talked herself into a job there, both as a hostess and a bartender. Once there, she served a different kind of clientele, and she had impressed the owner of a high-end antiques store with her knowledge of the resale value of 16th century antiques while pouring him a single malt scotch shot that cost more than she made in an entire night.

She introduced the antiques dealer to a middle-aged divorcee, who preferred extra dry martinis, and who was quietly looking to divest of her ex-husband's collection of antiques. As a thank you, the antiques dealer had offered her a job in his store. Strictly commission only, but she'd found that the commissions made selling furniture and artwork worth tens of thousands of dollars added up quickly.

She'd embraced her new life, dropped out of college, and made more money than she'd ever imagined selling antiques and promoting parties at clubs all over town. School was a distant memory.

She'd been part of an It Crowd, defined by parties, shopping, and living the good life. She found that if she played her cards right, she never had to pay for anything. Someone with daddy's credit card or a trust fund was always part of the party, and that was who paid her way. Her name was always on the right list for the newest club opening or the hottest after party.

As long as she kept bringing her bosses clients, whether for antiques or drinks, they were happy, and so was she. She put it all on her blog, of course, and she was a minor celebrity. Life was good. When she thought it couldn't have gotten any better, she met Olivier. He had been the real deal, strictly old money. French, with an accent to die for—or actually to fall in love with

—he ran his family's antiques business. He had an antiques shop in Paris, the best of the best, an apartment in town, and a country estate, with a crash pad in New York.

She had been swept off her feet, and the rest of the story had unspooled according to a time-worn formula that she had come to recognize after it was too late. Debonair older man flirts with younger woman who sorely needs a daddy figure. Long romantic dinners followed by a kiss, and soon she'd moved to Paris and found herself a woman about town, the brash American who could speak French, helping Olivier with his business. Her blog had continued, featuring their "lifestyle" including plenty of mentions of his store. It had been good for his business and their partnership.

She'd turned those customers into her own interior design clients, advising people with more money than sense on what to buy to fill their apartments and country homes. Colleen's sense of style was in high demand and her life had felt very European, very glamourous, until she got pregnant.

She'd been scared to say anything to Olivier, but he had been delighted. It was an alpha male thing, the pleasure that he could produce children. He had been happy, but that was when things began to change. She was something different for him, no longer a girlfriend, or as she had come to realize, the favored mistress. She was, too, she'd come to see, just one of many girls Olivier kept. He was generous and kind until you asked for too much.

Financial support he provided in abundance. Excellent doctors and, after Adele was born, a night nurse and a housekeeper. Her rent was paid and money was deposited in an account for her, but Olivier's presence had slowly slipped away.

Then he got engaged. Simone. She was from an old, aristocratic family, a woman who had grown up with city apartments, a summer house in the Rivera and skied in the Alps for winter break.

Simone was the kind of woman that Colleen could never truly be. Sure, she might have re-invented herself into someone who seemed like that, but it would all have been a fraud. Underneath it, she was girl from the wrong side of the tracks who had figured out how to give people what they wanted, whether it was a cool night out, a perfect martini, or the perfectly designed dining room.

Olivier's engagement had been a surprise, since she had seen a mention of it in the paper rather than hearing it from him. She had felt the fool when she realized what was happening, but then she would look at Adele and all regrets faded. Olivier had dismissed her with his usual insouciance, as if she had been a fool to think that he might actually have married her, Collen McShane, an American of Queensbay rather than Simone Des Robles of Paris, London, and Geneva.

Still, of course, he had promised, things didn't have to change between them. He adored her, Colleen, and their daughter; they'd just have to be discrete. And so, since Colleen didn't know what to do, she had stayed in Paris, in the apartment Olivier paid for, accepting referrals of clients from his store, while she worked on her book and her blog.

After four years of watching Adele grow and working on her blog and book, taking on interior design clients, selling her repurposed flea market finds, she found herself at a crossroads. She was almost thirty, Adele would start school soon, and it was time to think of what was next, to forge the next chapter of her life. She could go anywhere in the world, start over.

Thank God for Phil, and his help with that, though she wished he would have said something about being sick. She would have come home sooner, come to see him, and helped him in his final weeks. But she had known nothing about it.

Instead the catalyst to come home had been two-fold. Phil's estate needed settling, but she could have done that over the phone and by email. Rather, what had cemented her decision was when Olivier had come to her and had made the very casual suggestion that they rekindle their relationship. He had offered to set her up with her own shop. Not in Paris though, of course. New York was suggested, though London was a possibility.

She had realized, without having to ask, that he had no intention of becoming unmarried to his wife. He wanted them both. But Colleen had learned over the last few years that she could be on her own. That only Adele mattered, and that, in truth, she no longer loved Olivier. So she had told Olivier that she needed to come home for a while, to sort things out in person before she could give him an answer.

And truly she had meant that, to sort things out, to figure out what to do next. Maybe she would consider Olivier's offer to set up a shop. London or New York would be ideal. A business relationship only, of course. But somewhere along the way, as she cleaned and inventoried, moved in with her mom, found a pre-school for Adele, and settled into life in Queensbay, a plan formulated, including the decision to open her own shop. Except, not in Paris or London or even New York. No, *La Belle Vie: A Parisian Emporium* would begin its life in Queensbay.

Elated, she had splurged on a brand new sign for the shop, just as she realized how much work the place really needed. Her list grew and grew, and she was adding to it even now. The floors were a good solid wood but scarred and scratched. They should be refinished. Or, if that was too expensive, maybe painted, and the walls and ceiling. Everything had once been white but was now a dingy gray. She had put paper up on the windows, to keep prying eyes away, but she knew that curiosity about the place was running high. With the tourist season coming soon, she needed to be ready to open.

She was jolted out of her list-making by the rattle of the door and the sound of voices. Somewhat tempted to ignore it and keep working, she reminded herself that telling people she wasn't quite ready was almost as good as telling them she was almost ready. She went to the door, undid the lock and opened it, stepping back a bit as she did. Then she stopped when she saw who it was.

"What are you doing here?" Jake asked, obviously surprised. Next to him stood Jackson Sanders, his best friend, and, if Colleen remembered correctly, current business partner.

"I own the place," she said, then tried to look cool as if she were used to being the owner of something. She greeted Jackson, to cover the fluttery feeling in her stomach.

He smiled politely and nodded at her. He was as

tall as Jake and slimmer, his build that of a baseball player rather than a football player. Unlike Jake, he was dressed in a well-tailored suit and tie. Jake wore his usual khakis, boots, and polo shirt, the sleeves tight around his muscles. She told herself not to look at those but instead focus on Jake's face. It was all strong angles and blue eyes and dimples and almost as distracting as his muscled arms.

"I thought you worked at Quent's?" Jake said, clearly confused.

"I do," she said, deciding that the less information she doled out the better.

"I thought you worked at the Osprey Arms," Jackson said, his voice mild.

"I did. Didn't work out," she said, her answer sharp and clipped. Jake shot his friend a dark look.

Jackson nodded, a knowing look crossing his face. "Darby give you a hard time?"

Jackson had gone to high school with them too, and no one could fault his grasp of the complicated history of relationships that bound them together.

"Something like that," Colleen said and shrugged, one shoulder going up, a distinctly Parisian gesture she had adopted. It kept people guessing, and she liked that.

"What are you doing here?" Jake asked again. He took a step forward, and she took a step back and before she knew it, she had let the two of them inside the shop.

"Where did all the junk go?" Jake asked, walking around. He stopped, tested a column, bent down, touching his hand to the floor.

"In the basement, for storage," she answered, folding her arms over her chest. Jackson stood there, his hands in his pockets, a slightly amused look on his face, watching the two of them. He could sense, Colleen was sure, the tension between them. She had the feeling that Jackson knew everything.

"Where's Phil, in the basement too?"

"He died six months ago," she said, shocked, then saw the smile on his face.

"I know. I went to his wake. What are you doing in his shop?"

She paused. The word was bound to get out. "If you must know, he left it to me."

"Why?" Jake asked and turned around to look at her.

"I used to work for him back in high school, and we stayed in touch after I left."

"You stayed in touch with Old Phil?" he said, disbelief in his voice.

"I did," she said and raised her chin up. She had nothing to apologize for. She and Phil had been friends, and if people thought anything otherwise, well, that was their problem. But, she felt the familiar niggle of doubt. She was used to getting second glances. After all, she'd always been the girlfriend, never the wife, and there had seldom been a father figure around for Adele. Let them talk. Even at preschool, she had spent the first weeks dodging questions about the whereabouts of Adele's father.

"Old Phil," Jake said, still having trouble wrapping his head around the idea.

"Yes. Phil and I were friends. We kept in touch, and he even visited me in France. Turns out he didn't have anyone else to leave the building to, so he left it to me. Now I own it. I plan on having my own shop here," she said and waited a beat before she added, "Do you have a problem with that?"

"No," Jackson answered promptly and then pretended to be interested in a spot on the wall when Jake glared at him.

"What kind of shop?"

"Furniture, French antiques, design services, housewares. In case you have clients that are interested," she said.

"So the bartending is just biding time?"

"A part-time gig, while I get everything sorted out." Bartending was quick, easy money, and she liked the social aspect of it.

Jake said nothing, and the silence hung between them.

Jackson looked at them, shook his head in resignation, and said, "Hey Jake, I've got to go. Colleen, always nice to see you." He slipped out quickly, and Colleen imagined he was glad to get out into the sunlight and leave the complications of old relationships behind.

She was alone with Jake again. If it unsettled him the way it unsettled her, he didn't show it. He was bending down, running his hands over the floor, and when he looked up his expression was considering. He looked serious, and somehow, it was even sexier than his usual lazy, relaxed grin. This Jake was all business, and she supposed she had an understanding into why his company was so successful.

"These floorboards need reinforcing and a nice sanding, staining, and buff wouldn't hurt. Paint job too. White or were you thinking something warmer? Or gray? Gray is the new white, or so I've heard."

"Something like a creamy white," Colleen answered, surprised.

Jake stood up, arms folded. She didn't quite believe she was talking building renovations with Jake Owen, but so she was.

"Outside could use a paint job as well. I have a construction company in case you haven't noticed."

"It's on your shirt. You can't miss it."

"Best advertising there is. I could get you a shirt too? Or maybe you just want to borrow mine sometime?"

His voice had dropped and was suddenly playful. She decided to ignore the subtle little flip in her stomach. She found Jake Owen sexy. This constant temptation to go against her decision to remain uninvolved was really annoying. He was all of those things, but she was stronger than that, stronger than him. There was no place in her life for anything resembling a complication.

"I don't think so. Somehow, embroidered polo shirts don't quite say Parisian style," she said, proud that she was taking a stance against flirting. She wondered if his shirt would smell like him, like soap and sawdust and pine sap.

"You might change your mind," he said, and the double meaning of his words was obvious to both of them.

She looked at him and said, "I don't think so."

There was a pause, and he smiled. Her heart skipped a beat. It was time to get back to business. She had to pick Adele up in less than an hour.

"I have things to do. Did you come here for something in particular, or were you just being nosy?"

"Would it be so bad if I just stopped by?" He came closer to her, and she wanted to take a step back. He was just so damn big and hulking, and smiling. She had brushed him off so many times, yet he always came back with the same cocky, self-assured grin.

"Grand opening will be in a couple of weeks. I'll have some free wine and cheese. You can come back then."

"Too bad, I like pretzels and beer. It looks like you could use some help now. Maybe I can stop by later and help you paint something. Or, better yet maybe help you strip something off?"

She avoided closing her eyes, avoided even giving into the temptation that stripping anything off of Jake Owen might just be the most excitement she'd had in years.

"I'm busy later," she said.

"At Quent's?"

"No," she said shortly. She had a date with some swings and Adele at the park. But she didn't need to give him any ideas. He nodded and moved back just a fraction. She could breathe now.

"I did come here for a reason. If I remember, Phil used to have some old postcards of places around town."

His voice had lost the flirtatious edge, which she appreciated, even if she missed it. She thought for a moment. She had seen something like that downstairs. At the moment they had seemed completely unsellable so she was considering just donating them to the Maritime Center.

"Sounds familiar. Why?"

"A little research project," he said evasively.

85

She wondered at that, but decided that if she didn't want him nosing around in her business, she couldn't nose around in his. Besides, if he really wanted them, he could pay for them.

"I'll see what I can find," she said finally.

"I'd be mighty grateful to you. Maybe I could send some of my boys over to help you out, at least with the floors. Hard work, but worth it, and my guys are fast and good."

"I'll think about it."

He turned, as if he were about to go, then stopped and stared.

"Did you do that?"

She crossed over to where he stood.

"Yeah, I finished it yesterday."

It was a small set of drawers, something she had picked up at a yard sale in the neighborhood. It was a solid, but old-fashioned piece, made of real wood but of no historical value. So she hadn't felt bad removing some of the fussier details, stripping it of its stain and using a cool white-blue for a whitewashed, slightly distressed effect. She loved it, as she did all of her pieces, developing a maternal-like attachment to them. Still, she was pretty sure she could make a decent profit on it. Or maybe she'd just let it be a display item.

"It's good. Really good," he said, surprise obvious in his voice.

"Guess I'm more than a girl who can sling a drink."

"I never thought otherwise," he said, then turned to look at her, his blue eyes thoughtful.

She took a breath, steadied herself. Out of all the people she could be around, why did it have to be him?

Every time she looked at him, she was reminded of that night, of how sweet he'd been and then how ferocious the need for him had been. Now, with the filter of years, she could see that it had been yearning. Poor Colleen McShane had been looking for her daddy, and instead she'd found Jake Owen, who was the clean-cut hero type right out of central casting and still as sexy as hell. The kind of guy you could count on, who'd taken a girl to the prom because he was the only guy her father had trusted. Yup, Jake Owen didn't run away.

After the brief frenzy of that night, she had seen that Jake was dependable and that his dreams and hopes and goals were steady and consistent. He knew he wasn't destined for bigtime football. He'd wanted to get done with college so he could come back home and start building houses. He was a small town guy, and she had been eager to fling herself out into the world. Now here she was, bruised and battered and washed ashore, and he was still the same small town guy, albeit with a thriving regional business, just where he wanted to be.

He faced her, took her hand, and as if he could read all of the thoughts flitting through her mind, said, "I don't know what brought you back, Colleen, but it looks like you're here to stay. It just might be more enjoyable if we got to know each other again."

She shook her head and said, "I don't think you've changed much. You're right where you wanted to be."

He dropped her hand and took a step back as if she'd slapped him. She hadn't meant to insult him, but she saw that she had.

"Nothing wrong with knowing what you want and sticking to it," he said stiffly.

"Jake, I didn't mean to say there was."

"As I recall, that's exactly what you said when you left. Wasn't it something like," he paused for effect and then threw her words back at him, "'Jake Owen, you're never leaving this town. And I am, leaving here and seeing the world and never coming back.'"

She smiled, blinked back sudden tears, and replied, "Well, I'm back now. You're a good guy, successful, well-established. I'm still finding my way, and I need some space to do it, to breathe, and to be clear-headed about it."

He took a step closer, so close that she thought they were going to kiss. For one brief moment, she let herself imagine what it would be like. She could feel the heat between them, feel the desire from him. She closed her eyes halfway, almost felt him leaning in, then she stepped away. She did not need a man to help her, as easy as it would be to fall into those arms and say yes, Jake, send a crew over. She couldn't do that. She had learned the hard way that nothing came for free. She had learned her lesson, and she needed to teach her daughter the same thing, if only by setting the example.

He stopped midway through his move toward her and nodded.

"Okay, we'll take it slow," he said.

"We'll take it nowhere," she said firmly as she came back to her senses.

"If that's what you want to tell yourself. Colleen, it's been a long time, but I think you and I both know there's some unfinished business between us. You could be anywhere in the world, but you're here, now. So I think we can both count on figuring out just what's going on between the two of us."

He smiled, turned around, and walked out the door.

"Don't let the door hit you on the way out," she called after him, trying not admire his tall, athletic build. *So not my type*, she told herself.

The sun had come out, so he stopped a moment to slip on his sunglasses. He couldn't quite keep the grin off of his face. For some women it was shoes, some it was flowers, others chocolate. For Colleen it appeared to be old furniture. Good thing he had a whole warehouse full of stuff he had pulled off of job sites. Never knew when you were going to need something, whether it was antique floorboards, an old-fashioned clawfoot tub, or some old piece of furniture begging for a little tender loving care.

He was whistling as he headed to the truck. He'd always known she was something special.

Chapter 10

J ake's words bothered her, leaving her feeling nervous and unsettled. What did he mean by unfinished business between them? She sighed. She knew exactly what he meant, and the only question was what was she going to do about it? The walk to the preschool was doing nothing to settle her nerves, but she felt the familiar tingle of happiness as she turned the corner toward the day care. Adele loved it here, and that was one bright spot. Adele was happy to see her, even happier when she suggested that they stop by the park on the way home. Together they walked hand in hand to the small playground next to the library, Adele happily chattering about her day.

She loved to talk about her teachers and the still strange mannerisms of the kids, especially one, Josh, who only ate white food. Adele was French enough to not be a picky eater, and the thought someone could not like to eat almost everything incomprehensible. Colleen smiled down at her daughter, noting with wistfulness that her little face seemed to be getting more and more grown-up by the day. Adele's words came out in a tumbling stream and when she did not know the English one, she substituted the French one, and Colleen followed along, nodding in all the proper places.

This late in the afternoon, the sun was still strong, so she was glad to see that at least one of the benches at the playground was shaded by a sprawling oak tree. She took Adele's assorted things and sat down. Adele ran off, and Colleen watched until she saw her talking to some other girls. Soon there was a game going, and Colleen relaxed, thankful that at least one of them was finding her place. In the moment of relative peace, she tried to relax but found that her mind was racing. Jake, the store, Olivier, Phil, Darby, Adele.

It was so hard to be sure she was doing the right thing. There was no way of knowing, which was the hardest pill to swallow. Where would all of her choices up to this point and all of them past this point lead? Would it ever be alright?

Caught up in her own thoughts, it took a while before she registered the stares directed in her direction. She looked across the sandbox at the park bench at the two women who sat there. Colleen knew one of them. Amy Anderson, formerly Amy Waters. Married, with one kid, Mackenzie who went to Happy Faces with Adele.

Colleen sighed. Though she and Amy had gone to high school together, they hadn't exactly been what you would call friends. But unlike what had happened with Darby, Amy had brought that incident on herself. Still, hadn't enough time passed that they could move on? Perhaps they could laugh about it over drinks, maybe while their kids had a play date. Isn't that what mommies did here? Wine Wednesdays and Tipsy Tuesdays or something like that?

Adele had moved from the slide to the sandbox,

which featured a concrete sculpture of a mother turtle and a baby turtle. Kids played on and about it, and Adele was soon in the sand, building something with two other girls. Colleen decided it was now or never. If she was going to be in Queensbay and run a business, she needed friends. Colleen wiped her hands on the skirt of her dress. They were just a little sweaty as she idled her way over to the general vicinity of the bench where the two mothers were sitting. One had a stroller with a bundle of blue in it. Colleen could just make out the tip of a nose and eyes closed tightly in slumber. She would compliment the baby, Colleen thought, that would be a good place to start; she couldn't go wrong there.

"Oh my, what a lovely baby," she said, pitching her voice low, so as not to wake him up.

Amy turned to look at her, a challenging, direct look, while the other woman gave her a tentative smile, which faded as she saw the look on Amy's face. The silence stretched into rudeness, and Colleen straightened, readying herself for the fight.

"I'm Lisa," the other woman said, taking pity on her.

"Colleen."

There was still silence from the other woman, so Colleen decided to take the plunge. "Amy, nice to see you again."

Amy continued to stare frostily at her. Colleen swallowed. This wasn't going to be easy. Luckily for her, Lisa was an easier nut to crack.

"You're from around here?" Lisa asked, against the silence.

"I used to be. I grew up in Queensbay, but I've

been living in Paris."

"Paris," Lisa breathed, and Colleen saw real excitement in her eyes. "I love Paris, I mean I only went once, for like three days, and it was on a bus tour."

"Don't worry, it still counts," Colleen said, though she knew her Parisian friends would frown at such a touristy way to see the city. To get to know Paris, one had to walk and walk some more.

"Oh my, why did you leave? I mean, if I lived in Paris, I don't know that I would ever leave there."

Colleen smiled, tried to hide her nervousness. "I decided to open a store in Queensbay. Grand opening is in a few weeks. I hope you'll stop by." There, it was out. She had said it, and now she knew she needed to make sure she really did it.

Lisa was about to say something when Amy finally decided to chime in. "I heard you're back because your sugar daddy kicked you to the curb."

"Amy," Lisa hissed, her voice horrified. The little blue package made a fussing sound, and Lisa's hand automatically went out to push the stroller back and forth as she bent over and began to make soothing noises over the baby.

Colleen froze and then turned to Amy. "What did you say?"

"I heard you had to leave. That your baby daddy's wife told you to get out."

Colleen laughed, or at least tried to. She wondered how Amy had struck so close to the truth. Who could know about all of that?

"I don't know what you're talking about."

"Oh, I think you do. I mean, it's a pattern with you, stealing other people's boyfriends. Started with

93

Jake and the prom, then you find some French prince to shack up with. Now that he's turned you out, you're here with your little bastard. And, don't get too cozy with Jake Owen. He might just be taken as well."

Colleen tried to collect her swirling thoughts, trying to decide just where this antipathy was coming from. Lisa, who looked embarrassed by her friend, stood up as the baby in the stroller's fussing became more agitated.

"You, know I really should get him home. Kylie, come here, Henry needs to go home."

There was a bit of fussing from Kylie, but in the end she skipped to her mother, and they took off, a neat unit walking down the block, after a quick good-bye.

"Mackenzie, come here," Amy said, throwing a baleful look at Colleen.

Mackenzie, who looked to be in the middle of telling Addie some secret, looked up. She was about to protest, but one look at her mother's face told her that there was no room for negotiation.

"Nice to see you too, Amy," Colleen said as the woman led her daughter off.

Colleen sank down on the bench and let the colors of the park swirl around her. Bright pink jackets, the green of the trees, the early flowers. She wondered just who had been talking and what sort of stories had been going around about her. She had come back home to regroup, to start over, but somehow she wasn't finding things quite as inviting as she thought they might be.

Adele came over after a moment. She had dirty hands and a smudge of dirt on her face.

"Why did they leave?"

"Do you know those girls?"

"They go to school with me," Adele said.

"Are they friends with you?"

"Yes, Mama. Why wouldn't they be?"

"No reason, just asking. Is it time to go home yet?"

"Swing?" Adele said hopefully instead, and Colleen smiled and nodded.

A swing, a playground. If that's all it took to make Adele happy, then that was what mattered. Adele ran over to the swing, where a little boy was being pushed by a tall blond woman. Adele said hi, and waved her mother over. Colleen swallowed, took a breath, not sure she could handle an encounter with another person, but Adele wanted to swing, so swing she would.

She walked over and started pushing, giving a small nod and smile to the woman. They pushed the kids in silence until the other woman broke it.

"Those women." It was just two words, but there was something in the way that it was said that managed to convey both shame and something close to solidarity.

Colleen looked at the other woman closely. She really was much taller than Colleen, even in her flat bottomed red Converse sneakers. She was dressed casually, in ripped faded jeans, a plain gray t-shirt, and a brown suede jacket.

"Do you know them?" Colleen asked, returning her attention to the woman's face.

"They go to preschool with Josh," the woman answered with a nod. "I call them the Queensbay Meanie Queenies."

Colleen stifled laughter, even as the woman explained.

"Everyone here is like the Stepford Wives. They all have the same jeans, flats, and expensive bags and strollers. And, that's just the kids. The moms are even worse. Makes me want to vomit. I mean, I thought high school was the last time you had to dress to fit in. Come on, we're grown-ups. We should be allowed to wear what we want, right? And let our kids do the same."

"Adele goes to preschool with them too."

"I'm sorry, I didn't mean to insult anyone," the woman said and looked mortified.

"I'm not friends with them," Colleen hastily assured her. Especially not after what Amy had said to her.

"Oh, good. I mean, well, they just don't seem very nice."

Colleen considered and sighed. They weren't, but the sad fact was that she hadn't been much different, once upon a time.

"Sand box, please. Josh and I are going to build a castle." Adele turned and Colleen let the swing slow, helping her out. Josh, impatient, jumped off the swings and the two of them raced off toward the sandbox.

"So, Josh goes to Happy Faces too?" Colleen asked and wondered if this was the same Josh Adele had told her about, the one who only ate white foods.

"For now," the woman said matter-of-factly. They drifted toward the bench that was near to the sandbox.

Colleen wondered what was behind those words. There weren't a lot of preschools in town, as Colleen had found out. Any of the other places would have required Colleen to drive Adele, and she preferred, for the moment, that her life was mostly contained within a relatively small radius of her house, the preschool, the bar, and the shop. A far cry from Paris, but that was going to have to be acceptable.

"I'm Colleen."

"Lydia Snow." The other woman stuck out a hand, and Colleen took it. The grip, as she expected, was firm and enveloping, and there was a hint of roughness over it, as if Lydia worked outside or at least worked with her hands a lot.

"It's not fair!" A bellow came from the sand pile, and then there was a shower of sand.

Before Colleen could realize what was happening, Lydia was on her feet and heading over toward the children.

"Josh, what did I say about throwing sand?" Lydia's voice was weary, as if she had said it a thousand times before.

Colleen stood too, her eyes scanning Adele, who looked unharmed but unhappy.

"My dress is ruined," Adele said icily, and Colleen had to smother a smile.

"Darling, it's not ruined. Nothing a little detergent can't take care of," Colleen replied.

She had tried to explain to Adele that it might be better to dress in more casual play clothes, but Adele was part French after all and could not be swayed from wearing dresses even to pre-school.

"He," Adele said, and pointed at Josh, "threw sand."

"You didn't want to play cops and robbers," Josh said, his voice hurt and his arms crossed over his chest.

"I said I would play after I finished building my

castle."

"Well, your castle is done."

Colleen looked, seeing no evidence of a castle.

"Because you stepped on it," Adele said.

"You made me," Josh said.

Colleen didn't have to check her watch to know that it was probably time to go.

"I did not."

"Did too."

"Josh," Lydia said testily "You did too, I saw you."

"Well, she didn't want to play."

"She did, just not right away."

"Hailey always plays with me."

"Hailey gets paid to play with you, Josh."

Colleen was shocked and waited for the outburst of tears. Instead there was none, just the stamp of a foot, oddly defiant and heartbreaking.

"How about this. Why don't we build a castle over here and a city here and then connect it with a bridge. New and old," Lydia suggested in the same matter-of-fact voice.

"Like Paris," Adele said, her mind captured.

"Yes, like Paris," Lydia said. "Here, I'll start over here."

"Mama, come help."

Colleen smiled, glad she had worn jeans today. It didn't take long before Josh and Adele were busy enough that they didn't need help. Carefully, Lydia took a seat on the concrete edge of the sand pit, and Colleen followed her.

"That was a good idea."

"Yes. Josh's therapist says that he needs to work on his deflection and compromising skills."

"Oh." Colleen wasn't sure what to say.

"At least that's what my dad told me. Who knows? I think he's just a kid who hasn't had someone tell him 'no' a lot. His babysitter pretty much gives him what he wants."

"So you're not his mother? Or his babysitter?" Colleen had been trying to figure out the exact relationship between Lydia and Josh all afternoon but hadn't wanted to ask outright.

"Oh no, couldn't pay me enough. I mean, I like kids," Lydia said, then paused, and then frowned. "Actually, I don't know much about them."

Colleen was well and truly confused. It must have showed on her face, and Lydia took pity on her.

"I'm Josh's sister. Hailey is his babysitter. She's on her vacation, and if the gods are willing, she'll be back next Monday."

"His sister?" Colleen was pretty sure there was a solid twenty-year age difference between Josh and Lydia.

"Yes. Let's see, his mom, Charlene, is my dad's fourth wife. I'm from my dad's first marriage. So technically we're only half siblings, but that's a mouthful. And it's just the two of us. There weren't any other kids. Dad is, well, not exactly the fatherly type, unless you count marrying women who are young enough to be his daughter."

"So you live with them?"

"Oh no . . . are you kidding? I grew up in Georgia with my mom. I live in Savannah now. I'm just visiting. I mean, my dad and I, well, close might not be the right word, but we're not estranged, either. He's always supported me, so he called, because Hailey's gone, and

Charlene is out in Arizona. I think she's in rehab, or maybe it's just an extended stay at the spa, so my dad asked me to help out."

"So you're just watching Josh temporarily." Colleen wasn't quite sure she had kept everything straight.

"Yup, I get to be the bossy big sister," Lydia said and smiled sincerely. "It's a new role for me so I'm trying to figure out how to do it. You think I was too harsh when I told him about the babysitter? That she gets paid to play with him? Just seems like better be honest with the kid, and let him know that's why Hailey is soft on him."

Colleen thought for a moment. "Well, it was honest and at the end of the day, kids are pretty good at detecting lies." She looked at Adele and wondered just how much the girl had figured out on her own.

"Yeah, that's what I thought. I told him right off the bat, after he had thrown his third juice box at me, that I wasn't the babysitter, and I wasn't being paid to be there. I could leave any time. It sort of quieted him down and made him think. Since then he's gotten better, plus I like to keep him active."

"Keeping kids busy is never a bad idea," Colleen agreed.

Lydia held up her hands. "I'm an artist, well, a potter, and so when Dad offered me a place to stay, the starving artist in me thought that a free place to crash meant that I wouldn't have to teach as many classes to pay rent, which meant more time to just pot."

Lydia flexed her hands and watched the children playing contentedly in the sand.

"I think you'd be a good teacher," Colleen said.

Lydia smiled shyly. "I am. I mean I don't really

teach kids, at least not the little ones. The little buggers are hard, you know what I mean."

Colleen smiled ruefully. "I know what you mean."

"I like teaching older kids, the surly adolescents and adults too. The ones who don't think they are artistic or creative, or who are angry at the world. Then they get their hands on clay, and all of that crap just falls away. Of course, it's true that most of them don't have any real talent, but they're happy."

Colleen smiled and said, "I hadn't thought about it that way."

Something beeped and Lydia jumped as if she had been prodded. She took a phone from her pocket. "I set up all these alarms. This one tells me it's time to get Josh home, hose him down, and feed him. Otherwise he gets cranky."

Colleen looked at her watch, surprised at how late it was already. The sun was slipping lower into the sky, a gentle breeze stirring the leaves of the tree. It was time to head home for dinner, plus she had a date with a cup of tea and reviewing manufacturers' catalogs. Lydia pushed herself up to her feet, sand shaking off of her. Colleen got up too, dusting herself off.

Adele and Josh were in the middle of the sand pit, around the elaborate city they had created. Looking at it critically, she could see where Lydia's artistic talent had worked its magic, from the detailed windows in one of the skyscrapers, to the decorations on the outside railing of the bridge that connected the two worlds, down to the simpler, lumpier structures the kids had made themselves.

"It's really something else, kids," Lydia said, approving.

"Take a picture, Mama," Adele said, and while Colleen thought she knew what was coming next, she was surprised. "You should send it to Gran-mere. She'd want to see.

"Can we do this again?" Adele asked as she came up to view the picture on Colleen's phone.

"Sure," Lydia said. "What do you say, little man?"

Josh nodded vigorously, sucking on a dirty thumb. It didn't seem to bother Lydia, and Colleen decided that a little dirt never hurt anyone. Besides, Adele was covered in it too, a thin gray dusting on her face and hands.

"Now that's a picture," Lydia said. Josh was trying to give Adele a hug, and she was trying to teach him the European way of greeting, a kiss on both cheeks. The ensuing chaotic affection of the two dirty children truly was adorable, and both of the women smiled.

"Well, there you go. Little buddies."

Colleen smiled. Her daughter seemed tired and dirty and happy. Just like a kid was supposed to be. "Thank you," she said to Lydia.

Lydia looked at her, surprise in her big green-brown eyes. "For getting the kids dirty? Can't wait to see what the bath water looks after they get in it."

Colleen smiled. "Gray at best. By the way, I sometimes work at Quent's Pub in town. If you can ever get away, come on in. First drink's on me."

Lydia nodded. "I just might," she said. "Never understood why moms were talking about all the wine they needed, but I'm starting to get an inkling about how hard a job this is."

"But totally worth it at the end of the day," Colleen said.

Chapter 11

Colleen walked up Main Street, smiling. She had enjoyed yesterday afternoon, once she had met Lydia, and felt that she had started on the beginnings of a friendship. She had seen Lydia again at drop-off that morning, where Lydia had been trying to corral the unruly Josh. Colleen had felt a rush of sympathy for Lydia as the other moms had steered clear of her and Josh. The avoidance had tugged at her heart for the little boy. She had suggested they meet that afternoon in the park again, and Lydia had immediately agreed.

It would be nice to get to know Lydia better, Colleen thought as she wandered up the street, assessing the store fronts of the other shops, cataloging ways to complement but not compete with them. A healthy and thriving downtown served them all, and the last thing Colleen wanted was to be seen as a threat. With that in mind, she saw that Joan Altieri, owner of the Garden Cottage, a shop filled with water fountains, garden gnomes, sun dials, and other things outdoorsy, was sweeping her front stoop. Colleen squared her shoulders, deciding that her public relations campaign could begin right now.

"Hello," Colleen said and stopped.

Joan looked up. She wore her hair short and slightly spiky and red reading glasses dangled from a chain around her neck. The look Joan returned was not exactly comforting, but compared to the response she had gotten from Darby and Amy, Colleen decided it was good enough to push through.

"I'm Colleen McShane. I'm the new owner of Phil's old place."

"Aye yuh," Joan responded in classic New England style, just a little bit frosty, which was why Colleen was going to ply this with woman with her brilliant Parisian charm.

"I just wanted to say hello and introduce myself."

"I remember you," Joan said.

Colleen waited, bracing herself.

"You used to work for Phil back in high school. He showed me your postcards; said you were living in Paris running an art gallery."

"More like an antiques store, but close enough," Colleen said and nodded. "I was just as surprised as anyone when Phil died, and well, I guess you know he left me the store."

"Some inheritance," Joan grunted. She picked up her mat and shook it out so dust flew out into the morning air. She swept the dirt away and replaced the mat before she said anything more.

"Thing's a firetrap. And the junk. Don't know how he stayed in business. You'd be better off just selling the building to a developer who will knock it down," Joan pronounced and looked at her expectantly, as if daring her to agree.

"He did have eclectic tastes, but the building isn't so bad."

"Roof leaks, doesn't it? Built like a sieve. Heating bill must be a fortune." Joan's assessment was pretty accurate.

Colleen smiled, tried to stay positive. "It's not too bad, and, since the weather is getting warmer, I have a few months to make the repairs."

"So you're not selling?" Joan's voice sharpened with interest, as she leaned on her broom and fixed her brown eyes on Colleen. "What you going to do? Throw out all of his so-called treasures?"

Colleen acknowledged the jab with a shrug of her shoulders. "Well, as it turns out there is a healthy on-line interest in some of those treasures, as you call them, but I've actually decided to open up a totally new shop."

Now she had Joan's attention. "What kind?"

"A French-inspired boutique with housewares, clothes, jewelry."

"Garden things?"

"Not really," Colleen assured her. "I wouldn't want to compete, but I do believe that the more vibrant stores we have downtown, the more we can help each other."

"Complement each other rather than compete," Joan assessed.

"Exactly," Colleen agreed. "I'll probably also do some home design and furniture as well."

Joan pursed her lips, her silence speaking volumes. Though it was hard to do, Colleen stood her ground, waiting.

"Interesting. You going to keep the name?"

"No," Colleen said and shook her head. "The new sign is almost ready. It will be called *La Belle Vie*. I've been doing some work inside as well."

"I might have noticed."

Colleen couldn't tell what Joan was really thinking, but she decided that it was better to keep going than to overthink it.

"I hope you'll stop by. Pop in anytime I'm there and take a look around, tell me what you think." It took a lot for Colleen to make that offer. She didn't like being told what to do, but still, she needed friends, not enemies and Joan, she knew, was dialed into just about everyone in town.

"Maybe I can find some time later this afternoon," Joan said.

Colleen smiled and added her last bit casually as if it were an afterthought. "There's one more thing. I was thinking that maybe we should have a sidewalk sale, you know, to kick off the summer season."

"A sidewalk sale?" Joan's tone was sharp, but finally, Colleen detected some real interest.

"Yes, all the merchants could put up canopies along the sidewalk, and we could have tables outside. Almost like a festival."

"Not much time to organize it," Joan pointed out.

"True, but I figure that this first time could be like a test run. We could do it the weekend of the regatta when there's usually a lot of extra foot traffic in town, so we wouldn't have to spend too much to promote it, but it would be fun, something to do. Especially for all those who prefer shopping over sailing."

"Might work," Joan said, pursing her lips as she considered the idea. "You'll need permission, of course. Agnes Sampson is good place to start."

"I think I remember her. She runs the Maritime

Center, right? She's head of the Historic Committee."

"That would be her," Joan agreed. "Runs just about everything in town. Like I said, if you can get her behind it, there'd be no stopping it."

"Well, I am happy to do all of the legwork: get the permissions, tell the other merchants about it, but it sure would be a big help if I could tell everyone you're on board."

Joan thought for a moment, her eyes narrowed. "Could be an interesting idea," she said.

"So, that's a yes?" Colleen asked, knowing she needed to seal the deal.

"Aye yuh, we'll do it. Downtown needs a bit of a shaking up. Restaurants are good, but the shopping isn't what it could be. Getting everyone out and excited about the shops sounds like a good idea. Go see Agnes soon, ya hear?"

Chapter 12

Colleen nodded, and after saying good-bye, headed over to the front door of her shop with a spring in her step. The idea of a sidewalk sale had been swirling around her head for a while, but she'd been putting off saying anything about it. Now, though, it had a hard date, a stake in the sand, so to speak, to get her to go ahead and get the store ready to open. More pressure to actually open the store. She opened the door to the shop, stepped in, and surveyed the space. She was crazy. The place screamed Phil's Treasure Emporium more than it did La Belle Vie. Could she ever get junk shop out of the shop and replace it with something totally different? Or was junk shop woven too tightly into the store's DNA?

She closed her eyes, remembering the stores she had worked and shopped in during her time in Paris. She needed to channel that vibe and bring it to a small town in New England. It was the mix of merchandise, but more than that it was the atmosphere. The right atmosphere and no one would care about the prices. That was one trick she had learned from Olivier. His sales skills were impeccable. Everything in his family's store had screamed old money, from the way everyone dressed, to champagne or tea served, to the understated way the prices were displayed. When a customer walked through that door, they felt special and their white-glove treatment justified the sky-high prices.

Not that she needed to recreate that experience. She wanted something a little less stuffy but with a vibe that said everyday could be a little special, a little glamorous when just enough attention was paid to the details. Her mind flipped through images until a picture began to form. She opened her eyes, pulled out her little notebook and began making notes.

A few days later, Jake was walking down the street, a cup of coffee in one hand when he paused in front of the store. He could see a shadow in there and knew that it could only be her. He decided that he wouldn't think about why he wanted to go in and just do it. Besides, he had a surprise in his truck. He went to go knock but found the door open. He took her by surprise when he said, "Are you going to lock it? Or just let anyone walk in?"

"What are you doing here?" she said and turned suddenly, obviously startled. Her eyes were wide and surprised, but they narrowed when she saw it was just him. He took a sip of coffee and waited, taking in the sight of her. Usually he didn't care about clothes, except for the relative amount of them. For the most part, Colleen covered up more of herself than she needed to, but he appreciated the way her dresses fit and flared against her body. She was more beautiful than she'd ever been.

"We're closed," she added, as if he couldn't tell by the fact that the store was empty.

"It's looking about the same," he remarked as he came in and looked around. True, the place looked cleaner and emptier. But she didn't appear to be any closer to the grand opening than she had been a couple of days ago when he'd first come in.

"I'm about to start painting," she said.

She stood in the center of the floor, with her arms crossed over her chest. The light was slipping in through the paper she'd put over the windows, hitting her hair, giving the brownish blonde a pretty gold tint. There was nothing pretty in her face; instead, she looked thoroughly annoyed with him. *Good,* he decided, since it was better than her usual indifference.

"In that dress?" he said. "Sure you don't want a painter's cap? I have one in my truck. Has my logo on it and everything."

"No thanks. I don't need anything from you," she said.

He smiled at her, and he could see that her eyes were bright as if she were trying hard not to feel something.

"You know I run a construction company. Your floor would take ten days tops," he said, keeping the same affable smile on his.

"I'm on a budget."

"Most of my clients are. I'm known for doing excellent work at an affordable price. Besides, maybe we can work out a deal."

"What do I have that you want?" she said before she realized her mistake. Jake let it just hang there for a moment.

"I've got six dining room chairs in my truck. Been promising my mom I'd fix them up for months. Just never seem to have the time to do it. I thought maybe if you'd help me out with that, I could help you out with the floors, a paint job, maybe even add some shelves to the back wall."

"Six chairs for floors and a paint job?"

He looked around. "Plus, I'll fix that countertop for you. And plaster the cracks in the wall. I'll give you the family and friends discount. My mom needs the chairs next week." He took a sip of coffee and hoped he hadn't pushed his luck. But his mom was having some garden club luncheon, and he didn't want to disappoint her.

"A week? That's a rush job, you know," she said, beginning to bargain. He could see it in the way her eyes lit up that she was assessing the deal and that she might actually be thinking of taking it.

"Word is you're trying to have a grand opening regatta weekend too. We're both under a deadline."

She raised an eyebrow, and he felt compelled to elaborate: "Joan Altieri is all fired up with your idea for a sidewalk sale. Word gets around."

"Okay, so I can do the chairs in a week. How much for the work I want done?"

He named a price, and she kept her face blank. It was a fair price, he knew, almost too good for her to say no, which was sort of the point.

She crossed her arms, tapped her foot and named something twenty percent lower.

Jake was shocked but smiled. He figured with that deal, she'd feel compelled to let him take her to dinner when it was all done, so he offered a just a bit more than she had, in order to save his pride.

"You have a deal. Can they start tomorrow?"

"Sure. I've got the chairs in the truck just outside," he said and held out his hand. She looked at him, looked at it. She shook it quickly, then pulled it away. "You were awfully sure of yourself, bringing the chairs with you," she said.

He looked at her, held her gaze. "Just remember, Colleen, I'm not as dumb as I look. I usually figure out a way to get what I want."

When he left, she leaned back against one of the columns. She was about to run out of the door, tell him never mind, but she stopped herself and looked around at her big, blank canvas. She needed help. His crew, she told herself, not him, would be doing it. And she was paying. It wasn't a favor, it came with no obligations. But why then did she feel she was slowly sliding down a slippery slope when it came to Jake Owen?

Chapter 13

E llie sat on her bar stool nursing her white wine, idly watching Colleen. The girl looked worried, as if she had something on her mind. She moved along the edge of the bar, collected glasses, made small talk, threw her smile around like there was nothing wrong, but there was a definite air of distraction to her. Ellie didn't know why, but she felt slightly protective of the younger woman. Colleen was confident, but you could tell her confidence was bruised. But she was a hard worker, stylish, funny. And a single mom trying to do her best for herself and her daughter. Ellie knew Colleen reminded her of herself, just a little bit, and she could not help but like her.

Another woman came in, a long tall drink of water, with long blonde hair swept up in a messy ponytail, wearing jeans, paint-spattered sneakers, and a flowing peasant blouse. She took a seat near Ellie, sending her a wide, friendly smile.

Colleen greeted the newcomer, cheerily. "Lydia. You came. Nice to see you. What it'll be? White wine?"

The other woman laughed. "Hell to the no. Bourbon, neat, to start, then we'll see."

Ellie's ears pricked in recognition. Another

Southern girl.

"What's got your knickers in a twist?" Colleen said, pouring a shot of bourbon into a glass and sliding it over.

"What doesn't?" the woman, Lydia, said, sighed, took a sip, and savored the bourbon as it went down.

Colleen smiled at Ellie.

"Lydia, this is Eleanor DeWitt. Ellie, this is Lydia Snow. We met each other at the playground."

"Pleasure," Ellie drawled, and she caught Lydia's smile. She had green-brown eyes and sandy blonde hair that appeared completely untouched. The girl was a knockout, with little or no makeup and an earthy, take it or leave it kind of beauty.

"Oh, a fellow refugee from the South? Where you from, and are you any relation to Bobby DeWitt?" Lydia's words tumbled out in a stream of questions.

"He was my husband," Ellie said and smiled, trying to press down the feeling of sadness at the mention of his name. Besides, it had been over a year. She could finally say it without tearing up.

"Wow." Lydia looked suitably impressed. "My dad was a big fan. I remember the commercials from when I was kid."

Colleen paused, leaned on the bar. "You mean Bobby Dean? The guy in the car oil commercials? You were married to him?" she asked.

Ellie nodded, feeling her hands wrapping tightly around her glass. "That was my Bobby."

"Wow," Lydia said again. "I mean, sorry for your loss."

Ellie looked up, touched by the obvious sincerity in Lydia's voice.

"It's been over a year, more like two now, but me and Bobby went way back."

There was a silence, the dead air filled with the pity that she had grown to dread. She needed to change the subject quickly before things turned more morose.

"So where are you from and why do you need bourbon?"

"I'm from Georgia and I need a drink because of a man."

"Isn't it always the case," Ellie agreed.

"Too bad this one happens to be three feet tall and only five years old. I can only imagine what a little hellion Josh will be when he reaches teenage years."

Ellie wasn't sure what to make of this.

"Don't worry," Lydia said, as if reading her apprehension. "Josh is my brother, well, half-brother, if you must know the truth. I am only temporarily in charge of him. Still . . ." She took another breath and shuddered.

"No word on when his mother will be back?" Colleen asked sympathetically.

"His mother?" Lydia snorted. "I am still hoping that his babysitter shows up soon. Apparently she's taken a detour to Ibiza. You know, in Spain. I am not sure when I'll see her again. I once spent what I thought were two weeks there."

"What do you mean?" Ellie asked.

"I mean two weeks turned out to be two months. It was during art school, but that place has a way of making time slow down. And no one minds a bit."

"I'll be happy to meet you at the park tomorrow. We can let the kids run around like hellions and get some of that energy out," Colleen said. "Ellie said she'd meet us too."

Colleen and Adele had met Ellie while out on a walk, and Adele had immediately charmed Ellie by asking if her suit was vintage Chanel. Ellie had decided that she and the little girl were kindred spirits.

"How's she treating you, luv?" Quent boomed as he appeared from the back. His arms were folded across his chest, and Ellie could see that Colleen had to suppress a slight jump at the way he had snuck up on her.

"Wonderfully as always. A real treasure you found here."

"I know. Too bad she's leaving me to sell pretty French fripperies and the like."

"You know she wasn't meant to work in a bar all her life," Ellie said, enjoying trading banter with Quent. She had to admit that this was part of the reason she kept showing up at the pub. She could easily be sitting on her balcony, enjoying a glass of wine while staring out over the water, but something about Quent's smile kept pulling her back. It was almost enough to stop her thinking about Bobby.

"She's good enough at it," Quent said, clapping Colleen on the back.

"When's the grand opening?" Ellie asked, turning to Colleen.

"About three weeks. Regatta weekend," Colleen answered.

"I'll be there with my checkbook in hand," Ellie promised her.

"Make sure you invite me to your grand opening. I have something for you," Lydia chimed in.

Ellie passed a few minutes listening to Colleen and Lydia talking about something one of the other moms had done at school. She was trying to follow along when she noticed that Quent was still standing in front of her, drying a glass that he'd already dried. She looked at him and was surprised to see he looked nervous.

"How are you doing, Ellie?"

"Lovely, and how are you, sugar?" she drawled. Quent looked good, she decided. There was something very nice about the way his v-neck shirt settled over his chest and his arms. His arms. She had never been a fan of overly muscled men, but Quent's arms were massive and he looked like he could crush a tree limb with them. For a moment she wondered, very briefly, what it would like to be in those arms. Would she be crushed or comforted?

"I'm fine," Quent said, then he took up another glass and began to carefully polish it.

She waited, then asked, "Everything turn out okay with that family emergency of yours?"

Quent nodded sheepishly. "They're distant family but, yes, everything is settled for now. Enough about that. I heard there was a spot of trouble that night," he said, glancing over at Colleen.

"She handled it well, got him out the door and into a cab."

Quent nodded, and then said, as if trying to be casual, "You've been coming here a while now."

Ellie nodded. She looked around. The pub was mainly empty, and though Colleen and Lydia were still chatting while Colleen restocked the garnishes, she had the distinct feeling that they were very interested in her and Quent's conversation.

"That I have. Looks like a fine summer you have

coming up," she said, not knowing what else to say. She started to take a sip of her wine, then put it down. She reached for the glass of water that Colleen always poured for her and had a sip of that instead.

"Weather is lovely," Quent agreed, seeming happy to talk about it. "You know, it's good boating weather."

"I suppose," Eleanor said. She knew Quent liked to fish, since there were a few pictures of him on the wall, on a boat, holding up the obligatory fish.

"Well, I was wondering if maybe if you'd like to go out on my boat with me sometime. See the harbor?"

"On your boat? Fishing?"

"Well, no, not unless you wanted to?" Quent smiled hopefully, then added, "Maybe just a tour. See the sights. The weather's going to be fine for the next week or so."

Eleanor was shocked and didn't know what to say. "Well . . . I . . ."

It was on the tip of her tongue, ready to find some excuse, then she looked at Quent. He looked earnest and hopeful and without any trace of guile about him. She realized that he was asking her out. On a date. She swallowed. It had been a long time, a long time since she had gone out with a man.

"Of course, if you're busy, no worries. Summer lasts a long time," he said, giving her the option of an out, but she knew in an instant she didn't want to take it.

"Why, that would be lovely, darling," she answered, keeping her voice casual as if it were no big deal that she had been asked out by a man.

Quent seemed to finally breathe, and a big smile

cracked across his face. There was another awkward pause, then he scratched his cleanly shaved head. "Well, I think there is some stock in the back that needs to be checked. Would Tuesday work?"

She nodded. Quent smiled again, then lumbered in the back, muttering something about a refrigerator hose that was acting up. Ellie stared at her drink until she became acutely aware of the regard of both Lydia and Colleen.

"What?" she asked, trying to keep her tone filled with innocence.

"Nothing," Colleen said. "I don't think Quent has ever asked a woman out on his boat. From what I hear, it's strictly for his fishing buddies."

"It's just a boat ride."

Colleen shot a look at Lydia. "Hey Lydia, down south, what did a guy ask you to do when he wanted to get you alone."

Lydia laughed and answered, "You'd take a drive in their truck down to the creek."

"And then did they pretend to run out of gas?"

"Something like that," Lydia confirmed.

"Well, Ellie, when a guy from Queensbay asks you out on his boat, it's just about the same thing as getting asked to take a ride in a truck."

"It was just a friendly gesture," Ellie protested, though she wondered if that was all she thought it was, why she felt so twitchy in anticipation of it.

Colleen mixed up a gin and tonic. "Yup, just a friendly gesture."

"Oh please, why, he'd have to be crazy," Ellie protested.

"He'd have to be crazy not to," Colleen said.

"You're just being nice."

"Not from where I'm standing. I hope I look half as good as you when I'm your age."

"Who says I'm older than you?" Eleanor said, but it was an automatic question.

She had learned never ever to confess to her age. She'd been so much younger than her husband, but it still hadn't stopped him from chasing after anything in a skirt. She had been a mother so young too, always hiding her age, sometimes trying to be older, sometimes trying to be younger, that she'd forgotten she wasn't old at all, that she still had a lot of years left.

She'd given her best years to Bobby Dean, and then he had died. Now it was a new chapter in her life, one she was easing into. She wanted more time with her son, Colby, helping him with his business, watching him and his fiancé, Tory, fall in love and begin to settle down. Beyond that, she hadn't really thought about what came next for her.

"Quent's one of the good ones. I know he plays the tough guy card," Colleen said. "But he gave me a job, always works around my schedule. Not sure he really needed another bartender, but he did the right thing."

Ellie played with the little red plastic stick that came with her water. Not that she had any aversion to a real drink, but she had started to spend quite a bit of time here, and she couldn't keep up the drinking to match it. Still she came. She wondered why.

It might have been the way Quent had smiled at her when she first walked in, frazzled after her first day at work. She had ordered bourbon neat, thrown it back, and nursed the second one as Quent listened to her talk. She had told him her story, maybe more than she should have, but he'd been a good listener and she found it easy to talk to him.

"It's just a boat ride," she said again and looked down when Colleen sent her that knowing smile.

Just a boat ride. And what the hell did one wear on a boat ride? Shopping, she would have to go shopping. The right outfit almost always made her feel better and ready to conquer new challenges.

"I haven't a clue what to wear."

Colleen laughed with her. Ellie, though, quickly sobered up.

"What's the matter? I mean, you obviously like him," Lydia asked.

"Well, of course I do, but well . . ." Ellie paused, took a sip of her wine. "It's been a while. I was married to my husband for a long, long time. I'm not sure I remember how to do this," Ellie confessed.

Colleen laughed. "Well, I wouldn't ask me," she said. "I've made a hash of my life. But I have a feeling you'll figure it out. And Quent, like I said, he's one of the good guys."

Lydia shook her head. "I only date down-on-their-luck artist types. Once they find out that I actually have a few bucks in my bank account, I can't shake them. Seems like you could do worse than Quent."

Ellie looked up, glanced toward the end of the bar where Quent was pouring a drink, and smiled. Quent must have felt her gaze because he looked up and threw Ellie a broad wink. She couldn't help the smile that lit up her face. She was going out on a date. She looked down into her drink, suddenly feeling shy, and decided she really needed to think about what to wear.

Chapter 14

C olleen was running late of course, something she had tried desperately not to do. Such was the life of a mom. Bunny had been sticky, which set off a cycle of events that led to a rush getting Adele ready, hustling her off to school, and then getting to the shop. She had been stopped by a few curious people eager to know just what was going on at old Phil's Treasure Emporium. Word was out that something new was coming to town. She had a to-do list a mile long, and she was eager to get to the shop before the morning was gone and it was time to pick Adele up again.

The door was slightly open, and loud noises emanated from within. She pushed open the door and stopped. She took a look around and couldn't quite believe her eyes.

"What is going on here?" she asked, quickly zoning in on Jake who was standing in the center of the chaos, sipping a cup of coffee.

"As you can see, we're working. We like to get an early start. Good thing you gave me an extra key." He took a step toward someone, ducking as some lumber swung his way. "Hey Manny, watch what you're doing."

"I thought you were just going to paint and do the floors."

"We are. But that column needs reinforcing and the ceiling patched."

She took it all in. It looked like the shop was crawling with people though she quickly realized there were only about four or five workers, but they had set up lights, spread drop cloths. She could see how Jake's promise to have this all done in a few days might actually be possible.

"And, I think you should have some built-in shelves here, to match the ones on the other side, which we can also patch up for you. They look like they've been carrying a heavy load for a century or so."

She saw what he was talking about. It would look nice to have flanking bookshelves on either side of the back wall. She had thought of doing something like that herself but hadn't really thought about how to get from idea to actuality.

"I can extend the run of this countertop so you have more space for wrapping," he said. "You said you were thinking of doing some design work, and unless you want to redo the back office, you probably will want more space to spread out up here in the front."

She stopped, looking for a place to put her coffee, so that she could focus on what Jake was saying. Music was blaring from a big radio in the corner, and the energy was high.

"Here." He took her coffee from her, placed it on a stack of paint cans and handed her a folded sheet of paper. She opened it up and looked around, then at him.

"You drew this?"

He nodded and rocked back on his heels, looking

slightly embarrassed. "Look, I know I'm no Rembrandt, but I think it captures what you were thinking of doing."

"No," she said and looked at the drawing. It was done in a charcoal pencil, she guessed, bold black lines against the heavy white stock. It was perfect, a perfect rendering of what she would have imagined the store to look like in her dreams. "It's perfect. How did you know?"

He ducked his head, didn't meet her eyes. "I did some research online," he eventually answered. "You know, looked at some Parisian boutiques, antique stores, plus I did the renovations on the dog bakery in town. Figured there were certain similarities in how a retail space should be set up."

She nodded, looking at the paper, felt her stomach clench with the war between desire and practicality. "It's a bit more work than we discussed."

"True, but it will cost you a lot more if you go back in and do it later," he said, as if a complete renovation was entirely possible and within her budget.

"I'm under a deadline," she reminded him.

"True. I think the work will take an extra week."

She looked around, the disbelief clear in her eyes.

"I have a break between jobs, and it's better to keep the crew busy, otherwise they get into trouble, and I have to go and bail them out."

She looked at him, directly. He grinned sheepishly.

"I'm joking, really," he said, "but I still have to pay them to make sure they don't go off and find better people to work for. So you'd be doing me a favor. I can give you my wholesaler's discount on materials, and then I'll just charge you for the labor."

"Why?" she asked. "Why are you doing this?"

Even with all of the noise surrounding them, it seemed as if it was just the two of them, caught in a bubble.

"I think you know why," he finally said.

Her breath hitched as she waited for him to go on.

"I just got appointed to the Business Improvement Council," he said. "It's my civic duty to bring new business in. If I can do it in such a way that doesn't exactly cost me money, that's great on both fronts."

She smiled, trying to hide her disappointment. Of course he wasn't doing it because of her.

He waited a beat, then reached out and touched a strand of her hair, tucking it behind her ear. She had to remind herself that they were surrounded by people, that they were not alone.

"I am doing it, so you'll go out with me. But I know you'd say no if I said that, so why don't we just tell ourselves we're striking a deal to make the town a better place."

He dropped his hand and kept her gaze as her eyes opened in surprise. She wondered why it was so hard to accept that she had feelings for him.

"Okay," she finally said, putting her misgivings firmly away in some other part of her, telling herself she would deal with them later, much later.

"All right then," he said and smiled, a full on, patented Jake Owen grin that had all of her misgivings rushing back.

"Here's your coffee, now give me back my sketch. You'll probably want to get out of here today. Come back later or, better yet, tomorrow. It's not pretty while it's happening, but trust me, you'll be amazed at the end result."

"Thank you," she said simply, then nodded and turned to go.

"Any time," he said.

She went around the back and down the narrow alley that divided her shop from the other building. She could smell the aroma of coffee and croissants wafting toward her and sighed. She hadn't seen Darby again and knew that she needed to make it right. At the very least she needed to get Darby on board with the sidewalk sale, but not today. Another thing she would just push away and decide not to deal with until later. She opened the door to the back and headed down the stairs, pulling on the light cord. The basement was a single long room, the whole length of the building. Harsh, bare bulbs illuminated just about every corner. This was her storage space and her workshop. There had been shelving here already, and she had picked up some cheap ones from the home supply store. She'd ruthlessly cleaned and purged, bringing a military-like organization to the place.

The chairs she had promised to redo for Jake were there. They were a good, solid set, but definitely needed cleaning, stripping, and refinishing. They had upholstered seats, the fabric faded and grungy. She had picked out new fabric, a classic red, gold, and creamy white striped pattern and was working on the cushions. She wasn't an expert at upholstery but luckily, seat cushions weren't that hard. Still, she stopped and looked toward the shelves. Jake had asked her about old postcards of Queensbay, and finding them seemed like it would be a nice gesture, considering the amount of help he was giving her. She was pretty certain she knew where they were, and with all the workers upstairs, she figured now was as good a time as any to go through things.

Plus she had a few things to box and send out through the mail, the result of successful online auctions. Thank goodness Phil had set that up. Between that, her bartending, and her savings, Colleen's money situation was slightly better than she could have forecast. At the end of the day, she wasn't too worried about the bill Jake would hand her, and she would make sure she paid him promptly.

She had been surprised to see the sketch, but then realized she shouldn't have been. He had been a good artist back in school, especially if he was sketching something real. No, the football player with the talent for pencil and paper hadn't been creating underground comics. He had just enjoyed sketching things. Buildings mostly, now that she remembered. It was a shock to see his work around town. She realized that half of the houses and buildings in town had been fixed up and rejuvenated by his company. He was part and parcel of Queensbay. She listened to the sound of music, saws, and voices of the men working. Phil's legacy to her was in good hands with Jake. She knew she'd made the right decision hiring him. The least she could do was to find him some old postcards.

She found some old shoeboxes and began pulling them off the shelves. Postcards, chairs, and then later on, she would go down and see someone at town hall about the sidewalk sale. The day pleasantly mapped out, she smiled and got to work.

Chapter 15

"I was thinking that it could be something like this," April Worthington said, pulling a glossy picture book with pages marked by sticky tabs toward them.

He nodded, though he wasn't really paying attention. April was a lovely woman, probably in her early fifties, and he was renovating a house for her and her husband. April was sweet and could bake morning glory muffins like nobody's business, but on her best of days, she was a little scattered when deciding what she wanted. This had led to him redoing several days' worth of work. Usually he didn't mind because April's husband adored her and pretty much gave her a blank check to do as she wished, but Kevin had finally cried uncle and told Jake that he and April needed to finalize their plans and stick to them.

"I just love how she did the living room. I was thinking we could do something like that in here."

"You know I'm not a designer, Mrs. Worthington. I am just the builder."

"You give yourself too little credit. I saw what you did for Adrianna Biddle and the Schumachers. Those plans were just lovely."

He looked down at the picture in the book. It was a nice room, showing both restraint and taste, a bit grand, but April's new house was designed to be a bit grand. Kevin had just been promoted to CEO, and he and April wanted someplace where they could "entertain" clients and friends alike.

"I can do the built-ins and the moldings, but I suggest you call in a decorator for the rest," he said, resisting the urge to sigh.

It was a beautiful day outside, and he had several job sites to check out. Not to mention he'd managed to get a meeting with Agnes Sampson to discuss the future of the Showhouse. He was eager to keep moving forward on that project and his head was filled with ideas he wanted to put to paper.

"I love her work. Her blog is amazing, and the book, the pictures are just gorgeous. You know she grew up around here. You didn't know her, did you?" April asked and helpfully flipped the book over and showed him the back cover.

He sighed again. It was a photo of Colleen McShane standing on a cobblestoned street with a row of shops behind her. She was dressed in jeans, boots, and a short jacket, a colorful scarf arranged stylishly around her neck. She looked beautiful, glamourous, like she had the world at her fingertips.

He didn't really need to look at the back cover or any of the pictures in the book because he had his own copy. He had stopped reading the blog a while ago because it was torture. The same masochistic feeling had led him to buy the book, which he had read through, memorized, and buried on his bookshelf behind Tom Clancy and *Principles of Construction Management*.

"We went to school together. Not the same grade though," he added, as if that made a difference.

April put her chin on one hand, her voice dreamy. "I hear she's opening up a shop, right here in town. Said so on her blog. I can't wait."

He looked up, inspiration hitting him in a moment.

"She is. I'm her contractor."

April's mouth dropped, and she actually squealed as she hit him on the arm.

"Can I meet her, could you arrange that?" she said, sounding like a tween fan girl.

He nodded, looking like he was considering it and judging how hard it would be. "I think she said she'd be interested in taking on some design clients. How about I tell her to give you a call, and maybe the two of you can work something out."

"That would be amazing," April said, drawing the last word out.

This referral would be another mark in his favor if he could help Colleen get her business off the ground. April was loyal if nothing else. If she and Colleen hit it off, April would give credit where credit was due, and Colleen would have her fill of business, and he'd be off the hook with Kevin. Jake would be able to do what he was best at, which was building, not deciding on which style of couch looked best in the family room. It promised to be a win-win for everyone concerned.

Chapter 16

T he beautiful spring day seemed full of promise
and anticipation. Sun bright, sky blue, clouds
puffy and white. Jake felt both keenly. Colleen's project was proceeding nicely, and on schedule.
He'd solved the problem of April Worthington, and her
cost overruns, and today he was going to sweet talk
Mrs. Agnes Sampson, head of the historic commission,
president of the Maritime Center and all around de
facto ruler of Queensbay. It was too bad she scared the
piss out of him.

Maybe scared was overstating it, but she had
been his first grade teacher, in fact just about everyone
in town's first grade teacher until she had retired and
been appointed to run the historical society and the
Maritime Center. She was also on the town council, but
who was counting? None of the jobs paid, but Agnes
Sampson did wield an unholy amount of power among
anyone who wanted to build, buy, or change any sort
of structure in town. She ruled the town with the same
firm hand she'd run her classroom.

Jake had set his sights on just about the biggest,
most iconic building in all of Queensbay. Sweet talking
wouldn't even begin to cover what he wanted to do.

He'd be lucky if he could keep the outside as a shell. Renovating the Showhouse was a huge job, and he was crazy for wanting to take it on.

Jax agreed, but was too good a friend to tell him no. He felt the anticipation, readied for it, welcomed it because he knew he'd use it to his advantage. He took one last look in the mirror, decided he couldn't do any better and grabbed his jacket and his portfolio filled with sketches and designs and headed out into the morning. He got out onto the boardwalk, took a deep breath, drawing in the sun and salt air. He looked out across the harbor at the Showhouse.

It leaned tipsily, like it wanted to slide into the harbor. What if it did? He had no idea about the condition of the place, not really. He knew that the floorboards could support approximately four hundred pounds of weight, which was about what he and Jackson were combined. He knew that while birds got in and out, he hadn't seen that much water or wind damage. The whole place was like some great pile of dreams, and it had been his to do something with it for as long as he could remember.

He was at the point in his life where he was able to indulge in dreaming again. He'd worked hard to build a successful business, and now it was time to take a risk, to see if he couldn't make a leap forward. He tapped his notebook with his sketches, like it was a talisman. He could sweet talk all he wanted, but he firmly believed that pictures were a lot more powerful than words. He started the walk toward the Maritime Center, which was in an old warehouse along the docks. A community center had grown up around it, with a small park with a fountain and benches where people could enjoy some ice cream and watch the sea birds.

He opened the big glass doors to the Maritime Center, which was dedicated to the history of Queensbay from its beginnings as a small settler trading post, to its history in the whaling and shipbuilding trade, then its transition to commercial fishing town, and finally to its heyday as a summer place for robber barons and artists. The historical map skipped over the declining fortunes during the last century and finished with a relatively optimistic view of current prospects for the town as a shopping and foodie destination. And, a great place to live, he reminded himself, that would need high-end apartment buildings with boat slips.

He saw Mrs. Sampson, her white hair creating a sort of halo around her head, as she stood near the glass case in the center of the floor that held a small-scale replica of how the village had looked two hundred years ago. He stopped.

Colleen was talking to Mrs. Sampson. He swallowed, couldn't help but take a good look at her. She was wearing one of her dresses, the gauzy, flowy kind that managed to both cling to her body and flare away, reminding him of a movie star. Not Audrey Hepburn, no, more like a Grace Kelly. He suspected that image might just visit him again tonight. He hadn't expected to see her, and he didn't want to think that was throwing him off of his stride.

If Colleen saw him, she didn't acknowledge his presence. The sun was coming in from the skylight, and it bathed her in a soft warm light. Her lips were red, cherry bowed and puckered in concentration as she and Mrs. Sampson looked over something together. He caught snatches of conversation, things like "great for the community . . . a unique event. I have some other support . . ." and figured that Colleen was doing her own version of sweet talking. He decided not to interrupt her but started to do a slow circuit of the building, pretending to take an intense interest in the pictures and the facts listed on the walls. He looked for photos with the Showhouse, and, as luck would have it, that placed him directly in Colleen's line of view. He knew the moment she noticed him, because her voice trailed off, paused before she started again. He smiled, liked knowing that the sight of him was as much a distraction for her as it was for him.

Colleen tried to concentrate, but it was almost impossible with Jake lurking there. She was close to getting Agnes Sampson to bless her plan for the sidewalk sale. Sure, there would be some permits to get, but all that would be easier once everyone knew Agnes was on board. Jake was in the Maritime Center now, and she couldn't help but notice him because that bastard had put himself directly in the line of her sight. He smiled and winked at her, behind Agnes' back. For once she could see that he wasn't wearing his khaki pants and polo shirt and work boots. In fact, Jake Owen was in a suit, a charcoal gray one that fit him so perfectly he must have had it custom tailored. In it his shoulders looked even broader and more powerful, his whole presence that much more commanding.

Colleen snapped her attention back to what Agnes was saying. They had bonded over Paris where it turned out Agnes and Arnie, her husband of over fifty years, had gone for their thirtieth anniversary. She had brought some lavender-scented soap, triple milled, as a small present and now they were talking about the Moulin Rouge and the can-can, which apparently caused Agnes to blush with some memories. She was pretty certain she was about to seal the deal when Agnes turned sharply. For a seventy year old, the woman had the hearing of a bat.

"Jake Owen, stop lurking in the shadows," she demanded. "Have you taken a look at that gazebo in the park yet? We're almost at the summer season, and the thing is falling down. You told the mayor you wouldn't charge us for it, but that doesn't mean you can take your own sweet time doing."

Jake stepped forward into the light. His blue eyes danced as they lit briefly on her face, and she had to force herself not to turn away, even though his gaze had the predictable reaction on her traitorous body.

"Are you looking for my niece's number? Seems to me she mentioned you hadn't called her back after you took her out for dinner," Agnes said, her voice tart.

Jake rocked back on his heels, and Colleen tried to look like she didn't care at the mention of another woman in Jake's life.

"This boy has quite the reputation as a ladies' man around town and, to tell you the truth, I've never seen him with the same one twice," Agnes said to Colleen, shaking her head.

Jake looked like he was about to protest, but before he could, Colleen urged Mrs. Sampson to go on. Maybe some uncomfortable truths about Jake would be just what she needed to get him out of her mind.

"Nieces, little sisters, this man has left a trail of broken hearts all over town. Someday it will come back to you, Jake Owen, when you meet the girl who won't give you the time of day."

"Trust me," Jake said, his eyes drifting to Colleen, holding them. "That day seems to come every morning."

Agnes glanced between the two of them as if she was trying to catch them doing something they shouldn't, but Colleen kept her expression serene and didn't meet Jake's gaze.

Agnes snorted and shook her head and said, "I know we had an appointment, Jake, but you just go on over there while I finish up here with Colleen."

Colleen glanced at her watch. Convincing Agnes had taken much longer than she anticipated, and she was going to have to rush to pick up Adele on time.

"That's okay," Colleen said. "I really must be going. But I do hope..."

Agnes interrupted her: "Seems like a good idea if you can pull it off. You have my blessing if that's what you're looking for. You'll have to head to town hall to get the permits set up and convince the rest of the shop owners that it's a good idea, but see what you can make of it."

"Thank you," Colleen said, her voice full of relief and warmth. Before Agnes could rethink things, she gathered up her papers and started toward the door. Jake was holding the door for her, and she had to brush past him to find her way out.

"Wish me luck," he said quietly.

"Maybe you should have just called her niece back," Colleen said in the same lowered tone. She popped out into the sunshine, and chided herself for her comment but she hadn't been able to resist. Jake needed to know she wasn't just going to be another one in his string of conquests.

Chapter 17

C olleen stepped gingerly on the brown paper covering the refinished floors of the shop. She stopped, bent down, and pulled up a corner and nearly wept at the beauty of it. The wood gleamed, a lustrous, dark mahogany. It would be a bright, crisp contrast to the perfect shade of white she had selected for the walls.

After looking at countless swatches and asking for endless opinions from Lydia and Ellie, she had settled on what she thought of as the perfect shade of white. Not a bright, bold white, but something creamy that reminded her of rich French vanilla ice cream. Already the walls had one coat and they glowed softly in the light that filtered in from the still papered-over windows.

The shelf unit and countertop Jake had promised her was just about done. The wood was still raw, so she figured that it just needed sanding and painting. One more coat of paint on the walls, she estimated, and the shop would be finished. She would finally have her store. She turned around slowly, taking it all in.

She tried to remember how it had looked when she first opened the door after it had been sitting, alone and unloved for weeks. The store had been dusty, musty, and dark; the shelves stuffed to the rafters, and so crowded you could barely thread your way through the store without knocking something over. She'd been certain she'd heard the scurry of rodent feet. The exterminator had been her first call, and then when she had reopened the door a few days later and looked through the papers Phil had left her, the reality of the opportunity finally struck home. Here was the answer she needed, the chance to change the course of her life.

Once, when confronted by such an opportunity, she would have charged ahead with her barely formed plans, making calls, ordering things, creating a maelstrom of activity, in order to feel that she was moving forward, making things happen.

This time she had decided to go about things differently, more deliberately. There was no rush, she had realized. She was glad she had taken her time, moved slowly, deciding on what she really wanted to do. Opening a business was a big step, a commitment to a place and the people in it. When the going got tough, you had to dig in, not run away. The permanence of that scared her. Part of her had believed what she had told Olivier, that she was only in Queensbay temporarily, to handle Phil's estate. Slowly, days had slipped into weeks, and weeks into months. She had gotten a job, then another one. She had cleaned, inventoried, and dreamed and was starting to make friends.

She had found a place for Adele and had begun the process of living with her mother again, which had gone surprisingly well. True, Maura was not a morning person, but as long as Colleen remembered that about her, her bark was worse than her bite. And she was great with Adele, doing puzzles, coloring for hours. All of the things her mother had never done with her. Colleen pushed that uncharitable thought away. The past was the past. No way but forward. She placed the box she had carried in carefully on a wooden sawhorse that held a flat sheet of plywood and served as a makeshift table for the crew. The radio was plugged in, but silent. The crew was off today, Jake had told her, to let the countertop dry. A day of drying, then the final painting. Two, three days more, max, he had promised her and then she could start to move her stuff in.

This information had come mostly via texts from Jake. She hadn't seen him since their run-in at the Maritime Center. She had found the box of postcards he had asked for, and she had sorted through them last night. They were interesting, a true glimpse of history, but she still couldn't quite imagine why he wanted them.

As if on cue, the bell over the door tinkled, and he was there. He stepped in, and she watched him as he did a slow, thorough inspection of the work. He was nodding in satisfaction and then his gaze zeroed in on her, and she felt a familiar fluttering that started in her stomach and settled in her chest. She had to admit that pretending that he didn't have an effect on her was getting harder and harder.

"It looks good in here," she said, though that statement couldn't begin to cover the gift he'd given her.

He grinned, delight sparking in his eyes. "Good? It looks amazing."

His tone was slightly self-congratulatory, and part of her wanted to say something to deflate it, to make him realize that he shouldn't be so cocky, but she couldn't, not when he clearly deserved the credit. He took a step toward her.

To deflect him, she said, "I have something for you." She turned and picked up the shoe box and held it toward him.

"What is it?"

"The postcards."

His eyes filled with interest as he came over, took the box from her and set it back down on the plywood. He started to rifle through everything.

"Is this what you were looking for?" she asked, trying not to sound anxious, but eager to have found what he needed.

He looked excited. He held up a postcard, one of the Queensbay Showhouse, from its glory days, and said, "Exactly what I was looking for."

"I went through them, tried to organize them," she said and shook her head. It had taken her a while to decide on which method to use, but locale seemed to be the most logical categorization, and she had become absorbed in them, swept away by seeing familiar places as they had been.

"I am sure Phil had them all in one big pile," Jake said, laughing as he hands flipped through them.

"Worse than that," she said. "I sorted them by location, then I tried to group them by people. There are plenty of the Osprey Arms. And the beach. Look at those swimsuits."

She held up a black and white picture showing a serious-looking group of people staring at the camera wearing what could only be described as bathing costumes. Just about every part of their bodies, for both the men and the women, was covered in some sort of black fabric. The only nod to summer was the jaunty straw boater hats the men wore.

"They look hot," he said.

She nodded. "They'd be shocked at the beaches today, wouldn't they? Everyone with their shirts off."

"Maybe in Europe," he said. "Last I saw in Queensbay, it was tops on."

"That's not what I meant. And that's all anyone ever thinks about European beaches. That we all go around topless."

He was silent, looking at her with a speculative twinkle in his eye. She blushed.

"I did not," she said firmly and sighed. "I guess I was too much the American to be able to do that."

"Too bad," he said. "Though, I'm happy that the whole world doesn't know you as well as I do."

She blushed again. It brought complicated memories of that night after the prom. To hide her embarrassment, she pointed to another postcard.

"Here's some showing the shipyards and the boat builders. Hard to imagine the waterfront as anything but the t-shirt shops and the ice cream place."

He nodded, but he was still flipping through the pictures of the Showhouse. Mostly exterior ones, though here and there were ones that showed the interior. He paused at those, looking at them carefully.

"Why are you so interested in this stuff anyway?" she asked.

"Seems a shame no one's paying any attention to it," he said, nodding to a postcard of the Showhouse, his tone noncommittal.

She wondered at it but decided not to push. They

were both entitled to privacy.

He looked at her, his hands gathering up the postcards. They were big, capable hands, with a scrape across the knuckles on one hand and a bandage wrapped tightly around his thumb.

"Still having trouble hitting the nail?" she asked, her voice light.

He held up his hand and smiled. "Even after all these years, I still miss a few times. But you've got to keep swinging."

She swallowed, suddenly wondering if they were talking about nails or something else. She needed to change the subject: "So, how much do I owe you? I have a check right here." She reached for her bag.

He held up his hand. "No rush. The job's not done. Never pay the contractor until the job is done, don't you know that?"

"I trust you," she said automatically.

He put out a hand to stop her, and she froze. His touch was firm, with an electric pulse beating between the two of them. She could not, should not be feeling this way. It wasn't that she had sworn off men. Well maybe she had, but only until Adele was eighteen and safely away at college, which would make her a withered old spinster. And she was fine with that, really she was, because if she stayed away from men, she would stay away from mistakes. Right now, with her second chance taking shape, she couldn't afford any mistakes.

"Then you'll let me do this," he said and leaned in.

She didn't know if she would have let him her kiss her, only that she wanted, at that moment, for him to do it more than anything else. But good reason returned, just as the bell on the door tinkled, letting them know they were no longer alone.

She took a step back, looked up, and saw that Lydia and Ellie were standing there watching them, frozen. It took her a moment to pull herself together and right her tilting sense of equilibrium.

"Well now, Jake, Colleen, hope we're not interrupting anything," Ellie drawled.

Colleen took a deep breath, steadied herself. She had been saved by the bell, and she didn't quite know what to think.

"Ladies," Jake said, without a trace of embarrassment in his eyes, Colleen noted. She clasped her hands together, trying to find a place for them, trying to find a place for herself, unsure of just what to do.

"Nice work," Lydia said, and Colleen was certain of the double meaning behind those words. She shot a look at Lydia, who just smiled wickedly.

"Well, thanks for the postcards, Colleen. I need to get going. But here." He stopped and pulled a slip of paper from his pocket. "You should give her a call," he said, handing her the paper. "I'm doing some work for her, April, that is, she's a big fan of yours and looking for a decorator. She has a signed copy of your book and gets the auto updates to your blog. At least that's what she told me. She's looking for a decorator to save her from herself, in my opinion."

"Umm, okay," Colleen said and took the scrap of paper. "I'm not really . . ."

"Huge favor for me," Jake interrupted. "Kind of already told her I knew you blah, blah. Nice woman, doesn't know what she wants but has the money to pay for it. You treat her right, she'll sing your praises, and you'll have more work than you can handle. At least that's the idea."

"Umm, okay," Colleen said. She was speechless. What had just happened? One moment Jake had been trying to kiss her, of that she was almost sure, and the next he was talking about business and thanking her for digging up some old postcards.

Jake took his box and his smile and sauntered out of the shop, calling out one last thing as he did: "Boys will be back tomorrow to start painting."

There was a pause as Ellie and Lydia eyed her with amusement and interest.

"Well darling, there's enough heat in here to make an alligator happy," Ellie said.

"Uh-huh. Are his muscles always so big and rip-ple-ly?" Lydia asked, teasing; her Southern accent grew more pronounced when she was around Ellie.

"I have no idea," Colleen said. She needed to sit down, but there was no place. Her legs felt rubbery, as if she'd just run a mile.

"Oh, I think I get the idea," Ellie said. "That boy has his sights set on you."

Colleen shook her head. "I do not need anyone with their sights on me. I have too much going on."

"I wouldn't worry about it," Ellie said. "I don't think Jake does complicated."

Colleen paused, then asked: "What do you mean?" The Jake she knew had been looking for something that was inevitably complicated. Their brief, ro-bust emotions had been too much for Colleen. Just an-other one of the reasons why she'd left town in a hurry.

"Just that Jake never sticks with one person for long. Least that's what I've heard. From the younger ladies of course. Not from personal experience."

Colleen nodded. She was quite certain that if Ellie had been interested, Jake wouldn't have stood a chance, no matter the difference in their ages.

"Love and leave 'em Owen. At least that's what the other moms say around Happy Faces," Lydia chimed him.

"What?"

"Well, it's mostly Amy Anderson."

"Amy?" Colleen said, her voice faint.

"She and Jake dated a few years ago, until Jake called it off. I guess Amy didn't take it well, even though she found a husband nice and quick. Lisa seems to think she may still be carrying a torch for your man Jake."

"Jake is not my man," Colleen said, but she could tell from the look Ellie and Lydia passed between them that they weren't buying it.

"Well, she certainly has it out for you. Apparently, Amy's still mad at you for something that happened during high school too."

Colleen sighed. Not one of her finer moments, but really, Amy had started it.

"I was the better cheerleader," Colleen said. "Amy was a senior, so she was named the captain. Then it just happened she needed to keep her grades up. We happened to have the same history class. She forced me to give her my essay, which I did, but not the one I turned in."

Lydia looked at her, prompting her for more

"I wrote one just for her. It had some passages that were copied verbatim from a well-known source. Just enough so she got in a little trouble; you know, detention and extra credit. Course she couldn't rat me out otherwise she'd be in even worse trouble. I was already not going to be co-captain. At least not until she graduated, but I had to let her know I wouldn't be pushed around."

"Well played," Ellie murmured, and Lydia nodded in agreement.

"Needless to say, we were never friends after that. But Jake and I were not together then, either."

"Then?" Lydia asked, and Colleen realized her mistake.

"It was nothing," Colleen said, hoping that her friends would drop it.

"No way," Ellie said. "You don't drop that on us and expect to us not to follow up."

"It was nothing. It was a long time ago. We were just together a few weeks, really, right before I left for college." Colleen tried to make her voice sound airy as if what she and Jake had had been just that, when in reality it had been intense. The night of the prom, then a few stolen moments afterward when they had talked about everything. The connection had been real, intense, and had seemed potentially life changing. Those feelings had made Colleen want to run away as far and as fast as she could.

"Doesn't seem like he's forgotten you, has he?" Ellie said.

"Amy does not like that one bit," Lydia added, with a little shake of her head.

Colleen sighed and reminded herself that was all the more reason to stay away from Jake. She did not need any more enemies in her life. She had come back to Queensbay to start over, raise her daughter, and build a business that would support them both. She didn't need to be pulled into any sort of drama.

Ellie took pity on her and changed the subject. "So what are you planning on selling here?"

Colleen turned gratefully to her friend and started in on the grand tour.

Chapter 18

Ellie and Lydia had left and Colleen was trying to focus and sort through her to-do list, but what Lydia had said about Amy was bothering her. It reminded Colleen of her long-ago self, which was an uncomfortable recollection. She hadn't always been nice. She had, in fact, been a mean girl. Not that she ruled the school with a clique of acolytes, or maybe she had, but she'd definitely tried everything she could to make sure that people knew Colleen McShane was someone to be reckoned with. Sure, she might have been from the wrong side of the town, with a less-than-perfect family, but Colleen had wanted people to know she belonged.

She had schemed, manipulated, and done what she needed to stay on top. It had seemed so important then, and for a lot of her life after high school as she sought to make her way in the world. She had kept manipulating and scheming, from one job to the next, from one relationship to the next, chasing after some mythical brass ring.

Until she met Olivier, and she had met her match. When she first was with him, she had felt for once like she could relax, that he would take care of things. And, he had, until he got tired of her. She had realized, once again, that she needed to take care of herself. But she didn't have to do it the way she had done it before, did she? Couldn't she could still look out for herself and Adele and be nicer about it?

She had never really apologized to Darby, which was why she was now standing outside the Golden Pear Café, with a flyer about the sidewalk sale in her hand. She pushed open the door and let herself into the café. It was just about empty, with Darby starting to clean up and pack away things. She looked up at Colleen but said nothing.

"Hello, could I please have a cappuccino?" Colleen said.

Darby looked at her as if she'd grown another head.

"You know, just espresso, steamed milk. You make it with the machine back there," Colleen kept her voice friendly.

"I know what a cappuccino is," Darby said tartly.

Colleen squared her shoulders, told herself not to back down.

"May I have one? I did say please."

"Fine." Darby busied herself with the gleaming machine. Colleen put the flyer down. "I'm organizing a sidewalk sale, same weekend as the Harbor Cup Regatta. Figure it would be good for business. Osprey Arms said they'd run a special, so I am sure everyplace, including here, will be busy."

Darby turned around, flicked her eye over the flyer. "I heard about it."

She slid the white cup with the perfectly foamed milk toward Colleen.

Colleen picked up took a sip. "It's delicious."

"It's a good idea," Darby said.

"Thanks. I thought of it while I was working at Quent's," Colleen said. It was a deliberate provocation, and she waited.

Darby wiped her hands on her apron. For a moment it looked as if she would say nothing, then she finally threw up her hands.

"Look, I'm sorry about that. I overreacted. If it means anything, Sean told me I was being ridiculous, and you were one of his best employees."

Colleen allowed herself the smallest of smiles. "He looked like someone had run over his dog after you left."

"You heard?"

"Whole staff heard. I am pretty sure they know just what type of gal I am."

"What . . . I mean, I never . . . I just . . ." Darby was at a loss for words.

"Someone seems to know a lot about me. Been keeping tabs on me?"

Darby shook her head. "Not exactly. But Amy Anderson still has it out for you."

"She deserved it," Colleen said, but stopped there.

"She did. I thought what you did was brilliant."

"I am sorry that I ran off with your prom date. It was a bad move. I could have handled it better," Colleen said as she put her money on the counter.

Darby paused, looked thoughtful, and said, "It's a little anticlimactic, hearing those words after all this time. Somehow I thought this moment would be more momentous."

"A public encounter with a slap fight?"

Darby smiled, almost chuckled, and said, "Not quite. But I've thought about it, more since Sean and I had that discussion, and I do seem to recall that I was the one who ditched Jake to find Aaron Miller."

Darby sighed. "None of us is blameless for that night. So, fine, apology accepted. I am sorry for making you think you had to quit."

Darby shook her head. "That Amy . . . she just kept filling my head with things."

"Like what?" Colleen asked.

Darby turned away, pretended to be busy with a rack of cupcakes.

"What did you say?" Colleen said more clearly.

"That your sugar daddy Parisian count's new wife kicked you out and told you to never come back."

Colleen took a deep breath. "She's not entirely wrong," Colleen admitted. "Olivier was older, and wealthier, and my boss. But he didn't get married until after he dumped me, and I have never had the pleasure of meeting his new wife. And I doubt I will."

Darby was silent as her eyes took in Colleen.

"What else?"

Darby sighed, put down the tray. "That this wasn't your first relationship of this type."

"So she thinks I am a gold digger?"

Darby scrunched her shoulders noncommittally.

"I'm not a gold digger," Colleen said, and struggled for what else to say. "I never expected to get married to Olivier. I've always worked, and I had a few relationships before Olivier, but they weren't like that. I didn't date anyone just for the money."

"But it was nice that they had it?"

It was Colleen's turn to shrug noncommittally. "I wouldn't have cared if Olivier hadn't been successful and rich, but somehow I don't think he would have been the person he was if he wasn't, if that makes sense."

Darby nodded. "It does, in a weird sort of way."

"There's still more," Colleen said, prompting her.

"People know you inherited the store from Phil."

"They don't think that there was anything going on between us, Phil and me, do they?" Colleen was horrified at the thought.

Darby put cookies into a plastic container and sealed the lid. "Phil made a big deal about going to visit you in Paris a few years back."

It took a moment for Colleen to figure out what Darby was driving at.

"They're not saying that my daughter is . . ." Colleen giggled, then laughed outright. "So he left me the store as a secret inheritance for his love child?"

Darby looked uncomfortable. "I'm just the messenger."

Colleen looked around and pulled a chair out from one of the little café tables and sat down. She might as well get comfortable since this seemed like it was going to take a while.

"That's some message."

"I know it's not true," Darby said after a moment.

"Of course it's not. Adele is not Phil's love child. Phil and I were friends."

"I know," Darby said, picked out two chocolate croissants, put them on plates and came out from behind the counter. She put a plate in front of Colleen and the other across the table and took a seat.

"Phil used to come in here, every day, pretty much. He was always talking about you."

"Did you know how sick he was?" Colleen asked. It hurt a bit that Phil hadn't told her, that he'd kept that from her.

Darby shook her head. "He kept that quiet. It was fast, so fast."

"Did you know he wanted to leave the shop to me?" Colleen asked.

"Yeah, he told me. Just in case anyone decided to make an issue of it. He told me that he was of sound mind and body and all of that. He told me a little about you and your relationship. I'll be honest, I thought he didn't sound like he was a fan of Adele's father."

Colleen nodded. "Phil knew the score even before I did. Probably knew I needed to get away before I did."

Darby paused. "Honestly, I thought you'd sell it. Didn't expect to see you here, and when I did and found out that you were 'the Colleen' Sean was singing the praises of, guess I went a little crazy."

"Hormones?" Colleen asked.

Darby flushed, then smiled as her hands drifted down to settle protectively over her still-flat belly. "How did you know? Only Sean knows."

"Like I said, he looked like a man who would do anything for his wife. And you have that combination of exhausted and glowiness about you. Don't worry, I won't say anything."

Darby smiled, and Colleen thought about just how lucky she was. Darby had had everything Colleen had ever wanted. Loving parents, a stable home life. Her father, Big Reg, had been over-protective, and Darby had complained about him, but Colleen had been envious. Her own father had been gone all the time, never cared how well his daughter had done on her algebra test or whether or not she'd get into trouble on prom night. Her father hadn't even bothered to show up for graduation, instead getting married in a quickie wedding in Vegas to his third wife.

"You messed him up when you left," Darby said, and Colleen knew that they had moved on, that she was speaking about Jake. "Badly. He was a wreck. He was in love, and after a couple of weeks, you just up and disappeared, without a word."

"I went off to college early. He was going back to school. It was never going to be more than a summer fling," Colleen said, knowing that while the reasons sounded logical, rational, it had been one of the hardest decisions of her life.

They had been intense and had scared her because for once she had second thoughts about getting out of Queensbay, thoughts of maybe what it would be like to be with Jake. He was the favorite son of Queensbay, too handsome for his own good with a business that was going to be handed to him. He was steady and faithful, caring and sweet. He paid attention to her.

All the things she had never experienced from a man. But if she stayed with him, envisioned a future with him, she'd never go to college in the big city, never travel, never meet tall dark strangers who would whisk her off to foreign cities. She would have never found herself.

"I figured he'd get over me."

"He did, sort of. Pined for a bit, then took up dating with a vengeance. None of them stuck around though. None of them were you."

Colleen laughed. "That's ridiculous," she said. "It was over ten years ago. We knew each other for a couple of weeks, not counting the semester we took art together. I mean, seriously."

"Trust me, I think he's tried to get over you," Darby said. "He hasn't been a monk, not at all. But no one, except for Amy Anderson, has managed to keep him for long. Everyone thinks they can change him, make him settle down, but I think he's been waiting for just the right person."

Colleen shook her head. "It was Phil who made it easy for me to get away. He found me a job at an antiques store near college and a place to rent. But, I had to leave right away."

Phil had found her one day, crying over it all. It was after she had gotten another letter from her father, a "hey honey, sorry about missing graduation, here's a fifty go buy yourself something nice" type of message. Her mother had been crawling back from another episode with the bottle, her last, if Colleen remembered correctly, and was no help.

Phil had listened, given her some tissues, and told her that dreams weren't to be taken lightly. That she needed to fly, fly far and fast. Within a few days, he'd told her he had a friend who needed some summer help in an antiques shop, near her new college. He'd even found a room to rent, but told her that she had to take it now, or risk losing the job and the room. It meant leaving Jake. Picking up and going had been easier than trying to explain it, so that's what she'd done. Run far and fast.

She figured that Jake would get over her. After all, he had everything going for him. There were lots of girls who would let Jake Owen cry on their shoulders.

"Sounds like Phil wanted to make sure you didn't stick around back then," Darby said.

"And now it seems like he wanted me back," Colleen said, thinking about it.

Darby shook her head. "I never thought you'd come back and make a go of it."

Colleen shrugged. "It was time for a change and this seemed like the perfect opportunity, to start over."

"Funny how coming back to Queensbay seems like a way to start over for a lot of us."

"Sometimes you don't know how much home means until you've been away," Colleen said quietly.

It was community, a network of people you could trust and count on, whether it was because you served them a drink at a bar, met them at the playground, or did business with them, turning over money in exchange for something they'd put blood, sweat, and tears in. Colleen took a bite of the croissant. Darby always did have a way with dough.

"Good?"

"Oh yeah," Colleen said. "It's good."

"Good," Darby echoed.

Chapter 19

Colleen spent the next couple of days in a frenzy of activity. Darby had agreed that the sidewalk sale was a good idea and had come on as the official co-organizer. Colleen had printed up flyers and postcards, and Darby had posted them in the Golden Pear Café, town hall, the library, and the Osprey Arms. Colleen had spent the rest of the time up and down the shops on the street, building up buzz, answering questions, and providing encouragement.

She'd also written a press release and sent it out to all the local papers and community sites. A blog post had drawn lots of comments, and she heard that the Osprey Arms was just starting to book up for that weekend. A reporter from the local lifestyle magazine was even going to do a story on the event. All in all, Colleen was feeling pretty good about things as she looked at her new sign.

It was here, the design she had hemmed and hawed over, debated, and seconded-guessed everything from the font to the background color, and was ready to go up. She felt a small pang of sadness as the letters spelling out "Treasure Emporium" came down, but her excitement grew as she finally saw the sign with *"La*

Belle Vie" go up above the window of the storefront.

"Thank you," she whispered up to Phil as she swelled just a little bit with pride.

There was still a lot to do, including the set-up of the shop itself, but now, the sign meant that there was no turning back. Even her mother had stopped mentioning nursing school or systems administrator school and quietly accepted the fact that Colleen was not selling the building. Colleen was inside now, looking through catalogs and working on her spreadsheet. All afternoon there'd been visitors, eager to congratulate her on the sign and check on the transformation of the space. She thought nothing of it when the door opened once again, even though she was packing her things up, getting ready to go pick Adele up, get her settled before she went in for her shift at Quent's.

"Well, well, look who's here. My day just picked up," a voice said.

Colleen's heart sank, but she tried to keep her face neutral, as she saw who it was. Chino Charlie, the drunk from the bar. Colleen took a deep breath. She could handle this. It wasn't the first time a guy hadn't taken the hint. Charlie was a little more persistent than most of them, but he was just a guy.

He wandered around, poking a finger here and there, and making approving comments. Colleen began to gather her things, hoping that he'd get her not-so-subtle hint.

"What's your hurry? I've been out of town on business. I missed you. Thought maybe I could take you out. You never did take me up on my offer of breakfast."

In broad daylight, he looked like a successful businessman, without any of the air of menace that drinking gave him. Darker hair swept back from a high forehead. Just a little bit of gray, she noticed, so subtle, it made him distinguished. He had a full face though, which showed the combination of too much drinking and eating out and not quite enough exercise. He looked like a man who had worked hard and now was enjoying the fruits of his labor. He'd once been muscular, now was just big.

In a small way he reminded her of Olivier. Not in looks, though they shared dark hair, but in the general air of self-satisfaction that came from being rich, a certain smugness, as if they were certain of their charm. Olivier, though, had the slight benefit of French charm. In Chino Charlie's case, it came off as arrogance.

"I'm meeting a friend," Colleen said, hoping the generically bland excuse would suffice. Her hopes were disappointed.

"Invite her along. The more the merrier. My boat's down at the marina. Why don't we take it out for a spin, a sunset cruise in the harbor?"

"I don't think so," Colleen said, wondering if she should admit that her friend was a five year old, but she didn't want Chino Charlie to know anything more about her than he already did.

"We can swing by your house and pick up anything you need," he said grandly. "The Jag is just outside."

She wondered if he knew where she lived, and she felt just a little bit creeped out. He had moved closer to her. She was glad that there was a counter between them, but still it wasn't enough to hide the overpowering smell of his aftershave. He had on a watch, a big fancy timepiece. He glanced at it conspicuously. She saw too that he wore a wedding band. Her eyes deliberately lingered there for a moment before she looked up at him.

He smiled, as if he didn't care, and said, "My wife and I have an understanding."

"Good for you," she said, gathering all of her things into her bag and moving just a little around the counter, giving him the clear signal that she was ready to go, and that it was time for him to leave.

He reached out a hand, fast, and his grip was surprisingly strong. She tried to stay calm, knowing that even though it was broad daylight, the shop's windows were still papered over, and the door, though unlocked, was closed. She didn't know if anyone could see them, and she fought down the rising tide of panic. The relative privacy seemed to give Charlie Chino the incentive he needed to make a play for it.

"I'll make it worth your while. Spend a little time with me, and it'll beat your best night of tips. Bring your friend, and I'll make it really worth your while; we'll have a real party. I know your type: once a party girl, always a party girl. Girls like you need a sugar daddy, and I might just be your type."

Colleen had to swallow the bile that rose in her throat. She wasn't scared but didn't know if she were truly strong enough to fight him off. She was reviewing her options, trying to think of how to talk her way out of this, wondering what she could say that would get him to leave her alone.

The bell above the door tinkled and Lydia burst in, her usual energy rolling into the store ahead of her. Charlie took stock of the interruption and released Colleen. She backed away quickly, absurdly glad she was free and tried not to rub her arm where he had grabbed it.

"Hi, I thought we could get the kids and go to the park," Lydia said, looking at the two of them, a confused expression on her face.

Charlie beamed at Lydia, as if he had done nothing wrong and then looked directly at Colleen.

"Guess we'll be catching up later?" he said, then turned and left. The store was absurdly silent then, and Colleen felt her hands start to shake.

Lydia came over to her, concern in her eyes. "Are you okay?"

Colleen nodded and sucked in a deep breath. She had been too lulled by the small town to think properly about security. She needed to think about a camera system and an alarm button underneath the counter. Simple measures but that would do a lot to make her feel safer.

"Do you want to tell me what that was all about?" Lydia put her hand on Colleen's arm.

Colleen smiled at her, warmly comforted. It was nice to have a friend. "Just a typical jerk move. It's someone from the bar. I don't know how he found me here. I'm sure someone talked. He wanted me to take a boat ride. I told him I had to meet a friend, and he said to bring her along."

Lydia snorted and rolled her eyes. "Bet he doesn't know your friend is a five year old. All four of us could go. Josh would ask him about a million questions. It would make sure he didn't want to have anything to do with us."

Colleen smiled, her heartbeat returning to normal as Lydia's joking calmed her down.

"We better get going, or we're going to be late for pickup. And, I don't know if I can live with the guilt Miss Carol throws my way if I'm not there on time."

Colleen nodded, and she and Lydia walked out. Colleen carefully locked the door. Yes, she would call the alarm company tomorrow and talk about her options. Just the thought made her feel better, and she was happy as she and Lydia made their way down the street toward Happy Faces.

Chapter 20

J ake threw down the pencil. He was having trouble concentrating, and he knew why. He looked at what he'd doodled in the paper's margin. He'd been working on some drawings for the Showhouse, trying to get a sense of what the space could look like. He'd reviewed the research on other apartment complexes built out of warehouses, piano factories, and even old movie theaters. Plenty of inspiration was out there, and judging by what the developers were charging once projects were finished, these types of renovated spaces were very desirable and lucrative. Empty nesters loved the idea of being close to town but without the up-keep of a house. Amenities were what they wanted, and that's what he was grappling with.

He was trying to figure out how to use the main amphitheater space. Maybe a performance center or a community center or a library, game room, or café would be appropriate. Unfortunately, little sketches of Colleen's face had appeared along the margins, along with some ideas for her store. If he had more time, he would have liked to expose the beams, distress them and add more built-ins. The guys had done a great job so far, he'd made sure of that, and he'd even had them throw in some extras.

Jax walked in, suit jacket off for once, shirt sleeves rolled up. "I heard the Tanner site is behind."

"Managed to catch up," Jake replied. "The vet building is behind, for sure, though. The solar panels you wanted are on back order. Think you can call your guy and get us something sooner?"

Jax nodded and stepped over to the drafting table, looking at Jake's plans. "These for the Showhouse?"

Jake nodded. "Mrs. Sampson likes the idea in theory. She warned me that there's a long road ahead, but I could see her mind working. She told me that the more pictures the better, and that I'd better be ready to present to the council next month for some preliminary approval. In the meantime, she did give me permission to go in and do a full inspection to get a sense of the place."

"Good, no more breaking and entering."

Jax pulled one of the sketches toward him. Jake almost stopped him but Jax was too quick.

"Showhouse or Colleen McShane?" Jax said, chuckling. "Man, you've got it bad."

"Shut up," Jake said darkly. He didn't need the obvious pointed out.

"Have you had this obsession since she dumped you or just since she came back into town?"

Jake walked over to the window, ran a hand through his hair. Jax was his best friend. There was no bullshitting him.

"Both, I guess. Let's just say she's a hard girl to forget."

"That's an understatement, judging by the number of pictures you've drawn of her. It's a little creepy, if you ask me."

"What?" he turned to Jax.

"It's like some sort of weird stalking thing."

"I am not stalking her. We talk."

Jax raised a blonde eyebrow.

"Sometimes I think she likes me, but every time I get close, she pushes me away. I don't know," Jake confessed.

"Maybe there's someone else."

Jake shook his head. "No, she said there isn't, but she said that it's complicated."

"Always is. You know, it's softball night. We're playing North Coast. They beat us last time, so in order to keep the family honor I thought we'd bring the big guns to bear."

"Softball?"

"I can't let Chase win again," Jax was begging.

Chase was Jackson's brother and the owner of North Coast Outfitters. The softball rivalry between the two and their companies was legendary.

"So?"

"Lynn's umpiring."

Lynn was Jackson's pregnant wife. She wanted to play, but despite her protests that she was fine, he insisted that she only play umpire.

"And I heard Tory tell Lynn that afterward everyone is heading to Quent's for a few beers. Pretty certain Colleen will be there. Maybe you just need to keep showing up."

"Isn't that stalker-ish?"

"Well, my sources say that the chemistry between you two could light up the streetlights in town."

"Sources?"

"Ellie mentioned something to Tory, Tory said something to Lynn, and Lynn told me. Something about Ellie almost walking in on you guys the other day."

"More of those mixed signals," Jake said.

"Well, maybe give her one more chance. Then after she shoots you down one more time, you can get back to work and stay focused there," Jax said, tossing the sketches back down.

Chapter 21

T he pub seemed unusually quiet tonight, just one middle-aged couple at the bar, and only a few of the tables filled. Lydia and Ellie were here of course, but she thought of them as friends, rather than customers. Colleen wasn't too worried about the size of her tip jar. It was softball team night, and, win or lose, they usually came to Quent's to relive the game.

The place would soon be hopping, the energy amped up. Spring was definitely in the air, summer not far behind. The time had come to remind people of that, to have them thinking about fireflies, warm summer nights, and the sun blazing on the sand. She'd created a special cocktail just for it, using her favorite lavender lemonade as the base.

She had control of the playlist and had selected a round-up of summer hits of the past, just to put everyone in a good mood. The door opened, bringing in a gust of evening air and more customers.

"Here's my working girl."

She looked up, and tried to hide her annoyance. Chino Charlie came swaggering in, and he had a friend with him who was also giving her a long, slow once over. Everything in her screamed to tell him to get out,

169

but this wasn't her bar, and he was a customer, a paying one, who so far hadn't done anything wrong. Still, she knew that if he gave her trouble, Quent would back her up. Quent was talking to Ellie and a little bit oblivious to what was going on, which was a good thing. He wasn't always the best at customer relations. Then again, he didn't have to be, since booze usually sold itself.

Charlie and his buddy sat down at the far end of the bar, and she could tell that they had already been drinking. Their faces were flushed, and the slight staggers and disjointed gazes reinforced Colleen's deduction. It was a public place, she reminded herself, and she had plenty of support. Nothing would happen. Still, she had to fight to keep her expression calm and friendly as she felt their stares undo her confidence.

Charlie slapped his friend on the back, tipped his head toward Colleen and said, loudly enough for the whole bar to hear, "Told you she was worth the walk."

"Hiya, hot thing," he said directly to her.

Colleen ignored him and kept wiping down the counter. Her creep-o-meter was definitely going up. They hadn't done anything. Yet.

"We'll have two bourbons, neat," Charlie said, his tone already a little less friendly, more suggestive as he realized that he was being ignored.

"Whoa, hitting it a little hard, Charlie, aren't you?" his friend said, but Charlie shrugged.

"Hell of a day at work. Good thing the sexy bartender is here to listen to our tales of woe, right?"

"Hey, Colleen, can I get another?" Ellie called her over politely, and Colleen was grateful for the diversion. Quent had disappeared into the back, and Ellie was warily watching the two guys. Colleen was pretty sure Ellie had heard everything they'd said.

"Take your time, getting my refill. Hasn't he been here before?"

Before Colleen could say anything, Lydia chimed in, "He was at the shop earlier today too."

"That's more than a little upsetting. You should let Quent know." Ellie's voice had an edge of concern in it.

Colleen shook her head. "He'll get angry. Besides, this isn't the first time I've dealt with overeager customers. They get the picture. Eventually."

Ellie looked unsure, but didn't say anything. The bar was starting to fill up, people coming in to watch the baseball game, and now she saw the first of the softball teams were filing in.

There was safety in crowds, and she'd be too busy to have to pay too much attention to Charlie and his friend. She glanced at the uniforms. Queensbay Construction and North Coast Outfitters. She sighed and it figured that it had to be Jake's team. He wasn't here yet, so maybe that meant he hadn't played, and she would be spared the double complication of Charlie and Jake together in one place. She recognized a few faces. Tory Somers for one, who gave her a nod and held up two fingers for the number of pitchers she needed as she walked over to Ellie and gave her a hug.

"Who won?" Ellie asked.

"We didn't," Tory said in disgust. "Jackson decided to play, and it was all over."

Colleen listened to them chat about the game as she filled the two pitchers all the while aware that Charlie's eyes were boring into her, watching her every move. Intense had just been upped a notch. She knew she would have to deal with Charlie soon, but she still wasn't quite sure how to do it.

"Hey Mama," said a tall man wearing cowboy boots, dark jeans, and a button-down shirt. He came over, pecked Ellie on the cheek, and pulled Tory to him. Colleen noticed the way both of them lit up in his presence and pushed down the wave of sadness that suddenly welled up. It had been a long time since a man had lit up when she was around.

"You don't have to do that. I'll put it on the company account. We lost fair and square," Tory said with a sigh as Colby tried to lay some money down on the bar.

Colleen filled more pitchers and made a note that she would have to ask Quent how to handle company accounts when he returned from dealing with the walk-in freezer. That and a hundred other little things kept her occupied as the night wore on and more people came in. Colleen felt good. There was an energy in here that not even Charlie's stares could dispel. But Colleen was grateful that Ellie stayed at the bar, nursing a white wine while she chatted easily with Colleen and Lydia, Tory and her son Colby, keeping her for the most part out of Charlie's orbit.

She was pouring a club soda for Eleanor and closing out the softball team's tab when she felt it. It wasn't so much the gust of fresh air that came in as a shift of attention. People called his name, and eyes went toward him, including her own. Jake caught Colleen's attention, and he gave her a long, slow, meaningful look that reminded her that the last time they had been together, they had almost kissed. She had wanted it, wanted him.

Looking away quickly, she drew her attention

back to the bar, surveying her customers. Ellie was fine, chatting with Colby and Tory, sipping her club soda and nibbling on a potato wedge. Lydia was talking to a couple of guys from the softball team, who looked like they were doing their best to impress her.

The rest of the softball teams, what was left of them, were rowdy and buoyant, but judging by the number of sodas at the tables, they had already sorted out who the designated drivers were. Then there was the middle-aged couple at the bar, she two drinks in, him one, and sharing a plate of calamari. The guy seemed like a good tipper, so Colleen asked if they wanted a refill, but he shook his head and his wife beamed at him. Happy and temperate, she thought, and didn't worry about them.

A few other tables were scattered around but no one had ordered too much. A nice, respectable evening had shaped up, except for Chino Charlie and his pal. They were both watching her. She had replaced their beers with bourbons because they were customers, and so far they had done nothing to cause her to cut them off. But Quent's Pub was not an all-night kind of place.

"Last call soon," she said as she pulled a few empties off the bar. She set out two glasses of water and filled them up to make her point, slid them over to Chino Charlie and his friend.

"Doesn't seem to be quieting down," Charlie said, his eyes more than a little glassy.

"Still, it's almost closing time," she said, sweeping some empties off of the bar and into the sink. Other patrons were getting the hint, reaching for their checks or their wallet. She went out onto the floor, passing right by Charlie and his friend.

"You know, you remind me of a girl I used to know. Works up at a place on the highway. That isn't your other job, is it?" Charlie's voice carried across during a sudden lull in the music.

His friend laughed. Colleen paused. She had a sneaking suspicion she knew exactly which kind of place they were referring to.

"Sorry, you must be thinking about someone else," she answered without turning around.

"I don't know," Charlie said. "I can almost see you there, dancing, or maybe you'd just do a private show for me? I am sure I could make it worth your while? Better than working for shitty tips in dives like this."

Before she knew it, Charlie had her arm and was pulling her closer. His eyes were glassy, his breath fumy, and his lips wet, his tongue running over them in anticipation.

She looked down at his hand on her arm and then up at him, trying to stay steady. She couldn't let him see her rattled. It would only make it worse, goad him on.

"Hey Charlie, leave the lady alone," his friend, who was a fraction less drunk, said, his good sense starting to take over.

"I don't think she's much of a lady, not if she's working here."

"Do you kiss your wife with a mouth like that?" was all Colleen could think of to say.

"My wife's a frigid bitch, that's why I need to find hot stuff like you."

She was dimly aware that Ellie was calling her from the other end of the bar.

"Sorry, I've got to take care of another customer," she said, pulling her arm away.

She walked over to Ellie, trying to smile but she saw that the older woman had seen everything, knew pretty much exactly what was going on.

"Thanks," she said as she cleared some glasses.

"Anytime. Some guys can be such jerks."

"Is there a problem here?" Quent was there, his arms folded across his chest.

Colleen shot Ellie a look. "Nothing I can't handle."

Ellie raised an eyebrow but said nothing. Colleen didn't want Quent to know what was going on. She didn't want the boss to think she couldn't handle herself.

"Take a break, luv," Quent said. "Get some fresh air or get off your feet."

Colleen almost nodded, but just shook her head instead. "I'm fine. Let's get this place cleaned up so we can all go home."

She turned, intent on a couple of empty pitchers at a table across the floor, but all of sudden he was there.

"I've been waiting all night for you, dear," Jake said, a huge grin on his face as he swept her up in a bear hug. She froze stiff, not sure what had happened, as he set her down, leaned in, and kissed her.

She was on the spot, frozen, not half an arm's length away from Charlie, kissing Jake Owen in front of a bar full of people. Everyone was watching, and she was fighting the urge to not slip into his arms, let him take her away from all of this.

He whispered in her ear, barely heard above the din of the bar and the pounding of her heart. "Kiss me back. Otherwise he won't get the point."

His lips came down on hers again and her brain

got it. Her lips parted and they kissed, his touch insistent, possessive, and full of show. His arm was around her, pulling her close and she had to stand on her tiptoes to reach him. The other hand held her cheek; it was rough and warm, and the touch as he brushed her hair back was just enough to make her body shudder.

She pulled away finally, feeling her heart thudding, wondering just what the hell had happened. They had garnered more than a few stares, including Ellie, who was looking at her approvingly. She could feel the anger from behind her, but Jake spun her around, his arm draped over her shoulders. "I'll take you home when you get off," he said loudly enough, just an edge of possessiveness directed toward Charlie and his friend.

Charlie was glaring at them, his eyes narrowed. He got up, drew himself up to his full height, and took a step toward Jake. Then he reconsidered, taking in all six foot three of Jake's solidly muscled, ex-quarterback body, which Colleen felt herself nestled against. The arms of steel, the muscled chest—she could even feel them through the shirt he wore. She'd always been into guys who were slimmer, slighter, more elegant, but there was something to say about being enveloped by strength. Then she shook her head and made to move away. But Jake held her firmly there and whispered again, "Stay still, he's about to get the point."

She wanted to scream that she didn't need his protection, but out of the corner of her eye she saw Quent moving down the bar, his own thickly muscled arms bulging, a look of disgust on his face. Behind her, she was aware that the bar had quieted down as if everyone was sensing a fight. Colby had slipped up behind Jake and the other members of the softball team had arrayed themselves in a loose circle behind them. It was shaping up to be a classic townie versus tourist showdown.

Charlie considered his odds, looked at his friend who was pulling out his wallet. He slammed some cash down on the counter top and grabbed Charlie by the arm.

"Hope you didn't leave a tip. The service sucks here," Charlie said into the general quiet of the bar.

They hustled out. Jake turned toward them slowly, his arm still around her. He gave a nod to two of the guys from the softball team.

"Make sure they get back to the rock they crawled out from."

"No problem, boss," they said, and they disappeared. They weren't quite as tall or muscular as Jake, but Colleen was pretty sure that Charlie and his buddy would think twice before hanging around.

Finally, he loosened his hold on her, and she pushed him away, both hands flat on his chest. He barely moved. The bar returned back to the usual noise level.

Quent looked at Jake, and said, "Thanks, mate. Colleen, I can close up here. Why don't you head home."

"I can finish my shift, just like I could have taken care of those guys," she told both Quent and Jake. Jake stood there nonplussed, arms folded over his chest.

Lydia came over. "That guy, he was at the shop earlier today. He's stalking you."

"He was what?" Jake turned to her.

Colleen didn't answer.

"You need to call the police and file a report."

"Has he hassled you before?" Quent asked. His

voice was sharp.

This was just what she wanted to avoid. She didn't need a bunch of guys handling her problems for her.

"It's nothing," she said, but Jake cut her off.

"It wasn't nothing," he muttered.

She turned on him, suddenly furious, not quite sure why, except she felt that somehow Jake had all of a sudden made a big deal out of nothing. She needed this to be a little deal. She did not need this to be any deal. She was going to get security in the shop, and she'd have Lydia give her a ride home. She did not need Jake. She did not need his protection, and she did not need him kissing her in front of everyone just to make a point.

"Oh, don't worry, thanks to your goons, I don't think he will be coming back here."

"My goons," Jake laughed, "are an electrician and a plumber and they'll do nothing. I hope." He thought for a second, whipped out a phone, and texted something.

"Just making sure," he said without being quite able to meet Colleen's eyes with his own.

She shook her head and walked back behind the bar, clearing the empties away. Quent was standing next to Ellie, who had her hand on his arm and was talking intently to him. Ellie noticed her look, sent her a small smile, and Colleen breathed a little easier. She had a feeling Ellie was on her side, whatever that was, and that maybe, just maybe she'd keep this job for another day.

She surveyed the bar. Most of the customers, excitement over, had gone back to what they were doing. She went over to where Charlie had been sitting, saw that his friend had left just enough to cover the bill with a generous two-cent tip. At least she wouldn't owe Quent any money at the end of her shift.

She sighed. Being a bartender was supposed to be a fun, uncomplicated job.

"Here." Jake was there, and he was counting out some money from his wallet.

"I don't need your charity," she said stiffly, keeping her hands busy cleaning glasses, sweeping up damp napkins, anything to avoid looking at him in the eye.

"I want a beer."

"Last call already went out. See if there's any in the pitcher over there," she said and tipped her head to the tables where the remnants of the softball team were getting up.

She saw Colby and Tory come up, say goodbye to Ellie. Tory looked over at them, and when she knew that Colleen knew that, she said, "Bye Colleen. See you around."

Colleen smiled. It was nothing, just a pleasantry, but it made Colleen feel ordinary and at home.

"You too. Better luck next game."

Tory nodded, and she and Colby disappeared into the spring night, arms wrapped around each other.

Colleen took the pitcher Tory had brought up and poured what was left of it into a glass and pushed it over toward Jake.

"On the house," she said.

He looked down at the warm, foamy beer then at her, and said. "I was trying to do something nice for you."

"I told you, I can take care of myself, and that wasn't help. That was practically assault."

"You didn't push me away," he said.

"You had no right. Kissing a girl without asking is just as creepy as following her from bar to bar."

He didn't reply.

She paused, thought for a moment. "Why are you here tonight, anyway? Are you following me?"

He spread out his hands. "I didn't know you'd be working here tonight. The team always comes here after softball."

Colleen knew he was lying and was about to call him on it when he said, "Besides, you kissed me."

"I what?" She stopped in her tracks. "You told me to."

"I didn't think you would actually do it," Jake said.

She turned and stared at him. A lesser man would have walked away, but Jake just sat there, casually looking at her.

"You're joking."

"Teasing, maybe."

She shook her head.

"Maybe I was just testing your feminine wiles for myself."

She froze, her whole body stiff with rage, and she knew it for what it was, a sudden all-consuming anger. She knew that she couldn't let it get to her. That she couldn't let him get to her.

"I don't know what you heard or thought you heard, but get out of here. If I kiss you, I am not trying to get something from you, or steal you from someone else."

He eyes narrowed, saw the look on her face, then reconsidered. "It's not your place, you can't kick me out."

"Bartender rules: I can kick out anyone I want to."
She raised her voice just a little and knew that Quent
had heard her, saw the small, swift smile cross his face.
Quent liked to play the tough guy, and knowing that
Quent had her back made her bold.

Jake looked around. Saw Quent standing there
with his arms folded over his chest.

"You looked like you needed help," Jake said.

"I can take care of myself."

"Fine. Next time I'll let you," he said, and there
was just a bit of a sulky edge to his voice.

"Good," she said and knew hers sounded just as
petulant.

Jake scowled back at her, and Colleen felt slightly
ridiculous as if she had just had a battle of wills with a
three year old, not a thirty-year-old man.

Apparently there was nothing left to say because
Jake huffed, turned on his heel, and stormed out. She
watched him go, sure that if he could, he would have
slammed the door, but it closed softly and slowly on its
well-oiled hinges.

She sighed, looked around. Most everyone was
gone, except for Ellie and Lydia, who were looking at
her.

"Well, honey, that was a show," Ellie drawled.

Colleen said nothing, just turned away and found
some more dirty pitchers to gather up.

Chapter 22

Lydia drove her home. She climbed into Lydia's Jeep, grateful for once to not have to make the walk home. It had been a rough night. She didn't know why she was so angry at Jake. He had been trying to help. His method was a little heavy-handed, and it had in a resulted in a kiss that half the town had seen. The kiss had been . . . well, amazing didn't quite cover it, but she didn't need to build that kind of reputation around town.

Lydia didn't say much, just kept shooting concerned glances her way.

Colleen sighed. She appreciated the concern, but wanted to tell everyone that she'd been taking care of herself for a long time. She maybe had been overconfident because Queensbay was such a small town, but luckily she'd been reminded that it was always right to take some basic precautions.

"I already told you I'm calling the security company first thing tomorrow," she told Lydia. "Cameras, panic button, whole nine yards in the shop."

"Good thing, but I was thinking more about the kiss."

Colleen shrugged his shoulders. "It was just a

kiss."

"That was not just a kiss," Lydia pointed out. "And it seems to me that Jake has his sights set on more than kissing you."

"Just not going to happen," Colleen said empathically.

"Why not? He's perfectly good looking, you know, and I bet he's pretty good with his hands."

"No comment," Colleen said, though her lips twitched a little as she fought the smile.

"Then what is it?"

Colleen sighed. "When I came back home, I promised myself that this time I would do it by myself, make a life for myself and Adele without relying on anyone, especially a man."

"Not one of us makes it alone, you know," Lydia said.

Collen looked out the window as Queensbay, dark and quiet, rolled by.

"I just want to prove to myself that I can be my own person."

"To yourself or to Adele's father?" Lydia asked. "I've never met him, but I don't like him. Sounds a bit manipulative if you ask me, coming to you and telling you he'd buy you a store if you became his mistress."

Colleen tried not to remember how he had reacted when she had suggested that she run her own shop. He had said something along the lines, of "you silly little girl." Okay, so *La Belle Vie* wasn't on the Parisian High Street, but at least she was starting somewhere. Nothing to say she wouldn't be selling all over the country through her website or opening another store. Queensbay today, maybe New York or London tomorrow.

"He just didn't believe in me," Colleen said. And he was a jerk. She didn't need him and she needed to prove that to him once and for all. The money he sent, she had been carefully banking in an account for Adele, for college, for her future. He could contribute to his daughter, even if he wouldn't acknowledge her, but Colleen was determined to live on her own.

"I think Jake believes in you," Lydia said as the Jeep pulled up to Colleen's house.

"I am just afraid that he'll want too much of me. Olivier wanted all of me, but he didn't give any of himself."

"Like a little kid who doesn't want the toy but doesn't want anyone else to have it?"

"Exactly," Colleen said. She looked up at Adele's nightlight in the window. She was eager to go in, get into her pajamas, give her daughter a kiss, and remind herself that it was all going to be okay because they had each other.

"Jake seems like the type of kid who was pretty good at teamwork, if you know what I mean," Lydia said.

Colleen leaned her head against the glass window, letting the coolness transfer to her, trying to still the mix of thoughts and hormones in her body. She wanted Jake Owen, but she needed to not need him. How to untangle the two was never something she'd been very good at.

Chapter 23

"What are you doing here?" Quent asked Jake as he appeared out of the early morning fog.

Jake stopped his perusal of the boats moored at the marina. He'd been reading names, looking for the right one. It was still early, and a light mist clung to water as the rising sun inched above the horizon. Quent looked dangerous in black jeans, black boots, and a black motorcycle jacket.

"You're up pretty early for a bartender," Jake said, not answering the question.

"I've got some business to attend to," Quent said shortly.

"Your boat looks pretty ship-shape to me," Jake said and gestured toward Quent's neat little runabout.

"That's not the business I was looking for," Quent said. He nodded in the direction of the coffee cup Jake was holding.

"Meeting anyone for coffee?"

"Just thought I'd have a friendly chat with someone."

Quent nodded, cracked his knuckles. "Same thought occurred to me. Can't have the patrons hassling my staff like that, not with me trying to run a decent, family-friendly establishment."

"Can't have lowlifes hassling my girl like that," Jake concurred. It didn't matter that Colleen had yet to agree to be his girl.

Quent smiled, looking pleased. "What do ya say we pay this chucklehead a visit together and make it clear he'd be better off in another port of call?"

Jake squared his shoulders, smiled. "Sounds good to me."

Charlie had been surprisingly cooperative. A quick chat with the harbor master had helped them track down the boat, a sweet forty-foot cabin cruiser, equipped for deep sea fishing. Charlie had been asleep, but they had roused him, sat him down in his skivvies and laid the situation out for him, making it very clear that he wasn't welcome in Queensbay again. Jake had done enough research between last night and this morning to know just enough about Charlie, like where he lived, his wife's name and that he had two teenage daughters. All of this was more than enough to convince Charlie to take his business elsewhere.

As they stepped off the boat into the bright morning sun, Jake saw that the fog had indeed burned away. Behind him, he could hear the engines firing up.

"Shaping up to be a glorious day, what do you think, Quent?"

"Absolutely," Quent agreed, shaking his hand.

They parted ways, both whistling, ready for the day.

Chapter 24

"That was some lip-lock last night."

Jake looked up. Ellie had stepped out onto her balcony. As usual she was impeccably dressed, ready for work.

Jack said nothing. After he and Quent had taken care of Charlie, he'd come back to his place. He decided to enjoy his own cup of coffee as he watched Charlie's boat head away from the dock. Ellie leaned on her railing. A partition divided the two balconies, but with them both leaning out, it as if they were next to each other.

"The guy was upsetting her," he said. He didn't regret what he'd done.

"You could have said something to him, told him to get lost. You kissed her in the middle of the whole damn bar. Pretty over-the-top way to send a message."

"So?" he said. His good mood was rapidly deteriorating.

"I don't know all of the details, but it seems like you two have a bit of a history together."

"Maybe. Sort of," he admitted.

Ellie nodded. "Going to be a beautiful day. Maybe you should try to get to know her better."

"I know her. I've known her all my life."

"People change, and maybe you want to get to know her before you go in and start kissing her."

"I don't know," he said, running a hand through his hair. "Ever since she's been back, I sort of can't stop thinking about her. I try to avoid her, and I run into her and then I think about her and then, I don't know, I see some guys giving her a hard time, and all I want to do is..."

"Kiss her?"

"Something like that. What do you think I should do?" He didn't want to tell Ellie any more, but she and Colleen were friendly and he needed all the help he could get.

Ellie thought for a moment. "Maybe, you know, you need to be honest with her. Ask her on a date. You know, treat her like someone you're interested in and not some sort of sketchy high school fling."

"She wasn't some sort of high school fling. And that's not what I have in mind."

Ellie shook her head slowly. "Like I said, maybe you need to stop kissing girls in bars and take one on a date. Just saying. Maybe she has her reasons for being serious and not just falling into your arms."

"We're two healthy, unattached adults," Jake said.

Ellie paused, as is she were thinking, then said, "Doesn't mean you can't be a gentleman about it."

"I thought I was," he said. That had been his intention last night. To show that creep that Colleen wasn't just some girl he could hassle.

"You kissed her in front of her boss and half the town. You didn't really give her a chance to say no or, you know, have that moment in private."

"So you're saying, even though I thought I was being a good guy, I was being my usual moronic self?" Jake said, sighing. He wasn't good at relationships. Never had been. Colleen had run out on him, and then after that, he never was able to get close to anyone. Or, as the women he had dated liked to point out, he had commitment issues or was "emotionally unavailable." But the problem was that since none of them had been Colleen, he hadn't wanted to be committed. Now that she was back, she wanted to have nothing to do with him. And it was eating away at him.

"Something like that," Ellie said. "I'm just saying that you've both changed, so maybe you need to take it slow, like grownups."

Ellie smiled at him and slipped back into her apartment, leaving Jake alone, staring at the water, considering his options. He could be grown-up about this. He could go over to the shop right now, apologize for being overbearing, and ask if they could go on a date together. They needed to reset the whole scenario. They weren't horny teenagers any more. They were adults, grownups, and he could act like one. And, now that they weren't horny teenagers, they could take their time getting to know each other. No more worries about being found out or burst-in upon. As he drained the last of the coffee and soaked in the morning sun, he decided that he was going to ask Colleen McShane out on a date.

Chapter 25

Colleen took a step back, admired her handiwork and then decided that it looked like crap. She was setting up her merchandise, trying to decide how the store was going to be laid out. The vision she had in her mind's eye was just not coming together, and she knew why and who to blame.

Jake. And Chino Charlie. But mostly Jake. He had kissed her. A real kiss in front of everyone, and she had kissed him back. It had happened exactly thirty-six hours ago, give or take, and she hadn't been able to do anything but think about it. She'd barely slept, hadn't eaten, except for coffee, and now she was trying to work, and all she could think about was the kiss. She sighed and checked her watch, mindful of the time. Lydia had agreed to do her a favor, pick up Adele, and walk her and Josh over to the shop. Then, they'd all go the park. Being in the fresh air would be good for all of them. Still, she wished she had more time.

There was a knock on the door and shake of the handle. She had decided to keep it locked if she was there alone. The security company was coming tomorrow to do an evaluation.

She stepped toward the door, saw who it was and

almost told him to go away.

"I know you're in there. I can see you," he said, his voice insistent. She hesitated, not sure what she should do. To let him in would be to invite him in and could be the start of something. She wasn't sure she was ready for that.

"You can't ignore me forever," he pointed out. She sighed. He was right about that. She needed to cut this off, stop it, nip it in the bud, and plainly tell him that she was not interested. Not if he was going to treat her like something that needed protecting. She pulled herself together and unlocked the door.

He came in and looked at her. She blinked, swallowed as if she were about to say something. It wasn't supposed to be seductive but it was, and suddenly he had to be close to her. If she pushed him away, well fine, but he needed to kiss her, really kiss her, while they were alone, when it wasn't for show, when it was just the two of them. No distractions.

He moved to her, so that they were so close, no space between them. He took his hands and rested them on her shoulders, angling his head down. He moved in, and she said nothing, just rose to her feet and met him, kissed him back, hungrily, full of want.

But she broke the kiss off, gently, a look of worry on her face.

"Jake."

He opened his eyes and looked deeply into hers.

"I can't," she said.

"Won't or can't?"

"It doesn't matter."

"It does to me," he said. She was shaking, and her

hand was on her throat.

"What do you want?"

"To kiss you again," he said. He took a step forward, and she took one back.

He stopped. "Sorry. I didn't mean to be a jerk."

"Just take a step back."

"Done." He took two steps back, and she seemed to calm down.

"It's not you, Jake."

He held up his hands. "I get it, it's not me, it's you. Heard it before." He couldn't hide the frustration in his voice.

"No, I don't think you understand," she said, struggling to get the words right. "I just, you . . . you don't know me. You should stay away."

"I don't want to. I can't stop thinking about you. I haven't stopped for ten years, and, well, I thought we had something together and then you just left, disappeared. Why? What did I do?"

"Nothing, Jake. I had to get away. I had plans, dreams, and you were . . ."

"A distraction? What? A complication?" He knew her biggest desire had been to escape her shitty dad, her unhappy mother. Colleen had dreamed of big things, bigger things than life in a small town.

"Yes," she said softly.

"And what am I now?"

"Something I want but shouldn't have."

It was what he wanted to hear. She came to him, this time, and he kissed her. He could feel her falling into it, totally and absolutely. This time she didn't pull away, and he let her feel his need for her, let him run his hands along her shoulders and down her back, pulling her tight to him. *This must be how people become junkies,* flitted through his mind.

He broke away for just a moment and looked at her. She was smiling, a small, tentative, hopeful smile. And then it faded.

"Jake, there's something..."

There was the tinkle of the bell, the sound of voices, a little girl's voice and Colleen jerked back, a look of horror on her face.

"Mama, we stopped for cookies," a little girl called.

There, along with Lydia, who held onto the hand of a little boy, was a little girl. A little girl who came over to Colleen, who held out her hand and enveloped her in a hug.

"Hey sweetie," Colleen said and gave the girl a smile.

The girl turned, big blue eyes fixed on him and asked, "Who are you?"

The resemblance between her and Colleen was unmistakable.

"Why were you kissing Mama?" she asked.

"What?" he managed to get out. It was if his tongue wouldn't work. He'd never thought that being caught kissing someone's mother would be worse than being caught kissing someone's daughter.

If he had any hopes that Colleen would save him, he was sorely mistaken.

"Now that's an interesting question," Lydia said, her Southern drawl only emphasizing the question.

"I'm Josh," the little boy said, standing there with his arms folded, staring up at Jake, as if he too were looking for an explanation.

"Josh," he repeated, then turned to look at Colleen.

"I am Adele," the girl said.

"Adele," he repeated, but that was about all he could say.

"I umm, well, I have to go," Jake said. He looked at Colleen, who raised one shoulder and shrugged, as if to say, I told you it was complicated.

He couldn't get out into the spring afternoon fast enough.

Chapter 26

"Well, that went well," Colleen said with a sigh, as the door slammed on Jake.

Lydia shook her head. "There's more heat between the two of you than August in Georgia. Who are you trying to kid?"

"He ran out as soon as he saw Adele."

"Honey, that was embarrassment. I have a feeling he's never really thought of you as a mother. Nice guys get funny about mothers. Not a bad thing. Probably just needs to wrap his head around the reality of dating a single mom."

"I have to protect Adele." Colleen said firmly.

"From what?" Lydia asked, a puzzled expression on her face.

"I don't want people to judge her, because of me."

"What, that you're not married?" Lydia asked, shaking her head. "In case you haven't heard, it's a modern world out there. Things like these don't matter anymore."

"It's not that," Colleen said, groping for words. How could she put it in a way her friend would understand? She had left Queensbay after high school, shaking the dust from her shoes and vowing never to come back here. She was bound for glory and greater things, the first of her family to go to college. She wasn't going to repeat the mistakes of her own mother and her absentee father. Colleen McShane had meant to make something of her life, to show the good residents of Queensbay that she was better than the girl from the wrong side of the tracks.

And here she was to all appearances a marginally employed, unwed mother, living at home on the wrong side of the tracks. She knew that she was more than that. She had money in the bank, a career, and now her own business, but to anyone else it would look like she had essentially wound up right back where she started. She didn't need a big house or a fancy car to prove that she had made something of herself. She wouldn't fall into that trap. She just needed to be enough for her daughter, to know that Adele wouldn't grow up feeling abandoned and neglected as she had. She would be both mother and father to Adele, and she wouldn't let anything distract her from moving them forward. And Jake was definitely a distraction. Something, someone she could lose herself to.

"You know," Lydia said. "History has a way of repeating itself, unless you make a real effort to change it. You have to have the will and gumption."

"Gumption?"

"Moxie, *cajones*, you know what I mean. Seems like you've taken a few licks, and maybe you're a little down and out, but at least you found someplace to rest your feet and that's something. Don't stay down."

"Onward and upward, something like that?"

Lydia nodded. "Exactly," she said. "Now it's a nice day, so can we go to the park? Josh needs to run his crazies out before he breaks something in here."

Colleen looked over to where Adele and Josh were. The boy was trying to climb some shelves. Colleen nodded in agreement. Fresh air would do them all a world of good.

Chapter 27

T he park was quiet, and she was thankful for that. She was brooding, and Lydia, sensing her mood, rounded up Adele and Josh and took them to the swings, leaving Colleen alone with her thoughts. The encounter with Jake had left her riding a roller coaster of emotions. One of which was most definitely guilt. She never should have let Adele see her kissing Jake. She had been careful to keep men, even Olivier after he had made it clear he did not want to be a father to their daughter, out of her life. She was human and had her needs, but she had tended to them discretely, if at all. She wanted Adele to know that she was the most important thing in her life. Now that she had been caught kissing Jake, what would her daughter think?

On the walk over to the park, Adele had been quiet but Colleen knew that her brain was working furiously. She waited for the inevitable questions a four year old would have. She sighed and picked at some imaginary lint on her skirt. She didn't know what to do. There was a part of her that enjoyed kissing Jake. Every part of her body responded to him. But she was more than a collection of physical needs. She had to be, even if it would feel good to respond to them.

Jake took a while to work up the courage to go find her. It had been a shock to see Colleen's daughter. Sure, he had known about her, in theory, but he realized she had never once talked about her with him. And then, being caught like that, kissing Colleen in front of the girl, had made him feel like a jerk. He'd panicked and ran out of there. Which, somehow made it worse.

Jake paused, paced a bit. If there was a daughter, there had to be a father. Was that why Colleen had said it was complicated. He took a deep breath. If Colleen were married, if there was a dad, he could, would respect that. Jake shook his head. But if there was a dad, where was he? Colleen was living in Queensbay with her mother and her daughter. It didn't quite scream nuclear family to him. And the way she had kissed him. There hadn't been a hesitation like she was conflicted, not once she had let herself fall into him.

He needed to know, so he found his steps heading toward the park. They could talk, in public, if that was best, but he needed to know the score. And, if Colleen was spoken for, well then he would walk away. He would stop pressing her, stop being anything more than friendly to her. He would respect her wishes. His gut wrenched, even as his mind made the logical arguments. He didn't want to think what he would do if that turned out to be the case.

She was meant to be with him, he was meant to be with her. Jake saw her finally, in the park, sunlight from the giant oak tree that kept guard over the playground, bathing her and the swing she was pushing in a hazy, dappled kind of light. He caught his breath, fought the fierce feeling of possessiveness and longing that rose in him and tried to settle his nerves as he walked over to her.

"Why are you here?" she asked without turning around.

He was casting a shadow, and she knew it was him from the smell of fresh wood and sawdust that he always carried with him.

"I promised Mrs. Sampson I'd take a look at the gazebo and see what it would take to repair it," he said.

She glanced at the gazebo. It stood as it always had, under that shade of a spreading elm, but she could see that it was starting to look a little the worse for wear.

"Looks fine to me," she said.

"Wood rot," he said authoritatively, watching her push the swing.

"Higher, Mommy, higher," Adele said, delight coloring her words.

"Here, let me try," Jake said, and he stepped in and gave a good push.

Addie squealed as she went higher, but not too high. Jake's next push wasn't quite so forceful, and Colleen was able to breathe a sigh of relief. Last thing she needed was Adele to fall off the swing and hurt herself. Jake pushed for a while, and they stood, not talking, the only sounds the squeak of the swing's chain as it moved back and forth.

"I take it you've gotten over your surprise?" she said when Adele was at the apex and less likely to hear them. Lydia and Josh had gone home a while ago, after Josh had another one of his meltdowns.

"My surprise?"

"I could have sworn that you were going to have a heart attack back there."

"It didn't seem right," he admitted. "Her seeing me kiss you like that. It gave me pause."

"Sand," Adele cried, her little legs slowing so that the swing's momentum slowed with them.

"She wants to play in the sandbox," Colleen explained.

Jake stopped pushing, and when the swing came back to the middle, he slowed it in his big hands.

Adele squirmed around and looked at him gravely. "Hi," she said.

"Hi," Jake answered, his voice friendly. Colleen watched their exchange carefully.

"You were at the shop," she said, and Colleen thought she saw Jake blush.

"I was," he answered simply enough and waited.

"Why were you kissing my mama?" Adele asked as Colleen helped her out of the swing. One of her pigtails was coming undone, but Colleen froze. Adele had been silent on this point, and Colleen had hoped that maybe she had escaped the host of questions that preceded Adele no matter where they went. But no, her bright, inquisitive daughter had just been biding her time.

Jake stroked his hand across his chin, but he did not meet Colleen's eyes, instead he kept his gaze focused on Adele.

"Because she smells nice," he said.

Colleen sighed in relief.

Adele nodded, as if it were true.

"And she's pretty."

Adele nodded again.

"I'm Jake, by the way."

"Adele McShane," she said and held out her little hand.

Jake looked down at it for just a moment, then shook it.

"A pleasure to meet you," he said, and she was off, racing to the sandbox.

Colleen made her way to follow her slowly, and Jake fell into step alongside of her.

"Gazebo is over that way," she said pointedly. She liked it too much that he was next to her. That moment just before where he had pushed Adele on the swing and shaken her hand had been too perfect. He had known exactly how to behave with her.

It gave her a sharp sense of longing, for a sense of belonging and normalcy that she pushed away. She had always prided herself on being unconventional; it had been what led her away from Queensbay so long ago and why she had tried not to beat herself up for all the choices she had made since then. She hadn't lived an ordinary life by any means, and when the result of all of them, which was Adele, was so perfect, she couldn't pine after what she could not have.

"I'll get to it. Too nice a day to be working."

Colleen slanted her gaze up at him. Jake had never been one to shirk hard work.

He shrugged. "Can't I enjoy a day at the park?"

"Not if you don't have a kid. That's called being a creep."

"Told you, I have a job to do, and I am visiting with you."

Colleen waited, her shoulders tensed.

"Why don't you talk about her? To me, I mean."

"I . . ." Colleen faltered. "I don't not talk about it or her."

"You think it would have come up."

"Why would it? We've barely said two words to each other. I mean, you say, I'll have a beer and I say what kind, and then you thank me and that's about it. And then you just start kissing me. Sorry if I didn't quite know how to work in my whole back story."

"You won't say anything else to me."

"What am I supposed to say?"

"So how did this happen?"

"Do you mean how does a woman get pregnant? Do I really have to explain biology to you?"

"Where's her father?"

"What's it to you?" Colleen threw back at him.

He ran a hand through his hair. "Because if he's in the picture then I am out. I am not going to step on any toes. I will walk away."

"He's not in the picture," she said, and she didn't know whether to be annoyed or slightly pleased at his sense of decency. She didn't want to point out that it was up to her, not him to decide if there were any toes to be stepped on.

"That's all?" Jake asked.

"Why? Do you need to know more?"

He was silent, then he said, "I need to know you're free."

She twisted her hands. Was she free? What did free even mean? She had a daughter, and she would never be free from that gift, and the responsibility.

"He's not in the picture for me. He knows about Adele, but she doesn't know about him. I mean she doesn't know that Olivier is her father. She thinks he's just a friend of the family."

She sighed, reading into his silence, feeling she needed to explain herself. "He's married now. But before that, when we were together, I got pregnant. I knew right away that I would keep the baby. Olivier, I don't know, but he was already moving on, as they say. So I agreed not to name him the father. His new wife wouldn't have liked that."

Jake was still silent. She knew that she needed to give him more.

She shrugged. "Naïve girl goes to big city, gets swept up by the glitter and fast-paced life, and makes some dubious choices. Fast forward a few years, she has a kid but no husband and decides it's time to make a change. Simplest way is to go back to a place with free rent where she knows her way around."

He looked down at her, his blue eyes thoughtful. His silence compelled her to keep speaking.

"Our relationship was tapering off. He was more and more distant. But still I got pregnant. At first he seemed delighted. I never expected him to marry me. But then he got engaged, which I didn't expect either. But, he didn't leave me. I found out in the paper about the engagement, and he had the gall to say that nothing between us had to change, really."

Colleen took a deep breath. This was the part she was not particularly proud of, but she hadn't known what to do. "I stayed. I kept working for him, cashed his checks. Adele was born. He wasn't there. He was at his engagement party. He sent a present and set up a bank account in her name. He came by a few times. To see her. To see me.

"He even spoke to me about a promotion and opening a store in a new city. Where I suppose he could visit me, without his wife knowing. Except Adele and I were the worst-kept secret in all of Paris.

"Olivier, luckily, lost interest. And, I was happy, living my own life, with Adele. We had a roof over our heads, some money in the bank, but I knew that it was it at his sufferance. He kept mentioning the store, but when I asked about it, somehow it was always something he'd look into in another few months.

"I was ready to stop waiting. I had started to look into new jobs, to do something else when I got the letter from Phil. Well, from his lawyer. Coming back to Queensbay, even only to settle the estate, seemed like the best way to help me think through what I wanted to do next."

"Okay," Jake said. "It happens."

"Even before I left Paris, it had been three months since he'd seen Adele. I don't want to sound like I'm blaming him, but I didn't want her to grow up waiting for a dad that wasn't going to come home. Not like I did. I thought if I came here, just the two of us, that she'd only know that I was her family."

"He sounds like a real winner," Jake said drily. "Or is that just the French way of doing things?"

Colleen laughed, a bitter edge to it. It was the way Olivier did things. "Maybe. I told Olivier I was only coming over for a few weeks, a month or two to sort things out."

Jake looked at her. "It's been longer than that."

"I know. I'm pretty certain Olivier knows we're not coming back, but he hasn't said a word. So that's my story. I'm just a single mom who's trying to get back on my feet."

Jake shook his head. "You went out, you met someone, and you made some choices. You had a baby. And you're raising her, starting a business, working a second job."

He turned to her and held her hands. "I don't see anything wrong with what you did."

Jake's hands were warm and strong, and she couldn't deny the comfort she felt as he held hers. She had never felt this comfort from a man before. Excitement, but not comfort or security. She wanted to pull her hands away and tell herself not to trust it.

She looked at him. "I shouldn't have left like I did."

He knew exactly what she was talking about. "What were you afraid of?" he asked. "Getting knocked up by the ex-quarterback and being stuck in a small town?"

She laughed. "Something like that. Guess the joke's on me."

He looked at her, and while his hands radiated warmth and security, there was an entirely different look in his eye. "Well, we're both here now. You have a kid. I suppose that means no late nights or sleepovers just yet."

"What?"

"I want to get to know you again, Colleen. I want you to get to know me. I think they call it dating. You have a kid who you want to protect. I get it. So you tell me what the ground rules are for dating a single mother, and I'll abide by them. But don't try to just tell me to go away, because I'm a complication or a distraction. We both know you'd be lying."

She looked at Jake, finally admitting to herself what had been growing over the last several weeks. "Yes, I'd be lying."

"Good. We have a place to start."

She scanned his face carefully, trying to decide if he was teasing her, but for once she saw no humor in his face. She realized that she had seen many emotions cross Jake's face: amusement, satisfaction, anger, but what she saw now was different. Maybe it was sincerity. When had she had last seen it in a man? She almost laughed because the answer was the last time would be when she had been with Jake, a long, long time ago.

She turned away, unsure of what she was feeling.

"Mama, Mama, swings."

Colleen pulled her hands from Jake's and looked down at her daughter. It took her a moment to pull herself back into the reality. Where had she been? Daydreaming about something, pulled down memory lane. It was a dangerous place to be.

She looked at her watch. "We have to go home to dinner."

Adele looked at her, and she could sense the pleading that was about to begin. All of a sudden though, she needed to get away from Jake and his too-close presence.

"Tomorrow," she told Adele. "I can bring you again tomorrow. Remember tonight, *croque monsieurs* for dinner. And I said we would make *madeleines*."

Adele looked torn. She already loved to cook, and Colleen could see the fierce struggle going on inside the little girl's head between more time in the park and the siren call of the kitchen.

"Tomorrow I will leave work early, and we can

have an extra half-hour in the park."

That sealed the deal. She was smart enough to know when the offer was too good to refuse.

"I can walk you home," Jake started to say and took a step in their direction. Adele looked curious and, Colleen thought, pleased by the idea. She had a horrible thought of the questions Adele would ask or the information she would surrender without much of a fight and it seemed quite clear to her that Jake could in no way accompany them home.

Colleen shook her head firmly. "We will be fine. Another time."

Jake nodded and took a step back. "Think about what those rules are," he said, his voice low.

She took Adele by the hand, and they started to walk away. She felt rather than saw Adele twist around, knowing that her daughter must be giving one final wave to Jake, before she turned around and skipped ahead, doing her best to avoid the cracks in the sidewalk. As for herself, Colleen did not trust herself to turn around, and so marched straight on, aware of Jake's lingering gaze at her retreating figure.

Chapter 28

"Wow. What a difference a couple of days makes."

Colleen looked up and smiled when she saw the tall blonde woman step into the store. Lydia was dressed up for her, in a pair of black leggings, flats, and a flowy oversized blouse. Enormous black sunglasses acted as a headband, holding her hair away from her face. Not a paint splash or clay splatter was to be seen. Cradled carefully in her arms was a cardboard box with a sparkly blue bow.

"Lydia," Colleen greeted her friend happily.

"I thought I'd check up on your progress, see if you needed any help."

Colleen looked at her and guessed. "Artist's block?"

Lydia nodded sheepishly. "I wasn't getting anything done in the studio, so I decided to get out. I thought something mindless like sweeping or painting or cleaning might relax me. And I wanted to bring you this."

"That's so sweet of you," Colleen said taking the box. She set it down on the counter and opened it up, peeling back the layers of newspaper until she uncovered what was in it.

She lifted the candlesticks and they caught the sunlight pouring in through the now-uncovered windows.

"They're beautiful, luminous," she said, and they were. They were light, airy, and a beautiful color between blue and green that reminded her of the water in the harbor just before a storm rolled in.

"I thought maybe you'd like to take some of my pieces, on commission of course, so no risk to you. I've been experimenting with a new glaze, trying to get the color right. It reminds me of the green of the harbor in the evening as the light is fading. There's also the tint when the wind is stirring up the whitecaps, and it froths it into something more translucent." Lydia's voice had gone airy, and the look on her face was dreamy as she talked about her art.

"They'll be perfect over here," Colleen said as she walked toward a spot where the light came in. "No one will be able to miss them."

"Oh good. I am glad you like them. I have other pieces, but you can start with that."

"I had no idea..." Colleen said, then hesitated, unsure of the phrasing.

"What? That I wasn't just some crazy lady who likes to play with clay?"

"Well . . ." Colleen hadn't wanted to admit that she'd thought Lydia might just be spending her daddy's money to play around with clay.

"Nope, I am a real art school grad. I teach too, in Savannah, but I took the semester off to help with Josh. I told Daddy I would come but on the condition that he had to have a kiln installed. It's been really great for my work, you know, just being able to focus on Josh and creating. I am glad he's in school a couple of hours every day. Still, there are days that are harder than others."

"Do you sell anywhere else?"

Lydia nodded. "Oh, yes. Some places in Manhattan, L.A., New Orleans, and down in Florida. I am trying to get into San Francisco too."

Colleen nodded, slightly overwhelmed. "Very impressive. Thank you so much."

"Cool," Lydia said, and she seemed suddenly nervous. "I'm supposed to give you this. My dealer, I mean my art dealer, says you're supposed to sign it, that way I know I'll get paid."

Colleen took the papers Lydia handed her and glanced over them. She stopped when she saw the name. "You're repped by the Norman Gallery."

"Oh, have you heard of them?"

Colleen nodded. "You might say."

The Norman Gallery was huge, with outposts in Manhattan, London, and Paris. She'd dealt with them when she worked for Olivier. The gallery took on established artists as well as up-and-coming ones. Lydia Snow was much more than some woman who played with clay indeed.

"Well great," Lydia said. "If you sell them, I told Josh I'd take him for ice cream. And he wants Adele to come along too. He's taken quite a shine to her—probably because she doesn't cave into his narcissistic bullshit. She's just cool."

"It seems like I should be buying you the ice cream," Colleen said, slightly overwhelmed that she was going to be displaying Lydia's work in her own small store.

"No way, I'm trying to teach the kid about delayed gratification. I am sure it will all be undone once Hailey gets back, but a big sister has got to try."

"Absolutely. I'll buy you a glass of wine when I sell this. You might want to get ready and create a few more. I have the feeling these aren't going to last long."

"Cool," Lydia said, and her face broke into a grin. "I think this place is going to be a smashing success."

Colleen shrugged, just a little bit nervous. "Sometimes it all feels false. Like I'm creating this life that I will never get to live."

"Well, nothing wrong with selling a dream. I get it: '*La Belle Vie.*' Name of the blog, name of the store; it all sort of ties together."

Colleen nodded as she fussed with where to place some towels. She had unearthed an old butcher block island. Actually, she had found it on the side of the road and asked one of Jake's crew to help her bring it back in his truck. She'd bought them all lunch as a thank you. Now it was sitting in one section of the shop as the anchor to her home goods section. She'd only had time to give it a quick coat of paint but with the candlesticks and her French linen towels, the vignette, as she liked to think about it, was starting to take shape.

"I like it. Nice complement to the Garden Cottage. She's going to take some of my flower pots, by the way," Lydia said, sounding excited and amazed. "Sometimes it's hard to believe that people really want to buy my stuff."

"You shouldn't be," Colleen said with a smile. "From what I've seen, your work is amazing."

"I don't know," Lydia said, "it's not like I'm kissing guys all over town."

Lydia put it out there, and Colleen looked at her.

"Sorry, had to ask. Smooth segues in conversation aren't my forte. So you better just spill, otherwise you'll be subjected to more of my heavy-handed attempts at finding out what happened."

"He came by the park later on." Colleen said.

"And?"

"He pushed Adele on the swing."

"Okay," Lydia said slowly.

Colleen stacked her folded towels. She needed to price these. She looked around for her sticker gun.

"Adele's father never once pushed her on a swing."

"Okay."

"I'm not looking for a dad for her."

"Okay."

"Can you say something more than that?"

"Nope," Lydia said cheerfully. "I want to hear what you have to say. What I think isn't important."

"So . . ." Colleen struggled to find words. "I don't need him coming into my life and acting . . ."

"Like a nice guy who might want to kiss you and push your daughter on the swing. Let me guess, you're a package deal, you and Adele."

"No."

"No?" Lydia was clearly puzzled.

"We're not any sort of deal. We don't need anyone in our life."

"Okay, I get how you can rock the single mom gig, but, I mean, you don't plan to become a nun, do you?"

"A what?"

"You are going to have sex again sometime."

"I haven't thought about that," Colleen said,

knowing her voice sounded prim.

"Oh, honey," Lydia drawled, "everyone thinks about that sooner or later."

"Fine," Colleen admitted. "I can have sex, but that part is separate. My needs can be met . . ."

"With a simple hook up? Sure, that might work for a while, but look around. You're a nester if I have ever met one. You're going to want to share that with someone."

"With Adele. And my mom."

"Okay, so that sounds like some weird version of *The Golden Girls*, but I think you may be selling yourself short."

"I've got a business to open up and run."

"All those sound like good excuses. You know that you can have sex when the shop isn't open?"

"I just don't want Adele to get her hopes up."

Lydia laughed. "Now you've hit the nail on the head. I buy that excuse more than anything else. Maybe you just start with the hot sex with the guy with the amazing abs and take it from there. If he occasionally pushes Adele on the swing, think of it as a bonus."

Colleen sighed. Lydia had been right about one thing. She was a nester, and there was some part of her that would always long for the things she had stopped believing in. Jake had told her that the rules of the relationship were hers to make. But once made, would she be able to navigate them? Or stick to them? And what happened when one of them wanted more?

Chapter 29

J ake stepped into La Belle Vie, shutting the door gently behind him. He'd been thinking about Colleen a lot since he had left her in the park. He'd kept his distance, respecting her desire to think about how she wanted to handle their relationship. He understood that she had someone to think about besides herself, but, after not hearing from her, he decided that he needed to give her a nudge, a gentle one, to let her know that he hadn't changed his mind. Sure, her having a daughter made things a little more complicated, but this was his second chance with Colleen McShane, and he was ready to take her on, child and all.

He glanced around, taking in the whole of the shop. The place looked good, especially now that she was stocking the store with her inventory. It smelled nice too, like lavender, he realized, and he saw a basket filled with little bags of it that he knew were supposed to go in your drawers. Well, not his. But maybe he should pick some up for his mother, or the women who worked in his office. There was a section with soaps and potions, then one with things for the kitchen, towels, dishes, and candlesticks.

He admired the butcher block she had found and

recognized how she had cleaned it up and transformed it. She appeared from behind the curtain that separated the main part of the shop from the back storage space. She had changed out the beads Phil had used for a simple linen cloth curtain. He missed the clack of the beads but had to admit that the curtain was more in keeping with the style of the store. She paused, then continued over to the butcher block where she put a stack of gaily patterned napkins down.

"Looks great in here," he said. "Totally amazing."

"Thanks to you," she said. "I must have been crazy to think I could have done it all by myself. Are you here to drop off the final bill? One of your guys picked up the chairs the other day. I hope your mom likes them."

Jake looked at her and smiled. She was wearing one of her dresses, the kind that both covered and revealed, a filmy concoction patterned with bright flowers. Her hair was up, in a messy sort of bun, and he wanted to pull it down and run his hands through it. But he could sense the guard she had up, the edge on her as she watched him.

He stuck his hands in his pocket, instead, determined, for the moment, to keep them to himself.

"What?" she said. "Why are you smiling?"

"Because you look pretty and smell nice. Can't I smile about that?"

Her hand rose to her throat.

"Don't worry, I'll send you the bill. It has to go through accounting first."

"Okay," Colleen said, and nodded.

He took a step closer and was heartened to see that she didn't step back.

"You haven't got back to me with your rules, you know."

She twisted her hands together.

"Jake, I want to ..."

"Rip my shirt off?" he said, smiling, his voice teasing.

"Yes," she said and sounded surprised at herself. "I am attracted to you, and not just because you have an amazing set of abs. I always have been, and maybe that's the problem."

"That's a problem?"

"It is when you tend to lose yourself. You have a way of turning my life upside down, Jake, and I came here to get my footing."

He came closer to her, and she didn't move away. One strand of hair had escaped from her bun, and he tucked it behind her ear. She trembled, and he smiled. He leaned down and kissed her gently on the lips, a short, sweet kiss. He broke it off and grinned at the confusion in her eyes.

"So we go slow," he said, "like I said. Rules. You make them. I'll follow them. But, like I said, I want to see you. I get you're a package deal. You tell me how that works."

"I've never done this before," she said.

"You're a smart girl, one of the smartest people I know. You'll figure it out."

He watched the emotions playing across her face. He wanted more, wanted her right now, but he fought every raging hormone in his body. She wanted it to be less intense. Well, he could handle that. Sure, it would mean keeping a grip on his feelings, but he could do that for now.

"Would you like to see something?"

"What?" she asked and looked up, surprised.

"Tomorrow morning. I want to show you something."

"Jake..."

"I can use your professional opinion," he said smoothly.

"My what?"

"Your eye for design. It's a project I'm working on."

"Does this have anything to do with why you wanted all those pictures of the Showhouse?" she asked, suddenly curious.

He thought about satisfying that curiosity but decided it would be more interesting for them both if he just shrugged. "It might."

"Okay, I'm in."

He smiled, caught the excitement in her voice. "You probably shouldn't wear a dress. It's a bit, umm, messy in there."

She looked as if she were considering it. "Fine. I'll see if I own sneakers."

He started to react, but she shook her head. "I'm kidding," she said. "I have work clothes too."

"Good," he said. "I was starting to think you slept in your dresses. Not that it's a bad way to picture you, but jeans might be more appropriate."

"So it's a date."

He swooped in, brushed his lips against her cheek.

"I'll pick you up tomorrow around ten o'clock, here."

She nodded, and he left, whistling as he went out

into the sunlight. There was something entirely satisfying, he thought, about keeping Colleen McShane off guard.

Chapter 30

C olleen didn't know why she was nervous. This wasn't even a real date. And she'd been on a bunch of those. They'd been sweet and boring, horrible and marginally tolerable. But none of them, not even the times she'd gone out with Olivier, had left her with such a case of jitters and anticipation as this nondate with Jake.

She had dropped Adele off at school, where excitement about the upcoming spring pageant was riding high. Adele fervently hoped she would get the part of the flower, but the competition was fierce. Colleen assured her that no part was too small and that a long and fulfilling show business career lay ahead of her. And then she had gone to the shop, determined to work on inventory and spreadsheets.

She had fussed with the window display she was working on and checked her watch a hundred times. She decided to think of it as a consultation, a work thing, not a date. There was no reason for the butterflies in her stomach. She saw his truck, white with the logo of his company on it, as it pulled neatly into a spot in front of the shop. She watched as he swung out of it and came to the door, opening it. She pretended to be busy with something.

"Sorry I'm running a little late. One of the guys was just about to hit a water main at a site, and I had to rearrange a few things."

She looked up. He looked a little harried, especially for Jake.

"If this isn't a good time, we can reschedule," she said.

"You're wearing jeans. That might not happen again anytime soon. We better take advantage of it, don't you think?"

She smiled and nodded.

He headed out of the shop, waiting while she locked the door.

"I heard you got some security cameras put in and an alarm system."

"Funny, the owner told me he'd been instructed to give me his best pricing, as a special favor."

Jake shrugged. "I steer a lot of business his way."

She wanted to know how he'd known she was even going to call the security company, but decided it didn't really matter. Someone had talked.

"Seemed like the smart thing to do."

"Good," he said and nodded. "Small town and all, but still, you never know."

He placed his hand on her back and guided her out onto the sidewalk. "How about a cup of coffee to go? My treat?"

"Sure."

He took her hand, a gesture that caught her by surprise.

"What?"

"You don't have to hold my hand," she said, but

she made no move to pull away. There was something strong and reassuring about holding it.

"It's just a hand," he said. "And it feels right."

She didn't disagree, and she didn't pull away as he opened the door for her.

The Golden Pear Café was warm and filled with scents of fresh roasted coffee, butter, and cinnamon. She had to stop herself from inhaling deeply. People were spread around the tables, reading the paper, chattering with one another, all against the background of soothing acoustic guitar. Jake strolled up at the counter, their hands still linked. To Colleen it felt as if everyone was looking at them, that there were more than a few stares and whispers. Just the normal small town interest, she reminded herself, and everyone knew Jake. It was something she'd have to get used to, she realized, if she and Jake continued.

"Do you want coffee?" Jake's voice was perfectly calm as if he weren't aware of the attention they were garnering.

She nodded, and he ordered for them. She looked over at the glass display case, admiring the cookies and croissants, the éclairs and the cakes. Darby emerged from the kitchen and Colleen caught her small double-take as she took in the sight of Jake and Colleen. But Darby recovered and took over their order from the other server, making small talk as she did.

"Maybe I'll swing by later," she said. "I had a few ideas about the sidewalk sale."

"That would be great," Colleen said, and meant it, glad that she and Darby had reached détente.

Jake's arm was draped around her shoulder, and Colleen wanted to both shrug it off and snuggle into it deeper. She wasn't sure how she felt about being part of this show, and she wasn't quite sure what Jake was trying to do. The coffees were on the counter. Colleen felt the presence of the other woman before she heard her speak.

"Well, well, Jake, look who you dragged in."

Colleen shifted, saw a woman standing there. She was tall, with brunette hair kissed by sunlight. She wore skinny white jeans, high heels, and a halter top. Expensive perfume competed with the smell of baked goods.

The whole café, including Darby, seemed to have gone silent as the woman stared at Jake.

"Hi Serena," Jake said, his voice neutral. He managed to remove his wallet without letting go of Colleen, even though she wanted to wiggle free.

Colleen wasn't sure what else Serena was going to say because Darby jumped in.

"Would you like some croissants with that? Maybe some cookies? Colleen, you'll have to tell me what you think. I modeled my recipe after the ones I tasted in Paris, but it would be great to get a second opinion."

Colleen snapped her attention forward. Darby had tongs in her hand and had removed the glass cover from a plate piled high with them.

"We'll take six of each," Jake said. "Office always loves when I bring back your cookies, Darby."

"Wonderful," Darby answered.

Jake took the coffees, and Colleen took the bag with the baked goods. There might have been some more small talk exchanged, but it didn't register with Colleen. She felt Serena's lingering gaze on them and was aware that others were looking at them. Just as casually, as if nothing was out of the ordinary, Jake led her out of there and into the bright summer morning.

She stopped.

He didn't, but said, "Everyone's still watching. I'll talk about it, but I think we'd both prefer to do so in private."

She nodded, and they both kept going and into the truck. It had grown hot in the sun, and she waited while he fiddled with the A/C and pulled away from the curb.

"What was that about?"

"What do you mean?" he asked innocently, taking a sip of his coffee and setting it down in the cup holder.

Colleen was thankful that Darby had come to her defense. "Don't play dumb with me."

Jake looked at her. "Just an ex-girlfriend."

"You don't seem like you parted on good terms," Colleen said, keeping her voice even. Amy, Serena . . . who else had Jake dated? Then she told herself that it didn't matter. She had a past. He had a past. She had a kid, which was more than a past.

"Maybe we didn't."

He looked at her. "She wanted to get married, and I didn't. For the record, I never said I would. I thought I was clear on that. She thought she could change my mind. She didn't take it well."

"Anyone else I should know about?"

He shot her a look and asked, "Why, are you jealous?"

She forced herself to smile easily. She could tell that Serena had been one of those girls who rode horses in the fall and sailed in summer, took trips out west to go skiing, and island-hopped when she needed a break. Colleen didn't even know her, and she hated her because Serena had everything Colleen had wanted but never had.

"Of course not," she said, trying to sound like she meant it. She took a deep breath. She wasn't going to be jealous of the past. Colleen had gone out and made her own life. She had learned to ride a horse, skied in the Alps, and sailed the Mediterranean on private yachts. It didn't matter what Jake and Serena's relationship had been because Jake was with her now.

"Sounds to me like you might care just a little."

"We both have pasts, Jake, right? So my past is my past and yours is yours. Deal?"

"Fine by me."

He started humming something, and she thought she recognized it as a country song about a jealous woman. She hit him on the arm. It was solid muscle, and he barely flinched. He stopped humming, and she reached for the radio, finding a station playing a song by Train. She cranked it up, rolled down the window, and let herself enjoy a ride in a truck with a good-looking guy.

It only took a few minutes before they were in front of the Showhouse. The white building always seemed poised to drop over the bluff it stood on and into the waters of Queensbay Harbor. They both sat in the truck for a second, taking it in. Despite the building's state of decrepitude, the view was amazing, and she said as much.

"I think there is much more to it," he answered, opening up the truck door. She watched him get out, deciding that there was nothing to do but follow.

No Trespassing signs were displayed prominently, and a chain hung haphazardly across the parking lot whose tarmac was filled with cracks. Healthy, vibrant weeds grew out of the cracks. Despite the fact that no one was supposed to be here, Colleen could see the evidence that plenty of people had been. Empty beer cans and cigarette butts were scattered around. She figured that the kids of Queensbay must still be using the Showhouse as a make-out spot.

Up close, she could see that the building was in terrible condition. Shutters hung willy-nilly and the fascia board was clearly rotting. As if to prove a point, she saw a pigeon fly out of a broken window.

"Looks like a real winner."

"Let me show you inside."

"In there? I bet there are birds in there. Spiders. And mice."

"All of the above," he said. "But I'll hold your hand." And as if to prove it, he did just that.

She followed him up the steps and onto the veranda, avoiding a rotten floorboard that gave under his booted foot. He lifted a bar off the door, put his shoulder into it, and heaved. The hinges squealed, then gave, and they burst into the cool, dark interior.

"Wow," she said as she turned around in it.

Light came through the high windows, filtering down softly, catching dust in the air and burnishing the faded red velvet curtains into soft jewel tones. She heard the cooing of the pigeons, but luckily the only evidence of mice was the slightly tattered edges of the curtains. The woodwork, elaborately scrolled and painted, was all still intact.

"Amazing, isn't it?" he said, and she could hear the reverence in his voice.

"An amazing pile of junk," she said and started to walk toward the concession stand.

"Be careful, the floorboards are a little weak there."

She stepped, feeling the give beneath her feet, but they held.

"Come this way," he said and pulled her toward a double door and flung it open. The auditorium was in front of them, with curved stage. But here, the sloped floor was bare.

"What happened?"

"Someone came in and took out all of the seats. Not sure when it happened. But this part was stripped. Scrap metal was pretty valuable a while back."

"Just a shell," she said, and he smiled.

"Just means it will be easier to remake it."

She caught his enthusiasm and smiled, decided to play into it.

"Okay, so what do you have planned?"

"I thought you'd never ask."

She loved the way his eyes lit up when talking about the project. The sketches he shared with her showed a sweeping vision for what the Showhouse could be. Apartments were a good idea, and she could imagine the panoramic views they would command, see their luxury, even if his sketches were only in black and white. And, if he could build a dock with some slips, she was pretty sure he'd have a home run.

They were still tossing ideas around when she glanced at her watch.

"I need to go," she said suddenly. She had to pick

up Adele.

"What?"

"Pick up time, for Adele."

"Oh, of course," he said. "Here, I'll drive you there. Do you want me to drive you home too?"

"I'll take the ride there. Adele and I usually walk home, stop by the park together."

He nodded, as if her brush off didn't bother him. "Of course. I should probably get back to work anyway."

She nodded, knowing that he understood, that he was following the rules. She didn't know what to make of it exactly, only that she'd found her morning with him, in a vermin-infested building that ought to be condemned, to be almost perfect. They'd touched, held hands, pored over drawings together, but he hadn't tried to kiss her and part of her was burning up with the desire to feel his lips on hers again. To have him pull her to him, to run her hands through his hair, to feel the strength of his arms, his shoulders.

He said nothing as he let her out just a bit before the school to pick up Adele.

"Thanks," she said as she slid out of the truck.

"Maybe I'll swing by Quent's some evening, see if you're working."

She nodded. "That would be nice." She didn't ask how he'd know if she'd be working, knew he'd find her if he wanted.

"Well, then, I'll be seeing you," he said casually. She swallowed, smiled and shut the door. He drove away with a wave of his hand and she stood there, letting her heart beat to return to normal. She was a goner, and part of her knew it.

Chapter 31

Rain. Not the soft spring kind that reminded you summer was on its way, or the kind that feathered you with soft touches and made you think of men dancing in trench coats on picture-pretty streets. Nope, this was a soaker, she thought, as she stepped out onto the sidewalk in front of Quent's. The village was settling in, lights flickering off as everyone closed up shop. She paused, assessed.

Quent had offered a ride home, but he was still closing up, and she didn't want to wait. It was just a little rain, and she wanted to go home and throw herself in a hot tub for a nice long soak. That, she thought, sounded perfect, and it was the thought that would keep her going on the walk home. An engine sprang to life behind her and she was aware of the sweep of headlights. She was on the sidewalk when the truck pulled up beside her and the window rolled down.

"Get in," Jake said.

She narrowed her eyes. "Why?"

"Because it's raining, and I'm offering you a ride."

"How do you know I need one?"

"Because anyone who had a car would be in one."

"Maybe I like the exercise," she answered. There

was a long low rumble of thunder somewhere behind her, over the harbor. He hadn't come to see her at work or stopped by the shop and she had found that annoyed her enough so now that he was in front of her, she was spoiling for an argument.

"At midnight in a rain storm?" he said. His voice was reasonable, and his face was shadowed and dimly lit by the dashboard lights.

"Fine," she said, because there was a cold trickle of water seeping down her neck. She didn't want to walk home, and her feet hurt, and she trusted Jake. Yanking the door open, she stepped up into the high cab. The light from the door flashed on, and she looked at Jake, knowing she looked and felt wet and bedraggled like a cat caught unawares.

"Seat warmer button is right there," he said and waved his hand in the general direction.

She turned it on. Who cared if it was May, and she was a hardy New Englander? The warm seat felt good. The car felt good, and she was suddenly aware that Jake was there and he smelled good too, like soap and maybe fresh lumber and just a hint of aftershave, nothing too powerful. She hadn't seen him in a few days, not since he'd dropped her off after visiting the Showhouse. She had half expected to see him at the pub, but he hadn't been in.

She closed her eyes and let the warmth and comfort seep into her. The truck started rolling, and Jake slowly began the drive through town. The radio was on, not too loud, the local rock station, and some tortured adolescent was singing about love and desire, and Colleen wondered how at sixteen the girl could know anything. The truck had stopped in front of the tipsy little Victorian. In the light of the sulfur lamp she could see that the flaws of the street were hidden. The houses didn't look quite so shabby in the dusky light and the soft screen of rain.

"I thought I'd see you before this," she said.

"I wanted to. I've been fighting not coming into the shop or into the pub."

"Why?"

"Because I've wanted to do this."

"Do what?"

Jake had unbuckled and had slipped over to her until he was just inches from her.

"Kiss you," Jake said, and he did.

It was tender at first, his lips coming down over hers, then his arms pulled her close, deftly undoing the seat belt she was connected to, so they were intertwined, and she was kissing him back. All thought had left her head, and she was able for a moment to forget that she was necking in the front seat of a truck with the high school quarterback in front of her mother's house.

Time tumbled and slipped, and she let her hands roam over him, touching his face, then feeling the muscles in his shoulders, his arms. There was only solidness here, strength and more strength. He stopped for a moment, looked at her, checking.

"Don't stop, just keep kissing me," she breathed.

She could feel herself tremble as he moved and then pulled her onto him. She was kneeling astride him and his hand was fisted in her hair, pulling her lips down to his, and then he was running his hands up and down her arms, then around her waist, sneaking up to get a touch of skin. His hands were hot against her, and she leaned down into him, savoring the feel of his body, of his legs, of his wanting her.

His hands were pushing up the edge of her shirt and she could feel, through the fabric of her simple white bra, the scrape of his callused thumbs over her breasts. Still her body responded to his touch, his caresses driving her desire for him, to be with him, just a little bit deeper.

For a moment she knew that this was crazy, that they were in a parked car, on a street lined with houses, where anyone could see them, but she didn't care, just knew that her need for him was pushing her over the edge. She wanted him, all of him.

Her shirt was off, and her hands were tugging his polo up and over his head, revealing his chest. She took a moment just to look. She had to admit his chest was more spectacular than she remembered, slightly tan, and perfectly flat, hard, and muscled. She caught her breath. Jake had always had a great body, and it was definitely part of his appeal.

Her body responded as his hand cupped her breast and caressed her nipple. She hissed at his touch and wanted more. She reached around and unsnapped her bra, freeing herself. She saw him swallow, mutter something, then he was kissing her breasts, his head buried and she arched her head back, letting her body savor the pleasure.

She dropped her hands to the waist of his jeans, slid down, and felt him. He groaned, and she smiled. As she toyed with the waistband, she looked at him, from beneath lowered eyelids. His eyes were dark, flushed with lust, and he looked like he'd just won the jackpot.

"Are you sure?"

"Do you have protection? I'm on the pill, but you can never be too safe."

He nodded, and a hand groped toward the glove compartment.

"Classic," she said with a smile.

He stopped. "I didn't give you a ride, intending for this to happen."

She laughed. "Really, didn't you? I don't care, you know. I might be more offended if you hadn't planned for this."

His silence gave him away, and she laughed again. She didn't care. Her body was humming like she was intoxicated, but she hadn't had a drop to drink tonight. She wanted sex, wanted to have it with Jake, needed sex. It had been a long time.

"Take pity on me, Jake. I'm all worked up, and you can't all of a sudden decide you want to leave me with a good night kiss on the cheek. Besides, I'm pretty sure you want it too." She dropped her hand down to make a point, felt him. He breathed in sharply and the smile left his face, replaced by a hungry, intent look.

"I'm a guy, of course I want it," he said. She kissed him, long and slow, and his resistance crumbled.

"What if I tell you I haven't had sex in over a year and that if you don't have it with me I might just explode?"

"Then I would say it would be my duty to rectify that situation."

"I thought you might say something like that."

He kissed her again and all she could feel was heat between the two of them. She felt his hands reaching, heard the glove box open and him rummaging around.

"You're sure?"

"Shut up, Jake, and kiss me."

He did, and his hands slipped her skirt up, around her waist, pulled her panties down, as she helped him slither out of his jeans. His fingers found her and slowly, maddeningly stroked her to pleasure. She felt her body tighten with anticipation and pleasure as his fingers pushed her higher and higher and her heart beat faster and faster, a wild drumbeat.

"Now Jake, I want you now."

She let her head fall back as he entered her, and then she was over him, kissing him, his arms holding her tight as they moved together, pushing each other higher and higher until they reached the edge. She came first, and then he followed with a final thrust and a cry of pleasure and then there was just the sound of their breathing, their hearts beating almost in time to the drumming of the rain on the windshield.

She laid her head on his chest, his wonderful, hard, muscled chest, just admiring it. She was dimly aware that her phone was buzzing, probably her mom, wondering where she was, and that she needed to go, to check on Adele, do some work, pay some bills, all of the hundred things a grown-up, single mom had to do. But she stayed still, just for a moment, savoring the connection.

His arms were around her, playing in her hair. She couldn't get used to this, couldn't get swayed by this.

"Okay, thanks, I need to go," she said, pushing herself up. She needed to find her shirt, her underwear, make herself look presentable. She laughed. It was raining, so she would be soaked anyway. She just needed to be sure her clothes were all buttoned.

"What?" he said, rousing himself.

"What? You think I'm going to invite you in, make you a snack?"

"I..." he stammered.

"Sorry, I've got a kid to check on, a mom to dodge; you know, the usual."

"Okay," Jake said, but he looked like he had been whipsawed, not sure what had just happened. She handed him his shirt.

"Thanks for the ride," she said, pulling her hair back into a ponytail and grabbing her bag, laughing at the double meaning. She was giddy, felt good, relaxed, better than she had in a long time.

Jake still looked dazed as if he wasn't sure what had hit him.

"See you around," she said as she opened the door and stepped out into the night. The rain had lightened, and it was warming up. Tomorrow would probably be a fine day, and she couldn't help humming, "Walking on Sunshine," as she opened the rickety gate to the garden and ran up the path to the sagging steps.

She threw one last glance at the truck, still sitting there, wipers going, but the windows too fogged up to see clearly.

Smiling, she waved good night.

Holy cow, Jake thought. He sat there in his truck, watching the wipers go back and forth, their rhythmic swishing a counterpoint to his racing heart. What in the name of all hell had just happened? Had he just had some of the most mind-blowing and amazing sex in his life with Colleen McShane? And she had just sauntered out of his truck, smiling, like she hadn't a care in this world.

The windows were still fogged, so he rolled one down, so he could get a good look at the house. There were lights on in the first floor of the house, but as he watched, they went off one by one, and he could imagine her making her way through the rooms and up the stairs. He saw one wink on upstairs for a moment, then wink off and then a dim light switch on in one of the upper windows. He waited for a moment, wondering if she would come to the window, look down, and see him. What was she was thinking? A dog started to bark, furiously, and there was a large, rolling boom of thunder, soft and muffled. *Spring thunder*, he thought, with the promise of a clear day tomorrow.

She wasn't coming back, he told himself, and there was no reason to expect that she should. He'd only be a fool if she caught him staring up at her window like some lovesick teenage boy. He pulled on his clothes, as best he could, put the truck in drive and pulled away, rolling slowly down the street, his heart still racing and his mind still whirling with the memories of her scent, her hair, the way she had looked as she told him she wanted him.

Chapter 32

"So what does one wear on a boat trip?" Ellie asked. She meant the question casually, but she needed some advice. She and Quent had finally set a date for their date and the question had been on the top of her mind.

Colleen considered it as she polished a glass. Lydia was at Quent's Pub too, sipping bourbon, after having left her little brother with her father and a temporary babysitter.

"White pants, a striped t-shirt, and a long scarf," Colleen said definitively, after a moment's thought.

"This isn't *To Catch a Thief*," Ellie reminded her, tartly so that Colleen had to laugh.

Ellie was glad to get a laugh out of her, since Colleen looked troubled.

"True, Quentin Tate is no Cary Grant," Colleen said. Quent was more like a Vin Diesel, Colleen thought, with his shaved head and amazing biceps.

"Trust me, I'm no Grace Kelly either."

"Carole Lombard, maybe?" Lydia suggested.

Eleanor smiled. "Sophia Loren. And let me guess, you always fancied yourself an Audrey Hepburn?" she said and looked at Colleen.

Colleen sighed as she polished another bar glass to a perfect shine, then said, "Sort of. My hair was never that dark, but I loved *Sabrina*. That was the movie that got me dreaming about living in Paris."

Lydia shook her head. "Give me a boat, sunshine, and a cooler of beer," she said. "Where I'm from, going for a boat ride means you put on your best jean shorts and a bikini top."

"To Southern girls," Ellie said and raised her glass, and Lydia lifted hers in response.

"So what should I wear?" Ellie asked intently. She did want to know. Dating was something she hadn't done in more years than she cared to think. She was pretty sure a lot had changed. She had looked into dating sites after Bobby passed, just a little bit, but had been horrified. Not that she was opposed to a good healthy hook up, at least she didn't think so, but there was absolutely no charm, no romance when she swiped through those apps or clicked through the websites. She didn't know if that meant she was old or just old-fashioned.

"Well, it's still a bit chilly out. So you'll want a sweater or something. White pants, striped shirt. No high heels," Colleen recommended.

Ellie put a hand to her chest. "I don't know what language you're speaking."

"Try cute white sneakers. It will keep you from slipping."

"Or poking a hole in the bottom of the boat with those spikes you call shoes," Lydia said, glancing down at Ellie's shoes. Lydia was wearing plain black Converse, a little bit of paint splattered on them.

Colleen leaned over the bar, took a good look at

Eleanor's shoes and mouthed, "Jimmy Choo?"

Eleanor nodded and sighed. "I suppose you have a point. Having to get fished out of the water is not a good way to start off a relationship."

"A relationship?" Colleen said. "I thought you said it was just a date."

"If a man asks you out on a date, he should be interested in starting a relationship," Ellie said, realizing that was why she had hated those dating apps. She wanted at least the chance to be appreciated.

"I guess catching a ride home from a guy in a truck doesn't qualify as going on a date?" Lydia asked from behind her glass of bourbon.

Colleen stilled. Ellie shot Lydia a look. Quent had said something to her about how Jake had driven Colleen home, and then she had mentioned it to Lydia. She just hadn't expected the other woman to ask Colleen outright about it. Still, it was a subject she was interested in hearing about, so she waited while Colleen decided if she was going to answer the question.

"Guess it depends what happens in the truck," Colleen said finally as she turned to grab a chit off the bar and ring it up.

Ellie looked at Lydia and whispered, "It's none of our business."

Lydia shrugged and rolled her eyes. "Why not? We're all friends here, right? I mean you two are kind of the only adults I know in this town, besides my stepmother, who doesn't really qualify, and my dad, who definitely doesn't qualify."

"As adults or friends?" Ellie shot back.

Lydia sighed. "Neither, unfortunately. But enough about me. So?" she said and turned back to Colleen.

"If the girl doesn't want to tell us, then she doesn't have to tell us," Ellie said. She wanted to allow Colleen at least the façade of privacy. Didn't mean she wasn't going to get the story out of her eventually.

"Oh, it doesn't work like that. You have to tell us. Girl code," Lydia said.

"He gave me a ride home," Colleen said.

"That's it? Just a ride? Not even a goodnight kiss."

"There might have been," Colleen finally admitted.

"Aha, now we're getting to the good part," Lydia said, smiling.

Colleen paused, then admitted, "It was a good kiss."

"So was it a case of don't come a-knockin' if the truck bed is a rockin'?" Lydia said.

"What? How, who?" Colleen said and blushed a deep red.

"I just shot an arrow in the dark. Looks like it found its mark," Lydia said and smiled at Ellie.

"In a truck?" Ellie said.

"I'm a single mom who lives with her mother. It's not like I can invite him up for a glass of sweet tea or however you're supposed to do it," Colleen said, her voice rising just a little and then she brought it down before the other patrons of the bar could catch on to the discussion.

"That's it? Oh no you don't. There's no way you're not telling us all of it," Lydia said.

"I never kiss and tell," Colleen said primly.

"So it wasn't earth-shattering, mind-blowing? A few morsels, please?" Lydia begged.

"It was . . ." Colleen started to say, then paused, as if searching for the right words and a slightly dreamy expression came over her face. "It was amazing. Sexy, exciting. Just what I needed," Colleen finally said.

"So are you going to do it again?" Again Lydia went for the direct query, but Ellie was interested in the answer too.

A troubled look crossed over Colleen's face and she set a clean glass down on the rack. "We have a history together. I have a daughter. It's complicated," Colleen said. "And I don't need complicated."

Ellie shook her head, thinking about her own life and said, "Honey, if it's not complicated, it just may not be worth it."

"Easy ain't worth much. It's what we have to work for that matters," Lydia agreed.

Colleen said nothing and moved away to pour a drink, while Lydia shot Ellie a meaningful look.

Ellie just shook her head. Jake and Colleen. If the two of them couldn't recognize the chemistry between them, then they were too pig-headed to deserve each other. So what if Colleen had a daughter. Jake would just have to man up about it. Which, if Ellie knew him, wouldn't be the problem. No, it would be whether or not Colleen could accept what Jake was ready to offer her.

She caught Quent's eye as he went about serving some customers at the other end of the bar. They'd set a time and a place for their date. She was nervous, more nervous than she cared to admit. *It was just a date*, Ellie thought, but then she saw the look Quent gave her. She knew that look. Knew that he wasn't looking for casual. Ellie took a sip of her drink to hide her confusion. For once in her life, she didn't know what she was looking for.

Chapter 33

J ake hadn't seen Colleen since that night in the truck, and he couldn't stop thinking about her. He had texted her, and she had texted back, but the messages had been meaningless, with no commitments or promises. Had he just served to scratch an itch on her part? he wondered. The sex between them had been explosive, better than he could have imagined, the feel, the scent, the overwhelming need he'd felt for her coming back to haunt him as he went about his day. He wasn't satisfied, not by a long shot. He needed her, wanted her. Couldn't imagine being without her. She'd given him nothing in response except a smiley face and the vague "had a great time."

Did she want to see him again? Would she see him again? He wanted her, all of her, and this time he wanted to take his time with her, to get to know every inch of her. He was waiting for her, an ambush, sort of, but he had tried to find her at the shop and at the park, but she hadn't been either place. He didn't want to see her at Quent's, not in public where the eyes of the whole town would be staring at them. He would respect Colleen's right to privacy, to discretion. So, he sat outside Quent's in his truck after last call, waiting. Tonight there was no hint of rain, no reason why Colleen couldn't walk safely home alone, but he wasn't going to let her. He would offer her a ride, and hopefully they would have a chance to talk. That was all he was going to ask for tonight.

He watched as she emerged from the alley between Quent's and the building next door. He could see her look around, and as he turned the truck on and the lights caught, he saw the troubled expression on her face. He rolled down the window and smiled. It was hard to read the look in her eyes, but it seemed to be a cross between wariness and thankfulness.

"Would you like to get in?" he asked.

"You don't have to keep driving me home," she said, and pulled her coat around her. Spring might have arrived, but the nights were still in the last grip of winter, and he could see her breath hang in the air, despite this being May.

"I don't mind. The cold is hanging on," he answered. She got into the car and leaned over and kissed him, but he pulled back. "You don't have to, you know." He wanted it to be clear.

"What?"

"I'm not driving you home because I want to get lucky."

She reached down, rubbed her hands down his leg. He shifted, but she had caught the lie in his words. Just seeing her made him want her, and his body wasn't very good at lying.

"You're not?" she said, her voice teasing as her fingers applied enough pressure to make him rethink his vow of just talking to her.

"I am not," he said firmly. She looked at him, surprise registering on her face.

"Well, you're not coming into my house," she said, her eyes drifting so they stared out the windshield. He couldn't quite read her voice, but she sounded both disappointed and relieved.

"I know that," he said, horrified that she would even think that he would suggest that. There was Adele and Mrs. McShane. There was no way he'd risk sneaking into or out of that house.

He wondered if she regretted what had happened. He wasn't exactly proud that their first time had taken place in his truck, like a couple of horny teenagers. He'd imagined it differently, but he couldn't deny that he wanted her again.

"I know you're tired, but maybe on your next night off you could come to my place, and I'll cook you dinner. You could stay, you know for a while. Not overnight of course, I mean unless you wanted to, but . . ."

"Are you asking me over to cook me dinner so you can get into my pants?"

"Yes. I would like to have more than twenty minutes with you," he said, though he doubted their encounter had lasted even that long. The rush, the pleasure had come all too quickly and now he wanted a chance to savor his time with her.

There was a moment of silence, and he kept his eyes ahead, determined not to push the point. He had said that he would let her set the rules.

"Okay," she said. "Not tomorrow, but the night after. I'll come over around six. My mom's working the night shift, but I'll get a babysitter." She was saying it to herself, almost as much as to him, but he didn't care. She'd just be like any other normal mom.

"Okay," he agreed and let out a breath, suddenly happy because this was a step forward with Colleen. The ride was short and, before he knew it, they were at her house. He could see the light in the window that must belong to Adele because it had a soft glow, like it was lit by a night light.

"I hope she's not waiting up for me," Colleen said, shaking her head.

"You're worth waiting for," Jake said before he could stop himself.

The look that crossed that Colleen's face seemed to indicate that what he had said was deeply unsettling. How could he admit that he'd been waiting for her for over ten years? That every other woman he'd met had been nothing but a substitute and that he'd never quite gotten Colleen McShane out of his head, not since they sat next to each other in art class, not until he almost gotten her fully undressed on prom night, and not since he tasted her lips and felt his body inside of her. Oh no, she was worth the wait.

But he knew that if he acted anything less than lighthearted, she'd run away. He wasn't going to hurt her or Adele; he just needed her to see that. So he let her go with just a smile, the kind of smile that he hoped hinted at fun later on. She slid out of the truck without a word and hurried up the steps and into her house. He watched the lights as they winked on and off as she made her way through the house until she got to Adele's room. He saw the flick of the curtain, knew that she was looking down at him. So he waved his hand and eased the truck away from the curb and left her.

Chapter 34

"This is your boat?" Eleanor asked, looking around, taking it in. It was nice, she supposed, as far as boats went, but how was she supposed to know? Cars, she knew. Boats, not so much. The boat was neat and clean, and from the way Quent was beaming, she knew he was proud of it.

"The Lady O'Brien," Quent said grandly, with more than his usual brogue slipping out, as he held out his hand so that Ellie could hop lightly aboard. The boat swayed beneath her, and she all but fell into Quent's arms, which were big and strong and easily steadied her. His brown eyes were gentle at first, then darkened as they stood for a moment in each other's arms. She shifted, and the moment passed. Quent dropped his arms in a rush as if he had been too forward.

Ellie took a delicate step forward. She had forgone the heels, on the advice of Colleen, and worn sneakers: cute white ones, of course, with a thick sole. Crisp white jeans, a blue and white striped shirt, and a navy blue canvas jacket completed her ensemble. She had pulled her hair back in a low ponytail but even so the wind was whipping it around. The breeze had been lighter in town, but out here at the docks, it was kicking up a ripple on the water. The air was cool, cooler than she had thought it would be.

"I thought I'd take you out to the lighthouse and back. We won't be out too long. The temperature is cooler than I thought."

He looked over her as if assessing if this was really happening.

"All righty," Eleanor said and realized that the boat smelled faintly of fish.

"Guess, I'll be casting off then," Quent said.

Ellie didn't know which of them was more nervous. Was she unsettled because of the gentle rocking of the boat or because she and Quent were finally alone? Eleanor took a seat gingerly on the white vinyl-covered bench, next to where the steering wheel stood. Quent bustled about and soon they were off. The roar of the engine was loud enough so that they didn't have to talk. Eleanor looked at the water and tried to gulp down some air. The boat moved slowly through the water, leaving powerful waves in its wake. They passed a thicket of boats moored close into the marina, and then they were out into the open water of the harbor. It was a sunny day. Not too warm though, and she was glad she had her jacket. Quent stood tall, one hand on the steering wheel, the other on the throttle as he carefully threaded his way through boats and buoys. Once they were clear of the mooring field, he pushed down the lever and the boat leapt ahead in time with Eleanor's stomach.

"Well, what do you think?" Quent asked, his voice necessarily booming above the roar of the engine. "Not too fast for you?"

She wanted to laugh. She'd been married to a race

car driver; speed didn't bother her, but this was a different kind of freedom, rocketing out here on the wide-open expanse of the water. The sun was starting to set, and as it was too loud to really talk, she leaned back and let the wind slide over her and through her and, for once, let the sadness that had been weighing on her slip away.

Chapter 35

C olleen knocked on Jake's door, trying not to feel nervous. She double-checked to make sure she had her phone with her, already knowing that she did. The neighbor was babysitting Adele, so there was nothing to worry about. Still, all of this made her feel guilty, as if she were sneaking away doing something illicit. She took a deep breath. She was a single, grown woman, and she was allowed to go on a date. Or just have sex, she thought as he opened the door. Jake was wearing jeans and a black t-shirt. His feet were bare, no hat or sunglasses. His hair was just a little longer than its usual closely cropped length, and crinkles around his blue eyes showed when he smiled as he let her inside. He smelled good, like Jake, fresh wood and soap, and her heart fluttered as he stepped back and beckoned her to come in.

She stepped into his apartment. It was a rental, one of the few on the top floor of the building they called the Annex, which was part of the marina and the restaurant. It was a nice, modern, simply finished apartment with a galley kitchen, the counter dividing it from the living room and eating area. A sliding glass door led out onto a balcony with a view of the harbor. A hallway with two closed doors led away from the front of the apartment.

He leaned down to kiss her cheek, but she met him mouth to mouth. After a moment, his arms wrapped around her, and he pulled her into him. She kissed him back, feeling the need rise in her. She turned him around, pushing him in the direction of the hallway, already thinking about the bedroom.

"Whoa, wait a second," he said. "There's no need to rush."

She put the bottle of wine she had brought on the marble countertop. "Obviously you've never dated a single mom before. Babysitter can only stay until ten thirty, so we have approximately two hours and thirty minutes."

"Um, okay," Jake said, "but we could have dinner, you know, and talk."

Her blue eyes were fixed on him. She had on a light coat over one her favored dresses. She smelled like lemon and lavender and already he wanted more, but he had promised himself that he would be a gentleman about this, take his time. Just because they were in a place with a bed didn't mean that they had to jump right into it. He hadn't counted on Colleen having other ideas.

"What's that song?" she asked suddenly, stopping.

"Sorry, I'm not sure how that got in there," Jake said. He grinned. "You know we never got to dance."

"What?"

"Well, we never got to dance at the prom. Want to try it now?"

"Jake," she looked at him. "We can't go back, you

know."

He nodded, looked at her, and tapped his phone. The song switched to something from Train.

"How about this one?" he said and moved over to her, slid her into his arms.

"You don't know how to dance, do you?" she said after a moment.

"Don't you just sway to the music?" he murmured into her hair. He didn't care that they were barely moving because she was in his arms. He could feel her, delicate, yet strong, her long lean body next to his own. He was lying; he did want to pull her straight into bed, but he warned himself to slow things down. They didn't have to rush, but he couldn't stop feeling this need for her, and he leaned down and kissed her.

She responded immediately, fire meeting fire, as she made an almost inaudible sound of pleasure. Every part of him wanted her, and when he took a moment, looked at her, he saw his feelings mirrored in her eyes. He let his hands run down her sides, and with one swift, smooth movement, lifted her up and carried her into the bedroom.

He put her down on the bed, took a moment to admire the full length of her. Her eyes never left his face, as she peeled her jacket off and tossed it aside. There was something so very sexy about her, as she leaned back on her elbows, with her hair splayed out behind her, her dress a bold countertop to the light gray bedspread. His eyes traveled over her, taking it all in.

Colleen reached out, hooked a finger in the belt loop of his jeans and pulled him closer. He didn't think anymore, just sunk down with her, kissing her, while his fingers found the zipper of her dress. She helped him peel it off, so that her creamy skin was a backdrop against her darker bra and panties. He ran a hand over her flat belly, felt her shiver. She lifted his shirt and pulled it off of him. He couldn't help but notice the smile as she looked at him, as she ran her fingers over him.

"Swinging hammers agrees with you," she said as her hands drifted down and gripped him between his jeans. He hissed and grabbed her hands, held them away from him and kissed her. She moved, but he held her still, teasing her with his tongue and his hands as he took his time, exploring every inch. He unsnapped her bra, releasing her breasts, kissing them so she breathed sharply. He looked at her, saw her eyes were unfocused, filled with need and want. He moved down, slipping his hand between her skin and the fabric of her panties, found her, warm and moist, and touched her. She arched and moaned under his touch and he drove her higher and higher. He could feel her, feel that she was ready. He let go of her hands, and she wrapped around him, calling his name.

He didn't wait, just felt her hands as they pulled at his jeans, tugged down his boxers. He was ready for her and he bit off a cry as she touched him.

"Now, Jake, now," she urged him, looking up at him.

He smiled and slowly he reached down and kissed her, starting with her lips and moving down her neck. She pulled his hips toward her and he entered her, slowly, deliberately. He moved slowly, letting his hands move over her, savoring the feel of her skin underneath him. He could see all of her and he took his time until he could no longer keep himself under control as she moved under him, her hands doing wicked things to him.

He moved faster now and she moved with him, her legs tight around him as she climbed higher and higher. He held her, watched her ride the wave of pleasure and then followed her over the edge until his mind blurred and there was nothing but heat and fire.

Finally, they slowed together, and he found his heart was thudding; he was slicked with sweat as he rode the crest of pleasure down. Her eyes were closed, and there was a relaxed look of pleasure on her face, an air of satisfaction over her whole body. He leaned over her, coming to rest on his side so that he wouldn't crush her, pulling her in tight to him, locking her in his arms.

Her breathing was ragged, slowly finding its pace.

"That was incredible," he said.

She made a sound, which he hoped was agreement. He hazarded a glance and saw that the look was still on her face. She shivered.

"Cold?"

"No," she said, her voice breathy. "Full of the tingles."

"I'm glad the truck wasn't a one-time thing. I mean, you caught me by surprise."

She laughed. "I figured we'd get the sex out of the way so we could enjoy dinner," she said, then there was a pause. "You did make me dinner?"

"I have something for you to eat," he said.

"Where'd you order from?"

"Donatellis," he answered promptly.

"Best clam-chowder pizza ever," she said.

"I got us chicken Marsala," he said and waited a moment. "Hungry?"

She moved a little in his arms, and he felt his reaction to her. He wanted her again.

She turned toward him and smiled, then said, "Yes, but not for dinner."

He drove her home, even though she said she would walk. But he refused. She'd just have to get used him taking care of her, he thought, even if it was only driving her home. He wanted, needed, to know she was okay. She had kissed him goodnight, a long deep, lingering kiss, and he realized that he needed to stop himself from asking her to stay or for him to come in, to sleep on the couch or something silly like that. He couldn't push it with her, ask too much too soon. He was beginning to see that was what had happened the first time they were together. He had wanted her intensely then, had spun out his dreams of a future. And it had scared her away. So this time, he'd be cool, casual, for as long as he could, until she wasn't scared anymore. Yup, this time around, he'd play the long game with Colleen McShane.

Chapter 36

"**L**ovely day," a voice said.

Ellie jumped. She'd been concentrating, working on some invoices, trying to track down a minor discrepancy, and it was only the sound of Quent's voice that brought her back to reality. She looked up. Quent was standing in front of her desk, a shy smile on his face.

"It is," she said and felt herself blushing, forced herself to stop it with a deep, calming breath. She had enjoyed her date with Quent. He had walked her home, kissed her sweetly, and she had gone into her apartment alone. Her legs had been shaky and her stomach jumpy and since then, for the last few days, she had avoided him, even though she had pointed herself in his direction many times.

It wasn't that she was playing hard to get. She didn't quite know what to do with the emotions he brought out in her. She was a grown woman. She'd been married for over twenty years. She knew what love and affection was supposed to feel like, and it worried her because Quentin Tate, that big lug of a man, made her feel young and happy again.

"Thank you for the flowers," she remembered to

say. A small but elegant bouquet had arrived for her, just after the boat ride. It had been a thoughtful gesture, and now it stood on her desk.

"Least I could do. Sorry you felt a little queasy afterward."

She frowned. That had been the one bad part. Part of her shakiness had definitely had something to do with the constant motion of the waves. "I might be a landlubber after all."

"No worries, there's plenty of things to do right here on dry land."

Quent leaned against the high counter that surrounded her domain. She ran the front desk of Colby's car dealership, and nothing got by her. Her desk, with its counter-height surround, was designed for customers to lean into, to stay and chat, but she could still feel it settle as it absorbed Quent's solidity. He was wearing a leather jacket that fitted his powerful shoulders and strong arms perfectly. She had yet to touch them, but she desperately wanted to feel those muscles for herself. The thought had her blushing even more.

"You brought your car in for a tune-up," she said, looking out at the parking lot. A classic Firebird Trans Am, silver with a thin red racing stripe. She decided to take a guess: "1978? Solid American heavy metal."

"Don't tell me you like muscle cars?" Quent said. He gave a low whistle and the look he gave her, a mixture of admiration and surprise, had her blushing even more and sent her pulse racing. She doubted he would like to be described as a teddy bear, since he so carefully cultivated a rough image, with his shaved head, bulging muscles, and semi-permanent scowl, but that's what he seemed to her, a big lug with a heart of gold.

She smiled and said, "I'm more of a roadster type myself. But I enjoy a ride now and then."

He leaned over the counter and smiled. "Then maybe you'll let me take you for a ride up the coast one of these evenings. I know a quiet place to have dinner."

She could see that he was less nervous than the first time he had asked her, but also that the skin around his eyes was tight as if he was worried about what her answer would be. She thought for a moment that it would be good to demure, claim to have to check her schedule, but in fact she wasn't getting any younger. There had been a damn good reason she'd kept coming back to Quent's bar when she much preferred the ambiance at the Osprey Arms. His kindness, his attention to her, and the way he had stocked her favorite wine behind the bar just for her had made her feel welcome, comfortable, and important.

She smiled. "I'd love to."

"Well then it's a date, luv."

She still hadn't quite figured out his accent. Sometimes it had a trace of British to it, or English, Irish, Scottish, she couldn't tell, but in the next sentence he sounded like an extra from a gangster movie. Colleen had confessed that Quent's origins were a mystery, and Tory had confirmed that. He had shown up one day, taken up tending bar at the Ship's Inn. Within a year, old Dan, the owner, had sold it and retired to Florida, and Quent had turned it into the upscale pub and sports bar where he reigned supreme. No one doubted that he wasn't quite as authentic as the décor, but no one had the gumption to ask him outright.

"Where were you born?" She decided she had to know.

"What?" Quent asked in surprise.

Eleanor stood up, hands on her hips, looked at him.

"If we're going out on another date, I want to know something about you. It seems most of our conversations have been about what wine I like to drink and the weather."

"Fair enough, luv." He took a deep breath before he continued. "I was born in Queens but moved to Long Island when I was five. My mother's from Liverpool, and my dad's from Queens. My grandma, also from Liverpool, lived with us. I got my way of talking and love of all things English from them. Never been married. Came close. No kids, but I have a deadbeat brother with two kids, a boy and a girl, who I've taken in from time to time. Both adults now, and are on their own. Mostly. Sometimes I have to go and bail them out of trouble." He said and looked at her, waiting.

She took a deep breath, and asked one more question.

"How'd you get your money to buy the bar?" She almost didn't want to know the answer, afraid that if the rumors were true, she wouldn't care.

He looked at her, puzzled, then laughed. "Have you been listening to those rumors about my supposed past?"

She smiled ruefully. "Some of them might have reached my ears."

He held out his hands. "I have a degree in restaurant management from Johnson & Wales University. I worked for years in big restaurants and fancy bars. After a while, I decided I wanted something different, something I could call my own. I started to look for a place someone wanted to sell, something that hadn't been managed right and needed a refresh, a place someone with some professional management experience could make profitable. Took a while, but I finally found my way to Queensbay. I worked with the owner for a while, and when he was ready to retire, bought the bar, took out a loan and renovated. Loan's fully paid off and I have money in the bank." He paused for a moment. "Boring enough for you?"

She almost laughed. "Just boring enough."

He nodded. "Your turn."

It was only fair, she decided. "I was born in a trailer park alongside a muddy river. Got pregnant when I was still a kid, left the baby with my mama, and ran off to the big city to make money. Worked hard and met Bobby Dean DeWitt, a race car driver, when I was still young, and he was growing old. We got married. I was faithful, he wasn't. Never lost his taste for fast cars and faster women, but I loved him and when he died, damn near broke me. I came up here to finally be a mother to my son. I hate the snow, but I love the water and every single day, life gets a little less gray, a little brighter."

She hadn't known what to think, how to act when she came to Queensbay. She had needed to see Colby, to see if she could mend their relationship after years of estrangement. It hadn't been easy, and they still sometimes butted heads. But family had a way of pulling you back in, of grounding you.

"Are you still broken?" Quent asked softly.

She shook her head and smiled, a true smile that came from the knowledge that she was ready to move on and that Quent, for some reason she didn't quite understand but wasn't going to question, just might have something to do with it. "I think I'm beginning to find my way to getting fixed."

He looked at her and said, "I'm no race car driver."

"And thank god you're not," she said. She didn't need or want another Bobby Dean. Quent was a good man, one who ran a business, saved money for a rainy day, and took care of the people in his life. She had heard that Quent had taken care of Chino Charlie, made sure he wouldn't dare show his face again at the pub and she appreciated Quent's caretaking of those around him.

"I'd still like to take you to dinner," he said.

"And I would like to go. You'll pick me up at six tomorrow?" she said, knowing that she would keep him waiting, just a little bit. She wasn't about to surrender all of her feminine wiles just because Quent was looking at her with adoring eyes. It felt good to be looked at like that.

"That would be lovely. Tomorrow then," Quent said.

Chapter 37

"Mrs. Worthington," Colleen said, holding out her hand and studying the woman who opened the door. Colleen was doing her best not to let nerves get the best of her, but she had a lot riding on this meeting. Her first new client, the start of a new business. The pressure to not mess this up was making her slightly sick to her stomach, but she smiled through the queasiness, trying to remind herself that April Worthington had asked for her, Colleen, specifically.

"Please call me April."

April Worthington was medium height, just a little on the plump side but had one of the biggest smiles Colleen had ever seen. Within seconds, April had her in the house and was pumping her hand.

"I couldn't wait to meet you. When Jake told me that he knew you, I was so excited I nearly peed my pants. I've been reading your blog for years. And your book—I've given it to my sister, my mom, my aunt. We love your recipe for lavender lemonade."

"That's great," Colleen said, truly happy that someone loved that recipe.

April was walking and talking and leading Colleen back through the hall on a whirlwind tour of the house.

"We've just finished the kitchen renovation and now we're starting on the rest of the downstairs: the family room, living room, dining room, and, of course, Kevin's study. That was the deal. He got his own space, and I got the new kitchen. The problem is if it's not a pot or a pan, I just don't know what to do. Kevin loves it when we entertain, swears my pot roast is his secret weapon to closing the deal, and I want the house to look perfect."

"Well, umm, okay," Colleen responded uncertainly. She wasn't usually at a loss for words, but the download of information from April was a little much.

April took a deep breath, then said, "I am so sorry. Everyone tells me that I can get a little hyper. I know I need to calm down but really, this project has been so overwhelming. Kevin is always working, which is only to be expected since he got the promotion, but like I said, he really wants the house to look nice and to be able to use it to entertain clients."

"Of course," Colleen agreed. "A welcoming home is very important."

April was standing there, wringing her hands, her eyes honed in on Colleen.

Colleen looked around, trying to take it all in. The house was vast. It was in one of the newer developments in town, in the wooded section, farther back from the coast. The lots were generously spacious, and the houses tended toward classical design—whether it was French chateau style, English manor house, or Colonial Williamsburg like this one. The house wasn't brand new, but the Worthingtons had bought it just a few months ago and had slowly but surely committed to a complete renovation and overhaul.

"Now that the kitchen is done, we decided to move in," April said. "We have the upstairs furnished, of course, but for now we just live in the kitchen. Jake and his crew are working on the finish work and built-ins. He told me he'd be done in two weeks, so it was time to start furnishing. I started to look, but I got so overwhelmed. I baked some muffins, would you like to try one? And I have coffee. Couldn't live without coffee."

"Coffee would be lovely," Colleen answered as she took in the kitchen. It was breathtaking—an expanse of marble counters and gleaming appliances. No expense, it appeared, had been spared. Even though the whole house smelled of new wood and fresh paint, the kitchen already looked homey with pots of herbs growing on a sunny windowsill, a bookshelf filled with cookbooks, and the plate of muffins set next to the glass carafe of coffee. The muffins and fresh coffee smelled heavenly.

"I went with marble since I like to bake," April said, one hand resting on a center island that seemed to be dedicated solely to the fine art of pie making.

"Why don't we set up here, and you can give me one of those muffins, and we'll start talking about what you're dreaming of."

Colleen put her things down on a long countertop with a couple of stools and smiled at April.

"Oh thank goodness, I just knew you'd be the answer to my prayers. I don't care what it costs if you can pull everything together.

"They're my morning glory muffins. I think Jake is quite fond of them too. Every time I brought them to the crew they disappeared—the muffins that is—and well, they got the job done ahead of schedule. Kevin does say that my muffins can work miracles."

April poured coffee and handed Colleen a muffin. There was something so endearing about her, her openness and friendliness.

Colleen took a bite of the muffin, then another. It was a seriously good muffin. "Wow, April, these are amazing. Morning glory, you said?"

"Oh yes; my grandmother's recipe. Of course I have made a few tweaks, but they are crowd pleasers."

The muffin was delicious, and Colleen found herself taking a third bite before she put the muffin aside. She wanted to eat the whole thing it was so good. Jake hadn't been lying about April's muffins.

"Now that Kevin has this new position, he is so excited. We've been looking at this neighborhood for years, and when this house came on the market, he bought it as a surprise. Can you imagine? Then he said as long as he got his traditional study, I could have the kitchen of my dreams. So we each got what we wanted, and now I have no idea how to do the rest. Do I want formal or casual or casual formal? I just don't know. And then I finally do make a decision, and I hate it, and I just don't know what to do about it, so I bake some more.

"So this time," April continued, "I said to myself, brand new house, brand new April. I looked over all of these magazines and blogs and websites, and I still didn't know what to do. And then Jake said he knew you and it was like a miracle."

Colleen smiled. She wasn't sure she was a miracle worker. But she could help April get started. "I brought some magazines and some books," she said. "I thought we could just flip through them, and you would show me what you liked without worrying about anything else."

Colleen wanted to get a sense of what April liked and, maybe more importantly, what she didn't like, before she made any recommendations.

"That sounds heavenly," April said, and they got to work.

Chapter 38

Ellie had agreed to meet Quent in the parking lot of her building simply because she wasn't quite ready to have him come up to her apartment. She was afraid that if she invited him in, they wouldn't ever leave. Not because Quent would be anything but the perfect gentleman, but because she wasn't sure she could be the perfect lady. She realized that something had tilted in her feelings toward him, that she was ready to move on, to embrace all that it meant. And so, because she wanted to force herself to slow just a bit, to enjoy it, she had him wait for her, and there he stood, leaning against the door of the Trans Am with arms folded as he watched her descend the steps.

No boat ride for her tonight, so she had dressed in her typical style, in a dark green dress that complemented her eyes, and her favorite stilettos. She had a wrap thrown over her arm and the tiniest of purses. Quent didn't move until she got to ground level, but his eyes watched her, and she had to work to hide her satisfaction. His smile, slow and easy, was definitely appreciative. He held out his arm, opened the door for her, and she slid into the low bucket seat. He came around, got in, and the engine roared to life and settled to a heady purr.

"Sounds good," she said. Close to him, away from the beer-soaked air of the bar, she noticed that he smelled like soap and a hint of spicy aftershave, nothing overpowering, just a lovely combination of maleness.

He took her hand and kissed it gently. "All tuned up for you," he said, and winked.

She smiled, settled into her seat. "So where are we going?"

"A little hideaway I know about, a bit up the coast."

She smiled. "Let's go for a drive," she said.

Quent couldn't decide it if was nervousness or lust that was coursing through his veins. He had watched Ellie descend those steps and wondered if he dared suggest that they scrap dinner and order in. But he knew he wanted a chance to woo her. The boat ride had been fine, but he had seen her turn green about half of the way through it and decided to cut it short. She had been apologetic and sweet, and it had taken some nerve to seek her out at work and try again. He had a plan, a trip to The Hideaway, a simple Italian restaurant, nestled along the coast at a small marina. The décor was wood paneling and dark carpets, but the wraparound deck had a splendid view and the food was amazing.

He powered the car out of town, then up the hilly road that hugged the coast. It swooped and dipped as the water stayed on their side, visible through breaks in the trees and the houses. The Trans-Am was loud and made conversation difficult, but he didn't mind, just liked being with Ellie. He'd known it from the first moment she had walked into his bar, after her first day of work, looking for a bourbon neat. She had slammed it back, the gesture in direct contrast to her ladylike appearance. He'd been tongue-tied, and when she asked for a water, he had put it in front of her, his hand brushing hers, and he had gotten a tingle. He'd been at her beck and call since then, for months, but he doubted she noticed. He'd been curious why she showed up at his place. She looked like the type who would prefer to do her drinking at the Osprey Arms, the luxury hotel in town, with a bar that had been named "Best Cocktail Lounge."

"You're the first watering hole I came to. Figured I wouldn't see anyone I know, either," she'd said as if she'd read his mind.

He hadn't known whether to be offended or pleased with his good luck. But it was her voice, the slow Southern drawl, along with her catlike green eyes, dark hair, and shapely body that had cemented his feelings for her. True, she wasn't as young as he had first thought, but she wore her years well, and he wasn't interested in some twenty-year-old bimbo who he'd have to explain every pop culture reference to. No, Ellie was magnificent in every way.

Despite her drinking that one bourbon straight down, he'd found out she wasn't a big drinker, even though she kept coming back to the bar. She wasn't a big eater, at least not of his typical bar food menu, though she would slowly work her way through a bowl of unshelled peanuts while she kept him company. She would arrive just after work and leave early, before the bar became crowded, so they'd have a chance to chat.

True, it was about the weather and what people were drinking, and maybe baseball or football. Nothing had been too personal, until now.

She loved the restaurant and for once, he was glad to see her eat; she seemed to really enjoy the pasta dish she ordered. She sipped at wine, enjoyed the view, and even had a bite of his tiramisu. After dinner, they stood on the deck of The Hideaway, a tall heat lamp warming them, nestled together. The sun was just about to set, just a bit of orange lacing itself against the deep purple of the darkening sky.

"I love the sunset over the water," she said and sighed.

"Best time of day," he agreed. The air was growing colder, and he could feel her shiver just a little. He put an arm over her shoulder, and she turned into him.

She looked up at him and her profile was caught in the soft glow of patio lights strung across the deck.

"I had a lovely dinner," she said.

"I did as well," He said, wanting to kiss her and trying to decide if that was what she wanted.

She seemed to sense his hesitation and one hand went up and brushed against his cheek. He caught it, held it and then leaned down. She met him, and the kiss was gentle, but then she wrapped her arms around him, and he could feel heat answering heat and something in him untwisted, the nervousness and worry relaxing. He placed his arms solidly on her waist, gently, knowing that she was fragile. She was tiny, a little woman, and he wanted to protect her, from what, he didn't know, because as far as he knew, Ellie was a woman without any demons in her life.

"You know, I have a pretty good view of the sunrise from the balcony at my apartment," she said.

It took him only a moment to grasp at the meaning behind her words. He smiled, looked down and said. "Why luv, are you inviting me over to see it?"

She smiled and kissed him again, before she pulled back and said in a sexy whisper of a voice, "Why darlin', you bet I am."

Chapter 39

J ake liked the quiet of an empty worksite, when it was just him and the building. He would never admit that the buildings he worked on seemed to talk to him, especially the older ones. If he walked into a house that had been built over a hundred years ago, it was as if he could see how it had been lived in, how it had been loved, the happiness and sadness that had transpired.

He believed a building, especially a home, wanted to be lived in, to be loved, which is why he loved restoring old and damaged buildings to glory. No building in Queensbay was quite as damaged and distressed as the Queensbay Showhouse. He'd come here often, ever since Mrs. Sampson had given her tacit approval for his proposal. There was still a long way to go, including the actual purchase of the building, not to mention permits and plans, but today, he was doing an inspection, the first step in creating a real, viable proposal for the Old Lady, as he had taken to calling the Showhouse. He was ready to hear her story, discover what secrets she was keeping.

He wasn't quite alone, though. The building was too big for that, so he grabbed some of his best guys for the day. Everyone said the building should just be torn down, and he should start over, but he was hoping that today would prove them all wrong. The five-man crew was swarming over the building. Two were looking along the foundation, while Jake and the other two got the ladders ready to start looking at the roof. The roof was very high, and as Jake knew from the interior avian residents, holes had to be in the roof because the birds were getting in somewhere.

Today, there was a spooky feel to the place, a vibe he couldn't quite shake. The sky was cloudy, and rain threatened, which did the old wreck of a building no favors. He dredged up an old memory from high school English, of another old house in dire need of some tender loving care. The Showhouse had always reminded Jake of Miss Havisham's house from *Great Expectations*.

He leaned the ladder against the side of the wall, tested it. Manny, one of the guys on his crew looked at him and shook his head, a clear indication that he thought Jake was crazy.

"What, you don't think it will hold?" Jake asked, trying to keep his voice light. He wasn't worried about the ladder, of course.

Manny muttered something under his breath that Jake couldn't quite catch. He looked over his crew. Robert was here too and though strong, he only weighed one hundred thirty pounds, max. He was the obvious choice to go up on the roof, and Jake knew if he asked, Robert would do it. But he wasn't that kind of boss, at least not yet. He was the hands-on type, the one who swung the hammer, who worked in the sun, and the one who prided himself on knowing how to do every job on the site, even if his main responsibility was paperwork, managing schedules, and keeping track of profit margins.

Jake climbed, not looking down, just up, focusing on the eaves above him, putting one step above the other. He got to the top of the ladder and reached the roof. Out to the right he could see the expanse of the harbor, flat, leaden, and calm, as if just waiting for the rain. The Showhouse was up on an embankment, higher than the beaches surrounding it. It was a tall building. He was up high, very high.

A bird rushed past him and he smiled. It was kind of like flying but not quite. He got up on the roof, carefully and gingerly. He walked, well, it was more like he crawled around it. He got to the pitch, peered down the other side and sighed. He'd seen enough, and it was starting to rain, which was making the slate tiles slippery. He went carefully back down the roof, to the ladder and began the descent. He hopped down when he was closer to the ground, and he almost felt the collective sigh of relief from his guys.

"Has to be replaced," he said.

Roof tiles were missing and there was clearly a small hole on the other side, which meant that it was probably the main point of entry for the pigeons. Redoing the roof in slate would be expensive, unless they could salvage a bunch of tiles. He'd have to see about that, he thought as he pulled out the notebook he carried in his pocket and jotted down something else to the endless list.

"Jake, you need to see this," someone called to him.

He went around the foundation and saw Manny pointing to a hole.

"Something's getting in there. Good news is the rest of it looks pretty sound."

Jake brightened up. "Really?"

"Well, the foundation is. I don't know what's holding up the floor," Manny amended.

Jake sighed. He wasn't a big fan of basements. Especially in old buildings, where no one had had the sense to turn them into a man cave. Old basements were creepy, and things tended to live down there.

"I have some flashlights in the truck," Manny said, trying to sound chipper.

They went inside and began investigating the old theater. Jake made it through the forest of cobwebs with only one rat sighting. Manny had sworn that it was only a mouse, but Jake hadn't believed him. Now he was in the actual theater room. The chairs had long been stripped away, but the orchestra pit and the stage remained, with the stage prompter box still visible. He vaulted up onto the stage and stood there for moment. The wood was good, so he'd have to find a way to reclaim it. He wasn't sure where he'd use it yet. There looked to be some water damage toward the far end. He walked toward it and suddenly he felt his legs give way. One moment he was standing, and the next he was sliding down, hard and fast, and everything went black.

When he came to, there was a ring of flashlights in his face. He was lying flat on his back and everything hurt. Which he decided was a good thing. He moved slightly, also a good thing. He sat up and felt woozy.

"Don't move, boss," Manny, said, hovering over him, concern lining his weathered face.

"Tell them to stop shining those lights in my

eye," Jake said gruffly.

His head hurt as he tried to get up.

"Wait boss, should we call the ambulance?"

"I'm fine," he said as he got up. He swayed a little but steadied himself before Manny could see.

He looked around. They were below the stage, the wood floor having given way. The break was clean. He looked around.

"I think it's the old trap door," Manny said.

Jake nodded. They were standing on it. It was a trap door so that actors could pop in or out, or things could pop up. They were only about six feet below the stage, so it was easy enough for the guys to lift him out.

Manny shined his light on him and said, "Boss, you don't look too good."

Jake brushed a hand over his face. It came away with a fine layer of cobwebs, tinged dark red. He touched the side of his head. Manny handed him a bandana.

"You should get that checked out."

"I'm fine," Jake started to say, but then a wave of nausea overtook him. He took a deep breath, and it passed.

"Fine, take me over to the clinic," he said, only because if it had been one of his guys who'd fallen, he'd make them go to the clinic. He needed to set an example and because lying down was starting to sound like a pretty good idea.

Still, it was pride that kept him upright as Manny took him to the truck.

"I'm driving."

Jake started to shake his head, but it hurt too much and just handed over his keys.

Chapter 40

The knock on the door interrupted Jake as he was flipping channels. Yet another good reason not to be home in the middle of the day. Nothing was on the television.

"Come in," he called out, not bothering to get up from the couch. He'd left it open and his arm and head still hurt. If people were going to insist on coming by all day, then he didn't want to bother getting up and down. He'd gone to the clinic, and the doctor had told him he didn't have a concussion. He did have a couple of nasty bruises on his back and a headache. A few days rest was all he needed, but he'd only made a few hours and he was going crazy.

The footsteps were light and hurried, and he made an effort to get up when he saw Colleen hovering over him, a worried look creasing her face.

"What the hell happened?" she said as she put a hand on his chest and pushed him back down.

"It's nothing," he said.

She looked pretty, in one of his favorite dresses, black with flowers over it. Her hair was pulled back in a low ponytail, which curled down over one shoulder. There was a look of unmistakable worry on her face as her hand hovered over him as if she was going to check his temperature.

"Just a bump on the head. I got checked out at the clinic. Hurts, but no concussion," he told her. Other spots were sore, and he had a nasty bruise on his side, but he'd had worse playing football.

"Thank goodness," she said, and he saw the worry ease from her face as she leaned back.

"You don't have to go, you know. Stay a while," he said with a smile, since she had folded her arms and looked like she was about to rush off. It was a gift, he decided, that she was here, in the middle of the day, an unscheduled, unchaperoned visit. She smelled nice, like lemon and lavender, and he didn't want her to go just yet.

"It's lunch time. I just thought I would run over and check on you. Why didn't you tell me?" A note of reproach was in her voice.

He shrugged. "No big deal. Not like a fall off of a roof or anything like that, because, let me tell you, that really hurts. And we're supposed to see each other tonight, and I figured I would tell you then."

"Oh no, no way. We're not going out tonight. You need to rest."

He grabbed her hand, pulled her down over the back of the couch and on top of him so that her slim length was nestled up against his.

"How about a kiss?" he said, brushing a hand over her ponytail. "I hear that makes everything better."

A smile played along her lips and sparked in her eyes as she searched his face. "That only works if you're under the age of six."

"We can pretend. Or better yet, you can examine

me and see if I sustained any other wounds."

"Report is that it was just a nasty bump on the head," she said as she buried her head into his chest. He rubbed his hands down her back, feeling the long, limber length of her.

"Just a little bump on the head," he repeated. "The old trapdoor gave out underneath me. I knew it was rotted, but I guess it was worse than I thought." She was warm and soft where she should be soft and strong where she needed to be strong. His aches and pains vanished as he pulled her mouth down to his and kissed her.

"Jake, you're hurt," she protested as she broke off the kiss.

He smiled at her, already feeling much better.

"Do I feel hurt?" he asked.

She didn't respond, but her eyes darkened as her hand moved down his shirt and down to his jeans. He closed his eyes and groaned just a little when she touched him fleetingly. He was, as he always was with her, ready for her. His body couldn't lie.

"The things you do to me, Colleen," he murmured as he kissed her again, pouring his need and want into it. He didn't want her to go, did not want to be stuck on a couch, pining for her.

He wrapped his hands in her hair, and then let them roam over her back, down to the skirt of her dress. He lifted it and felt the silky smoothness of her skin give way to the satin of her delicate underwear. She kissed him back and let herself sink gently into him, as his hands found every part of her, pulling and taking clothes off. She stopped him, smiled at him, and he was sure there was just a hint of a wicked gleam in her eye as she stilled his hands. He felt trapped, at her mercy, and knew without a doubt that once again, Colleen McShane had him dead to rights. There was nothing but her for him.

Her hands moved, pulling up his t-shirt, up and over his head, and then she traced her fingers gently down his bare skin so that he shivered. He reached up his hands, eager to see her flesh but she stopped him, and slowly reached behind her, unzipping her dress. He heard the slow agonizing sound and the dress split open, revealing her skin and the pale lacy bra beneath it. She shifted carefully and the dress was off, so that she sat atop of him, her hair undone so that it spilled over her shoulders. She let him touch her now, his hand finding her breast and touching her beneath the fabric of her bra, his fingers working her to arousal.

She unhooked the clasp and her breasts swung free. He moved up just enough so that he could trail kisses down her neck and along the creamy flesh of her skin, nipping at one nipple until it was hard and her breathing was quick and she moaned in pleasure. With his hands, he ran them down the length of her stomach as she shivered in pleasure, his fingers teasing between her thighs. He slipped down the satin softness of her panties and found her already aroused, so he pushed her higher, one arm holding her tightly in place while his mouth took his fill of her and his fingers drove her mad.

He felt her go higher and higher, even as her own hands worked on his button and zipper. Together, they pulled off their remaining clothes, and she mounted him, pushing him back down as he arched into her. Her moans of pleasure turned into a final cry of triumph as her head fell back and he could feel the convulsing waves of pleasure as he finally followed her.

They lay there afterward, breathing heavily, her head on his chest, while he ran his hand over her body. He didn't say anything, couldn't; he knew that if he did so, she would only run away. But the thought was clear in his head. He was in love with Colleen McShane, not just a dopey case of high school lust. She was an amazing, sexy, beautiful, accomplished woman, and he wanted her to be his and only his. He brushed back a stray bit of hair, and her eyes opened, looking at him warily. There was a worried smile on her face, and he could almost sense what she was thinking. Guilt and doubt. He could see the woman who was a mother, who had a business to run, who knew better than to be having a lunch-time quickie.

He didn't try to fight it, just let her eyes fly to her watch and then regarded her calmly as she rolled off of him and gathered up her clothes. He wouldn't push or ask her for anything more. He grabbed her hand, had her look at him.

"Don't worry, you still have half of your lunch hour left," he said.

She smiled, just a little bit, but he could tell that she was still worrying.

He walked her to the door, even though she told him not to. Still, she let him kiss her deeply. She knew she needed to get back, was already mad at what she had done. She had only meant to come over and check on him. She hadn't meant the desire, want, and need for him to sweep over her. God, she was doing it again, letting sex get in the way of what she needed to do, what she needed to focus on.

"I'll drive you," he was muttering as his arms

wrapped around her, almost pulling her back into his apartment.

"No way. You need to rest. It will be faster to walk; besides, I have to stop at The Garden Cottage," she murmured. She made herself get out of the apartment, stand on the small walkway that ran in front of it, and eventually down to the steps that would allow her to escape.

There was the sound of laughter, low and throaty. Colleen stopped. She would recognize that laugh anywhere.

"Ellie?" she said and glanced over. Ellie, who was in the process of pushing Quent out of her apartment door, froze. Colleen pulled herself away from Jake who frowned and then took a step out onto the landing. His eyebrows rose, amusement darting across his face. She elbowed him, as gently as she could. He'd better not start laughing, or she'd be a goner too.

Quent pulled himself up to his full height and put one arm around Ellie, who was blushing. It made her, Colleen thought, look younger and happy.

"What are you doing here?" Colleen blurted out because she couldn't really think of anything else to say.

Quent was blushing too and was, for once, tongue-tied. It was Ellie who came to all of their rescues: "Quent was just fixing my sink."

"You could have called the landlord," Jake said, and Colleen elbowed him again. He caught her arm, before she connected, but his face remained impassive.

"It's no bother. All fixed now, luv," Quent said, trying to sound breezy. Colleen hid a smile.

Colleen, reminded of what she'd just been doing,

fought the urge to check her own dress and fuss with her hair. They had all been caught, no doubt about it.

Ellie turned her catlike green eyes on Colleen and smiled. "I think perhaps a bit of discretion is best all around, don't you, sugar? Especially since I called in sick today?"

Colleen nodded. "Bartender code of honor. My lips are sealed."

There was another awkward silence, and then Colleen said briskly, "I have to go now. Jake, go and get some rest."

It took him a moment, but his door finally shut, and Colleen practically ran down the landing and took the stairs to the ground, fighting the urge to giggle all of the way.

Quent kept his arm around Ellie as he watched Colleen disappear. Jake's door had shut with finality, and now it was just the two of them, with just the tinkle of the wind chimes that hung from the eave, dancing in the breeze that was rolling in, gray clouds piling up.

"How long will they keep quiet about it?"

"I'm not worried about Colleen," Ellie said. "But I don't think Jake could keep a secret if his life depended on it."

Quent turned and looked at her, and a smile wreathed his face. "Guess we're going to have to go public with it. What do you think, luv?"

She turned to him, smiled, and said, without hesitation, "I'm ready if you're ready."

"I was ready from the first moment I laid eyes on you," he said and took her hand to his lips and kissed it.

Chapter 41

"**B**ut I want to go."

It was a whine that only a precocious five year old could muster, and it pierced Colleen's calm on many levels. She was irritated because Adele was being whiny, but she couldn't shake a feeling of guilt because she had made a promise, and now she was breaking it. And it was all too much to deal with on too little sleep. Colleen knew she was burning the candle at both ends between tending bar at Quent's, working on the shop, the sidewalk sale, and sneaking in time with Jake.

But things were coming together, the grand opening and the sidewalk sale coming up. If she could just get to that milestone, then she might be able to ease up a bit, maybe stop working at Quent's. She would have more time for Adele and for herself if she could quit bartending.

Adele was coloring, but it was with angry slashes of her crayons, in bold, dark colors, as if to show how displeased she was with her current situation. She was supposed to be at Happy Faces nursery school practicing for the spring finale. Adele, if nothing else, took her responsibilities as a tulip seriously.

"I know you want to go to the rehearsal, and we will, honey, I promise." Colleen checked her watch.

She was waiting for a shipment that she needed to sign for, a container of soaps, and if she missed the UPS guy again, the shipment would be taken back to the depot. She'd have to drive out and pick it up before it was returned to sender, which happened to be a small producer in the South of France. Something like that would only complicate her life, so she was determined to wait, hoping that Serge, her delivery man would appear, and she could still get Adele to rehearsal relatively on time.

"I promise you, the delivery will be here shortly; I'll sign for what I need, and then I can take you to rehearsal."

"Fine," Adele said, her arms crossed across her chest and her eyes narrowed down to small slits.

Colleen didn't know whether to laugh or to cry. It was cute now, at age five, but what would it be like when Adele was seven or nine or, god forbid, sixteen? She just needed to be strong and not be made to feel so guilty that she missed Serge. It wasn't like she had stopped for a three-martini lunch and forgotten to pick Adele up. She was working for both of their futures. Who knew, maybe *La Belle Vie* would turn into a chain of stores with a catalog or at least an ecommerce site. And all because she had remained committed to waiting for Serge.

The bell on the door tinkled. She looked up and didn't know whether to be pleased or dismayed that it was Jake and not Serge. Still, as Jake strolled in, she reflected that he was a lot better looking than Serge, who was balding with a slight paunch. Not that looks were the most important things, but she felt her mood lighten when Jake smiled at both of them.

"Hello ladies," he said, smiling. He gave Colleen a look but didn't kiss her or do anything that would lead to Adele asking questions. He'd come by the bar to keep her company while she worked, and they'd managed to sneak off once or twice to his apartment. Once, he'd stopped and met them at the park where he had pushed her on the swings, watched on the slide and even played tag with her and Josh. He was slowly integrating himself into their lives, and she wasn't certain how she felt about it.

"What's going on?" he asked, looking at Adele as he said it.

Adele gave him a sweet smile, her previous bad mood giving way to her natural good humor.

"We are waiting for the UPS man. Mama has a shipment," Adele said precisely.

"I think I just passed Serge. He was heading in the opposite direction."

"Mama!" Adele cried.

"Something bothering you, kiddo?" Jake asked.

"I will be late for rehearsal," Adele said as she slashed some angry red lines across a butterfly's wings.

"I need to sign personally for the package," Colleen explained. "And Adele is supposed to be a rehearsal for the spring show."

"It's called a Butterfly in the Garden. I'm the pink tulip. I have a song to sing. All the mothers and fathers are coming. And there will be a party afterward with cupcakes."

"Sounds lovely," Jake said, tweaking Adele's nose and getting a reluctant smile in return, even as she pouted.

"It won't be if I don't get to practice."

"Soon," Colleen said, trying to make her voice sound assuaging. She checked her watch.

"I have an idea," Jake said, glancing at Colleen casually, as if what he was about to propose was indeed no big deal. "How about I take Adele over to rehearsal, then I'll bring her back here. Or you can meet us at the park. It will give you a little time to work."

Colleen stopped looking at her watch and instead looked at him. "What?"

"I have a little free time this afternoon. I'd be happy to take her," Jake said and rocked back on his heels, his hands in his pockets. Colleen knew that while he was mostly healed from his fall, he was still supposed to be taking it easy, so maybe he really did have some free time. Or maybe not.

"I don't..."

"Please Mama?" Adele had already hopped off the counter, ready to go, an eager look on her face.

Colleen hesitated, looking at Jake, who had a carefully neutral look on his face as if what he suggested wasn't completely out of left field.

"It's just down the street, you know," he said. "And I am a responsible adult, part of the community. You can trust me."

"I know I can trust you, Jake, it's just . . ." Colleen wasn't worried about Adele's safety, of course. Not with Jake.

"It's just a favor, Colleen. You don't have to read too much into it," he said quietly so that Adele wouldn't hear, as if he sensed the doubts running through her mind.

"Please," Adele was trying hard not to beg, but it was clear that she was more than ready to go.

"Okay," Colleen finally said. "You have my cell phone number? I'll be right here."

"We know where you are and where we're going. Come on little lady, got what you need?"

He held out a hand and Adele slipped hers into his, and Colleen wondered why her heart gave a little hitch at the sight.

Chapter 42

"I liked your song," Jake said as he licked around the side of his cone of mint chocolate chip. Adele had chosen plain chocolate, and they were sitting at the park, side by side with their ice cream cones. He had texted Colleen that they would be back shortly, and she had said okay. He had decided that he wouldn't mention the ice cream, though, judging by the amount that was getting on Adele's shirt, he probably wasn't going to be able to hide it. He hoped that Colleen wouldn't mind, since Adele had assured him that ice cream was fine for an occasional treat.

"I like it too. I like the ending," Adele said and took a lick, like he had showed her, around the sides to catch the drips.

"You're not making a mess," she pointed out.

"Years of practice," he answered. The park was filling up. He recognized some of the kids and the moms from the rehearsal. A few he knew from around town because he had worked on their houses.

"The show is in just a few weeks. I do not know if we will be ready for it. Would you like to come? We can invite friends."

He froze. The invitation had been delivered

seamlessly as if Adele had given no thought about what it meant if he came. Because Jake knew that Colleen would have something to say about it, he paused, then thought, to hell with it.

"Sure, Adele, if you'd like me to, I'd be honored. I'll put it in my calendar," he said. He could do that. He was sure that Colleen wouldn't mind. Adele had asked him, and he wouldn't want to disappoint her. It didn't seem to bother her that she didn't have a dad around like the other kids, but still, he wondered if she ever noticed.

"I am going to play on the slide now," Adele announced, finishing her ice cream cone.

"Ten minutes," he said, "Your mom said to be back in ten minutes."

He watched her run off to the slide and start talking to a couple of other little girls. He settled in, but made sure he kept his eye on her. He wouldn't lose Adele, not on his watch.

A shadow fell over him. "Well, isn't that adorable."

He looked up, tried to school his face to neutrality, and said, "Amy."

"You hanging around with little girls now, Jake?" Amy asked. Her voice had a nasty tone to it.

He took a deep breath. He hadn't meant for things to end so badly between the two of them, they just had. If he recalled, her daughter was probably the same age as Adele, which would make sense since he'd seen Amy at the pre-school. Of course he had done his best to avoid her, hustling Adele off for some ice cream, but it seemed as if Amy had caught up with him anyway.

"Long time no see," he said easily and shifted so

he could keep his eye on Adele, who was now in an animated discussion with another girl on the top of the slide.

"Oh, it's been a while," she said. Her eyes followed his gaze and focused on Adele.

"So you're hanging out with Colleen McShane's little bastard."

He looked up, outraged at her tone. "What did you say?"

"You heard me. Adele's got no daddy. Think maybe that's what Colleen is looking for. If so, we know you're not that kind of guy. Better be careful you don't go breaking up any more lives."

She put her hand on his arm. The nails, as he remembered were perfectly manicured. She wore an engagement ring and a wedding ring on her finger, big, fat diamonds. He had not given them to her and that had been the point, hadn't it?

"I'm just doing a favor for a friend, Amy, that's all," he said. He waved at Adele. It was almost time to go, and he was ready to get away from Amy's gaze.

"You should be careful, very careful. You're not a fan of kids, remember?"

He turned to her. "That baby wasn't mine, and you knew it. Still you tried to get me to be something I wasn't. But you got what you wanted. You have your husband and kid. Leave me alone."

"What will happen when Colleen finds out you're a runner, Jake, not a family man?"

"People change," he said.

"Oh, I don't think so," she said.

He shook her hand off and left her, calling for Adele. It took a little cajoling for Adele to come down, but he promised her a piggyback ride and that made it easier. All he knew was that he needed to get away from Amy.

Chapter 43

J ake pushed open the door to the shop and gave himself the gift of being able to watch Colleen for a moment before she turned around and realized he was there. She was wearing cropped white pants, a simple black t-shirt, and a pair of impossibly high heels while balancing on a stool. She teetered a bit, and he instinctively moved closer to her, saying as he did, "I heard you were putting up the shelves. I thought you might need some help."

She half turned. Jake's arm came around her, steadied her.

"How about you hand them to me, and I'll slide them in. That way you won't fall off the stool."

"I'm handling it," she said, knowing she sounded cross.

He looked at her then asked: "Would you let Adele climb up on something like that?"

"Of course not."

"Well, I am not going to let you either," he said.

"You're not my father."

"I don't want to be," he replied, and because she looked very pretty with her hair pulled back he had to kiss her.

"What was that for?" she asked.

"Because I like you," he said and watched the expression on her face. Before she could think it through too much, he decided just to go for it. She needed to stop overthinking everything. "Because you smell nice," he continued, hooking an arm around her waist and pulling her toward him. She fell into his arms. She felt light, almost insubstantial. He knew she was working a lot, that she had put a lot of pressure on herself to get the opening of the store, along with the sidewalk sale, just right.

A lot of talk was going around town. The merchants were excited by the idea, and he'd heard that the Osprey Arms had a surge in bookings thanks to the blog posts from Colleen and the press releases she'd sent out. He wanted to tell her that it would all be okay but knew she wouldn't listen. The most he could hope for was to see if he could take her mind off of things for a while.

He kissed her again and felt as she relaxed into him and returned his kisses. Her arms came around his neck, and he swung her off the stool and nudged her back against the counter. He ran his hands over her back and cupped her backside with his hands. She made a sound, halfway between a moan and purr at his touch, and he ran his hands up her side and lifted up the edge of her shirt so he could feel her smooth, cool skin. She shivered under him, and he could feel as her body tensed with desire. He took a step back, saw the look in her eyes and was satisfied.

"The door is open," she said, her voice breathy with desire. It was a turn-on, and he decided that he wasn't going to let anything like an unlocked door get in their way.

"In here." He pushed her back through the curtain into the back storage room. There was a table there, spread with some stuff. He didn't quite clear it with a sweep of his hand, but he shoved enough aside and hiked her onto it.

Their hands were all over each other, and he pulled her shirt off to expose the swell of her breasts. He touched his lips to them, kissing one then the other and then sent a trail of kisses down her flat stomach. She trembled, her hands in his hair. Slowly he undid the snap of her jeans and pressed at the juncture of her legs. He was rewarded with a hiss of her breath, and he explored deeper with his fingers, peeling away her jeans with the other.

He kissed her thighs, and used his fingers to drive her higher and higher until he could feel her coming to her peak. He slowed the rhythm down, letting her ride the wave as her hands fumbled with his belt and pants. They slid down around his ankles, and she touched him through the fabric of his boxer briefs, and it was his turn to moan.

"God, I need you now," he whispered, and she pulled him to her. It was brief and intense and it was over all too soon, but she was smiling at him, half-clothed.

"*Bien?*" he couldn't help but ask, some long-ago learned French resurfacing, as he brushed a lock of her hair away from her face. She was warm now, her pale skin flushed and her chest heaving.

"*Tres bien,*" she said and leaned her head into him for one brief moment. He wanted to stay like that forever, joined together, but she pushed away, ready to disentangle herself.

He stopped her for a moment, put his hand under her chin and kissed her. It was a simple kiss and he meant it that way.

He ended it, and she blinked as if unsure.

"*Tres bien*," he agreed and handed her top back to her.

There was a tinkle of the bell, and she cursed as she hurriedly pulled it over herself.

He took a step back and pulled up his pants.

The curtain parted.

"Well, well, well," Darby Reese said.

Colleen felt the slow flush of red crawl up her cheeks. Of all the people who had to come in.

"Hey Darby, how you doing," Jake said as if nothing had happened. Darby stood there with hands folded over her chest and a smudge of flour on her nose. Colleen decided to focus on that. She hopped off the table, and Jake draped his arm around her.

"Fine. I had a question for her," Darby said and inched her chin toward Colleen.

"Well, don't let me hold you up. I've got to be going. Hey Colleen, how about I pick Adele up and take her to the park? You can meet us there."

Colleen opened her mouth and looked up at Jake.

"I know you wanted to spend some more time getting things set up," he coached her.

She nodded.

"Good, see you later. I left a coffee for you up front," he said and swaggered out as if nothing had happened.

Colleen wasn't sure what to think. Was she mad at him for leaving her alone with Darby or was she thankful that he showed no embarrassment? He'd been possessive though, what with the arm draped across her shoulder and the offer to pick up Adele, but she could use the help.

Colleen raised her chin defiantly. She was a grown-up, unattached. And so was Jake. He was no one's prom date, least of all Darby's. Darby was happily married with a kid, and another one on the way. The silence stretched between the two women as Jake's footsteps receded and the door clanged shut.

It was Darby who broke the silence first. "So you and Jake," she said. "Guess you're doing a bit more than drinking coffee together."

"Me and Jake. Jake and I. I assume you don't have a problem with that?"

"No. He's free. I'm assuming you're free."

"Yes," Colleen said shortly.

Darby shrugged. "None of my business."

Colleen raised her eyebrow and said, "No, you have something to say. Go ahead and say it."

Darby looked uncomfortable. "Jake doesn't just take someone's kid to the park because he wants to get into their capris."

"So . . ."

Darby sighed. "Just you know, be kind to him."

"I am. I will," Colleen said and shifted, then said what she was thinking: "It's complicated. With Adele. And well, I just don't want anyone to get their expectations up."

Darby gave her a shrewd look and said, "I think you're way past that."

"I don't need him. I don't need a father figure. Adele is just fine."

"I am sure she is. She looks fine to me. Looks like

you're doing fine here. You might not need Jake, but he wants you. In a bad way. Just go easy on him. He's not as tough as he looks."

Colleen snorted. "You don't have..."

Darby shook her head and said, "I do. Kind of. This is a small town, remember. We all go way back. It is complicated. That's all I am saying."

Colleen took a deep breath and was about to protest, but it died on her lips before she could give voice to the thought, because Darby was right. They were all connected. Something she hadn't thought about too much when she decided to move back. She had just assumed that it would be a good, safe community for her and Adele. Phil's legacy had opened the door for her, and now she had walked right through it. No getting away from it. And she didn't want to. In fact she wanted to be in it.

"Now that that's settled, I have a few ideas," Darby said as she flipped open the portfolio she'd brought with her.

Darby left finally and Colleen was smiling to herself. The former valedictorian turned lawyer, turned baker had had a number of good ideas about how to make the sidewalk sale a success. Colleen had enjoyed working with her, and it had brought back memories of high school when they had worked together planning pep rallies and dances.

So there was more at stake here; both their businesses, and the whole town, could benefit from this. Queensbay was still up and coming, Darby had explained, and could do with a little bit more discovery from the tourists. Together they had mapped out a plan, and now Colleen's to-do list was even longer. It had felt good to be working with Darby. She checked her phone. She had a text from Jake. She smiled. He had sent a photo of him and Adele smiling in the camera. They looked like they were near the pet store, but he had said for her to meet them at the park.

She knew that it was dangerous to let Jake spend time with Adele. She couldn't let him get too close, let Adele grow to like him too much. As she looked into the picture, she realized that it wasn't Olivier she had missed, no, not at all, but the sense that she had a partner in raising Adele, and to some extent living life. She had missed having someone who could take Adele to the park or weigh in on decisions about how Adele should be raised.

Of course she had Lydia, who seemed to have assumed responsibility for Josh, but Lydia was even more lost than she was. Who was to say that Jake knew any better than she did? After all, he'd never had a kid. He'd been one: the cute, carefree, get dirty, go out and play all-American kid. Something that Adele needed and could use a little more of.

"Want to come play?" Jake's text was accompanied by a smiley face.

She smiled. It was a sunny, gorgeous spring day. Of course she wanted to play.

She texted back: "BRT"

Chapter 44

"Are we going to the park?" Adele looked at Jake, running to him as he waited outside of Happy Faces. He studiously avoided the glares Amy was sending his way.

He took a moment, pretended to think. "Only if we get ice cream."

Her eyes lit up for a moment and then her face settled in a small frown. "Too many sweets aren't good for you."

"Who told you that?"

"Mama. And Grand-mama, but she was eating a donut when she said it, so I do not think she meant it."

He had to smother a smile. There was something about the preciseness with which she spoke that got to him. Maybe it was because she was thinking in one language and speaking in the other, but it made her sound wise beyond her years.

"How about a small one?" he suggested.

Adele's gray eyes grew serious as she thought about this for a moment.

"Yes, that sounds good."

"Okay, good. Are we going to walk or drive?" he asked, even though he already knew the answer.

"We walk, of course."

"Of course," he murmured and followed Adele out the door. She jumped up on the ledge of the small stone wall, arms out, balancing. The sky was a brilliant blue; a few puffy white clouds dotted it. A light breeze pushed the clouds along, but the sun stayed strong and bright, and he laughed as Adele danced and skipped her way along. He was ready for her when she came to the end of the wall, his hand out as she jumped down, and they continued in the direction of the park. They had fallen into a routine, the two of them. Colleen had objected at first, when he said he didn't mind picking up Adele every once in a while. Besides, Colleen was working her tail off getting everything ready for the grand opening of the shop, so he figured it was the least he could do.

"Look," Adele said, pointing to Barks and Wags, the new pet boutique.

"What?" he asked suspiciously.

"Puppies," she said and tugged his hand. Jake suddenly had a bad feeling about this.

There were puppies, all big paws, chubby bellies, and floppy ears. They were some sort of mutt, but Jake was pretty sure they had Labrador in them. Adele was already down on her knees, her hands and face pressing into the wire cage as the puppies swarmed her. She was shrieking with laughter.

"Mama says that I can get a puppy someday."

The puppies were awfully cute.

"Did you used to have a puppy?" Adele asked and looked up at him, one of the puppies already squirming in her arms as she tried to contain it.

"I did."

"What was his name?" she asked.

All of a sudden, Jake had the sensation he was being played. "Boomer," Jake said. He had really liked that dog. He had taken the dog to the beach, on the boat, everywhere. Boomer had loved the water. His mother had tolerated Boomer, who was always wet or sandy or both, but Boomer had been his best friend.

"If I had a puppy, I would name her . . ."

"What if it's a boy?"

Jake couldn't believe he was playing along with this, but he knew how much Adele wanted a dog, and since in his mind she had been through a lot, he was leaning toward that idea that she should have a dog.

"I like this one," Adele said. She looked up at him. He looked down at the puppy and knew he was a goner.

Chapter 45

"What is that?" Colleen looked at the wiggling heap of soft yellow fur.

"A puppy, Mama."

"You didn't," she began as she looked from the puppy to Jake.

"My puppy," Jake said carefully, heading off the panic he saw in Colleen's eyes.

"Her name is Boomer," Adele said. "Jake used to have a dog named Boomer, so this one is also Boomer. I wanted to name her Chloe, but Jake said that Boomer was fine, so we decided to name her Chloe Boomer Owen."

"Adorable," Colleen said, leaning down. The puppy *was* adorable, a brownish gold color, all soft fur, wrinkled nose, and big eyes. Her paws were entirely too big for her body. She was chewing on something, which turned out to be her leash. She stopped when a leaf crossed her path and looked as if she were going to chase it.

"You got a puppy," Colleen said. She couldn't quite look at Jake.

"Well, I've sort of been thinking about it," he said defensively. Somehow, while it was happening he'd had the sense that this was a bad idea. Not because he didn't want a dog. Already, he was charmed by Boomer, who tended to trip over her own feet, but because he was sure that Colleen would read too much into it. And he could see from her tenseness, the look on her face, the way she watched Adele play with Boomer that she was upset.

"I am sure you were. I mean it's your life, you have every right to get a dog."

"Jake said I could play with Boomer anytime I want to."

"I am sure he did," Colleen said, feeling the tight lump in her throat. What was Jake thinking? She looked up at him, and his eyes darted away. This was moving too fast for her. She needed to put a stop to this, but then she looked at her daughter who was jabbering at the puppy and at Jake, and she'd never thought she'd seen a guy so happy.

"Mama, Jake has invited us over to dinner. He says that he has a view of the water from his apartment."

Adele was rubbing the puppy's belly, and the puppy was wiggling in bliss underneath her touch.

"Oh really?"

"It doesn't have to be tonight," he said hastily. "In fact, I was thinking tomorrow night might be better. I thought we'd have steaks and watch a movie. Adele's given me a list of age-appropriate choices." He was stumbling over his words, and he ran a hand through his hair. Colleen almost took pity on him, since he looked so guilty, but then she quashed the thought.

She looked at Adele who was telling Boomer not to chase squirrels. Boomer had turned back over on her stomach and was yawning, looking very much like she was ready for a puppy nap.

"Adele, Jake and I are going to talk. We will just be over there," Colleen said and pointed toward the bench below the spreading leaves of the big oak tree, which was unoccupied and close enough to keep an eye on Adele but far enough away from the attention of the other moms at the playground. Because Colleen could tell that she and Jake might be about to have a scene, and she had no desire to be the subject of gossip around Happy Faces.

Jake stuck his hands in his pockets and followed her over to the tree where he stood, one booted foot kicking defiantly at the ground.

"I didn't know you were planning on getting a dog."

"I guess I didn't know either. You know how some things are just meant to be."

She shook her head. She didn't believe in rash decisions any longer, and she couldn't allow Jake to drag her and, more importantly, Adele, down that sort of path.

"I just want to see you, like a real person," he said, changing the subject.

"You do realize you invited my daughter over as well. What exactly do you think will happen?"

"I'll make steaks and baked potatoes, we will pop in a movie, something with princesses and cute talking animals, Adele will probably fall asleep, and then I'll drive you home."

"And?"

"What do you think I think will happen? What kind of guy do you think I am?"

The dangerous type, Colleen thought, because Jake

knew that exactly nothing would happen between them if Adele was there.

He took a step closer to her, dropped his voice but it was still laced with anger when he said, "If I wanted sex, I would stop by the shop and lock the door. Or I'd ask you out on a date and tell you to get a babysitter. Or I'd pick you up from work in my truck. You seem to have no problem having sex with me, Colleen, but now I'm asking you to dinner."

"With a five year old," Colleen pointed out.

"Exactly. And a puppy."

"Jake, I don't need to play house," she said. She'd done that and it had only led to broken dreams. He looked at her, and she could read the look in his eyes. It wouldn't just be playing with him.

"Adele says you like chocolate chip cookies. It's just dinner."

She wanted to say no, wanted to back away but knew that she was sliding, falling far too deep. She glanced over at her daughter, who was waving enthusiastically at them to come back over. She needed to make a decision, and she just didn't want to feel that it was so fraught with importance.

"Okay, for just a few hours. Adele's bedtime is eight."

"So is the puppy's, so it will work perfectly," he said and smiled.

She couldn't help but think that his smile was utterly charming, utterly irresistible, and her heart slid just a little bit further, just a little bit harder over the edge from which she knew there would be no coming back.

Chapter 46

Lydia watched the wheel go around as her fingers shaped the clay, then she stopped and smashed it all together. It wasn't working. She glanced at the clock. She had an hour before she needed to go pick up Josh, then they'd head to the park with Adele and Colleen. She sighed, absentmindedly wiping her hands on her shirt. It was an oversized flannel that had belonged to an ex-boyfriend. She couldn't remember which one.

She had on a clean Lady A t-shirt on underneath. So as long as the clay smears didn't soak through she should be okay. As far as she was concerned, a clean band t-shirt was totally appropriate to wear to pick up Josh. But then she'd never been overly concerned about fashion.

She got up from her stool, looked out the window. She had to admit that the view was priceless. Her father's house, which was practically a mansion, was in the Bluffs section of Queensbay on the highlands that ringed the hills with a water view. Not of the harbor; they were too far out of town for that, but of the Sound itself. All she could see was blue meeting the horizon, maybe a long, low-slung dark hump of land that was

Long Island.

She'd grown up a country girl, where water had come from creeks and lakes, then she had lived in cities like Savannah and Atlanta, and this was country again to her. Queensbay was quiet, and she could distract herself for hours watching the seagulls wheel and play in the sky.

She stood in the square of light, basking in the warmth. True, it wasn't exactly cold, but she was a southern girl, and she expected it be much warmer by this time of year. She knew she had needed to get out of Savannah, so when the deal with her dad had presented herself, she leapt at the chance. Plus, she'd felt Josh had deserved better. Her only condition had been that she needed a place to work, when she wasn't busy with Josh.

Her dad, true to his belief that money could buy the best, had spared no expense. He'd had an outbuilding erected with running water, electricity, and heat. He'd had a kiln installed, of course, along with shelving and plenty of counter space. She couldn't fault her dad because this was a potter's dream space, and now that she didn't have to worry about teaching classes, she should have plenty of time to focus on her work.

More time than she'd had in Georgia, in fact, hours of time to study, shape, and create. Still, it was harder than she had thought it would be. She realized that right now she was thinking about Josh. Had he liked what she packed for lunch? Was he getting in fights with the Wallach twins? Had he thrown the type of temper tantrum that was going to have the school calling her? And it was her they should call. Her dad had made that clear. With Josh's mom out of the picture and

Hailey, the nanny, away in Ibiza, just about everything Josh-related came to her.

At first it had bothered her, but her dad had never been the fatherly type. True, he was generous with his money, but not with his time. And since Josh was her only brother, she wanted better for him. There were worse things than taking him to the park and getting to hang out in a waterfront studio.

At least the cook and housekeeper hadn't left. She could handle the babysitting part of it, but she was sure everyone was glad she wasn't supposed to cook or dust. She tended to forget about those things the more absorbed she got in her work. In fact, she smiled as she watched a gull over in the wind current, this gig was sort of like being an artist in residence someplace.

She sighed, pulled out her phone, saw that she only had an hour left before she needed to get Josh. She sat back down, took a deep breath and closed her eyes. Slowly, as the wheel began to turn, she coaxed something to life underneath her hands. She and Josh had been out for a walk yesterday, a winding path along the bluff, and they had been looking in the trees, watching for birds and squirrels. Josh loved being outside, and the great outdoors was just about big enough to absorb his energy.

They had seen a wasp nest high up in the tree, somewhat camouflaged by the brilliant green leaves, but she had been struck by its shape, the conical nature of it. She had a commission from a store out in Seattle to make some vases, but the shapes were eluding her. Her long, delicate fingers kept working, shaping. Maybe Colleen would want some vases too, in that same shade she'd taken to calling Queensbay blue.

Lydia hummed to herself in satisfaction as the form rose up beneath her hands. Inspiration had found her or she had found it. Whichever it was, she wasn't about to question it.

Chapter 47

"**I**s Boomer sleeping? I brought her a toy," Adele said, almost as soon as the door was open. She was about to rush in when Colleen put a restraining arm to hold her back.

"Adele, wait until we are invited in."

It was no use. Jake had been trying to hold the puppy back with one of his feet, but Boomer broke loose and found Adele. The two of them were happily rolling around on the door mat in no time.

"Boomer, come," Jake commanded.

The dog's ear popped up and she paused for the barest of instances. It was enough time for Jake to scoop her up and for Colleen to right Adele.

"Sorry, she's very excited to see you. Won't you come in?" he said and stepped back.

Adele walked in, followed by Colleen. Her eyes were guarded, as if she still couldn't believe she had agreed to this arrangement. He wanted to kiss her, but Boomer wiggled and licked his face.

"Adele, I'm going to put Boomer down. Are you ready?"

"*Mais oui*," she declared, and Boomer leapt toward her. She had a toy ready and soon they were playing tug of war.

"Hello," he said and turned to Colleen.

She was wearing jeans, ones that cropped off near her ankles, and bright red flats. They contrasted with her black and white striped t-shirt. The neck was cut so he could see just enough of her skin to make him want to run his hand gently along it, if only to see her shiver and her eyes flicker with awareness.

"Hello," she answered and stood there. He wanted to kiss her, but was acutely aware that she was aware that Adele was there. So he leaned in, brushed his lips on her cheek and stepped back.

"For me?" he asked, taking the bag.

"Just a bottle of wine. We were going to make cookies, but Adele assured me that you had everything covered, so we should relax and enjoy what you planned for us."

"Pretty simple, I'm afraid," he said. "Steak, baked potatoes, and asparagus. If she won't eat that I have apple slices. Sources say that works for most kids."

"She'll be happy with anything."

"And I have popcorn for the movie," he said.

"With butter and salt?"

"Is there any other way?" he assured her.

"Adele, why don't you take your paper and pencils and see if you can draw a picture of Boomer," Colleen suggested and handed over a bag that he saw contained a coloring book, some paper, and colored pencils.

"I also have a puzzle for her, but we might have to play Old Maid with her as well."

"Sure we can't teach her poker?"

Colleen laughed, and he could sense that she was

relaxing just a little bit.

Adele and Boomer found a spot on the floor where Adele started to draw while Boomer chewed on one of her treats.

Jake walked over to the counter, and Colleen followed.

"Have a seat. How about a glass of wine?"

She accepted, and there was silence except for the background music as he poured a glass of wine for her and opened a beer for himself.

"Nervous?" he asked.

She shrugged. "I've never really done this before."

"Had a glass of wine with a guy?"

She glanced over at Adele. "Had a glass of wine with my," she started to say something, then hesitated, "friend while my daughter is here as well."

"Well, we're just two friends having a relaxing dinner together. Would it be weird if it were you and Lydia or you and Ellie?"

"Of course not," she answered quickly.

"It's just dinner, Colleen, I promise, nothing weird."

"It's a slippery slope, Jake. Especially when there is a child involved."

"I understand," he said evenly. He didn't want to tell her that it was the whole point of having her and Adele here together. The little girl had already won his heart, and now he just needed to make sure Colleen understood his full intentions toward them.

"I don't want her to think . . ."

"That a guy should be able to cook?" he asked and was rewarded with a flicker of a smile.

"A false sense of family," Colleen corrected, her

voice low.

"Families come in all shapes and sizes, Colleen, and like I said, it's just dinner and a movie. So we happen to have a chaperone," he said and looked at Boomer who was on her back getting a stomach rub from Adele. "Make that two. I think I can keep my hands off of you for one night."

She nodded and took a sip of her wine.

"So how was your day?" he asked, just when he saw that she was relaxed. Her eyes widened, then she accepted that he was joking.

"Smashing, and how was yours?"

"Got the permits for a new house. Talked to the mayor about the Showhouse. Jax still thinks I'm crazy."

And so they continued while he made dinner, prepping the asparagus, the potatoes, and the steak. He stepped outside onto his deck to light up the grill, and she came with him. She talked about things, her life working in shops, some things about college. He noticed the holes, or the parts that she carefully skipped around, kept to herself. He knew that they must be about Adele's father. He let her have her secrets for tonight, aware that Adele kept popping in and out, peppering them with questions.

Adele deemed the steak *tres bien*. She liked the baked potato and adored the asparagus. The chocolate chip cookies, made from a tube of refrigerated dough, got fine marks, especially once he let her lick the spoon when Colleen wasn't looking. And then came the popcorn. He made a big bowl, salted and buttered, and they sat down on the couch. Adele sat between them with Boomer on her lap. He had the lights dimmed and the movie all ready.

"What's this about?"

"A dog and another dog," he said as the opening credits of *Lady and the Tramp* came on. He could see the smile on Colleen's face, and they all settled into the movie.

Colleen had finally relaxed, though she couldn't quite lose herself in the movie. Her mind was racing. Everything about the night had been perfect, simple, but perfect. Jake's cooking had been simple but perfect. Not trying to impress her, but she'd barely lifted a finger. So what if cookies came from a tube? Adele had just discovered the timeless appeal of cookie dough. Wait until she found out it came in ice cream. The popcorn, the movie, and the warm, comforting presence of Adele between the two of them was wonderful, too good to be true. Jake's arm had stretched across the back of the couch, but it hadn't quite reached her. He didn't seem upset by it or the fact that somehow Adele's feet had kept poking at him after she'd fallen asleep. At no point had he seemed upset or bothered by Adele's questions, the need to cut her steak up into small pieces or any of the hundreds of little complications an evening with a child inevitably included.

Jake had said that he wasn't trying to play family, but she couldn't let her guard down. Men didn't really want to play family, or, if they did, it was only to get to what they really wanted: something with no strings attached.

Jake couldn't be any different, especially with his reputation around town. He had said that he had made no promises, that he had raised no expectations, but Colleen wondered if he had ever done something as ordinary and simple for anyone else. Sometimes expectations were not created with expensive gifts and fancy dinners, but by the fact you were just there to tie a shoelace, to fix a simple dinner, to help with homework. She had grown up hoping for those things from her father. And he hadn't been around to give them. Her mother had tried her best, but she had been too devastated by the inattention from her husband to give much of anything to Colleen.

Colleen wouldn't let the same thing happen to Adele. Adele's father didn't want to be involved, and that was fine. Colleen was going to be enough for Adele, so that she would never miss the fact she didn't have a dad. Just as Colleen strengthened her resolve, she looked over at Jake. He was watching the movie, smiling, as if he were truly enjoying the cartoon world of dogs. She sighed, her heart heavy. A slippery slope indeed when you started to play house.

Adele made it almost to the end, before she fell asleep. Boomer had been out for most of the movie. Jake lifted the sleeping dog, and put her on the pink bed Adele had helped to pick out. Colleen was standing up, folding the blanket. She stretched, turned, and he was there. He bent down and kissed her, a real one. She returned it, and then they finally broke apart.

"Thank you," she said simply.

"I'll carry her down to the truck and drive you guys home," he said. It wasn't a question. He knew that Adele and Colleen liked to walk, but it was dark, and Adele looked very cozy.

"That would be great," she said.

Chapter 48

Colleen had added some Kenny Chesney songs to her playlist, in deference to her helpers. Ellie and Lydia were singing along, something about no shirts and no problems and while Colleen didn't consider herself a fan of country music she had to admit that there was something upbeat about the tune.

She'd been fretting about her to do list, all the things she needed get done so that shop was ready for the grand opening. Ellie and Lydia had stepped up and offered to help. So here they were, setting up the shop, with a bottle of Ellie's favorite white wine and some takeout pizza.

Colleen hummed along as she stacked packages of paper cocktail napkins, printed with elegant egrets, in the entertaining section of the shop.

Ellie had slipped off her high heels in favor of a pair of flip flops and was wielding the box cutter with expert skill, opening cardboard boxes and calling out their contents while Lydia dutifully noted everything in the computer inventory system Colleen had set up.

"Twelve linen tea towels," Lydia said.

Colleen took them from her and walked over to

the butcher block counter and set them out on a hand painted tray.

"Oh sugar, that sure does look good," Ellie drawled in approval.

"They look great with your candlesticks." Colleen said, throwing a smile at Lydia.

"Oh, stop it. It's the way you put everything together, Colleen. You sure do have an eye for it."

She smiled. She took it as quite the compliment coming from Lydia with her artist's background.

"It doesn't take much to recognize beautiful things. I wish I could create like you"

"Oh no, putting things together is just as much of a skill," Lydia insisted.

"I will say, this place is shaping up to be something spectacular. From what I've heard, used to be a true junk shop, just filled with odds and ends." Ellie said. She had run out of boxes to open and had pulled a stool up. She sat and had a sip of her wine.

Colleen sighed. "Phil was a bit of a hoarder. I never realized how bad it was until I first opened the door."

She shook her head. "My first thought was just to close it, hand the keys back to the lawyer and tell them to sell it as is. Let someone else deal with it."

"Why didn't you?"

Colleen thought for a moment. "I couldn't do that to Phil, of course. He wanted me to have this place, so I screwed up my courage and just started in. The sorting took a while, but somehow, as I went through everything I realized that the real treasure was the space. A blank slate that I could make my own."

She would never be able to say thank you to Phil, of course, but she couldn't stop feeling grateful to him, especially now that the transformation was just about complete. The gleaming floors, the smooth walls, the beautiful countertop and custom bookcases. It was all too perfect.

"It's better than I could have imagined it. Jake's quite the miracle worker when it comes to buildings."

"Your fellow did good work," Ellie said approvingly.

"And he's some fellow." Lydia said, taking a sip of her wine. "Multi-talented. Wood bends to his will and stalkers leave town. Sort of a like an old-fashioned marshal."

Colleen turned, not sure she'd heard correctly. She looked at Lydia, then at Ellie, who was giving Lydia a look that was clearly meant to get her to stop talking.

"What?" Lydia shrugged. "Don't tell me she doesn't know?"

"Know what?" Colleen said. She put down the candlesticks she'd been holding, straightened the towels even though they didn't need to be straightened. There was a tightness coming over her chest and suddenly it felt hot, way too hot in here.

"Oh darlin' it was nothing." Ellie said. She came over and put a hand on Colleen's arm.

"Doesn't sound like it was nothing." Colleen

looked at Ellie.

Lydia seemed unconcerned by the tension in the room, but then she'd helped herself to more wine than the rest of them.

"You don't think Charlie just disappeared on his own? Those kind never do." There was an edge to Lydia's voice and Colleen looked at her, concerned.

"Sorry. Just in my experience, jerks like that don't take no for an answer. He would have come back, Colleen. And maybe you wouldn't have been in a crowded bar, or I wouldn't have walked in. You would have been alone. You should have called the police, but you didn't want to."

"But..."

"No, Colleen." Ellie shook her head. "It wasn't nothing. Something had to be done."

"What?" Colleen said faintly. She had been aware that Charlie hadn't come around again, but hadn't given much thought as to why.

"Jake and Quent paid him a visit the morning after, made it very clear that he should do his drinking in some other place."

Lydia gave a little smile at the thought. "I can only imagine them all having a little sit down. All muscle and quiet menace."

""Look, darling, it wasn't anything much. Quent and Jake, well they didn't want you to feel hassled or worried."

"They threatened him?" Colleen said. She felt unwell, not sure of her emotions.

"Of course not. Just made it clear to Charlie that you had someone looking out for you."

"I don't need to be looked after." Colleen said.

"Of course you don't, but they are men, you know and well, Quent thinks the world of you dear, and he wouldn't want you to feel unsafe." Ellie was still patting her arm.

"Fine." Colleen took a deep breath. It was Quent's bar and he had a right to serve or not serve anyone. But Jake. Jake should not have gotten involved in this.

"You have to admit it's kind of sexy, Jake telling Charlie to stay away from his girl." Lydia sighed and her expression had gone a little dreamy.

"Sexy? It's overbearing. And sexist. And…" Colleen couldn't think of anything else to say.

"I think maybe you're overreacting."

Colleen threw up her hands. "Doesn't anyone think I can take of myself? I can, you know."

"Of course, you can," Lydia said. "You do more in an afternoon than most people do in a week. But you have to see it from Jake's point of view."

"What do you mean?"

It was Ellie who spoke. "Oh darlin' if we have to explain to you why he did what he did, then you have bigger problems."

Colleen sighed. She didn't know what to say, couldn't really think. She took a deep breath, looking at her friends. In the background, Sheryl Crow sang about having fun.

It was Ellie who brought them back. "Well, what don't we get back to work. Clean this place up."

"Finish the bottle of wine?" Lydia said hopefully.

Ellie laughed. "Only if you promise to sleep on my couch tonight."

"Deal."

Chapter 49

Colleen woke up, her head hammering. She blinked, groaned. Lydia and Ellie had left together, but Colleen had stayed behind a bit longer, fussing with things, trying to get everything just right. Really though, she was thinking about what her friends had told her about the way Jake had taken care of Charlie.

Part of her was upset. She rolled over, stared at the celling. No, part of her wanted to be upset that he'd seen fit to take care of things. But it was something she should have expected from him. There was no way he wouldn't have taken care of it. Taken care of her. She wanted to be upset about it, wanted to be mad at him for it, but she wasn't.

She rolled over and saw that the window was open. The white eyelet curtain was fluttering gently in the warm breeze. She listened, realizing that the pounding was coming not from her head but from outside. Sitting up, she pulled the sheet up around her. She could hear voices too, a deep, throaty one, that she was sure was Jake and the little girlish peal of laughter that was Adele's. She looked over at her watch and saw that it was after ten o'clock. How could she have slept this late? She was never this late. Luckily, Adele didn't have school today. Still, she had meant to go back to the shop for a bit, and her mother had agreed to watch Adele.

She got up, pulled on the light cotton robe to cover her nightgown and padded down the stairs, following the sound of a saw against wood. *What the hell was going on?* Opening the screen door, she took in the scene, silently watching as all of the other participants went about their work, too busy to notice her.

"Just what do you think you're doing?"

Jake turned, smiled. He glanced over, saw that they were alone and said, "I've been hoping to see you in your nightgown for a while. Just never thought it would be without me being able to peel it off."

Colleen frowned, wrapped her robe more tightly around her.

"Seriously, what is this?"

"I am repairing the stairs," he said, amicably.

"Why?"

"Because the boards are loose," he said, around the nails in his mouth. "Hey Adele, honey, hand me that tape measure, will you?"

"Sure, Mr. Jake," Adele said, appearing from around the corner, where she was holding Boomer's leash in one hand and the tape measure in the other. She had a sticky, slightly chocolatey-looking smile. Colleen could see the culprits were a box of donuts, set up on the plank and sawhorse work table Jake had set up.

"Donuts and lumber. That's quite a combination."

"Stairs were a hazard," he answered and now he looked up at her, stopping what he was doing as if he had finally gotten a bead on her mood.

"I thought I told you not to bother," she said, as Adele came over and sat on the upper step, the one that Jake had already replaced and took up a piece of sandpaper and began to carefully rub it along the length of the board.

"That's it, nice and long strokes. She's a good helper," Jake said, though he couldn't quite bring himself to look at Colleen. She wasn't pleased, and he could feel her disapproval radiating over them.

"I see. Adele, honey, why don't you go inside see if there is any lemonade, Mr. Jake must be getting thirsty."

"But we already had lemonade, Mommy."

"Then it's time for another cup, I guess."

"But . . ." whatever else Adele was going to say was cut off by a look from Colleen, and she rose and went into the house. She wasn't pleased and to show it, she stomped across the rickety porch and the whole house shook as the screen door slammed.

"I can pay you for this, if you just let me know what it cost."

Jake walked over to the sawhorses he had set up, took out his tape measure, marked the board and then lifted down the saw. He let it cut through before he looked at her.

"No charge."

"That's ridiculous. There's the lumber, and I see paint, and then there's your time."

"I work for free. And the lumber is scrap left over from another job."

"Don't."

"Don't what?" he said and laid his pencil down.

"Don't patronize me."

"Patronize you? I'm fixing your porch."

"But why? I didn't ask you to."

"True, especially since you'll barely talk to me. You ran off the other day and I haven't seen you."

"I've been busy," she said.

"I heard. Grand opening and sidewalk sale. Just thought that maybe you'd want a little help with it all."

"I can take care of myself."

He stopped and looked at her. "I was trying to do something nice for you," he said.

"Like beating up Charlie?"

"I didn't touch him."

She drew herself up straighter. "But you did talk to him, didn't you?"

"I did. I just wanted him to know he wasn't welcome around here."

"I don't need you to fight my battles for me, Jake. I'm a big girl."

"I know that." He said, but his voice was testy.

"I told you Jake, not to keep pushing it. First Charlie, then the porch."

"I am doing that for Adele. She tripped, you know, the other day and got a splinter."

"She's five," Colleen said by way of explanation. "She bumped her head at the playground too. I don't see you going there and child proofing the monkey bars. Admit it, you're trying to become involved with us."

"Dammit, Colleen, It's just a porch," he said, but knew his face was showing too much. She seemed to see it too, because she looked at him, long and hard and then took a step away.

"You're going to get hurt, Jake. You're asking for more than I can give."

"It's a porch."

"Fine, it's just a porch. But what's next? Are you going to get up on a ladder and fix the roof?"

She laughed when she saw the expression on his face. "You were, weren't you? Why do you have to take care of me? Why do you want to?"

He took a step closer, swallowed. "It's just a porch."

She shook her head and darted around him. "You keep telling yourself that, Jake, otherwise you're going to get hurt. I warned you."

"So what if I want more? I think things are going great, and you keep pulling back from me. I think we have something together."

"I have things to do."

"I know, the big day's coming. You've got this, Colleen."

"Why do you have to be so nice?" she said and sagged against one of the columns, trying not to notice how it gave slightly with her weight. He was right, the whole house needed fixing, more than she could possibly do herself. Why couldn't she just let him help her?

He came over to her and put his arms around her. She didn't try to pull away, just pressed her head into his chest.

"What, you only go for the bad boys? The ones who take you to bed and leave? There's nothing wrong with nice. Nothing wrong with a guy fixing your steps, or a leaky roof, or telling a creep to buzz off. When people care about each other, that's what they do for each other. There doesn't always have to be a quid quo pro, you know. Sometimes I do nice things for you; sometimes you do nice things for me."

"I don't have anything to give you," she said simply.

He took her by the arms. "I just want you."

She started to say something, but he cut her off. "I know you're a package deal. You and Adele. I don't have a problem with it, and I don't know why you do."

"Jake," she started to say, but he hushed her.

"Don't push me away, Colleen. Tell yourself it's just a porch if that makes it easier and we can take it from there."

She stood there in his arms, trying to push her misgivings away, wondering if she would ever be able to give Jake Owen what he truly wanted, or if she was just too damn scared.

Chapter 50

Time both sped up and slowed down, in the final days before the grand opening and sidewalk sale. Colleen anxiously watched the weather, hoping and praying for clear skies. Jake told her not to worry and gave her some convoluted explanation that seemed to take into account the number of duck nests and cherry blossoms. Finally, he told her that he had asked Madame Robireux for a prediction, and she foretold nothing but sunny skies. Jake was right, of course, at least about the weather. They had reached a truce, as she saw it, when he was around but not too much. He was busy too, finishing up a few jobs and making plans for the Showhouse. He had stopped by the store to drop off some flowers, swung by Quent's, even gone with them to the playground, but he had said nothing more than pleasantries.

She knew that it couldn't go on like this, that he wasn't happy with the situation. She appreciated that he was giving her space, even as she admitted that he had wormed his way into their lives. For her part, Adele was ecstatic every time she was with Jake and the dog. Boomer had become her constant companion, except for the nights when she went to sleep at Jake's.

Colleen took a final look around the store. It was as ready as it ever could be, she decided. She had forgone the sidewalk tent, wanting instead to draw people into the space, to see the transformation from Treasure Emporium to *La Belle Vie*. A small table, placed near the door, a piece she had refinished herself and embellished with some *trompe l'oeil* handiwork, held cups of lavender lemonade, while extra copies of her book were piled near the cash register. All the displays were in place and the inventory stocked. She took a deep breath, closed her eyes, and opened them. She smiled, letting the ball of tension wash out of her. This was everything she had dreamed it would be and more. It had come out perfectly: her store and the start of a real life for her and Adele.

She took a step outside, breathed in the warm, sunny air. Tents and pavilions were stretched along High Street, the merchants out and about, doing as she was doing, checking and fussing over their displays with last-minute pride. Now all they needed were people to show up. Shelby, the manager at the Osprey Arms, had told her that they were all booked up, so she had to figure that everyone was getting up, eating their eggs and toast, sipping their coffee while they pored over the maps she'd had made up, highlighting all the different storefronts.

There was an early rush, as shoppers made their way around. And now, just before lunch, a bit of a lull had settled in. She took a breath and tapped a few numbers into her calculator. Yes, it had been a good morning. She had sold candles, some shirts, a few pairs of earrings, and twelve sets of tea towels. She smiled at that as she straightened the scarves draped with what she hoped was Parisian chic around the old tailor's mannequin she had found in the basement and then checked on pots of lavender she had made up, right next to the soap the Spillways Farm had brought her. She checked and double-checked prices.

"Well, well, what do we have here?"

Colleen stiffened, then told herself to relax her shoulders. It was just Amy Waters, trying to make trouble.

"What a lovely day to be out shopping," Colleen countered, even as she was overpowered by the scent of expensive perfume, too heavy for this spring day. Amy, model thin, dressed in tight white jeans, a sleeveless blue and white shirt, walked into the shop. Colleen was reminded of what Lydia had called her: a Stepford wife. Colleen thought Amy looked too angry to be a robot, but there was something so tightly drawn about her that Colleen wanted to give her a lavender sachet to help her chill out.

"And what a charming little place this is," Amy said and sniffed as she started to wander around. Colleen fought back her irritation. She was tired of everyone referring to this as her "little place." It was a real-life, brick-and-mortar business, with a profit margin and operating capital, business cards, and even a website, for goodness' sake.

"You should check out the ceramics," Colleen said smoothly. "They're by the artist Lydia Snow. She has pieces at The Met and is represented by the Norman gallery in New York and London."

Amy actually lingered for a moment in front of the selection of Lydia's pieces. She had given Colleen a few more pieces, and they were all stunning. Already a vase and a bowl had sold, and Colleen was betting the candlesticks would go before the end of the day.

In a monotone voice, Amy said, "You know he won't stay. You may think he will. Maybe he'll fix your sink or put together your bookshelves, talk about the house you could live in someday, but he won't have any intention of doing it. He'll just build up your dreams to crush them. You don't know what he did to me and my daughter."

"What?" Colleen said. She wanted to say nothing, to not react, but she couldn't keep it in.

"Oh, I guess he just told you his side of the story. That it didn't work out? We were going to get married. And then he just changed his mind. You can't trust him. Like I said, you think he's in there, playing daddy, playing the good boyfriend, and then some other broken thing will catch his eye, and he'll need the protect her, not you, and leave you high and dry."

"Look, Amy . . ."

Amy didn't let her finish. "You'll get what you deserve. Your type always does."

Colleen watched her go, for once, completely speechless.

She tried to put Amy's words out of her mind, even as she concentrated on the flow of customers. The candlesticks sold, and she had a request for a few more. She was ready to close up, wind down, rest her tired feet when she heard the tinkle of the bell, somehow knew it was him before she really saw him. He was grinning.

"I was going to bring you champagne. Haven't seen this place so crowded in years. I think all the merchants are locked away, counting all of the money they made. What an amazing job."

Normally she would be thrilled at his words and with seeing him. He looked handsome, and his words and manner were charming, irresistible. He stood inside the door of the shop in his work boots, khakis, and polo shirt. His hair was neatly combed, and his blue eyes twinkled. Everything about him screamed good guy, but she hadn't been able to get what Amy had said out of her head. Thoughts about how she had let him into their lives, how she had violated her own rules about not getting involved, swirled.

It was making Colleen sick to her stomach to realize that she may have betrayed her own interests, and, worse yet, her daughter's.

He came to her, as if he was going to swing her up into his arms. She held up a hand, flat, so that he almost ran into it, and said, "Are you going to tell me about what went on between you and Amy Anderson? Or is she treating me like this because she is still holding a grudge about that essay?"

Jake looked at her uneasily, then finally answered, "It's me she doesn't like. We dated."

"I could tell."

"I thought it was pretty clear that it was a casual kind of relationship, but I think she had other ideas. I mean in high school we dated, I mean before you, and then about five years ago, she came back to town, and, well, we took up again. I think she wanted more than I wanted to give."

"Like what?"

"You know: marriage, kids, the whole thing. It's what she wanted."

"She has a kid," Colleen said, thinking about the math of the whole thing.

"Mackenzie's not my daughter," Jake said quickly.

"I wasn't accusing you of that," Colleen said. She knew that wasn't the case. At least no one around town had said that. Amy was married to a man named Chad, who seemed like another nice guy, maybe a little mild-mannered, a little in awe of his wife.

"I thought we had broken up, and she was okay with it. Apparently she wasn't as clear on that as I was. She came to me and said she was pregnant. And that it was mine. I was pretty certain it wasn't. Things got contentious. But let's just say we all know for sure who the baby's father is, and it's not me. Chad is Mackenzie's father and he wanted to marry Amy. Be a family. That should be that."

She swallowed. "You sound pretty callow about the whole thing."

"I'm not. She tried to . . ." he started to say, but stopped.

"Trap you?" Colleen said.

"I made it clear from the beginning, what it was, what we had."

"And it was . . . ?"

"Casual. She thought she could change me."

"But you don't want to be changed, do you? Are you going to go around and chase girls for the rest of your life?"

"You're putting words in my mouth. Look, you're the one who keeps pulling back from me," he said.

She stopped, struck by the accusation.

He went on: "I want more, Colleen. I have always wanted more with you. That's why it never worked with anyone else. I know that now. Maybe I always knew it, and now you're here, and I want all of you, and you don't want me."

Colleen felt her stomach churning and her breathing grow more and more shallow.

"Breathe, Colleen, you don't need to panic because someone says they care for you," he said, looking at her intently.

Colleen knew that if tried to touch her, her resolve would break.

"What do you think of me?" she asked quietly. She had to know.

"What?"

"Do you think I tried to trap Adele's father?"

"What? No. Did you deliberately get pregnant so he'd marry you?"

She laughed, but it was bitter. "Adele was definitely unexpected. By the time it happened, it was pretty clear Olivier was on his way out of the picture. I never asked for anything from him. But I took his money. For her. And before that, I took the job he offered, and the apartment . . ." She trailed off, wondering what he thought of her.

"It's different."

"Why?"

"Because you're different. Trust me, if that child had been mine, I would have taken responsibility for her."

"Would you have married Amy?"

"I didn't love her. I don't love her. That would have been wrong, don't you think? I would have provided for that child, I would have been a parent to that child. But I wouldn't have married someone I didn't love."

He took another deep breath. "But if I had loved Amy, and she had a child by another man, then guess what. I would love that child too. Because it would be a part of the woman I loved."

"Jake, I can't," she managed to say. Suddenly things were closing in, and she was feeling trapped.

He started to take a step forward, but must have seen the panic on her face because he took a slow and deliberate step back. "Colleen, I know what you mean to me. What you have always meant to me. There is room in my heart for you and your daughter. There. Let it settle in."

The bell tinkled again, and she half turned. More customers, she thought, now of all times.

"I'll be going now," he said, moving away.

She nodded, then took a breath and focused. She had work to do.

Chapter 51

Amy wasn't that hard to find. She looked up from where she was sitting on a bench, watching her daughter play on the swings when Jake sat down. He didn't want to loom over her, figured this would be easier if they could keep it casual, friendly.

"You look like a man who could use a little pick me up," she said. Her hand reached out but he caught it before it could graze his arm.

"Don't try it," Jake said. "You have a husband. And it's not me. So go home to him." It was blunt, but maybe he hadn't been clear about it before this. She needed to know that there was nothing between them, and that, more importantly, she couldn't come between him and Colleen.

"I don't ..."

"Amy, don't say something you'll regret. I am not her father. He is. You made your decision. Think about what you're doing to Chad, to Mackenzie. Chad is a good guy. He's a great father. Don't throw that away."

"But I don't love him," she said, her voice low, plaintive.

"And I don't love you. Either way, you're screwed. Maybe you and Chad won't work out, but you should give it a try. Get over me." It was cruel and God knows he didn't like to be cruel, but he couldn't let Amy see this as an opening, not when he knew she had a family. Chad was a man who, despite everything, loved her, and she had a little girl who loved her too.

"You're a parent. Don't be selfish," he continued. If he had learned anything from Colleen, it was that a parent needed to do what was right for their child. Even if doing that meant putting what they wanted aside.

Colleen saw them, she could hardly help it. She stopped at the entrance to the playground, scanning for Adele, who was with Josh and Lydia when her eyes were drawn to where Amy and Jake sat on the bench, their postures tense, angled toward one another. She drew a deep breath. So what if Jake and Amy talked? He didn't seem to be enjoying it.

Suddenly someone tugged at Colleen's hand. She looked down. Mackenzie Anderson was there, tugging at her. Next to her was a man wearing khaki shorts, crisp polo shirt, and sunglasses. He looked nice, and from the way Mackenzie was holding on to him, she figured this must be her dad, Chad. Colleen had to smother the slightly hysterical laugh that almost bubbled up at the thought of the rhyme.

"Where's Adele?" Mackenzie asked her. Colleen looked up and saw that Chad too was watching his wife with a look she couldn't quite read on his face.

"In there, with Josh," she said automatically.

"Daddy, will you take me in?" Mackenzie asked and looked at her father who broke off from staring at his wife.

Colleen saw the smile Chad gave his daughter, full

of love and adoration. "I would love to go to the park. But only . . ." he paused, and Mackenzie watched him intently. "If you let me go down the slide too."

Colleen fought the lump that had risen in her throat. Chad obviously loved his daughter. *What more could a mom ask for?* She glanced at Amy, who was watching Jake walk away, a look of hurt and fury on her face.

"Hey pumpkin," Chad said, "why don't we start with the swings? Mom can join us later."

Colleen eased herself back from the park entrance, knowing it was cowardly and walked away. She'd text Lydia and ask her to bring Adele back to the house. For now, she just couldn't face Amy, Jake, or, maybe, even her own daughter.

Chapter 52

J ake stalked off from the meeting with Amy at the park. He fumed his way down the streets of Queensbay until he found himself in front of the pub. It was on the early side for a drink, but despite his best efforts, he was free to do as he pleased. No one needed or expected him. No one wanted him, except the wrong person. Colleen didn't need him, and he realized that he was okay with that. He liked her independence, the fact that she had built her life back up all on her own. It was her stubborn refusal to realize that they were meant for each other that was frustrating him.

"What are you doing here?" Quent boomed. He was standing in the mostly empty bar, wiping glasses with a towel. Ellie was there as well, a glass of sparkling water in front of her. Midnight Oil played on the radio.

"Give me a drink," Jake said as he slid onto a stool.

Quent pushed a beer toward him and slapped down a vinyl-covered menu. "It's happy hour. Order something," Quent said, as if reminding him that if he were going to take up a bar stool, he'd better order something more than a beer.

Jake pushed it away and said, "Burger." He wasn't really hungry but he didn't want Quent to bother him.

"Coming right up," Quent said, and he moved down toward the end of the bar.

Jake watched the bubbles fizz up in his beer. He wasn't really thirsty either, but what else was a man supposed to do when the going got tough besides have a beer and eat some fries. He loved Colleen. He didn't understand why she didn't love him back. She did like him. He could feel it; he knew it from the way she was with him. When they were together like that, things were perfect. It was everything else. He couldn't buy her a damn cookie without her accusing him of trying to bribe her. It was true that he wanted to help her and Adele. Something about them tugged at him.

"Girl trouble?" Quent asked laconically as he put the burger down in front of Jake. A bottle of malt vinegar appeared even as Jake reached for the ketchup.

"Why do you think that?"

"Because you're drinking alone in the daytime. It's the sign of a desperate man."

"Takes one to know one," Jake muttered as the ketchup poured out. He pushed the fries around so that the ketchup made a little pool.

Quent glanced down at Ellie who had stealthily slid up next to Jake.

"You and Colleen have a dust-up?"

"Something like that," Jake said. He still wasn't sure why she was angry with him. He'd kept something from her; that was true, but it hadn't seemed relevant at the time. He didn't pry into her past, did he?

"What do you know about Adele's father?" he asked Ellie as she snagged one of Jake's fries.

"Not much," she said. "Sounds like a real piece of work, though. But she won't talk about it."

"Her own dad was a loser," Jake said. The whole town had known it, how Sean McShane had breezed into town, gotten nice girl Maura Higgins knocked up, married her at the proverbial end of a shotgun, and had proceeded to booze and womanize his way through town until he'd hit the road as some sort of traveling salesman. The whole town had looked with pity on the sad, sad story of the McShanes as a cautionary tale of a good, hard-working family slipping down the rungs of respectability. It hadn't helped that Maura hadn't coped well with her husband's failings. She'd been a drunk for a while, everyone knew that, just as they all knew she'd kicked the bottle and gotten a job as a nurse.

Colleen had always been looked down on, even as she had racked up the accomplishments. Sure, Colleen had won spelling bees and art contests, gotten straight A's, been a cheerleader, but none of that had stopped them from whispering about her. She was the girl from the wrong side of the tracks, and there were plenty of people in Queensbay who hadn't wanted to let her forget it.

"I never cared about any of that," he said almost to himself.

"Any of what?" Ellie asked, taking a sip of water.

"Colleen had it rough growing up. Not her fault, her parents', but somehow the blame always fell close to her."

"Happens," Ellie agreed.

"But she showed them all. Just kept proving them wrong, but still it was always 'that Colleen McShane girl.'"

Jake shook his head. Even he'd been thinking about it at prom night, when he'd found her. Even though he knew her, knew she could draw and that she could name the artist of any picture put in front of her, knew that she read both Jane Austen and Stephen King. He had found all of that out during their sweet, brief time together. And she was just Colleen to him, and he was amazed by her, all of her.

"She dumped me," he said, pushing his plate away. He wasn't hungry. Wasn't really thirsty either, with the way his stomach was twisted up.

"What, back when you were kids? I don't think you should hold that against her. Sounds like she needed to focus on getting the hell out of Dodge," Ellie said.

"No, I think she did it again, today." He said and put his head in his hands.

"Well, if you only think it, there's probably some wiggle room."

"What?" He looked up.

Quent was there again polishing a glass. Ellie traded a look with him, and it was so full of affection and happiness that Jake wanted to break something.

"If you're not sure, you probably have a second chance," Quent agreed.

"She has trust issues. And daddy issues," Ellie said.

"I've never been anything but there for her."

"The girl's blind," Ellie said. "I know. You built her store, fixed her steps, bought a puppy for her daughter."

"Boomer is my dog."

"Oh please, sugar, everyone knows why you bought the dumb puppy. Because Adele looked at you with those big eyes of her, and you were a goner."

Jake shrugged. The McShane girls had gotten under his skin. He had thought about the future, and he wondered how he could fit a car seat in his truck. Or whether it might be time to kick the renters out of the house he had bought up in The Heights and start the renovation he'd been dreaming about. They'd need at least three, possibly four bedrooms, because Adele would want a brother or a sister. And, well, he hoped Colleen might want to have another baby someday. With him. That was the future he dreamed about with Colleen, evenings on their porch overlooking the harbor, watching the kids catch fireflies while the sun set over the harbor.

"I am not going anywhere. I am not Sean McShane or the Prince Charming she met in France. I'm me, Jake Owen."

"Darlin', I know that. And I think she knows that."

"What do I do, Ellie?"

"Give her some time," she answered. "She'll realize she's just scared. Girl's so broken she doesn't even know it. Every man has run out on her. Sure, she'll make it sound like she and Adele's daddy had an arrangement. That they were all grown up and sophisticated about it, but it's no doubt he made her plenty of promises he never intended to keep just to make sure she didn't run off on him. I am sure she doesn't love him anymore, but she sure feels abandoned by him. Trust me. I've been in her shoes. Doesn't know what she can trust or can't."

Jake nodded. A thought was coming to him about one thing that would, he hoped, show Colleen that he meant what he said. He pushed back from his chair, pulled some money from his pocket, and slapped it on the bar.

"Where you going?" Ellie asked suspiciously.

"Don't worry. Not to crowd her. I've got an idea."

Ellie and Quent watched him go. Ellie reached her hand almost unconsciously across the bar, and Quent, just as unconsciously took it, and pulled it gently to his lips, giving her a kiss.

"Think they'll figure it out?" Quent asked.

"I hope they will," Ellie said.

Chapter 53

"**W**hat is it that you're afraid of?" Ellie asked. Colleen sensed a point to be made lurked somewhere behind the offhand way Ellie asked the question while she swirled the lemon in her club soda with the thin red plastic straw.

"I'm not afraid of anything," Colleen said as she looked for the Grand Marnier. The I-just turned-twenty-one girl at the end of the bar was ordering fancy drinks just to prove how sophisticated she was. If she kept it up, she'd feel like hell in the morning, but Colleen was in no mood to lecture.

"Oh sugar, everyone is afraid of something."

"Like monsters in the closet? Okay, you will never find me camping. Did it once with the Girl Scouts and a bear came to our campsite and stole the hamburger rolls. I spent the whole night in my tent lying awake, listening to every nature sound and telling myself that I only needed to run faster than the girl sleeping next to me."

"Bears? I don't think there are many bears here. And fine, if you don't want to go camping, I get it. Trust me, you won't find me camping. We have air conditioning and walls for a reason."

"Amen sister," Colleen agreed and deposited the drink that was mostly cola and maraschino cherries in front of college girl, who was trying to impress the college guy who was drinking a gin and tonic. She wanted to pull the girl aside and tell her to stop laughing so hard at the guy's dumb jokes and that she didn't have to do anything with him just because he was buying her a drink. Colleen wanted to tell her to stay in school, to figure out how to code or program and start her own business. She shouldn't want or need a guy.

Instead, though, she took a deep breath and steeled herself. She couldn't go around preaching to every younger version of herself. Sometimes a person just needed to make her own mistakes.

Ellie wasn't done. "So what are you really afraid of?"

Colleen shrugged. It wasn't that she didn't have fears. She didn't like mice or spiders, but that was pretty routine as far as fears went.

"And I'm not talking about bugs and vermin. Or snakes. We're meant to be afraid of those, unless they're turned into cowboy boots, in which case you better be afraid of the fellah who wears them," Ellie said.

Colleen laughed and said, "Don't tell me you're afraid, even of those."

Ellie shrugged one elegant shoulder. She had gained a little weight, Colleen noticed, and it looked good on her. The gauntness was gone, and now Ellie looked like a commanding women of a certain age.

"I was afraid of being alone," Ellie said. "And of being poor. So afraid of being broke and alone that I made some questionable choices."

Collen shrugged. "Sometimes being broke and alone is better than the alternative."

"What?"

"Being with someone and miserable."

"Was that what you were? Miserable with Mr. Fancy Pants."

Colleen nodded. "Not at first of course, but when it became clear to me that I was never going to be a priority in his life, I started to think about who I was and how I ended up where I was."

"Who did you blame," Ellie asked. "Your mom or dad?"

Colleen stilled for a moment.

"Sorry, sugar, you don't have to answer it. None of my business. But sometimes until we can figure out why we did what we did, we can't really move on."

"Have you moved on?" Collen asked.

"I'd like to think I have, but maybe not. I still think about Bobby a lot, but now I remember the bad as well the good. I was beating myself up for how I lived my life, for all the mistakes I made, and then I decided, if I wanted to change, then I could. As simple as that."

"Can you?"

Ellie gave a wry smile. "Only if you really want to. Not saying it's easy. Just that the decision is simple. Follow through is a bitch though, and you're bound to fall off the wagon once in a while, but as long as you keep trying, you'll get there."

Colleen thought about what Ellie had said to her while she walked home after her shift. It wasn't too late, and the night was warm. She didn't know what to say to Jake, and it had seemed easier to avoid him.

But the avoidance had slipped into days of silence between them. She missed him, and that was the problem. Somewhere along the way she had gotten used to him being around, and he had become a part of the life she was starting to build with Adele.

He had walked out on her, part of her told herself. But it hadn't been like that, really. He had told he loved her and then given her space. What was she supposed to do with that? And she was pretty sure he'd told Amy Anderson to go to hell, given the way Amy glowered at her during pre-school pick up.

She came to her house, opened the gate, which swung silently on well-oiled hinges. Jake must have taken care of that, since it had been on her to-do list for days. She stopped, looking at the steps. There was a white piece of paper there, taped on, with the words "Wet Paint" scrawled on with a marker. She smiled, almost started to cry. He must have come while she was working, painted the step for her, taken care of the gate. She imagined he'd asked Adele to help and how patient he would have been while he showed her how to hold the brush, how to paint in long, even strokes.

Gingerly, she went up the steps, avoiding the wet one and sat herself down in one of the ancient rocking chairs. She needed a moment more to herself. *He was a good man,* she thought, as she rocked slowly and looked at the step. A good man.

Chapter 54

J ake took a good long, look at the house. He sighed, acknowledging that the view was the best thing about it. He'd meant to do more to it, but this particular project had fallen by the wayside, with all the other things that had been going on. The house was a sturdy Craftsman style that had once been charming but was now in dire need of new everything, inside and out. The roof, the porch, bathrooms, kitchen, plumbing, and electricity all needed replacing. But it had generously sized rooms, a master suite, and three additional bedrooms, and it was a good solid house. He had bought it from the previous owners, an older couple who'd finally had to move in with their family out of state. He hadn't done much with it over the last few years, which was good because it still boasted the original trim and some of the beautiful stained glass windows that were characteristic of the type.

What Ellie had said to him had gotten him thinking. Sure he'd been a good guy, doing all the right things. He'd thought Colleen would get the picture, but she hadn't because other people, particularly other men in her life, probably, had done some of the same things. Colleen had traveled, stayed in fancy hotels, dined in gourmet restaurants, but none of the past versions of him in her life had given her what couldn't be bought. She was afraid that she wasn't good enough for anyone to actually give her what she most wanted and needed: love and commitment, security and respect. She couldn't see it, but she was doing just fine on her own. Sure, he'd helped, but she could have hired any contractor for the store. True, he hadn't cashed her check yet, didn't intend to, but she had taken what she'd been given, a run-down junk shop and her vision had turned it into a first-class retail store.

All of those thoughts had gotten Jake thinking about what Colleen had said and what she had really meant. He knew he needed to show her, really show her that he wasn't going anywhere. He'd done all of the small things. Now it was time for the big one. He knew she would love the house. This was her favorite part of town; once, a long time ago, she had told him that, and had even pointed out this house to him.

He ran a hand along the wood railing of the porch. More solid than he had thought, which meant maybe he could just have it sanded and painted instead of replaced. He followed the porch along the whole front of the house. Good and solid. Inside was another story. Bathrooms and the kitchen would need to be completely redone. The floors needed refinishing, the walls repainted of course. The woodwork, if he remembered correctly, would need refinishing. Not a gut job, thankfully, but a thorough overhaul.

Jake took the steps down and walked around the side of the house to the back. The lawn stretched away from him, a good flat piece of land that sloped a bit before it dropped to the bluff. A stairway led down to the beach, but the view gave the house its million-dollar potential. Queensbay Harbor stretched out in front of him, the mid-morning sun and blue sky turning the water into a mix of sapphire and diamonds. A clean, light breeze ruffled his hair and stirred the leaves of the trees that helped to separate this lot from its neighbors.

A flagstone patio would be lovely out here, with a fire pit and some seating. A nice new grill and maybe even a countertop and refrigerator to keep the beverages chilled. Great for relaxing on summer evenings. She'd probably want him to string lights from the house to one of the trees. It would be nice to sit outside as the sun went down, hear kids running around looking for fireflies. He'd have to get a fence installed, a low one with a safety gate, so as to be sure to keep kids and dogs from heading down to the water unsupervised.

He nodded. Yes, this was a good house, and he could see it all coming together. Of course, there wasn't time to get it all perfect, and he was sure she'd want to have input. His crew could start on some of the basics, though. He pulled out his phone, fired off a few texts, and smiled. He loved it when a plan started to come together.

Chapter 55

Colleen finished her inventory while Adele sat on the counter, legs swinging. Adele was slightly miffed that they were working instead of going to the park, but Colleen needed to figure out what she needed to reorder after the success of the sidewalk sale.

"Can I have a cookie?" Adele asked.

Colleen almost said yes before she caught herself. "Nice try young lady, but didn't you have one yesterday?"

"That was yesterday," Adele said. Her eyes were big and solemn as if that settled the matter.

"I thought we agreed on half a cookie every other day," Colleen said. Darby's cookies were addictive, but they were also the size of Adele's head.

Colleen could see from Adele's expression that her mind was gearing up for a logical argument, but whatever else she was going to say was cut off as she caught sight of the man who pushed open the door and walked into the shop.

"Uncle Olivier!" she said, and Colleen turned as if in slow motion. Adele's little body had flung herself at him, and he caught her, giving her a little swing up into the air.

"My, my; let me look at you," he said.

Colleen felt cold suddenly, even though the shop was warm enough.

"You look *tres bien, ma cherie*," Olivier said. Adele was still in his arms, and Colleen couldn't see her face, but she could only guess that it looked rapturous. Olivier had that effect on females; she had to give him that.

He set her down, but Adele kept her hand intertwined with his. He turned and looked at her, and Colleen braced herself, waiting for it, the weak-kneed, stomach-leaping surge of excitement that had always accompanied his presence. She drew a deep breath. There was nothing. She still felt just the hint of annoyance, and now, she realized that she felt outrage as well. How dare he come here, to her town, without any warning? This was her town, her place. He had no right to chase them down.

"Colleen, you look wonderful," he purred. The accent usually got to her, made her practically swoon, but not today. It sounded fake, oily, and definitely not charming.

"Olivier, you're here. In Queensbay," she said. She had wanted to not sound surprised, not like an idiot, but knew she was failing. She needed to pull herself together.

"Charming little town," he said as he moved closer to her. He kissed her then, and she pulled away, but it was just the traditional European greeting, one kiss on each cheek, and she relaxed just a fraction.

He took her hand and looked into her eyes, as her senses tingled, warning her that he was trying to seduce her. "So lovely, my two belle mademoiselles. I have missed you. You said you would only be gone a little while, yet I find that you have a shop here, like you intend to stay, no?"

"Why are you here?" she asked.

"How long are you staying?" Adele asked at the same time.

Olivier smiled the smile that used to make her want to jump in bed with him and stay there all day. "For a little bit. I have some business that brought me to New York, and I realized this little town, this Queensbay, wasn't so far away, so I thought I would stop by and say hello."

"You're going to stay for a while?" Adele asked, and the hope in her voice was almost too much for Colleen to hear. She didn't stop to think about what her own thoughts were doing, the tumultuous brew of anticipation, excitement, and now dread that Olivier's presence elicited.

"For a while, *ma petite cherie*. Tell me, what do you do in this charmingly quaint town?" he asked Adele, but Colleen could see that it was directed toward her.

Olivier walked around the store, taking it in, Adele's hand still clutched in his, and Colleen found herself holding her breath. She hated herself for it, hated knowing that she was eager to know what he thought. It was her store, her life, her town. She should not care one whit what he thought.

"Ahh, *tres bien*. It reminds me of the shop on the Rue de la Nord, the one where we found the mirror."

"Yes," she said, letting out her breath. "I was trying for that. The way the space was open, with the light pouring in. Unfinished, but with a touch of the grand."

"Simple and elegant. I see you have some new

pieces in here as well?"

She nodded. "I've been adding some of my own pieces. They are being very well received."

"So business is good, *mais oui*?"

Adele pulled Olivier over toward something, but not before he gave Colleen a look. It was assessing, approving, and, yes, just a little bit sexy.

The bell tinkled, and she turned to greet the customer.

"I got your text, thought you ladies might like some lunch," Jake called out as he walked in, a box from The Golden Pear Café in one hand and a cup of coffee in the other.

Olivier, his timing impeccable, as always, rounded a display at that same moment. Jake stopped in his tracks, taking in the way Adele was wrapped around him. His face went blank, and Colleen could almost have kissed him right there for his understanding. She had texted him a simple thank you after she had found her porch step painted. And he had texted back. And now, here he was, bringing her lunch.

"Mr. Jake," Adele said and detached herself from Olivier to give him a hug. He managed to ruffle her hair with his hand without spilling the coffee or tipping the box.

"I didn't know you had a guest or would have brought another cup," he said as Adele went back to Olivier's side. He handed the cup of coffee to Colleen.

"Thanks. Jake, this is Olivier Martell. Olivier, Jake Owen."

Jake leaned forward. He didn't exactly tower over Olivier but Colleen couldn't help to note the contrasts between the two. Olivier, slim, elegantly dressed, very European and Jake, in his work boots, khakis, and polo shirt, the one that displayed his all-American muscles.

Olivier wanted to wince, she saw that, as Jake took his hand and shook it.

"Uncle Olivier is visiting, and he's going to stay for a while," Adele said, flitting around, and only her natural grace kept her from knocking over a display of vases.

"Uncle Olivier," Jake said, and Colleen shot him a warning look.

"Yes, quite a charming town. Adele was just telling me all about you."

"Yes, Colleen and I go way back."

"Really? She never mentioned you."

Colleen decided to step in. This wasn't how she had envisioned her next meeting with Jake going, but she needed to avoid any sort of scene while Adele was watching.

"Are the pastries for here?"

"Yes, I was getting a box for the office, and I picked one up for you. It's on me. A thank you to a customer."

"Customer?" Olivier's voice was curious.

"I work in construction. I fixed up the store for Colleen."

"He let me help," Adele chimed in, from where she had taken the box to the counter and was examining the contents.

"So you're a handyman?"

Jake laughed easily. "Something like that," he said.

Colleen interjected. "Jake is being modest. His

owns one of the largest construction companies on the coast."

"Still, personally fixing Colleen's shop. How nice. Please, send me the bill."

Smoothly, Olivier pulled a business card from his pocket and tried to hand it to Jake.

"No need," Jake said and waved the card away. "Colleen and I have already settled up."

Olivier looked between the two of them, and Colleen found herself seething. She wasn't particularly pleased that Olivier was here, but she certainly didn't like how she was becoming the object of a pissing match. Olivier had no claim on her, and Jake should know that he had nothing to worry about.

"Still, in case anything else needs fixing, please be sure to call me first," Olivier said and held out the card.

Jake's curiosity must have worn out. He took it without a glance and stuffed it in his pocket. Colleen wanted to scream in frustration. Most of all she wanted both of them to go and leave her in peace and quiet. It was disconcerting to have the two of them here, in the same place, as if her past, present, and future were colliding.

"I am sure Colleen can figure out what needs to be done. Must be going. Got some things to be handy with, you know."

Jake made his escape, but the look on his face was stormy. Colleen was about to run out after him and make excuses, but stopped herself. She hadn't invited Olivier here. She didn't want him here, but he had a right to see Adele. Of course he hadn't seemed that interested before now, but she pushed that traitorous thought out of her head. Olivier was here now, and she couldn't deny Adele the opportunity to spend time with him.

Chapter 56

C olleen stepped out of the car onto the brick walkway of The Lighthouse, an upscale restaurant, which was housed in the former Queensbay lighthouse.

"I am glad you agreed to go to dinner with me," Olivier said. He was waiting for her at the front entrance. He offered her his arm, and she took it, since to not do so would seem both rude and provincial.

The black Lincoln Town Car had arrived precisely at six-thirty for the half-hour drive up the coast. She had agreed to come to dinner with Olivier because she knew that the sooner she did, the sooner she would find out what he wanted. It was just dinner, at a restaurant, with dozens of other people. True, she hadn't realized he would have picked what the local papers called "the most romantic restaurant on the coast." He swept in, announced his name at the reception desk, and the hostess snapped to attention. The Lighthouse had a hushed and serene atmosphere. Cutlery clicked softly, candlelight flickered, and waiters in black vests and bowties moved fluidly among the tables.

They were led toward the back, to a small table for two. It was just central enough so that everyone in the dining room would see them together. Colleen knew that Olivier had carefully planned all of this. He was a big believer in appearances, and he wanted everyone to know that they were together. She let a rueful smile cross her lips. It was public yet intimate, and if pressed by his wife, he could claim that, true, he and Colleen had dined, but in full view of a dozen eyes. Subtle, clever, and totally Olivier. He wanted something, and Colleen braced herself for what was to come.

"I see they received my request for the champagne," he said as they were seated at the table. He checked the bottle, Colleen knew, to make sure it was the exact vintage he'd requested. Seeing it was satisfactory, he nodded for the waiter to pour a glass for her and then for himself. He lifted his glass, and she waited for the toast, wondering what he was going to say.

"To old times."

She nodded. "Cheers. To old times."

Their glasses clinked and she took a sip of the champagne. It was good, expensive, and she savored it as she leaned back and prepared herself for the show. He had obviously taken great pains with the evening, making all the arrangements ahead of time. The dishes paraded out before them without a menu offered for them to peruse. Even so, Colleen was aware that most of this wasn't even on the regular Lighthouse menu and knew she was being treated to the best he could offer.

Olivier talked about art, antiques, books, and work. He was charming, and it all flowed over her. She chatted back. He had been nothing all those years if not interesting. Still, when it turned personal, he didn't pry, just asked a few questions about her mother, the town, Adele and her schooling. She wondered about all of the things unsaid, and when he would get around to them.

After dinner, they walked out onto the terrace, overlooking the water, where it stretched out until it met the sky. The gentle breeze ruffled her hair and the silver sliver of moon kissed the water with its luminous glow. Restaurant sounds rose and fell behind them: laughter, the clink of dishes, while from below came the sound of the gentle lap of the water against the shoreline.

He took her hands. She realized that his seduction had been subtle. He hadn't tried to kiss her, had barely touched her. Instead, flowers had been delivered to the store and he had arranged the car, the dinner, and now a nightcap while they took in the amazing view. She realized this was no different than when she had first met him and his charm, carefully supplemented by money and sophistication, had swept her away. She had been blind and blindsided. Too young and too stupid to know where all of that was headed, but now, she thought, she wasn't the same person. So she waited, biding her time.

"I have been thinking, my darling, that I miss you. I miss what we had."

"What did we have?" Colleen asked. She was curious to see what he thought, how he characterized their relationship.

"Laughter, fun. Love."

"Yes. We did, and then you married another a woman and I'm a mother. It seems as if we aren't the people we used to be. We can't go back to what we had."

"There are many different kinds of relationships," he said softly.

She waited, wondering. He gave his most charming smile, even as he still held her hands. "I would like for us to find a way to be together more," he said.

"You're welcome to visit Adele anytime, but we would need . . ." Colleen started to say.

"Yes, someday, perhaps we can tell her who I am."

She kept the smile plastered on her face, but her heart dropped as he continued with his pitch.

"Would you like to open a store in New York for me?"

"What?" she said, taken aback. She took a deep breath, steadied herself.

"I think it is time Martell Antiques expanded across the ocean. You know our business, and your endeavor here is so charming, but really, here? A city is where you belong, not some place like this. I see great things for you in New York, with my brand name and capital behind you. You could manage it. I am negotiating the lease on the space now, and there is an apartment upstairs. It would be perfect for you and Adele. I am in New York frequently, so we would see each other, often."

So there it was. Olivier wanted to have his *gateau* and eat it too.

"Does Simone know about this offer?" Colleen asked pointedly

Olivier smiled briefly, then brushed off the mention of his wife.

"This is a business deal, with perhaps, some other benefits. Simone is not part of my business. You are, however, very good at what you do. My business is not the same since you left and I would hate to see you waste your talent here."

"So I get to be both your employee and your mistress?"

He paused, drew back as if offended by her blunt statement. She took her hands back, glad they were free.

Olivier, looked at her, considering if her words were merely part of a negotiating strategy. "Perhaps we could work out something more like a partnership. Some profit sharing, perhaps. I would of course hope that when I am in New York we could see each other outside of business."

"So you're bribing me?" she asked and smiled. She was starting to enjoy herself at Olivier's discomfiture at having his offer met with resistance.

"You are the mother of my child. I want to do what's right for you. I am offering you a chance of a lifetime. To build something."

"But the shop wouldn't be mine, would it?" she said, clarifying. "What happens when you get tired of me again? Or I get tired of you?"

"Tired of each other?" he said and gave a laugh as if the thought were impossible.

She waited and held her ground.

"My dear, obviously I am not tired of you. I cannot forget you," he said, and reached out and brushed a hand over her hair.

She didn't draw back but didn't feel anything. Her feelings for Olivier were clinical, dispassionate almost.

"Of course, I do not know what the future will bring, at least not in affairs of the heart, but I know that I miss you, and I know you must miss me and Paris and your life there. You gave it all up. I understand you were upset, but for what? To come back to this?" He swept his arm around taking in the whole of the grand scene, the water, the coast, and even the distant lights of Queensbay. "The village is charming, quaint, I give you that, but it is no Paris, no New York. You had big, grand plans once, my dear, I saw the fire in your eyes, and now you are settling."

"What I have done, Olivier, I have done on my own," Colleen replied stiffly. Okay, so maybe turning Phil's Queensbay Treasure Emporium into *La Belle Vie* was a far cry from what she had imagined her first store would look like, but she was slowly making it her own, on her own. Maybe she had had some help, but the help had come without strings. It had been freely given, as she thought of what her mom, Jake, Quent, Ellie, and Lydia had all done for her.

He ran a finger along the edge of her chin, lifting up her face so that she had to look at him. "Don't tell me you have become too fond of this place already," he said.

He made as if to kiss her, but she glanced her cheek away.

He stopped, looked at her, and then nodded. "Very well, you must think about it. I see. That is well. I will let you do so."

She ended the night after that and had him take her home, her head thick from the champagne, her heart feeling heavy with choice.

Later, she sat on the porch, curled up in her rocking chair, her hair up, out of her fancy dress and into a t-shirt and pair of comfortable pants. A blanket covered her bare feet, as the night, clear and beautiful, had just a hint of a chill to it. It was quiet, most houses in dim darkness as their inhabitants switched off their televisions and reading lights and settled into bed.

Colleen couldn't sleep, hadn't been able to, though she had tried. Better to do something, so she had come outside to rock and brood. She had a cup of herbal tea, untouched. As she watched, she saw a brief flickering light in the soft darkness. She smiled. The first firefly. In a few weeks, the nighttime would be thick with them, swarms of them lighting up the trees like twinkly lights. Then the summer sounds would start: frogs, bugs, birds, and she didn't know what else, but it would be as loud as the *Champs d'Élysées* at noon.

Her phone buzzed. She looked at the email, debated whether or not to open it. Olivier had titled the email "Your New Store" and attached pictures of a storefront. She could just make out the street name, recognized and knew exactly where it was in New York. Big plate glass windows, charming stone architecture. There was indeed an apartment above it. She could imagine it now, her own store in New York. What she had always wanted, far away from the quiet, soft dark that was enveloping her now. She put the phone down, breathed deeply, and watched the first firefly of the season zig zag through the night.

Chapter 57

"**D**id you enjoy your date last night?"

Colleen looked up in surprise. She had been a thousand miles away, true, but all of a sudden she was back in line, waiting for her coffee at the Golden Pear. Jake's voice was loud and definitely angry. A few of the people sitting at the tables looked up. Colleen saw Darby behind the counter, the flash of reddish hair as she looked up to see what the commotion was.

"My what?"

"Your date with your ex?"

She sighed. "It was just dinner, Jake. I did tell you," she said, and she had, trying to downplay it.

"He took you to The Lighthouse," he said, his voice accusing, as if she had booked a trip to Cancun with him.

"He read an online review. It had five stars," she said in exasperation. Jake stood there, big and hulking with a hurt look on his face. Colleen glanced around. People were desperately trying not to listen, but she could feel the interest crackling in the air. The downside of living in a small town.

"Can we talk about this later?"

"No, we're going to talk about this now."

"I don't want to talk about it. It's none of your business."

"None of my business?"

"Jake, really. Olivier and I have a . . ."

"A child together?"

She stilled, and then saw red. "How dare you. I told you it's none of your business," she hissed. She could feel her face coloring as all around her people tried to pretend they weren't listening.

"He's no father to her. He won't even claim her. What'd he offer you, a chance to be his mistress again? He's never going to leave his wife."

She wanted to hit him. She stopped herself just in time. She was trembling, and she closed her eyes, as if she could block the whole thing out. She opened her eyes, and everyone was still there, and they were definitely staring. She turned and walked out the door with as much dignity as she could muster. She kept her face set, cold and hard, until she made it into the shop. She let herself in, locked the door and let the tears come.

"I am not serving you," Darby said. Her hands were crossed over her chest, and Jake could see she was good and mad, which was exactly how he felt as well.

"What do you mean?"

"You were way out of line, mister."

He jammed his hands in his pocket, his right hitting the little square box he'd been carrying around for days, before Olivier had showed up. The café had settled around them a bit, but he could feel the stares.

"You just outed her baby daddy to half the town, something not even Adele knows. And you basically called her a slut. Shame on you."

"But she can't go back to him," he said, his voice a furious whisper.

"You're assuming the worst, you know. She was just in, asking about the craft and antique fair in Nattick next month, whether or not it was worth it to get a booth. Maybe she was just having dinner with an old friend. Or discussing some personal business. Like it or not, as you mentioned, he is connected to her."

He took his hand from his pocket and ran it through his hair. "What should I do?"

"Do you really have to ask?" Darby said curtly. "But first I would tell this crew to keep their mouths shut."

He looked around and nodded. He could do that.

Chapter 58

"Next," the nurse said and smiled serenely. Colleen picked Adele up, realizing she was getting heavy as the little girl's head fell against her shoulder. She was half asleep, poor thing. She followed the nurse down the hallway past brightly painted murals of sea animals and zoo animals and into a small room.

"The doctor will be in shortly."

Adele whimpered, and Colleen held her close. She hated these moments, when she felt powerless to make it better. On the one hand she knew that it was probably just a fever, and that it would pass, but she needed the reassurance of a doctor's diagnosis to know that it would be okay.

The fever had built slowly, the first signs some unusually irritable behavior, then it had been the flushed cheeks and the complaints of a sore throat. Colleen had tried cool baths, lots of water, but the fever had kept rising. She heard that something had been going around Happy Faces, that half the class was down with something. When she had checked on Adele this morning, she was burning up and listless. Colleen's mother had suggested a trip to the clinic, just to be on the safe side and now, though Colleen knew Adele would probably be fine, she was filled with worry, the gut-chewing worry of a mother over her child.

The door opened. The doctor was younger than Colleen had expected, maybe even younger than herself. She wore light blue scrubs, with a white coat that said "Dr. Lynn." There was a stethoscope around her neck, and her hair was pulled back in a ponytail. And, if Colleen wasn't mistaken, there was a small baby bump hiding under the white coat.

"Hi, I'm Dr. Lynn, and who do we have here?"

Adele barely stirred at the sound of another voice.

"This is Adele," Colleen said, "and I'm Colleen McShane."

"Nice to meet you. I'm married to Jackson—Jake's business partner. I've heard a lot about you from Jax and Jake. Nice to finally meet you. I keep meaning to get into the new shop, but there always seems to be sort of emergency."

Adele's head turned just a little. Dr. Lynn had a warm smile on her face, but Adele was having none of it. She turned her head back toward her mother, and Colleen whispered to her.

"French?"

"Yes. We speak French at home sometimes," Colleen said wearily.

"I barely made it through high school French. My Spanish is better, though."

"I think as long as you were good at biology, you could speak pig Latin for all I care," Colleen said, realizing too late that it came out more sharply than she had intended. "Sorry," she added quickly. "It's just I've never seen her like this. She's usually in excellent health."

"Don't worry. Straight A student when it came to science. But I do need to actually look at her. Can you tell me where it hurts, sweetheart?"

The doctor coaxed and cajoled Adele into talking, and together they figured out that she had a fever, which was bad, but not too bad, and that her throat hurt, and that there were a few red bumps. Colleen braced herself, a litany of diseases from strep to chicken pox to the mumps wandering through her mind.

Finally Lynn looked up, smiled and said, "No strep or chicken pox. Just a regular old fever. A cool bath, some medicine, and you'll be good to go."

Relief surged through Colleen. Her baby was going to be okay. "That's so good to hear."

"I know it's hard when they're hurting, but fortunately this time around it isn't anything serious."

"It is nice to be certain," Colleen said. She began feeling calmer and asked, "When are you due?"

Lynn patted her belly and smiled. "I have a couple of more months. It feels like forever."

"Having the baby is wonderful but enjoy this time too. After the baby, it's all sleepless nights and constant worrying. Well, I mean, since you're a doctor, you probably won't worry as much as the rest of us."

"I don't know, you think you know what you're doing. I mean I've studied, read books, treated patients, but I guess it's different."

"We're all just fumbling around blindly."

"She looks like she turned out all right," Lynn said as she smiled and produced a lollipop from her jacket pocket.

"Now, this is only because you have a sore throat, but it might help a bit. And only if your mother says it's okay."

Colleen nodded, and Adele's hand reached out and took the lollipop.

Colleen carried Adele out of the exam room and into the waiting room, more because she wanted the comfort of her daughter close to her than because Adele couldn't walk.

Jake's long body unfolded itself from the small chair he had been sitting in.

"What are you doing here?" she asked in surprise.

"I heard Adele was sick, and you had to take her to the doctor."

"Well, she's fine," Collen said, more brusquely than she had intended. Adele was getting heavier by the moment. Maura had dropped them off at the clinic, but now she was at work. Colleen hadn't thought too much about how she was going to get home, maybe call a cab, or call Lydia. She needed to put Adele down and figure it out.

"Here, let me help. I'll carry her out to my truck and drive you home," Jake said, his arms already reaching out for Adele.

"You don't have a car seat, I assume?" Colleen said, her voice deliberately snippy. If he thought he could just waltz in her and pretend . . . She stopped. She knew Jake wasn't pretending.

"I don't but you weren't planning to carry her all the way home, were you?"

Colleen was silent for a moment, not sure what to say. There was a small, discrete cough from behind them. Lynn, the doctor, was there, and Colleen was almost certain that she was smothering a smile that she managed to make disappear.

"You know, we have an extra booster seat here. You could borrow it for the drive home, then return when you come back to work, or, you know, later ..."

"Really, we don't . . ." Colleen said, starting to protest.

"Colleen, it's a far walk, and half of it is up the hill," Jake said. His voice was firm, logical even. Colleen was boxed in. It would be easier for her to take Jake up on his offer, and if Lynn had a car seat, then she was just being stubborn if she said no.

"Fine," Colleen said, "and thank you."

"Well, nothing like being gracious about it," he grumbled.

"I'll go get the car seat," Lynn offered.

Adele's sleepy eyes opened and fixed on Jake. She held her arms out to him, and Colleen, surprised, watched as he carefully took her into his arms.

She stared straight ahead, with Adele safely strapped into the seat. Jake had carried her out for her, and Colleen hadn't missed the way her daughter had smiled and nestled up against Jake, and the way Jake had held her close and whispered soothing things to her that had Adele smiling and even laughing.

"I was just trying to do you a favor, you know," he said as he pulled away from the curb. "I don't know why you're all twisted up about it."

"Don't you," she said, though she kept her head turned out toward the window, as if watching the quiet streets of the village flash by could make her feel any less out of sorts. He didn't say anything else, and they rode the rest of the way in silence, Adele dozing again.

"This is fine. I can take it from here," she said when they pulled up.

"I'll carry her in," Jake offered.

Colleen said nothing and watched as he carefully lifted Adele and carried her in the house. Together they put her into bed, tucking her in. He waited, and finally they walked down the stairs and out onto the porch. Fresh air seemed like a good idea, and she didn't want the risk of Adele hearing what they had to say.

"I have nothing to say to you," she said. Her words hurt, but it was the look that she gave to him that really pierced his heart.

"I'm supposed to say I'm sorry," he said simply, "and I am. Sorry. I never should have confronted you that way. I just ..."

"Got jealous?"

"Something like that," he said and rubbed his hands through his hair and leaned against one of the porch columns. "It's more that ... he doesn't treat you right, didn't treat you right, and that makes me mad. You and Adele deserve more."

"We do?"

"He won't even admit that he's her dad."

She shook her head. "That's my decision. Mostly."

"What?"

Colleen sat down in the rocking chair, thought about how to say it. "Look, I grew up with this idea of a dad, one that would magically appear and take me to out to the boardwalk and buy me strawberry ice cream. He was rich and handsome and had a cool car. He would show up at the school plays and concerts and games and all of that other stuff. Just like all of the other dads."

She looked down at her hands, folded in her lap.

"But he wasn't like that at all. He'd come into town for a few days, spread a little cash around, make some promises, and then disappear. And finally when he did come back, it was because he was a broken-down drunk who needed money. I learned that it's the hope that kills you slowly. That the idea of a family, the kind of family I was hoping for, was just a fantasy. At the end of the day it would have been better if I'd just accepted the reality that I didn't have a father. It would have been better for my mom too. We would have been a family, the two of us."

"And now, with Adele you think the same," he said. "If he won't be the kind of father who's around, better for her not to think she has one?"

Colleen sighed, nodded, and said, "I think it's harder to miss what you don't have. She doesn't have an absentee father; she has a benevolent uncle who shows up occasionally with some gifts. No expectations, no commitment. Olivier is not a bad man."

She saw his look and amended her words. "He's not a great man, but he's up front about it. He could never be the type of father I would want him to be. He wouldn't be there, I know that. Adele needs to grow up not waiting for some fantasy, some Prince Charming to make everything right. That way when she is a grown-up she won't set her sights on the first man who promises to take care of her."

"Is that what you did?"

"It doesn't take a therapist to see that my relationship with Olivier had daddy issues written all over it. He wanted to and did take care of me: new clothes, better job, nice place to live. Plus, other things. It just took me a while to sink into it, and for a while it was nice to let someone just take over, or take away the worry. Everything was okay."

"And then?"

"There's a fine line between being taken care of and being controlled, between opportunity and being beholden."

"Now he's investing in you?"

"What do you mean?"

"The shop in New York. Is that an investment or an opportunity for control?" Jake asked.

"What do you know about that?"

"Let's just say he's been dropping hints all over town, about how you'll be leaving for New York soon." Jake looked at her and thought his heart might break if she left again, but he couldn't force the choice on her. "Is that what you want?"

She looked at him, and he couldn't read the thoughts behind her face.

"It's what you wanted," he said. "You stood here and told me that it was your dream. Your vision. How can this ever compare?" he said and couldn't look at her, not the way she was looking at him, only knowing this was what it felt like to have your heart broken.

"You've always been running away from me," he said finally and waited.

She didn't say anything.

"Fine. I'm not pushing you. Not yet," he said as he rose up off of the porch and stepped onto the walkway. He didn't look back, just walked over the cracked flag-stones and out of the gate and into the blinding sun. He fumbled, found his sunglasses, and jammed them over his face. Ten in the morning and already a crap day.

Chapter 59

T he bell above the door tinkled, and Colleen
looked up. Her expression relaxed when she saw
that it was only her mother.

"I brought you some coffee from next door. And
something for you too, honey."

Adele, who was mostly recovered but still not
quite ready for school, was coloring in the corner. Colleen had decided that a kid's corner was a good idea and
had set up a little table and chairs with coloring books,
crayons, puzzles, and some games.

"Cookie?" Adele said, lighting up.

"Half," Maura said, "because the other half is for
after my lunch."

"*Merci, Grand-mere*," Adele said.

"Just call me gran, okay, kiddo," Maura said.

"Thank you, Gran." Adele repeated.

Colleen played with some flowers she was trying
to make into an arrangement that looked both grand
and natural.

"Looks good enough to me," Maura said, doing
a circuit of the store. "Looks good in here. I've been
telling some of the other nurses about it, and the doctors too. It's good for birthdays and anniversaries. Also

that you decorate. Couple of new doctors getting hired, thought maybe they could use a little help with their bare bones apartments."

"Thanks, Mom," Colleen said, though she would have preferred if her mom recommended her to the head of the hospital, but she had to start somewhere.

"Course I might have mentioned there would be a family and friends discount if they mentioned my name, but I figured any business is good business."

Colleen smiled. That was her mother. Her mother moved restlessly around and Colleen waited.

"You know, there are good ones out there."

"What do you mean?"

"Men."

"Mom?" Colleen said.

"I am not talking about Mr. Fancy Pants. I am talking about Mr. Jeans and T-Shirt who fixes your steps because your daughter mentions she got a splinter and helps you with your shop and who decides that there's always a few apartments set aside at below market rates for those that need them."

"What?" Colleen brought her full attention to bear on what her mother was saying.

"I am just saying you could do worse than Jake Owen."

"You didn't always feel that way." Colleen stilled her hands, watching her mother warily.

"You were eighteen. You had the chance to go to college. I didn't want anything to stop you. And nothing did. Your path might have dipped and jumped a bit, but don't let the thought of what you were supposed to do keep you from doing what you want to do now."

Maura nodded briskly, and, having said her piece

she turned and left the shop without another word.

Chapter 60

J ake wasn't nervous. He wasn't going to let a guy like Olivier Martell intimidate him. And he was going to show Colleen that he was here for her and Adele. He had been officially invited to the Happy Faces Spring Show, and he fully planned on attending and keeping his word. So he found himself with the crush of parents, grandparents, aunts, and uncles at Happy Faces. He had sat in the back of the auditorium and clapped as Adele delivered her line with a gusto that hinted at future talent on the stage. He recognized Josh up on stage too, caught a glimpse of Lydia and the older gentleman who must have been her father. Further up in the auditorium he saw Colleen sitting with Olivier.

He hazarded a glance at Olivier. The man was bored, but smooth about it, with a smile plastered on his face, though he kept checking his watch. Once Adele had departed the stage, he gave up all pretense of watching and instead typed out messages on his phone.

And now everyone was milling about the hallway of the high school, for which Happy Faces had commandeered the stage. He wasn't about to go, not without seeing her, but he braced himself.

"What are you doing here?" Colleen asked once she saw him.

He looked between her and Olivier. Olivier was wearing one of those suits, one that probably cost as much as Jake's first car. And Colleen was wearing a dress, a beautiful dress, white with a pattern of branches and flowers. He noticed with just a little bit of satisfaction that in her heels, she was a little taller than Olivier, which probably bothered him. Olivier's arm snaked around Colleen, but she shook it off, almost unconsciously.

"You came?" she asked

"I made a promise to Adele that I would be here to watch the show," Jake said simply.

"How charming of you. We will tell her you came," Olivier said.

Jake shook his head. "If you don't mind, I'll just tell her myself. Plus I have something for her."

He held up a box. "It's a necklace. Silver, with a small seashell. Just for doing a good job. If you don't mind, of course?"

He deliberately looked only at Colleen for permission.

Her eyes were dark but her smile was clear. "She would love that."

Adele came barreling out of the crowd of kids and into her mother's arms. "Did you see? Did you see?" she asked, her voice happy and bubbly. She turned, looked at Olivier, and gave a squeal of happiness. "You stayed."

"Wouldn't have missed it, *ma cherie*."

She hugged him and then she caught sight of Jake. She looked at him and the grin that spread over her face melted his heart.

"You're here," and he too got a full-barreled, full-arm hug.

She smelled of glue, crayons, and her fruity shampoo. He hugged her, put her down, then pulled the gift from his pocket.

"What's this?"

"Your congratulations card and a little something from Boomer."

"I thought you said she would come too."

"Well, she had some important puppy stuff to take care of, but I wouldn't miss it for the world," he said and meant it.

"A promise is a promise," she said, dropping her voice and doing a pretty fair imitation of him.

"That's right."

"Do you want to go to lunch with us? Olivier is taking us to lunch before he leaves. He said I could even have a soda."

He looked at Olivier and Colleen. Olivier had drawn himself up to his full height but even with his hair he was a shade shorter than Colleen.

A bemused expression flashed across Colleen's face and then she settled it into her neutral, shopkeeper's face. He wondered what she had been thinking.

"Thanks for the offer, but I have a big house going up, and I need to check in on it. Another time, okay?"

"Very well then," Adele said seriously. "Can I take Boomer to the park tomorrow?"

He hesitated, almost looked at Colleen, but decided not to, so he nodded, smiled, and patted Adele on the shoulder so that he did not ruffle her carefully braided hair.

"Sure thing, kiddo. I'll see you around."

He looked at Colleen, ignoring Olivier. "I'll see you around too."

She nodded almost imperceptibly, and then he decided to go. He'd done what he'd set out to do.

Chapter 61

Colleen looked at the address on the card, then checked the house number. This was the right place, but it didn't look very promising. The house was a Craftsman-style cottage set in The Heights, the section of Queensbay high above the town on the hills ringing the harbor. Houses here were close together, but almost all of them had a water view. She sighed and smiled. When she was younger she had dreamed about living in a house like this. This one was a bit on the rundown side, with the beige paint peeling and a roof that needed repair. The porch was deep though and shaded, and she liked the iron railing that separated the yard from the street.

Adele looked up at her and smiled.

Colleen smiled back down at her and hoped that Adele's good mood would continue. It was a risk bringing her along on a client visit, but things had seemed to go wrong from the get-go today. Her mother, who had agreed to babysit, had been called into work. Lydia, who was to be her back-up, had a Josh emergency. Quent had offered, but she really didn't want to leave Adele in a bar for half of the day.

The referral had come from her mother, who had

seemed a little vague on the details, only that this was someone who loved her work and wanted to have her in for a consult and needed to meet her today. So Colleen had put on a "Be Back Soon Sign" on the shop door and pulled Adele up the hill to see what this was all about.

She pushed open the gate, which opened smoothly, as if it had recently been oiled. The grass had been cut, but the garden beds, what was left of them, were overgrown. Her mind started to think about the flowers that could go in those beds, and then she reminded herself she was an interior decorator, not a landscape architect.

Adele looked up at her and asked, "Are you nervous, Mama?"

"No, of course not," she told Adele.

"You will do fine."

Adele had taken Olivier's departure soon after the show in stride and asked no more about him. She had asked about Jake and Boomer, and Colleen had done her best to put her off, until, thankfully, she had stopped asking. Colleen knew she and Jake needed to talk, maybe she even needed to apologize. She missed him, knew she needed him in her life, and knew that maybe she was ready to talk about what the next step could be. She just hoped she hadn't waited too long.

She knocked on the door, but it swung open under her touch.

"Hello," she called tentatively because the house appeared to be absolutely empty.

They stepped into a hallway. Adele tugged her over to the side of the house, to what was probably the living room. It ran the length of the house, flowing, she thought, into a kitchen. A stretch of windows ran along the back wall, giving a view out onto the sparkling water of Queensbay harbor. Colleen caught her breath. It was beautiful, the kind of space she loved. Cozy, yet open, not grand, but just the right kind of place to turn into a home.

"Thanks for meeting me here." Jake's voice was unexpected, and she jumped.

Adele did not seem surprised because she ran to Jake who swung her easily up by her arms.

"Did I get it right?"

"You did good, kiddo. Boomer's over on the other side of the house. She has a new toy she'd love to show you. Why don't you two play for a moment while I talk to your mom?"

He put Adele down, and she ran off to find the dog. Colleen's hand went to her throat, and she forced it down.

"What is all this about?" she asked, looking at him, drinking him in. Yes, she most definitely missed him. He wore jeans and casual loafers with a white button-down shirt. Not quite his usual getup, but it still suited him, suited his solid dependability, his handsomeness.

"Thanks for coming to check the place out."

"Is this your place?" she asked.

He shrugged. "Sort of," he said. "I own a few buildings, you know, but this one is . . ." he paused and smiled. Her stomach flipped, then settled, as he said, ". . . special."

Jake took a step closer. "I'm glad you decided to stay."

"I was never going to go, you know. No matter

what he offered me. You..."

"I should have known that," he said. "You're right. I shouldn't have doubted you."

She put her bag down because of all a sudden it all felt heavy, too heavy.

"Actually, you should have doubted me. I've given you no reason to think I wouldn't run away."

He looked at her, the ghost of a smile on his face, and said, "I think you may have given me a few reasons to trust you."

"I kept pushing you away."

He took another step closer, and his voice was low. "So, tell me, do you still want to push me away?" he asked. "Tell me now, Colleen, and I'll never bother you again."

She didn't hesitate. "No."

"Good, because I'm not going anywhere either. You and I belong here. You and Adele and I belong here." He gestured around them, and she frowned, not quite understanding.

"Here?"

"In Queensbay, yes. But here in this house, together as a family."

"What?" Again, she couldn't breathe, but it was different this time. Not panic, but a sense of everything dropping into place.

"Before you yell at me, don't," he said. "If you hate it, we can look at other houses. I bought it a while ago as an investment, but I haven't had the chance to fix it up. It needs work, a lot of it, but it has a pretty sweet view. And it has enough room for the three of us, and some room to grow." His voice ended on a hopeful note. "If you're still mad about me taking care of everything and not respecting your independence, I'll let you chip in too. It will be our house in every way."

"Why?" she whispered fiercely. She was standing with her arms wrapped tightly around her torso, as if she were trying to keep herself from spilling out.

"Why is that so hard for you to understand?" he asked. "Part of me doesn't know why, just knows what I want. From the moment I saw you in that courtyard, sitting by yourself, I wanted you. Something about you then spoke to me."

"So you want to protect me? I don't need protection."

"I know you don't, but I still want to do it. You make me want to do it, even though I know you'll yell at me or tell me to get lost."

"Do you feel sorry for me? For Adele?" she asked.

"No," he said and shook his head. "I love you. I want to be around you and Adele. I love her as much as I love you."

"But why?"

"Because you're sexy and smart and beautiful and strong, and I cannot get you out of my head. All those other girls, all the ones you accuse me of loving and leaving them; I am guilty of that. I tried to get you out of my head, out of my system, but each and every one, I would think of you, of our brief time together, and never once did I feel what I felt with you when I was with them. Then I saw you here, back in town, and my whole life turned around. You were just as mean as ever, but I couldn't stay away."

She took a step closer to him, and he could feel her, sense everything about her, from the way the sun shifted through the window and caught the light in her hair, to her lips, cherry red, to the delicate skin that peeked through the v-neck of her light sweater. Her eyes, blue, crystal clear looked up at him.

"You're a good guy, Jake," she said.

"A good guy? That's it? The kiss of death." He almost took a step back, but she stopped him.

"I mean you're a good man, a really good man."

"Who loves you," he said. "I know that maybe I might not be the most exciting of guys, but this is a good place, a good life. We can have a good life here, now. And we can always have more."

"Would you give me a New York store?" she asked.

"If that's what you want," he said. "There are ways to do both. Just because this is how you start, doesn't mean that it's where you're going to end up. I started off doing home repairs, and now I'm turning the Showhouse into apartments. Nothing wrong with being ambitious. There's a whole life ahead of us; who knows where it will take us, except I want to do it together, all three of us."

Boomer barked, and Adele squealed in laugher. "I meant all four of us," Jake said.

"And you want to spend it with us?"

"Can you believe in me?" he said. "I will be there for breakfast and dinner, for birthdays, for holidays, day in and day out, I will be there. It may not always be exciting or sexy, but I will be there for you, for Adele, and for our family."

"More kids?"

"Say the word," Jake said, and smiled at her.

"Are you going to build playsets and toy boats and teach them how to throw a ball?" Colleen asked.

"Yes. I will take them shopping and talk to their boyfriends before I let them out of my sight and watch them dance at ballet recitals and cheer at soccer games. I will build you shelves and check the oil in your car and make you call me when you get to work, just because. You mean everything to me, Colleen McShane, you and your little girl."

"What are you asking?"

"Marry me."

"What?"

He dug into his pocket and pulled out a box.

"When did you get that?" she asked.

"About the time I started to think how perfect this house was for us. I went and saw Guy at Queensbay Jewelers. I guessed a bit, so if you don't like it, you can always take it back."

"Shut up," she said.

He held out the little black box. Her hand almost touched it, but he pulled it back, and said, "Wait."

"Wait?"

"I'll be back." He ducked round the corner of the wall and onto the other side of the house. She heard a whispered conversation.

She peeked around the corner and saw that he was having a serious conversation with Adele. At least he was serious. Adele looked like she was ready to jump over the moon.

He returned, and she composed herself.

"I had to take care of something first."

"You're awfully sure of yourself."

"I just asked her if it would be okay if I were around more."

"And she said?"

"Yes, of course."

He opened the box, so that the ring, a solid band of gold with, a beautiful, brilliant diamond, winked in the sunlight.

"Colleen McShane, will you marry me?"

"Yes" she answered, and she could feel the world around her settle into place.

THE END

Want More Queensbay?

Truly Yours – Lydia & Lance's Story is now available in ebook and paperback. You can find out more here – Truly Yours – A Queensbay Small Town Romance

Lydia Snow left behind a glittering career as an artist to - temporarily - take care of her younger brother in the small town of Queensbay. Now it's time for her to her return to her old life. But there's just one problem.

Her father has disappeared, leaving Lydia answering questions from the authorities about his whereabouts. Now she's the only person her brother has. With the FBI telling her to stick around, and people following her, Lydia has to wonder - just what was her father mixed up in? And how is she going to make this right for her brother?

And to top it all off, she's totaled her father's fancy sports car. Luckily help arrived in the form for a Good - and good looking - Samaritan. Lance Morgan is a true Boy Scout and from helping her with her fender bender to giving her newly broke self a place to stay, he's undeniably helpful - and attractive.

He's almost too good to be true. And if he knows what's really going on – that her father is an internationally wanted art thief on the run and that authorities think Lydia knows more than she's telling, will he desert her too? Or is he hiding a secret as well?

Read Truly Yours, Book 7 of the Queensbay Series to discover the power of hope, family and small-town ties. *Truly Yours – A Queensbay Small Town Romance – available in e book & paperback*

Read A Preview of Truly Yours

Chapter 1

Feeling giddy at the size of the check she had just received, Lydia Snow stepped out onto the sidewalk. She checked her watch and made two decisions: one, she was starving, and two, she deserved to treat herself to a cup of coffee and a chocolate croissant at the cute little café across the street from the Nattick Art Gallery.

Shivering as she stepped out onto the street, she looked up at the sky. The sun had been out all day, throwing heat and humidity in a last showing of summer, but it had disappeared behind a scrim of sickly yellow clouds. The temperature had dropped, and the wind was a wild breeze, swirling fallen leaves in a devil's dance along the sidewalk in front of the quaint brick and clapboard shopfronts. The air was cool and wet as if it were a soaked blanket she needed to push her way through.

A storm was on its way, maybe a big one. She paused, considering, then decided she had plenty of time for that coffee and croissant before she headed out along the coast, back to Queensbay, and her dinner plans with friends. Humming, she crossed the street and pushed open the door to the café, inhaling deeply at the scent of freshly roasted coffee and buttery baked goods. Her stomach growled just a little, reminding her she'd been remiss and hadn't eaten anything, only gulping a hurried cup of coffee that morning.

But she'd had good reason, she mused as she wandered up to the glass display case and took in the tempting bounty of carbs. The owner of the Nattick Art Gallery had called to congratulate her on her pieces selling out so quickly and ask if she had any more available. It had taken a moment for Lydia to remember what she had consigned to the shop—a set of candlesticks and several serving bowls, all in a cerulean blue glaze she'd developed and quickly become entranced with.

Believing it best to strike while the iron was hot, she had happily told him she had a few more pieces for him and offered to drive them over that day. The time away from her work was even sweeter because he promised to have her commission check ready for her.

It had taken her longer to box up the new pieces and make herself presentable than she'd expected, and it was late afternoon by the time she had made it over to the gallery. Then there had been the chit-chat, the unwrapping and admiring of the recent pieces, and then the almost ceremonial writing out of the commission check. All in all, it had been a very profitable afternoon, especially since the owner, a charming older gentleman with salt and pepper hair, nattily dressed in a tweed jacket and bow tie, had commissioned her to create a set of dinner plates for one of his regular customers. After some good-natured haggling, they had agreed on a price and then air-kissed their goodbyes.

Now, in the peace of the nearly empty café, she bit into her chocolatey croissant and took a self-congratulatory sip of her cappuccino as she pulled out her sketchbook and phone and turned her attention to the alerts, messages, and texts she had ignored while doing business. Life had gone on at a gallop while she'd been in the gallery.

She reviewed the weather service alerts first and saw

with little surprise that it predicted poor weather. A glance at the sky could have told her that. Still, this storm had a name, Eileen, and came with numerous flash flood warnings. Lydia sighed in annoyance. She knew she couldn't control the weather, but if Eileen messed with her plans for this evening, she would be seriously upset.

There were several texts from her dad, asking her when she would be home, each one testier than the last. She had a few messages from Josh, her little brother, asking the same in a mix of emojis and misspelled words. She ignored the ones from her dad and emojied something back to Josh, hoping he would understand. It was her night off from babysitting, and dinner was strictly her dad's responsibility.

There was one from her old friend Dermot Baker, a reporter, asking her to check-in. Maybe he wanted a quote for a piece she was writing. Since she didn't want the attention, she texted *no comment* with a smiley face, hoping he'd get the message.

She froze, looking at the next one, from Bella. God, she could barely remember her last name, but they'd had some wild times together in Atlanta and Miami. Bella was a model, no a photographer, with an interest in documentary filmmaking. Or something like that. Bella always has a nose for a good party and a big enough trust fund to make the good times last.

She read the text.

Nate was asking about you

Lydia felt the little chill, the involuntary shiver that came over her whenever she thought about him. Then deliberately, she forced the slight tendril of disquiet down. Nate was her past, and she had done her best to make a clean break. He didn't know where she was, didn't have her new number, and he couldn't touch her.

Still, she needed to know, so she texted Bella back.

What did he want?

Your number

Lydia waited to see if there was more. She sighed in frustration and then asked.

Did you give it?

Another anxiety-filled pause while she waited. God knows what Bella was doing, maybe in the middle of a photoshoot, but still, she couldn't leave her hanging.

No. Told him I thought you were in Ibiza, right?

Lydia let out a sigh of relief, but then there was another text.

Haven't seen you in ages. Should meet up in Ibiza next month, just like old times.

Lydia gave her phone a rueful smile and texted back. *You never know! Ciao for now.*

Of course, she had no intention of joining Bella in Ibiza next month or ever. Still, she knew if she said maybe, by the time next month came around, Bella would have forgotten all about her and Ibiza, and her attention quickly refocused on the next bright shiny thing.

She put the phone down, satisfied that Nate Buchanan still thought she was half a world away. In fact, Lydia prided herself on doing a pretty good job of convincing her old circle of acquaintances that she was still partying hard in Ibiza.

She had actually gone to there, in an effort to get as far away as possible from him. As a matter of habit, she'd taken hundreds of pictures and then, when her father had asked her to come to Queensway to help with Josh, she had come up with the idea of that it might not be a bad thing if no one, especially Nate Buchanan, knew where she was.

The chance that Nate, a successful businessman, and confirmed urbanite, would venture out into the quaint seaside towns of New England was laughable. Then again, until a year ago, she wouldn't have been caught dead here either.

Personal growth, she thought as flipped open her sketchbook, had a way of sneaking up on you. She found that the very act of drawing served to relax her, pushing away the negative energy of Nate's intrusion into her life, her hand moving almost automatically, creating an intricate pattern out of a seemingly haphazard swirl of lines.

The waitress, an older, comfortable-looking woman, came over with a towel slung over her shoulder. She looked over at Lydia's sketchbook, watched for a moment, before saying, "Storm's coming up fast."

"What?" Lydia turned her focus toward the woman, who was bussing a nearby table. She smiled, and the woman, who was frowning as she wiped a sticky spot on the table, looked up.

"Storm clouds. We'll get clobbered with rain and a rising tide."

"Right." The storm. Lydia looked outside the big plate glass windows onto the quiet street. The sky had darkened, the scrim of sickly yellowish clouds replaced by angry gunmetal gray billows that had coalesced into a moving, writhing mass blown forward on wind so strong that the silvered-green underbellies of the leaves were showing.

It was dark, too dark for late afternoon, an unnatural, heebie-jeebies-inducing dark. Lydia shivered just a little. A storm was the perfect thing for when you wanted to lay about all day, but not when you had a plan for the evening.

Raindrops—big, fat ones—splatted against the window, and she could see the street lamps were turning on one by one, their sensors tricked by the inky sky into thinking it was much later than it was.

"Yup, Eileen's worse than they thought and coming in

a whole lot faster. Town's battening down the hatches. The road will flood, too." The waitress added that for good measure, with a cheerfulness that said she was a native New Englander and used to Mother Nature throwing hell at her.

Lydia's coffee had grown cold, and the croissant was a flaky, half-eaten mess. She looked up and saw that the other patrons were gone, except for a mother hastily bundling her small toddler into her raincoat.

The waitress set a chair upside down on a table.

Lydia could take a hint. It was only a half-hour drive between Nattick and Queensbay, then maybe another ten minutes to her father's house outside of town. She didn't know how far away the waitress lived, but her meaning was clear.

Time to get the heck out of Dodge.

She hoped to hell that Eileen would not get all bitchy on her and ruin her plans for the evening. She had finally finagled her father into giving her the night off from watching Josh, and she did not want to be stuck at home eating mac and cheese when she could be out. Just because her dad was a fancy-schmancy art dealer didn't mean he couldn't figure out how to boil water.

She'd get home, deal with the men in her life, and then she'd bitch about them with her friends. Leaving a generous tip on the table, she thanked the waitress and wished her a safe trip home.

The waitress glanced up, took in the tip, and gave her a smile and a cheery, "Drive carefully."

Lydia collected her things and left the café. As she stepped onto the sidewalk, she was hit by a blast of wind so strong, it blew her back a step. A cluster of leaves whipped past her, caught itself in her long blonde ponytail, and then just as quickly was ripped away. She crossed the street to the classic Mercedes roadster, one of her father's many prides and joys.

She was mature enough to admit she had driven his car because it felt like she was rocking the Grace Kelly vibe, tying her long blonde hair up in a scarf, and donning oversize sunglasses. It had made her feel just a little bit like her old self, but mostly she had taken the car because she was ticked off at him.

When he'd told her that something had come up, that he needed to go away on a business trip and asked if she could she stay just another week or two longer, she'd nearly lost it. She had been thinking about heading back to Savannah to her studio, maybe seeing if she could teach some classes at the college again.

That she too, had a life to live hadn't really crossed his mind. He hadn't given her much of a choice, so she'd assuaged her passive-aggressive anger by taking his favorite toy out for a joy ride. It seemed a reasonable trade-off, but looking up at the sky, she wished she'd driven her own car, a sturdy, reliable Jeep.

A large, cold drop of rain slid down her neck. She wiped it away and thought about her new suede boots as she hurriedly folded herself into the car.

In the moment it took to get her settled, the rain began, a pelting, thick curtain of water. She sighed and listened as the engine turned over and hummed with a gentle purr. A crack of something that might have been thunder and a sudden gust of wind made her jump in her seat.

She took a deep breath, laughing at herself. It was just a storm, nothing to be rattled by. She had her girls' night out, and nothing, not even the evil Eileen, could get in the way of that. Buoyed by the thought, she turned the radio to her favorite country music station, cranked up the volume, and started the car, singing along with a classic Reba tune as she started home.

Chapter 2

L ance Morgan watched the shiny roadster start and, with a lurch, slip out of the parking spot and head down the street. He waited until it was a fair distance ahead before pulling his SUV out of the parking spot and following it out of town.

The rain had begun as a few large splatters but was already coming down in a steady beat, the storm moving in hard and fast. Rain, along with an unusually high tide and the powerful wind, would push the seawater up along the beaches, causing flooding along the low-lying coast road.

He didn't worry whether his car could handle it, but he thought Lydia Snow taking that sweet little sports car along the coast road was a mistake. Even a medium-sized puddle would spell disaster for a beauty like that.

Still, his job wasn't to have opinions, only to observe and report. So far it had been a boring job. Good thing the client wasn't picky about the inflated hourly rate he'd quoted. It was work he didn't want to do, but the referral had come in from an old Army buddy and he'd felt obligated to take it, even though the client was turning into a major pain in the ass.

A few days into the job and he hadn't noticed anything out of the ordinary. The old man stayed holed up in the house. So, even though it wasn't part of the job, he'd been bored enough to refocus his attention. The daughter, a pretty, blonde daddy's girl, spent most of her time occupying the kid brother—taking him to the playground, going out for ice cream and shopping.

Today, she'd deviated from routine. He'd watched her get dolled up and head out in the shiny little sports car. He figured she might be meeting someone, a boyfriend or a lover, and he decided, not quite sure why, to follow her instead.

She'd set out in daddy's car with the top down, a scarf around her long blonde hair, for what seemed like a leisurely ride along the coast to Nattick, where she'd parked and gone into a little crafty type shop with a box.

She'd stayed there for a while, and then she'd stuck around to have some coffee, the expensive kind, and some sort of pastry. She seemed to be oblivious to the fact that a major storm was coming, which everyone in their right mind knew would be a doozy. Lance sighed. He'd had a protein bar and an energy drink and was looking forward to some real food as soon as he ascertained that the woman wasn't doing anything interesting.

His windshield wipers were working furiously as he turned onto Kirby Road. Grumbling with frustration, he slowed a bit, hanging well back to ensure he wasn't noticed. The tide was just reaching its peak, and it combined with the onshore winds and rain to create large, sheet-like puddles, the type that separated rubber tires from the road and meant a loss of control for the nervous or inexperienced driver.

But he figured that this rich girl—ok, so he had nicknamed her Princess—didn't think about things like the weather. Too far beneath her. Weather was for the poor suckers who had to work for a living. She seemed to shop and hang out most of the day.

A branch, freshly snapped off, flew right in front of him.

He maneuvered to avoid it, plowed through a puddle and felt, for a fraction of a second, the tires lose contact with the road. He kept his calm, got the car back on the road and sighed. It would be a nice night to be inside, out of the rain and the wind, but he reminded himself that he was being paid for what was ultimately easy work. So, he kept his speed slow and his eye on the Mercedes ahead of him.

Chapter 3

The storm was worse than she'd bargained for. And the car, a sleek, road-hugging beast on dry, winding country roads, was proving difficult to manage in the battering wind and bruising rain. Puddles formed, great big ones, making driving feel downright treacherous. It didn't help that she was stuck behind an ancient pickup truck that was crawling along, as if the storm was of no concern.

She wished she had brought the Jeep, with its rugged tires and extra height. Her anxiety climbed as her phone kept dinging with texts, Josh asking where she was. She was pissed that her father couldn't handle opening a box, boiling water and stirring in orange powder to feed his own son.

All she wanted was to make it safely home so she could go out with her girls, throw back a drink or two and eat some greasy bar food. She needed a night off from babysitter duty. Sure, she loved her little brother —well, half-brother—but being on 24-7 was getting to her. Thankfully, he started kindergarten soon, and if all went well, she would tell her dad she'd done her duty and would head back to her real life.

Except her dad didn't seem to be getting with the program, with his withdrawn attitude and now another trip planned. It wasn't her concern. Her father was a grown man. She felt a twinge of guilt about leaving Josh, since there was still no word from his mother about when she'd be home. Lydia reminded herself that her father's ex-wife was none of her business. God, she needed that drink. If only the guy ahead of her would hurry it up.

The Mercedes skidded and hydroplaned just a little as she hit a pool of water at the base of an incline. Lydia kept her hands clenched around the wheel, fought panic and wrenched the car back onto the road.

The truck ahead of her seemed in no rush, and they were headed up yet another hill. The roadster's engine grumbled beneath her, as if asking to be able to go flat out and run. Yup, she should have taken the Jeep. Anything but this high-strung lady.

Lightning cracked, and Lydia shuddered.

"Potato skins with bacon, potato skins with sour cream and chives," she chanted to herself while guiding the sporty little sedan behind the truck.

Dark was now rolling in—real dark, not just the heavy cloud cover. Sheets of water pooled on the road, and she skidded as she plowed through a puddle.

Ahead of her, the truck sped up and pulled away from her, as if the driver had suddenly woken up and realized he was in the middle of a storm. Though tempted to gun it, Lydia kept going slowly, maneuvering carefully down the hill, hoping to avoid losing control.

The world had become gray around her, a wall of clouds, fog and rain. Thunder rumbled so close she could feel the vibration of the air through the car. Another gust of wind made the car shimmy. Ok, so it seemed like Eileen wasn't joking.

The car picked up speed down the hill. She pumped the brakes, felt them engage weakly. Then she was at the bottom of the hill, plunging into the puddle.

Lydia fought the slide of the Mercedes as its tires

met water and hydroplaned for real this time. The car turned as if in slow motion, spinning 360 degrees as she wrestled with the wheel and tried to avoid slamming on the brakes.

Finally, she was out of the water and on the soft sand that edged the road. She hit something with a jolt, and the car stopped with a finality that had her whiplashed in her seat. The Mercedes listed slightly, and she felt the unevenness. Had a tire popped, or was it worse? Was she teetering on the edge of a ditch, the Mercedes poised to slide into the swampy marsh that would suck her slowly down into the muck?

Lydia took a deep breath. Except for her neck, she felt ok, and even that pain was fading. She was in much better shape than the car, since it seemed to make an odd rasping sound as steam billowed from the hood.

Just great, she thought. What would her dad say? She had made it throughout her teen years without wrecking a car, and now she'd smashed up one of his prides and joys, a favorite toy. This would take some explaining.

Chapter 4

As Lance turned onto the narrow side road, his SUV fishtailed for a moment before he managed to straighten out. Slow and steady was the way to handle this. He crested another hill, then started down, gently breaking as he took in the scene below. In a pool of water at the side of the road was the fancy roadster, sitting at a crazy angle as steam rose from its hood.

He considered his options. He should just drive on, maybe call the police. The car didn't look too damaged, and she shouldn't be hurt. There was no way he should stop, help her and risk exposure.

Except....

He slowed to a stop just behind the stuck car. He couldn't just drive by and let someone else handle this. What if she was hurt? He was on the scene, and it would take too long for anyone else to reach them. He put the car in park, took a moment to reach for the flashlight and emergency hammer he kept in the glovebox and prepared to head out into the rain.

Lydia looked up, her heart still pounding, her breath caught in her throat. She shook her head to clear it, but still felt the thrum of adrenaline shooting through her, setting her on edge. A vehicle, an SUV by the size of it, had pulled up behind her with its headlights on. The bright, disorienting light poured into the dark cabin of the Mercedes. She tensed, watching. She was all alone on the side of the road, and a small trickle of panic began to seep in. This was the stuff of horror movies, wasn't it?

Deep breath, she told herself. She needed to stay away from the scary Hitchcock movies and stick to the light-hearted ones, like *To Catch a Thief*. She needed to get away from any disturbing scenarios that would never happen in real life, right?

Grabbing her phone, she held her finger over the screen. Call 9-1-1? There was no way the police could get here in time. She was on her own, just like Janet Leigh in *Psycho*. She pushed that thought away. She was a lot more resourceful than some Hitchcock blonde, wasn't she?

Finally, she saw the door open, and a light popped on inside the SUV, illuminating someone. A man—tall, powerful, judging by the combination of height and broad shoulders—started toward her in a slow, measured stride.

Was there something in his hand?

A gun? A knife?

Suddenly, she felt the sharp prick of panic grow in her stomach and rush throughout her body. She was all alone, trapped in a tiny car that wasn't going anywhere. She was too far away to call for help.

She swallowed, told herself to think. She wouldn't go down without a fight. She pulled her pocketbook to her and rummaged through it until she found what she was looking for: a gift from her dad. For protection. He'd never said from what, but this seemed like as good a time as any. The panic receded, replaced by adrenaline. Hell, yeah, she would get this sucker.

Read Book 7, Truly Yours of the Queensbay Series to discover the power of hope, family and small-town ties. *Truly Yours – A Queensbay Small Town Romance – available in ebook & paperback*

GirlMogul Media
309 Main Street
Ste 101
Lebanon, NJ 08833

www.dreastein.com

V7

Books By This Author

Truly Yours

Lydia Snow left behind a glittering career as an artist to - temporarily - take care of her younger brother in the small town of Queensbay. Now it's time for her to her return to her old life. But there's just one problem.

Her father has disappeared, leaving Lydia answering questions from the authorities about his whereabouts. Now she's the only person her brother has. With the FBI telling her to stick around, and people following her, Lydia has to wonder - just what was her father mixed up in? And how is she going to make this right for her brother?

And to top it all off, she's totaled her father's fancy sports car. Luckily help arrived in the form for a Good - and good looking - Samaritan. Lance Morgan is a true Boy Scout and from helping her with her fender bender to giving her newly broke self a place to stay, he's undeniably helpful - and attractive.

He's almost too good to be true. And if he knows what's really going on – that her father is an internationally wanted art thief on the run and that authorities think

Lydia knows more than she's telling, will he desert her too? Or is he hiding a secret as well?

About The Author

Drea Stein

Drea Stein is the author of the Queensbay small town romance series. She lives in a small town New Jersey with her family, two dogs and chickens in an old farmhouse with a red barn.

Copyright

Publisher's Note: This is a work of fiction. Names,
characters, places, and incidents are a product of the
author's imagination. Locales and public names are
sometimes used for atmospheric purposes. Any resem-

v7